I0661315

Wings of Air

Heir to the Firstborn, Volume 4

Elizabeth Schechter

Published by Elizabeth Schechter, 2021.

Published by Raven's Wing Books

Previously published as **Wings of Air** (Elizabeth Schechter, 2021)

Editor: Michael Schechter
Cover design by GetCovers

Raven's Wing Books

ravens-wing-books.com
ISBN: 9781952598159

Table of Contents

To R, the sister of my heart.

And as always, to M and J. My reasons for being.

CHAPTER ONE

D el had lived his entire life in the Palace. It had been a sheltered life, and he knew it. By necessity, at first —he'd been years recovering from what Risha did to him, from the fall that should have killed him, and the subsequent mutilation. Years where his only glimpses of sky had been through his window. As he'd gotten older, and stronger, he'd gone to Forge with his father, and to Terraces. But those had been visits. Short ones. He'd never been able to handle anything longer than a few days away before the fear overtook him. Before the weight of the world started to smother him, before he started to panic and needed to flee to the sanctuary of the Palace, to the safety of his own rooms, the comfort of his own bed. He'd needed to hide away where it was safe. Where no one could hurt him. So he'd never lived anywhere else.

Now? He hadn't seen that room or that bed since the autumn. He hadn't been back to the Palace since the night of the storm that the Waterborn called The Mother's Rage. He'd spent four of the past five months living on canoes, out under the sky and the stars, and he wasn't even sure when he'd last felt smothered by the fear that something was going to hurt him. He knew he wasn't better. He would never fully recover. Not the way he'd teased his father the night this had all started. Loving someone wasn't going to undo the damage done. But being surrounded by love? Surrounded by people who didn't think he was broken? It helped.

He looked around his tiny bedroom and smiled. When he and Aven had moved in with the others at the house at Three Northwest, there had been that first night when they'd all piled like puppies into the large bed to sleep. But after that, with Aven's help, Del had made it clear to the others that he only used his bed to sleep. He had no interest in sex.

"None?" Aria asked. "Del, is this—"

"It's normal, Aria," Alanar said. "It's rare, but it's normal. Some people just like the opposite sex. Some people just like the same sex. Some of us don't care. And some...they don't want sex at all. Or maybe they do, but only if they care about someone very deeply." He shrugged, keeping his arm around Owyn's shoulders.

"What's important is that we don't have enough beds," Owyn added. "I mean, it's not fair to Del, is it? He needs his own space, so he don't get put out of bed because of the rest of us."

Del had raised his hands to start protesting, only to lower them when Aria arched a brow. "Were you going to say it isn't necessary?" she asked him. When he nodded, she shook her head. "It is. It is necessary. I won't have you made uncomfortable, or to feel pressured to do something you do not wish." She looked around. "And yet, I don't know how. I want you all with me, under the same roof. But we do not have another bedroom. Will we have to move houses again?"

"Nah," Owyn answered. "Let me talk to the carpenters. We can do something. I have an idea."

That idea had been turning a room that had been an unused, oversized closet into a small bedroom. When Owyn and the carpenters were done, there was just enough room in the space for a narrow bed and a small dresser. There was a shelf over the bed for books, and baskets under the bed for anything he might want to store there. Both were currently empty — he hadn't had enough time to acquire either books or possessions, and the only thing he really currently owned other than his clothes was the barbed spear that Othi had given to him. That rested on pegs on the wall beneath the shelf. There was no window, which Del didn't mind a bit — a lamp placed on top of the dresser gave him enough light to see. The room was tiny, almost claustrophobic, and Del loved every inch of it because it was his. When he wanted to be alone, he could come here to be alone. When he wanted company, there was almost always someone in the large sitting room in the front of the house, or the kitchen. If there wasn't anyone else home, there were other places he could go if he wanted company. Places where he felt safe going, leaving the house all by himself. He could go down to the docks, to where Neera and Othi were anchored. He could go and help in the healing complex, with Senior Healer Jehan, Alanar, Treesi and Aven. He wasn't allowed to help in the forge when Owyn went to work with Persis — he didn't know enough to keep from hurting himself. But he could watch, and Owyn was good about explaining things. He seemed to have a knack for knowing just what Del was going to ask, even if he was facing away from him and couldn't see the signs that Del used to communicate. The only place he didn't go was across the street, where Owyn's aunt Rhexa lived with her new wife, Ambaryl. Del knew he was welcome there, but Ambaryl had known him since he was a baby, and had been his first nursemaid after his mother's death. She meant well, but she tended to behave in what Del knew was the usual reaction of most of the Palace servants who had known him for his entire life — 'we must protect our poor, broken child from the world.'

Del didn't want to be protected. He'd stretched his boundaries over the past few months, and he wanted more. So he tended to avoid Rhexa's house, at least when he was alone.

Most of the time, Del spent his free time with his father. He couldn't remember Mannon ever being so relaxed, especially now that Memfis had been released from the healing complex. Mannon seemed to have appointed himself Memfis' caretaker, and Memfis didn't seem to mind too much. They shared a house on North, and seemed to be as comfortable together as Rhexa and Ambaryl. Del stopped in the middle of taking a clean shirt out of a drawer. Had his father paired off with Memfis? He considered it, while he finished dressing and tidying his little room. He wouldn't object — he liked Memfis. And it would make Owyn his brother, which...would be strange. He shook his head and grimaced. No, perhaps not. Besides, his father was so much older than Memfis — twenty years, at least! They couldn't be lovers.

Could they?

No. Absolutely not. It wouldn't happen.

But maybe he should ask Owyn.

It was early enough that Owyn was still in the kitchen, making something that smelled wonderful. He looked over his shoulder and smiled as Del came in.

"Good morning!" he called. "Go sit. Breakfast is almost ready. The porridge is done. The bread is just about to come out of the oven. And there's hard-cooked eggs this morning. I know you like those."

Del grinned and went to sit at the small table. He fished his tablet out of the pocket of the long vest that Aria had made for him, and scrawled a note that he left for Owyn to read. Then he waited.

Once he'd taken the bread out of the oven, Owyn came over to the table. "What's this?" he asked, tipping his head sideways to read. "Are your father and mine...no. No, absolutely not." He paused. "I don't think. Fuck, Del, why did you have to ask me that question? Now I'm going to think about it!" He grumbled, then leaned down and kissed Del on the cheek. Something else Del was getting used to. And, to be honest, enjoying. "Good morning. You're early enough to help me carry things to the table. No one else is up, but they'll be along once they smell the food."

Del nodded and stood up, helping Owyn carry bowls and trays and plates out to the large table in the front room. The bread, and pots of honey, jam and butter. A bowl of hard-cooked eggs. Another bowl of fermented sea oak, which Owyn put next to Aven's place. A large pot of porridge that Owyn insisted on carrying himself.

"Just get the bowls and spoons, would you?"

Del was just setting the teapot on the table when arms closed around him from behind. He leaned back into Aven's embrace, tipping his head back. Aven smiled down at him, then leaned down and kissed him. "Good morning."

Del nodded, tugging one hand free to sign, *"Good morning. Where's Aria?"*

"Finishing getting dressed," Aven answered. He took his seat at the table, then looked around. "More plates than people. Are we expecting anyone? Not Fa and Ama, I don't think."

"Yeah, I wasn't expecting them. Mannon said he'd be over this morning," Owyn answered. "And Mem, probably. They're usually together these days. And Granna Meris might come for some tea. But she usually doesn't eat breakfast, so I don't know. At the very least we'll have Mannon and Mem."

Aven frowned slightly. "About them. Owyn, have you asked Mem—"

"Don't you start!" Owyn warned, sitting down. "I'll serve when everyone else is here. And no, I don't think Mannon and my fa are pairing off. That's...no. Nope. Not at all. No."

"But what do you really think, Owyn?" Aria teased as she joined them. She kissed Del on the cheek, kissed Owyn on the lips, then sat down next to Aven and sighed. "I agree with you, Owyn. I do not think they are paired. I think there is something, but not a pairing."

"Well, what else is there?" Owyn asked.

"A life debt?" Del signed. *"Fa saved Memfis' life. Memfis owes him the debt."*

Owyn frowned. Then he shook his head. "I think I caught all of that—"

"That is better than I did," Aria murmured. "All I understood were the names."

Owyn nodded. "A life debt. That's old fashioned. But...yeah, maybe."

"What's a life debt?" Aven asked. "Is it a Fire thing?"

There was a knock on the door, and Mannon came in, holding the door for Memfis. "You weren't waiting on us, were you?" Mannon asked.

"We're all just sitting down," Owyn answered. "You're right on time."

Mannon looked around. "Mislaid your husband?" he asked, holding a chair out for Memfis, then taking the seat next to him.

"Mislaid my—" Owyn laughed. "No! No, he's sleeping in. Treesi, too. There was something at the healing complex last night." He started pouring tea. "I'm surprised you're awake, Fishie."

"They had me in reserve, in case they needed me, and so that someone would be awake and able to do rounds this morning," Aven answered. "So I didn't work nearly as hard as the others did, and I need to eat and leave."

"What happened?" Memfis asked. He leaned his elbow on the table. "I thought I heard alerts—"

"Another group of refugees," Aven answered. "This batch was from south and east of Forge. Took them this long to get around the areas where the ground is still smoking."

Memfis sighed and leaned back in his chair, rubbing his face with his hand. "Will we ever be able to go back?"

"What will there be to go back to?" Aria asked in response. "Has the Smoking Mountain ever erupted like this before?"

Memfis looked at Mannon. "You're the historian. Has it?"

Mannon looked thoughtful, taking the teacup that Del offered him and taking a sip. "I...don't think so," he said slowly as he put the cup down. "Not on this scale. Smaller eruptions, yes. On the south side. We have records of that. Eruptions on the north side? Never before. Can we rebuild Forge? Possibly. But maybe not in the same place. The ground there...it'll be too changed. It's a lava field now." He tapped his finger on the side of his cup. "I don't know what it will mean for the mines. Or the vents. We'll have to send scouts. Surveyors. People to find a site that's close to what Forge was—"

"What plans are you making behind my back, Mannon?" Meris asked as she came inside. Owyn jumped to his feet and hurried around the table, accepting a kiss from his adoptive grandmother before leading her to the table.

"Just wool-gathering, Lady Meris," Mannon answered. "The question was can we rebuild Forge. And I think we can, but not in the same place."

"And what prompted this question?" Meris asked. She shook her head when Owyn held up a bowl. "No, thank you, dear. I'll have a piece of bread, and some of that lovely jam you made. Now, why are we discussing building?"

"More refugees," Aven answered, taking a bowl from Owyn and putting it in front of Aria. "Last night. Fa might not have had time to send word to you. He and the others were up with them until late."

Meris nodded. "He hasn't. I'll go see them this morning. And see to him as well."

Del took his own bowl from Owyn, then helped himself to some of the fermented sea oak, stirring it into his porridge the way that Aven did. It made the cereal a little more pungent, and somehow more satisfying. And it always seemed to make Owyn look at him as if he'd grown another head.

"How can you eat that stuff?" Owyn asked. It was an old, comfortable question after a month, and Del grinned and took a big bite of seaweed-laced porridge. Next to him, he heard Aven snicker.

"He lived with us for four months, Mouse," Aven said. "He picked up—"

"Bad habits," Owyn finished.

"I was going to say refined tastes," Aven finished. He reached over and helped himself to an egg, and a piece of bread. He slathered the bread with jam, and handed it to Aria.

"So what is a life debt?" Aven asked again. "It's not something I've heard of out in the deep."

"It's an old idea, and all of the tribes held to it at one time or another," Meris answered. "Why?"

Owyn looked at Del. "It was your idea."

Del shrugged and laid down his spoon, picking up his tablet and writing, *"I was wondering if I had a new father. Owyn says no. So I thought it might be a life debt."*

He passed the tablet to Meris, who read it. She looked up at Mannon and Memfis, then chuckled. "I can see why you asked that question, Del," she said. She passed the tablet to Memfis, who looked at it, laughed, and passed it to Mannon.

"A new..." Mannon read aloud. He smiled. "Del, if I planned to marry, you would be the first person I'd tell." He paused. "The second person. No, we're not pairing."

"And yes, it is a life debt," Memfis added. "I owe Mannon my life. I need to repay that debt. And it's complicated by the fact that he—" He waved at Mannon with his spoon. "Feels responsible for me. At least until I'm ready to live on my own, he's insisting that I don't." He looked down at the empty right sleeve that was pinned up to the shoulder of his shirt. "I'm an old wolf. It's not easy to learn new hunting tricks."

"You're going to have to," Mannon said. He scraped the bottom of his bowl with his spoon. "Unless you plan on coming with me. Which I wouldn't mind—"

"Going with you?" Owyn interrupted. "Going with you where?"

"Back to the Palace," Mannon answered. "To get it ready for Aria. I haven't had a messenger bird in days, and I'm starting to wonder why. To tell the truth, I've already been wondering what's happening when I'm not looking. I've learned over the past month or two that a lot goes on behind my back. And there was someone in the Palace telling Risha what I was doing. I should find them before they do something rash."

"Oh, are you ready to go back to the Palace?" Aria asked. "When do we leave?"

CHAPTER TWO

M annon stared at her for a moment, then stammered, "I thought...I didn't think...I assumed that I would go ahead, and prepare things, and you would join me later." He stopped, setting down his spoon and resting his hands on the table. "You should join me later. You're safe here. Stay here. Have your baby here, where it's safe and you have access to the entire healing complex."

"She'll have three healers with her when we go to the Palace," Meris pointed out.

Aven shook his head, then turned in his chair to face Aria. "We haven't discussed this. At all. We should. This is more than just us leaving. This is taking three of the senior healers from the healing complex when refugees are still streaming in. This is taking Rhexa's assistant when she needs him to help organize and provide for those refugees." He nodded toward Owyn. "This is more complicated than simply saying 'let's go.'"

Aria looked thoughtful, then she nodded. "Council?"

"Council," Aven agreed. He looked up. "And I can't arrange it. I have rounds. Mouse, will you—?"

"I've got it," Owyn said. "When are you done in the healing complex? Or should I plan it around the evening meal? We can talk and eat."

Aria picked up her teacup and took a sip. "Please, do that. It will give me time to get my thoughts in order. And to ask the people I wish to be involved in the discussion to attend."

"How many am I cooking for?"

Aria tapped one finger on the table. "Us, of course. That's six, with Alanar. Mannon, you and Memfis. Grandmother?"

Meris smiled. "If you wish me to be, my dear."

Aria nodded. "I do. Thank you." She finished her tea, set the cup down. "I should have Jehan here, and Rhexa. Aleia. I am not certain about Pirit or Ambaryl."

Del snapped his fingers, and when Aria looked at him, he signed, "*You're going to need guards. You should have Karse in.*"

Aria narrowed her eyes slightly, then sighed, "I'm never going to learn this! I am sorry, Del."

"He says you need guards. He says that we should have Karse in. And I agree with him and with his choice. Karse is a good man. He'll make you a fantastic Guard Captain," Mannon said. "What I was able to do can never be allowed to happen again. You have to protect your future from the next Mannon."

"Mother grant that that shit never happens again," Owyn muttered. Del bit his lip to keep the giggles inside, but lost the fight when he looked at Owyn , who winked at him. They both started laughing.

"You're having fun without me again," Alanar grumbled as he came down the corridor. Owyn leaned back in his chair and smiled.

"Did you get enough sleep?" he asked. "You came in awfully late. I wasn't expecting you up for breakfast."

Alanar came over to the table and kissed Owyn slowly and deeply. Then he sat down. "I might nap later," he said. "I don't think I got enough sleep. But I was hungry, and I smelled bread." He cocked his head to the side. "There are more people at the table. Who's here?"

"Mannon, Memfis and Meris," Aven answered.

"A most pleasant and alliterative company," Alanar said with a grin. "Good morning, everyone."

Owyn took Alanar's hand. "So I'm cooking for ten? At least?" he asked. "Right. I'll go see Katrin. See what she has available. I'll start bread before I go out, it should be done by tonight. Bread bowls? With stew?"

"Oh, that sounds lovely," Aria said. "I do like your stew, Owyn. And the bread bowls."

"It's going to be crowded," Alanar said. "We'll need to borrow chairs from Aunt Rhexa."

"I'll ask her," Owyn said. He let go of Alanar's hand and stood up, filling a bowl with porridge. He set it in front of Alanar, then reached for bread and started cutting slices. Without looking up from what he was doing, he asked "Del, do you want to help me? Or do you have other plans for the day?"

Del blinked. *"I don't know what I can do to help,"* he signed. *"I am not good in the kitchen. Not like you are."* Before Aven could translate for him, Owyn answered.

"That's just practice. You'll learn. And until you learn, you can carry," he said. He put the bread down in front of Alanar, reached for the teapot. "And help move things. And run around and deliver invitations. Jam in your porridge, love?"

"It never ceases to amaze me how you do that, Owyn," Mannon murmured. "I've watched you do it for a month now. Memfis, how does he do that?"

"Do what?" Owyn asked, looking up. "What did I do?"

"You knew what Del was signing," Aven said. "Without looking at him. You never looked at him, but you answered him as if he'd said something aloud."

Owyn frowned. "I..." he stammered. "I did that?"

"You do it a lot," Del signed. *"I don't know how you do it."*

"Is it a Smoke Dancer thing?" Alanar asked. "Memfis? Lady Meris?"

"Not that I've heard of," Memfis answered.

"I've never heard of such a thing," Meris added. "But I've also never heard of a Smoke Dancer coming back from the dead. So perhaps I should test Owyn again."

Owyn groaned. "Again? You told me I'd only ever have to do that once!"

"You're a special case, my darling boy," Meris said. She smiled. "What is it that young Neera calls you? Twiceborn? So you have to be tested twice."

"Maybe you should have let me be dead, Aven," Owyn grumbled.

"No!"

Owyn jerked in shock as six voices chorused in unison, and they all started laughing. He sat down, and leaned back in his chair.

"Right. Testing. When, Granna? I'm going to be a bit busy today with planning for Council."

"I'll arrange it. It should be soon," Meris said. "But not too soon. It's not easy for me, either."

"Speaking of soon, I need to go. Rounds are soon," Aven added, getting up from his chair. He leaned down and kissed Aria, then made his way around the table, pausing to kiss Del, Owyn, and Alanar. He picked up his walking stick from where he'd left it in the corner of the room. "I'll see you all before the evening meal. Someone kiss Treesi for me. I'm off."

Del waved as Aven turned toward the door, then looked at Owyn. *What's so bad about the test?* he signed.

Owyn made a face. "Can't tell you," he answered. "I don't think, anyway. Granna, is it still forbidden to tell anyone about the testing?"

"I want to know," Aria said. "I'll have to do it at some point, won't I?"

"Not until you finish your training, which you won't be doing until you have that baby," Meris answered. "And yes, it is still part of the Smoke Dancer arcana. It is not something we share. I am sorry, Del."

Del nodded to show he understood, and reached for another piece of bread. He slathered it with jam and took a bite, then looked around and frowned.

"Del?" Aria asked. "What is it?"

He reached for his tablet, putting the bread down so that he could write, "*Now that we're thinking of leaving, I don't know if I want to go back. I like it here. No one treats me like I'm a child or an idiot.*"

Aria read the tablet and nodded. "I won't allow it," she said. "You are neither. I won't let anyone insult you so."

"He's neither what?" Mannon asked. Aria looked at Del, who nodded. She passed the tablet to Mannon. He read it, frowned, and looked up. "Who treats you like an idiot?"

"Nestor, for one," Owyn muttered. "D'ye know that he didn't believe me when I told him that Del was our Air? He called Del our poor, broken child."

Del nodded. "*Ambaryl does it, too,*" he signed. "*A lot of the staff do it. They think because my voice is gone that so are my wits. They treat me like a child. I didn't realize how much until I was gone. The Water tribe doesn't treat me that way. No one here does, either.*" He shrugged. "*Except Ambaryl. So I don't spend time with Ambaryl if I can help it.*"

"Which, if you're helping me help Auntie Rhexa, you don't have much of a choice about," Owyn said. "I'm sorry, Del. I didn't even notice!"

Del picked up his bread. He finished it, chasing it down with the last of his tea. "*It's not you. It's them. And even if you point it out, they won't stop. They never did when I said anything.*"

Owyn snorted. "Let me guess. They patted you on the head? Be a good boy and run off and...what? Play? Let us handle it?" Del nodded, and Owyn rolled his eyes. "Yeah, we'll be stopping that."

"Absolutely," Aria agreed. "It's rude."

"It's fucking insulting is what it is," Owyn growled. "Mannon, why didn't you ever stop it?"

"Because they didn't do it in front of me, or where I could hear," Mannon answered. "Del, why did you never tell me?"

"*What would you have done?*" Del signed.

Mannon looked puzzled. "Told them to stop treating you so," he answered.

"*And would that have changed how they thought of me?*" Del asked.

Mannon blinked. Then he frowned. "Oh. I see. Ordering them to change their behavior won't have changed their minds. It would have just driven it underground." He nodded. "I see now. Del, I am sorry. You'll have to change their minds."

Aria reached over and rested her hand on Del's arm. "We'll change their minds together, won't we?" she asked.

Del smiled. He took her hand and pressed a kiss into her palm. Then he turned to Owyn. "*Now what?*"

"Nothing until everyone has eaten," Owyn answered. "Have some more tea. I'll get a book and pen, and we can start making lists." He looked. "Good morning. You're up early for someone who was up so late."

"I didn't have time to eat last night, so I'm starving," Treesi answered. She came up behind Del and hugged him, kissing his cheek. She gave the same greeting to Aria, then sank into Aven's abandoned chair. "May I have some porridge, please? With jam?"

Owyn got up and started filling another bowl. "What else, Trees?"

"Tea. A lot of tea." Treesi turned and smiled. "Good morning. I'm sorry. I should have said that already." She looked around. "Did I miss Aven?"

"He just left for rounds," Alanar said. "He left a kiss for you."

"I'll claim it once I eat," Treesi said. She yawned. "I might go back to bed and sleep until tomorrow, as tired as I am."

"We'll be having Council tonight," Aria said. "At the evening meal."

Treesi sat up. "What? Why?"

"Because Mannon has proposed that he leave for the Palace, and I wish to go with him. To have all of us go with him," Aria answered. "But Aven pointed out to me that it is not a simple undertaking, and that we should discuss it properly before I decide."

Treesi smiled. "You're getting better at this ruling thing, Aria."

Aria chuckled. "I could hardly get worse than driving every one of you away, now could I?"

"Do you really want an answer to that?" Owyn asked.

Aria gave an indignant squeak, then burst out laughing. "I deserve that," she admitted. "And yes, I could have done worse."

"Of course you could have. You could have been me," Mannon grumbled.

ONCE BREAKFAST WAS done, Alanar and Treesi went back to bed, and Aria and Lady Meris went to meet with the new refugees. Del helped Owyn clean up, then took dictation for the invitations while Owyn started making bread dough.

"Let's see," Owyn said, measuring flour into his large bread bowl. "Ah...your presence is requested by the Heir this evening...no, that makes it sound optional. The Heir requires your attendance at Council, to be held this evening at Three Northwest. Supper will be served." He glanced over his shoulder. "How does that sound?"

Del nodded, and started writing, his pen scratching on the paper. Then he got up and took it to Owyn, who read aloud. "The Heir to the Firstborn has called a meeting of her Council, to be held this evening at her residence over the evening meal. Your presence is requested. Yeah, you make that sound a lot better than I did. Okay, can you write that up and deliver them? Then meet me at the dispensary?"

Del nodded. He set his draft down, then started writing. He wrote seven copies of the note as Owyn worked on the bread dough, and was sealing the last one as Owyn put the bowl on the shelf over the oven to rise.

"Seven?" Owyn asked, wiping his hands off on a towel. "Mem, Mannon and Granna were here. They already know they're invited."

"*It's polite,*" Del signed. "*They need to get official invitations, just like the others.*"

Owyn looked thoughtful. "All right. I need to learn this, don't I? How to be all...what's the word?"

Del laughed. "*That's funny. You asking me for a word. And the word is diplomatic.*"

"Diplomatic. Okay. I need to learn to be that," Owyn grinned. "And you know more than I do. More words. More everything. You had proper learning. I learned...well, what I learned is shit you never want to know, and we'll leave it at that. All right. I'll clean up here and meet you at the dispensary."

Del nodded and picked up the letters, tucking them into his vest pocket. He'd do the closest first, he decided. Get it out of the way. Get away from Ambaryl that much faster. He grinned at Owyn, and on impulse kissed him quickly on the lips.

Owyn smiled broadly. "Hey, you're in a good mood, aren't you?" he asked. "You're not usually the one to give those out." He stepped closer and met Del's eyes. "Do you want me to take Rhexa's letter over? You won't have to deal with Ambaryl."

Del smiled. "*Thank you. You have work to do. I'll go deliver that one first. Having to deliver the others will let me get out of there fast.*"

"Sounds like a plan," Owyn agreed. "Look, if she bothers you, let me know. I'll have a talk with Aunt Rhexa."

Del shook his head. "*I need to do this myself. But thank you.*"

Owyn nodded slowly. "I understand. All right. I'll see you at the dispensary."

Del patted his pocket to check for the letters and his tablet, waved to Owyn, then headed out of the kitchen and out of the house. Rhexa lived directly across from them, so he walked across the street and knocked on the door.

"Come in!"

He opened the door in response to Rhexa's cheerful call, and smiled to see Owyn's aunt alone in the front room. She was sitting at the table, looking over papers. She looked up when he came in, and smiled warmly.

"Well, good morning, Del!" she said. "How are you today, dear? Come and sit. There's tea."

Del shook his head. He took the letter to the table and placed it in front of Rhea. Then he took his tablet out. "*I can't stay,*" he wrote. "*I'm delivering these for Aria. You were closest, so you were first.*"

Her brows rose, and she picked up the letter and broke the seal. She read it, then looked up at Del. "She's decided to move on to the Palace, hasn't she?"

Del grinned. He wiped off the tablet. "*You're very good at that. Yes. Aven wants everyone who will be impacted by our move to be there to discuss it.*"

Rhexa nodded. "That makes sense. All right." She looked thoughtful. "I'm going to have to talk with Baryl. She seems to think we'll be going with you when you leave, and that I can simply drop everything in Jehan's lap. She has this odd idea that you don't know how to care for yourself, and she needs to be there to wipe your nose for you. It's ridiculous, but I can't dissuade her." Del rolled his eyes, and she chuckled. "I thought that would be your reaction. She's off at the dispensary. If you hurry, you won't see her this morning. Off with you. You have work to do."

Del nodded his thanks, and hurried back out.

Jehan and Aleia lived in One North, but Del doubted he'd find either of them there. He'd go to the healing complex as his last stop. Mannon and Memfis were in Seventeen North, and Lady Meris lived with Karse and Trey in Fifteen North, right next door. His father was waiting for him.

"I figured you would be the one to deliver these," Mannon said. He took the letters for him and for Memfis, brought them into the house, then came back out. "I'll walk with you a bit, if I may?"

"*What about Memfis?*" Del asked.

Mannon chuckled. "He kicked me out. He's tired of me at his elbow, and he told me, in very explicit language, to give him some room to breathe. I think I've been coddling him a bit too much."

Del grinned. "*I wouldn't know a thing about that.*"

"Did I ever coddle you, Del?" Mannon asked as they started walking.

Del shrugged one shoulder. "*Maybe when I was very small. Just after Mama died. But I think I needed it then. Once I was ready to stand on my own, you let me. Encouraged it. Pushed me when I needed it. Remember how I fussed at you when we were learning water signs?*"

Mannon chuckled. "You wanted nothing to do with it. Until you realized that it gave you a voice. Then...well, no one could have stopped you then."

Del nodded. He gestured for Mannon to wait for him, and walked up to Fifteen North. Meris met him at the door, took both letters, and gave him a warm hug in return. She waved at Mannon, then went back inside. Del trotted back down to the street and pointed back toward the healing complex.

"*Senior Healer next,*" he signed, and they started walking. After a moment, he started signing again, "*Fa, why didn't you treat me like that? Coddling. You're doing it to Memfis now. You never did it to me. Why not?*"

Mannon didn't answer immediately. They walked in silence up the street, and they were almost to the healing complex before he stopped. He turned to face Del and started signing.

"*When you started walking, you let me steady you for one day. Then you ran. You let me read to you for barely a year. Then you read to me. I'd seen what you could do if I gave you your head. I knew you had it in you to find your way.*" He paused, then shook his head and said aloud, "I knew you could. I just needed to steady you for a bit." He looked back down the street. "And I need to give Memfis the same courtesy." He turned back to Del. "Is that why you asked? To point out what I was doing?"

"*No,*" Del answered. "*I asked because you were the only one in the Palace who didn't. You never did. You even played along with the whole ridiculous slave idea so that I wouldn't panic.*"

"It worked," Mannon pointed out. "That means it wasn't ridiculous."

Del grinned "*Maybe. Maybe not. Thank you.*" He looked up. "*Let's go. I'm supposed to meet Owyn after this.*"

CHAPTER THREE

The healing complex was more crowded than usual. Del waved to the attendant at the desk as he and Mannon entered the building. It was Tancis, one of the newer healing students. Which meant that he was probably on punishment detail again, and Del wondered just what he'd done this time.

Mannon looked around and whistled low. "More refugees than I thought," he said. "Is there enough room for them all? Do you know?"

Del nodded. He'd spent enough time helping Owyn and Marik that he knew how much space there was above ground. And for anyone who wished it, there were the underground caverns. Some of the refugees had opted for those, which had surprised Del. He knew that the Air tribes made their homes in caves up high in the mountains. He didn't know there were entire Fire villages that lived in caves, too.

"*There's room underground,*" he signed, turning toward Mannon. As he did, he saw a woman staring at them. Maybe she'd never seen water signs before? "*I'll show you later, if we have time,*" he continued. Mannon nodded. He turned toward the corridor that led to Jehan's office

The woman screamed.

"It's him!" she shrieked. "It's the Butcher!" She pointed at Mannon, who went pale. The people around her jumped to their feet, all of them staring at Mannon and Del. The woman kept wailing. "He's here to kill us all!"

The crowd shifted. Men moved toward the front, some of them carrying walking sticks. Del put his hand on Mannon's arm, feeling the fear rising, feeling the cold panic threatening to lock him in ice.

"Go," Mannon whispered. "Go to Jehan. Just...go, Del." He held his hands up. "I'm not here to hurt anyone."

There was a low growl, and one of the men stepped forward. "It is you, isn't it? Mannon the Butcher."

"Not anymore," Mannon said. "I am nothing now. I surrendered to the Heir. My fate is in her hands now."

The man snorted. "She ain't here now, is she?"

"Actually, I am."

Aria moved through the group, and stopped next to the man who had spoken. "Were you intending to violate the healer's peace, Jassic?"

Jassic blinked. "You remembered my name?"

"I only just met you an hour ago," Aria said with a smile. "Of course I remember." She looked at Mannon. "Were you helping Del deliver the invitations?"

Mannon nodded. "I wanted to spend more time with my son. Apparently, that was a mistake." He sighed. "I'll go. I'll go back to the house."

"He gets to walk away?" Jassic demanded. "Why ain't he in chains?"

"Because I do not wish him to be," Aria answered, her voice calm. "That is reason enough."

Jassic growled. "Not reason enough for me," he snapped, and lunged toward Mannon, who dodged, moving away from Aria and Del. Del grabbed Aria and pulled her the other way, toward the corridor. His back hit the wall, and he froze – he couldn't move, couldn't protect his Heir, couldn't get them away from the ugly roar of angry men as they surged forward.

A sound broken by the furious roar of one particular angry man.

"What the absolute fuck is going on out here!" Aven's voice cut through the din. "Stop!"

There was enough command in Aven's voice that most of the men did stop. But Jassic didn't — he snarled and went for Mannon again...and dropped like a stone when Aven swung his walking stick, hitting him in the back of the head.

Aven turned, glaring at the assembled refugees. "Anyone else want to try to break the healer's peace?" he demanded.

"What's going on out here?" Jehan demanded, coming up behind Del quietly enough that his voice made Del jump. He rested a hand on Del's arm, dispelling the fear. "Sorry. What's the riot?"

"It was just that," Aria said. "Or near enough."

"Fa, I need to put Jassic's skull back together," Aven called. "Will you talk sense into these idiots?"

Jehan's brows rose. "Tancis, help Healer Aven move the patient. And someone explain to me why you're brawling in my healing complex?"

Jehan walked past Del and Aria, wading in to the group of refugees as they all started talking at once. Aleia took his place next to Del and Aria. She rested one hand on Del's shoulder and squeezed. "Are you all right?" she asked Aria.

"I am fine," Aria answered. "I thought they would stop—"

"Angry men don't always listen," Aleia said. "And they all have good reason to be angry." She looked past them, to where Mannon rested with his back against the wall. "And are you all right?"

"I'm getting old," Mannon grumbled. "Once upon a time, I'd have been able to take a brawler like that."

"*It wasn't just one,*" Del signed. "*Could you have taken all of them? And protected Aria? You know I'd be no help.*"

Mannon scowled. Then he deflated. "No," he admitted. "No, I couldn't. Aria, I'm sorry. I shouldn't...I'll go back to the house. And stay there."

"I'm not ordering that," Aria protested.

"I am," Mannon replied. He sighed. "I'm putting myself under house arrest until it's time for us to leave. It's not fair to them." He gestured widely, taking in the room full of refugees. "And it's not fair to you."

"Fair?" It was the woman who'd screamed, who was close enough to hear Mannon. "You're talking about fair?"

Mannon looked at her. "I was wrong," he said softly. "I know that. I learned that from Yana. Trying to fix what I'd done only made things worse. So I surrendered to my Heir. And when the time comes, if she tells me that I'm to be executed because of my crimes against the Mother, then I will go gladly. But until then, I am her servant."

The woman's eyes widened. "What d'you know of Yana?" she asked.

"I know...more than you would believe," Mannon answered. He sighed and looked at Del. "*I'll see you at supper,*" he signed. Then he bowed to Aria, turned, and left the healing complex.

"What did that mean?" the woman asked. "My Heir? What did he mean?"

"We weren't introduced," Aria said. "What's your name?"

"Afansa, my Heir," she answered.

Aria smiled. "Afansa, would you have believed him if he'd told you that he was Yana's Air? That he bears the gem still?" Aria asked.

"He...no!" She looked toward the door. "Really?"

"Yes," Aria answered. "I have seen it myself, and I know it is truth." She rested her hand on Del's shoulder. "My Del is Yana's son."

Afansa stared at Del in wide-eyed wonder. "Oh! But why...what will you do with him? With the Butcher. After everything he's done—"

"I know what he has done," Aria said. "And I know what he is doing, which I think you and your people do not. He is trying to make things right. He has stepped down. He has risked his life to save mine and the lives of the people I love, more than once." She shook her head. "It doesn't balance. I know. None of those things would have happened if he had not made the choice he did. But for now? He has surrendered. He has abdicated, and sworn his fealty to me, and I have chosen to believe him. At the moment, he is... useful to me. So I must decide on his fate. And it is my decision. Not yours. Not his." She pointed in the direction that Aven and Tancis had taken Jassic. "For now, I have not yet decided. And when I do decide... then it is my decision." She raised her chin slightly, and met Afansa's eyes. "We've had enough of people deciding to work against the Firstborn, have we not?"

Afansa caught her breath. Then she nodded. "We have, my Heir. We have."

Aria smiled. "Thank you, Afansa. I hope you'll be happy here in Terraces, until we are able to rebuild in the Fire tribe lands. We were discussing that this morning. Manron has some good ideas that I think we will have to explore further."

Del grinned. Now he could see what Aria was doing. He took his tablet out and wrote, "*He's always been better at organizing than ruling. He says it himself.*"

He handed the tablet to Aria, who read the note aloud. "Does he really say that?" she asked. "Well, perhaps I'll keep him to organize things for me. I'll be busy enough as it is." She nodded and handed the tablet back to Del. "Thank you. Now, you were busy. As was I. Let's be about our day. Grandmother is with the children, and I should join her." She leaned closer and kissed his cheek. "I will see you later."

She turned and made her way through the crowd, and Del turned to face Aleia.

"*What are you so busy with today?*" she signed.

"*Aria will be calling a Council meeting tonight,*" Del answered. "*I have invitations for you and the Senior Healer.*"

Aleia's brows rose. "Come to the office," she said aloud, and turned away. Del followed her down the corridor and into Jehan's office. She closed the door behind him and gestured to a chair.

"Council?" she asked. "What should we expect?"

"*Fa mentioned he was planning on leaving for the Palace, so he could arrange things for when Aria arrives,*" Del answered. "*She wants to go with him. Aven says that we need to consider the impact our leaving would have on everyone else, since we've all taken on important roles in Terraces.*"

Aria nodded slowly. "And she's listening. Good. She's getting better at this."

Del smiled and went into his pocket, taking out the last two letters. He handed them to Aleia. "*Leaving will be strange. I'm not sure I want to go. Why can't we stay here?*"

Aleia sat down behind Jehan's desk. She rested her elbows on the polished wood surface and studied Del. Then she said, "You tell me."

Del grinned. He should have known that would be her answer — she'd said it often enough to him when he'd asked questions about the ways of the Water tribe. He considered it. Why go to the Palace?

"*Part of it is probably tradition,*" he began. "*This is the way we do it because this is the way we've always done it.*"

Aleia chuckled. "True. Lore has it that the Palace was built on the site where Axia settled with her Companions, where they raised their families. But it's not the only reason."

There was more? Del frowned. He'd lived in the Palace for years. What made the place special? Why did the Firstborn have to rule from the Palace, when they would be able to rule from literally anywhere else? He heard the door open behind him, but didn't turn to look.

Finally, he shook his head. "*I don't know. Why?*"

Aleia smiled. "Access. The other reason is access."

"Access to where?" Jehan asked from behind Del. "What are we talking about?"

"The Palace," Aleia answered. "Want me to move?"

"No, you can rule the Earth tribe for a bit," Jehan answered. "I need a break." He came around the desk and shared breath with his wife. Then he kissed her before picking up one of the invitations and asking, "What's this?"

"*Aria has called a Council meeting tonight,*" Del answered.

Jehan arched a brow. "Right. And combined with the conversation I came in on, that means she's decided it's time to move north?"

"*Maybe?*" Del answered. "*That's what we're going to discuss tonight.*"

"All right," Jehan said. "We'll be there. So, what's the question about access to the Palace. Context?"

"*Why the Firstborn rules from the Palace and from nowhere else,*" Del answered. "*Also, why we're not staying here.*" He thought about it. "*Access? But the roads are barely there any more.*"

"But when they were, anyone could travel straight to the Palace gates, from anywhere in Adavar. There used to be regular caravans that carried passengers and goods between Forge, the Palace, and the Solstice village," Aleia pointed out. "The harbor will hold practically the entire Water tribe. The Palace is located in the one place that anyone can reach without too much effort."

Del nodded. "*I understand. We'll need to work on that, restoring access. Starting the caravans again.*"

"We'll add it to the to-do list. Which I think is now longer than you are tall," Jehan said. He grinned. "Where are you off to next?"

"*You were the last delivery,*" Del answered. "*I'm supposed to meet Owyn next, to help him with supplies.*"

Jehan nodded. "Well, then. Off with you. We'll see you later for Council."

Del stood up. "*Will Jassic be all right?*"

"He'll be fine," Jehan answered. "And maybe now he'll learn not to try and break the healer's peace."

"I somehow don't think he was expecting a healer to come up behind him with a club," Aleia said, her voice dry.

"Well, sometimes if you want someone to grow some sense, you have to crack their skull to let it in," Jehan answered. He winked at Del. "Go on. Owyn's probably waiting for you. And he's probably already heard about the brawl. I wouldn't be surprised if he was outside by now."

"*I'll go see. And catch him if he's not. See you later.*" Del bowed slightly and turned for the door.

OWYN WASN'T IN THE entry hall, which was empty except for the attendant. Tancis waved at Del as he left. For a moment, Del thought about following Mannon. He said he was going right home, hadn't he? House arrest? But if Owyn had heard about the fight, and Del didn't come meet him as he'd promised, then Owyn would worry. He turned toward the dispensary. He'd go see his father afterward.

Owyn was waiting for him outside the dispensary, pacing back and forth. When he saw Del, he waved and hurried toward him.

"What happened?" he demanded. "I'm hearing about a brawl at the healing complex. Are you all right?"

"One of the refugees recognized Fa," Del answered. *"And tried to go through Aria to get him. I got Aria out of the way, and Aven stopped him."*

Owyn frowned. "Stopped him how?"

"He broke the man's skull," Del answered.

"And now he has to go put him back together again?" Owyn asked. Del nodded, and Owyn sighed. "I'd wondered when that was going to start happening."

"You were expecting someone to attack my father?" Del asked. *"And you didn't say anything?"*

"I did!" Owyn protested. "To Jehan and Auntie Rhexa."

"But not to my father?" Del signed.

"Maybe I should have, but I thought they would," Owyn answered. "And maybe they did. I don't know."

"He never said anything to me. Not a word!"

"I don't know," Owyn repeated. "You'll have to ask him. Now, I talked to Katrin. She's putting together today's supplies for us, and stuff for tonight."

"How many baskets?" Del asked.

"Two. Maybe three."

Del whistled. The usual supply baskets were large enough to carry a small child, *"Can we handle three baskets?"* he asked. *"Or will we need another person?"*

"If we need another person, we'll find another person. There's usually someone around to help." Owyn dragged his fingers through his hair, pushing it back off his forehead. "I need to cut this," he muttered. "We've got a few minutes to wait. Are you sure you're all right?"

Del nodded. *"I think so. I didn't think anyone would do something like that in the healing complex."*

"I don't think anyone expected that. But from now on, they might. Which might mean two people in the entry, and one of them a guard," Owyn said. He looked up and smiled. "Is that Wraith?"

Del looked up, seeing the dark bird circling overhead. It was a familiar shape these days — before Del had arrived, Marik had befriended a shadow hawk from the northern mountains, and the bird had decided to stay in Terraces. *"I don't see Marik. But he's around somewhere, if Wraith is circling."*

Owyn waved to the shadow hawk. "Marik is always around somewhere," he said as the bird banked and flew off. "Now that's odd. Wonder why he flew off like that?"

"Maybe he's hungry?" Del suggested. *"Saw something to hunt?"*

"Or Marik called him," Owyn added. "Yeah, it's probably nothing. There's Katrin. Let's go get our baskets."

OWYN SOMEHOW MANAGED to carry two baskets, leaving the third for Del. It meant that they couldn't talk on the way back to the house. At least, Del couldn't talk. Owyn kept up a running commentary on what he was going to make for the evening meal.

"...Katrin said she had some nice venison, and some good wine. So what I'm going to do is get the venison cleaned up, and cut a bunch of little slits in it. Stuff garlic and herbs in the slits, and pour the wine over it. Then let it roast — yeah, I know I said I was making stew."

Del almost dropped his basket. He stopped in his tracks, staring. Owyn turned and looked at him for a moment, then his eyes widened.

"I...I did it again, didn't I?" he asked slowly. "But...you can't have signed it. I thought I might have just been seeing it without noticing. But...your hands are full." He licked his lips. "Were you thinking it? That I said I was making stew?"

Del nodded. Owyn looked down, then shook his head. "Once I get the meat in the oven, we'll have a few hours. We'll go talk to Granna. This...I don't know what this is."

"*Useful?*" Del thought.

Owyn's eyes widened. "You just did it, didn't you? I mean...I just heard you. How I think you sound, anyway. Yeah...yeah, it's useful. Useful and scary." He nodded. "Come on. Let's go get this taken care of."

Del followed Owyn back to the house, and put away their supplies while Owyn prepared the meat.

Owyn washed his hands, then held one hand in the oven for a moment. He nodded. "It's a good temperature. So, to explain, what I'm doing is starting the meat in the oven to roast. Then I'll take it out, cut it up, and use the cooking juices from the roasting to help flavor the stew. It'll sit in the oven for...maybe an hour? Then I'll let it cool while I get the bread bowls shaped and put you to work chopping vegetables. Then get the stew in the pot to cook until dinner. Make sense?"

Del shook his head. "*I'm taking your word for it.*"

"Ah, I'll teach you how to cook yet." Owyn looked around and smiled. "Right. Let's go see Granna."

"*You don't need to stay with the roast?*" Del asked. "*I can go ask her to come back. It's not far.*"

Owyn looked at the oven. He nodded without turning. "All right. Yeah. Do that. I don't want anything to burn. I'll get the bread bowls shaped now."

Del moved in behind him and slipped his arms around Owyn, pressing his cheek to Owyn's shoulder. Owyn clasped his hands over Del's.

"Thanks," he murmured. "I just...this is a lot weird. I don't know why this is happening."

Del nodded, his cheek scraping against Owyn's shirt. He tried to keep his mind blank as he let go — there was no reason to make Owyn even more uncomfortable. Owyn chuckled as he turned.

"I appreciate that," he said.

Del groaned and rolled his eyes, making Owyn laugh. Owyn pulled Del closer, met his eyes, then kissed him on the lips. Del closed his eyes and slid his arms back around Owyn, enjoying the warmth of his body, the sweetness of his kiss.

Owyn rubbed Del's back. "You know, if you ever decide you want to explore the bedroom, between me and Allie, we could show you a few things."

"Who's between us?" Alanar asked as he came into the kitchen. "And what smells so good?"

"Del, if he wants, and that's the venison for tonight's stew," Owyn answered. He looked over his shoulder. "Are you up for the day now?"

"I can't sleep any more," Alanar said with a grimace. "So I thought I'd get up and see what help I could be. I'm not on shift today. Neither is Treesi."

"You missed the excitement at the healing complex," Del signed.

Owyn translated for him, and Alanar frowned. "What excitement?"

"Someone tried to go for Mannon," Owyn answered. "Everyone is all right. But...yeah. There was a brawl."

Alanar gaped at him. "A brawl," he repeated. "In the healing complex?"

"Come sit and I'll tell you," Owyn said. He moved away from Del, going to his husband's side and taking Alanar's hand.

"I'll go and see if Lady Meris is back from the healing complex. I can ask her to come over," Del signed.

Owyn nodded, even though he wasn't looking at Del. Del brushed past them, heading out of the house.

CHAPTER FOUR

K arse met Del at the door. "You're back again?" he asked. "Meris said you were here already with the invitations. Was the Council called off?"

Del shook his head and took his tablet out of his pocket. *"Owyn needs to speak to Lady Meris, if she's here?"*

"She just got back a few minutes ago. Is it important?"

"Yes. If she can come to the house? He can't come here. He's started cooking for the Council meeting."

Karse read the note and nodded. "Come inside."

Del followed him into the house, seeing Karse's husband Trey sitting at the table. Trey grinned at him around a mouthful of something.

"Good morning," he called once he'd swallowed. "Do I get to come tonight, too?"

Del considered it, then nodded, wiping off the tablet and writing, *"I don't see why not. You're Karse's second. I think you should be involved."*

Karse read the note aloud, then added, "And any excuse to eat Owyn's cooking?"

Trey laughed. "Well, if you put it that way..." he drawled.

Del laughed. He wiped the tablet again and wrote, *"Is Lady Meris here?"*

"She went to take a nap," Karse answered. "I'll go see if she's still awake." He headed further into the house, and Trey waved Del over.

"Come sit," he said. "Have you given any thought to my offer?"

Del shuddered. He had thought about Trey's offer...for about five seconds. He cleaned off the tablet and answered, "*I don't want to learn to fight. If there's a brawl, I'm hiding behind Owyn or Aven. Or Othi.*"

Trey took the tablet and narrowed his eyes, his lips moving slightly as he read. "You can't hide behind them forever. I'm not saying you need to be at the front of the battle, Del. I'm saying you need to know enough to keep yourself alive until someone gets to you."

"*I don't go anywhere by myself,*" Del scrawled. Not if he could help it.

"You came here alone," Trey pointed out. "But Terraces isn't as safe as you want it to be. No place is that safe. And before you tell me I'm wrong, we heard about the fight at the healing complex already. Someone recognized Mannon. How long before someone recognizes you?"

Del stared at him. Who'd recognize him? No one knew who he was. He certainly wasn't anyone important. He wiped off the tablet and heard Trey sigh.

"You know, I never thought learning to read was important before I met you. Didn't matter what Karse said, or Owyn. Why the fuck did I need to learn to read?" He snorted. "Listen to me. I sound like you. And the answer is the same. Why do you need to learn to fight? Because someday, it might be important, you knob."

"Trey," Meris said as she came down the corridor. "You don't need to be rude."

Trey winced. "Sorry, Lady Meris," he called.

"I'm not the one to whom you were rude," she replied. Trey looked sheepishly at Del.

"Sorry, Del," Trey said. "I just...how is it going to hurt if you know how to use a blade?"

Del rolled his eyes. He picked up the tablet and wrote, then handed it to Trey. Who promptly handed it to Karse. Karse shook his head.

"It's a good thing you're good-looking," he grumbled. "Because sometimes, you're as dumb as a box of mice. Now do you believe me when I tell you reading is important?"

"Yes," Trey answered. "Now explain to Del why it's important that he learn to fight. It's the same thing!"

Karse looked down at the tablet. "No, he might have a point here," he said. Then he read what Del had written, "*Handing me a blade will be dangerous for me and anyone around me. When I get scared, I panic, and I freeze. Which means that whoever is attacking me gets another weapon. I had weapons masters at the Palace. And Othi tried to teach me to use the spear he gave me. It didn't work. So he told me to keep it for show, and to stay with Aven.*"

Trey's eyebrows were so high that Del couldn't see them under his hair. "You could have told me that!"

Del growled softly, then signed, "*No is a complete fucking sentence.*" He got up, bowed to Lady Meris, then offered his arm.

Karse handed him his tablet, then asked, "You going to translate that last one?"

Del shook his head and led Meris out of the house.

Halfway down the street, Meris tugged on his arm. "I realize you're quite upset, but the pace is a bit much for me. If we could slow down?"

Del froze. He turned, feeling his face burning, and bowed.

"Now stop that," Meris chided him gently. "Trey means well, but he can be somewhat overbearing. He tried to push me, much the same way he pushed you. And, like you, I had to be quite stern with him. Now, I am very much out of practice with Water signs. What did you say?"

Del's face grew warmer, and he took his tablet out. *"It was rude."*

"From the look on your face, I didn't think it was anything but." Meris smiled at him. "So?"

"I said that no is a complete sentence."

Meris frowned slightly as she read what he'd written, then chuckled. "You censored yourself here, didn't you? Because this is hardly rude." Del smiled slightly and nodded, and she laughed and took his arm again. "Let's go on," she said. "Slower."

They walked the rest of the way up the street at a slower pace, which gave Del the time to realize that he hadn't even thought about checking on his father. He glanced back over his shoulder, but he could no longer see Seventeen North. He did, however, see Trey following behind them.

"Del?" Trey called as he got closer. "I...did you tell me to fuck off?"

Del blinked. Then he shook his head. Trey looked confused.

"You didn't?" he asked. "You should have. Karse says you should have." He looked down, then sighed. "I just...you're important to a lot of people who are important to me. And Owyn would be the first person to tell you that I try to take care of my people. It's why I became a Guard." He clasped his hands behind his back. "I'm sorry I pushed."

Meris sniffed. "Perhaps you should volunteer to become his guard?" she suggested. "If you feel so strongly about it."

Trey frowned. "Then who'll look after you?" he asked. Then his eyes widened. "Oh. Am I...Lady Meris, are *you* telling me to fuck off?"

Meris laughed. "No, darling. I wouldn't. However, you have this uncomfortable habit of trying to wrap me in padding, as if I were breakable."

Trey swallowed. "I...I'm just..."

"Trying to take care of the people you love," Meris finished. "I know. And I understand why, too."

Trey winced. "I didn't take care of Tacen, and Fandor did for him. He never even got a proper burning. I told you. I promised myself I wasn't going to lose someone like that again."

Del frowned. Who was Tacen? He looked at Meris, who nodded slightly. He understood — if Trey didn't explain himself, then she'd explain later, when Trey wasn't around.

He wiped off his tablet and wrote, *"Owyn is waiting for us."*

Meris read it and nodded. "Of course," she said. "Are you coming, Trey?"

Trey blushed slightly. "Do you want me to?"

Del smiled. He put his tablet into his pocket, then held out his free hand. Trey's hand was big, warm and callused, and he squeezed Del's fingers gently.

"Thank you," he murmured. "I'll try not to push again."

Del grinned. He leaned into Trey, hard enough to throw him off balance. Trey stumbled, then straightened and burst out laughing.

"If I push, you push back?" he asked. "That's a deal."

DEL KNOCKED THREE TIMES on the front door, paused, then did it again before walking in.

"Does that let them know it's you?" Trey asked. Del nodded, and smiled as Owyn came out of the kitchen.

"There you are," Owyn said. "I was wondering what kept you. Good morning again, Granna." He grinned up at Trey. "And what are you doing here?"

"Groveling," Trey answered. "I'm groveling. Because I been doing it again."

"Doing...oh, did you go all protective?" Owyn chuckled. "Yeah, I should have warned you both about that."

"Perhaps, but there's been no harm done," Meris said. "Owyn, what was it that you wanted?"

"To show you something," Owyn said. "Ah...Del, I'm going to turn my back. You say something." He turned. Del frowned, then started signing.

"Yeah, no is a complete sentence, and you are going to have to show me how to sign fucking. I need to know that," Owyn said. He turned back.

"That's what you signed at me!" Trey gasped. "What was it, no is a complete fucking sentence?"

"Yeah," Owyn agreed. "That's what he signed. And...that's what I wanted you to see, Granna. I can tell what Del is signing, even if I'm not looking at him. And even if he can't sign. He was carrying a basket, and I knew what he wanted to tell me! It was like I knew what he was thinking."

Meris frowned. "Have you tried this with anyone else?"

"Alanar, while we were waiting. And...it's funny, but with him, I don't really hear him. Not like I do Del. With Allie, it's noise." He snorted. "He says it's because Virrik talks too much, and I'm hearing the both of them."

"He's still hearing Virrik?" Meris asked. Then she shook her head. "No, I need to focus. When did this start?"

"*You started understanding signs very fast,*" Del signed. "*Maybe that's why?*"

"And why I understand you better than I do Neera or Othi?" Owyn added. "But I understand Aven just fine." He blinked. "Oh. Oh, I know. I think I know." He looked up at Trey. "Think of something."

Trey looked startled. "What?"

"Just..." Owyn's face fell. "Oh, fuck. Tacen? Why are you thinking about Tacen?"

Trey went pale. "It's spring. I...you know we were born in the spring. It's just...closer to the surface today." He looked down. "I...does Del remind you of him? A little?"

Owyn frowned. "I don't know. I never knew Tacen. Never had the chance." He shook his head. "Okay, I know what it is now. I have to be close to someone. Like, really close." He smiled slightly. "Closer than just with a grandmother."

"I have no issues with you not being able to read my thoughts, Owyn," Meris said gently. "A close emotional bond, a lover's bond? Yes, I can see that. You're more sensitive than you were before, my Owyn."

Owyn blinked. "Granna, come sit down. I'll make a pot of tea. You know what's going on with me?"

"I believe I do," Meris answered. "And some tea would be lovely."

Owyn kissed her cheek and disappeared into the kitchen. Meris sat down at the table, and Del followed after her, sitting down in his usual chair. Trey sat across from him, his face still pale. On impulse, Del reached across and took his hand.

Trey smiled slightly. "Thanks," he said softly. "Tacen...he was my brother. My twin. I was older, by a few minutes. We thought. I don't know if we ever really knew for sure. But he always called me the big brother, because I was a little taller before we hit our growth. And...yeah, we...we were brothel boys. We were sold there by our uncle, after our mother died. He didn't want us, didn't want the extra mouths to feed." He looked at Meris. "How much of this did I tell you?"

Meris shook her head. "Some. Not all. You never told me all of it. I didn't want..." She paused, then smiled. "I didn't want to push."

Trey grinned. "Yeah. I'm learning. Slow, but I'm learning." He looked back at Del. "We were sold when we were seven. To Fandor."

Del shuddered, which made Trey look thoughtful. "Right. Forgot you knew him. We were kitchen boys for about five years. Then we were backroom boys. Fandor kept the younger boys hidden, because there were some guards who wouldn't look the other way when the kids were that young."

"Like Karse," Meris said.

"Like Karse," Trey agreed. "Who told me he suspected, but never could get the leverage to actually do anything about it. Fandor paid his bribes on time." He paused and sighed. "Fandor moved us up front at thirteen — two years before we were really old enough to be there. Brothel boys were supposed to be at least fifteen. But...yeah, we were up front. Two for one special, he called us. Matched set. A bargain at twice the price." He snorted. "Fuck, I haven't talked this much about it in years."

"You don't have to," Owyn said as he came back with the teapot. Alanar followed him, and sat down at the foot of the table. Owyn poured tea, then took a seat between Del and Alanar. "I can fill them in."

"No, I've said this much," Trey said. He picked up his cup and took a sip. "Tacen hit his growth first. We started looking less like a matched set, and I started getting picked out alone by the men who wanted a younger mark. And Tacen, he started making noises about getting out. He wanted us to get out, get away from Fandor and have a real life. Fandor, he must have heard. He already didn't like keeping mouths to feed that weren't paying their way, and he didn't like it when the boys got too old. So he—" Trey stopped. He shook his head. Del could feel his hand shaking.

"Fandor murdered him," Owyn finished, his voice quiet.

Trey nodded. "He did to Tacen what he tried to do to you, Owyn. He tied him down, poured Rut down his throat, and raped him until he died." He closed his eyes. "There wasn't anything I could do to save him."

"Wait," Owyn said. "You were *there?*"

Trey stared at him. "I didn't tell you that?"

"No, you did not fucking tell me that!" Owyn gasped. "Fuck, Trey!"

"That explains so much," Meris murmured. "Trey, I am so sorry."

Trey shrugged. "He called us both in. He'd do that — bring us both in. Have one of us tied up, have the other do things to them. He liked that. Liked to watch. Only...once I was secured, he..." He stopped and his fingers tightened on Del's hand, hard enough to hurt. "I couldn't stop him."

"Trey," Alanar asked softly. "How did you get away?"

Trey looked over at the healer and let out a broken laugh. "That would be your husband's fault. Sort of."

"Mine?" Owyn asked. "Wait...what did I do?"

Trey grinned. "You showed up with the winter ague. Tacen hadn't been gone but a week, and here you came, sick out of your mind. You gave me someone else to look after, when I was ready to give up." He shook his head. "I'm still not sure how I managed to hide you long enough for you to get well enough to leave. And I stayed in the brothel, partly because I had no place else to go, and partly because Owyn needed me where I was. So he had a place to go when the streets got really bad. I don't think Fandor ever knew that we knew each other. I'd have been in trouble if he did, I think.

And after Fandor turned on Owyn, I knew it was time for me to run."

"To me," Owyn interjected. "He ran right to me. And when I explained who he was to Mem, Mem hid him." He frowned. "I didn't tell you all about the hole. We had a hidden room, under the forge. Aven and Aria know about it because that's where we hid them. But we put Trey there first. That's where the both of us learned to be people, and not just wild things."

"You were more wild than I was," Trey murmured. "I'd had the wild beat out of me. But I stayed down there a full year, almost. Until I was of age and Fandor couldn't touch me anymore. And then I went into the guard, to try and protect other kids like me and Owyn. Like Tacen." He looked down at Del's hand, and his eyes widened. "Del, I didn't hurt you, did I?"

Del drew his hand back. He flexed his fingers and winced as sharp pain shot through them.

"Del, give me your hand," Alanar said. "I felt that all the way over here."

Trey looked stricken. "I broke him?" he gasped. "Don't tell me I broke him!"

Del put his hand into Alanar's, who cocked his head to the side, then nodded. "He has Air bones. Hollow bones, if you don't know, Trey. And it's a simple fracture. That's easy enough to fix."

"Oh, fuck!" Trey moaned. "Del, I'm *sorry*!"

Del sighed as the pain in his hand started to fade. He looked down at his other hand, then up at Owyn.

Owyn grinned. "He said that you're not allowed to punish yourself for it. You didn't know Air bones break easy," he said. "He accepts your apology. And if you can think of a way around him freezing up, he'll go along with you trying to teach him something. Maybe you can do something no one else could. You sure about that, Del?"

"I...he will?" Trey looked at Del. "Why?"

"Because now he understands what this means to you," Owyn answered. Del nodded.

"This is really weird," Trey said, looking from Del to Owyn. "You reading his mind. My mind. Is it anyone you've fucked, Wyn?"

"Not sure," Owyn answered. "Treesi is still asleep, so I can't check with her. And no one else is around." He turned in his chair. "Granna, you said you have an idea?"

Meris nodded. "I do, although I could wish that the archives still existed. I'd want to check—" She stopped. "Del, you're familiar with the library at the Palace. Are the archives there?"

Del glanced at Owyn again, who said, "He says Mannon would know better."

"Then I'll ask him. But I don't think you're reading minds. You're not hearing everything, for example." She gestured around the table. "You know this from your training. The mind is a very noisy place. If you were hearing all of the thoughts of all of the people to whom you have a strong bond, you'd be hearing them constantly." She smiled. "My darling, this isn't mind reading. You're having heart visions."

CHAPTER FIVE

"Heart visions?" Owyn repeated. "Wait. You told me a story about those, when I started training. That's a thing? I mean, you told me, and I've read about them, but that's really a thing? Really?"

Meris laughed. "Yes, it's really a thing. It's rare. I can't even remember when I last heard of someone who had heart visions." She looked thoughtful. "I don't think it's been in my lifetime."

"What's a heart vision?" Alanar asked. "I know there's a lot you can't tell us about Smoke Dancing, but can you tell us this?"

Meris nodded. "How to explain it?" she murmured. She picked up her tea and sipped it. "It's so rare. It's said to be a legacy of Axia — she loved all of her Companions, but she loved Abin deeply enough that she knew his heart and his mind as well as she knew her own. You know how some people who have lived and loved together for years just seem to know what the other is thinking, or feeling? Those are heart visions."

"Granna," Owyn said. "Are you sure? I mean, the story I remember is that one. Axia and Abin. One person knowing what the other person is thinking. Or feeling. This...I'm up to three, and if it's really everyone I really love, then we're going to be at..." he paused, clearly counting. "Um...six? At least?"

"Everyone you love," Trey repeated. "And you can read me, too. I...Owyn, I didn't know you loved me like that. I thought we were just friends."

Owyn blinked. "I...I thought you knew how I felt. We're a lot closer than friends. I mean, we're friends now. But we've been more. How long were we sharing a bed, once we both were out?"

"I didn't...I thought we were just fucking!" Trey blurted.

"Owyn doesn't just fuck," Alanar answered. He took Owyn's hand, rubbing his thumb over Owyn's knuckles. "If he's taking you to his bed, it's because he loves you."

Owyn felt his face warm. "Um...yeah. Because I promised myself that. After everything, I wasn't going to have sex with anyone if I didn't want to. And I needed to want it. And you were the first one. So...yeah, Trey. You really didn't know I love you?"

"You never said," Trey answered. "And occasionally I'm dumb as a box of mice."

Alanar frowned. "I'm sorry. A box of *mice*?"

"Karse says that, sometimes," Trey explained.

"That's not the sort of thing I'd expect a lover to tell someone," Alanar said.

Trey laughed. "He doesn't mean anything by it. Usually, it's just when he's frustrated at me."

Del signed, "*He did it today, because Trey couldn't read my notes.*"

"Couldn't read...Trey, you still haven't learned to read?" Owyn asked. "We could fix that."

"I'm going to have to, aren't I?" Trey leaned back in his chair. "If I'm going to be teaching Del anything, I'm going to have to know what he's saying. I should talk to Othi, see what he has to say about teaching you. Maybe we can come up with something together." He nodded. "Yeah, I'll go down to the docks and talk to him. Tomorrow. Del says I can come to the Council tonight." He grinned. "What's for dinner?"

"I'll tell you later. I want to hear more about heart visions, and why I can hear Del. We haven't done anything, but I can hear him," Owyn said.

"Love isn't just physical, Owyn," Alanar murmured. "You can love someone without sex."

"I know, but it's still a question. I have a lot of questions." Owyn picked up his own teacup and took a long drink. "Granna, what else can you tell me?"

AVEN KNOCKED AT THE Senior Healer's office door, then let himself in and smiled when he saw who was sitting in the desk chair. "Hiding, love?"

Aria returned the smile. "A little, perhaps. There are so many people. Are you finished?"

"I just finished my charting. And I spoke to Fa," He walked around the desk and leaned against it, resting his walking stick against his leg and feeling the deep ache in his hip that told him he'd been on his feet too long. "Fa says that Grandmother will be supervising the older trainees tonight so that Treesi and Alanar can both be at Council." Aria nodded, rubbing one hand gently over the swell of her belly, and Aven realized she was fighting sleep. He held his hand out to her. "Come with me. We'll go home, and we can tuck into bed for a while."

"We need to go to North before we go home," Aria said. "I want to see how Mannon is."

Aven nodded. Then he grinned. "Is it still strange to you, that he's part of us now? That we're trusting him?"

Aria chuckled. "It is still very strange. But it hasn't even been two months. I'm sure we'll get used to it." She smiled. "Eventually."

Aven smiled and nodded. "And how's the little one treating you? You slept well last night, I know."

"If you say so. I don't feel as though I did," Aria admitted. "They've been dancing, and quite a lot. So my back aches. And they've decided that they do not like that lentil stew—"

"The spicy one that Rhexa makes?" Aven asked. "You love that stew!"

"I love that stew," Aria agreed. "The little one does not. The smell of it turned my stomach when she brought some to me at midday."

"Does that mean you haven't eaten?" Aven asked.

"No, I did eat. Bread and cheese, and tea. And a lovely stone fruit. I don't think I've ever had one that tasted so good."

Aven nodded. "We'll see if we can get some for the allotment. I'll talk to Owyn." He offered his hand again. "Let me take you home."

"By way of North," Aria said as she put her hand into Aven's.

"By way of North," Aven agreed. He led Aria around the desk and out into the corridor, where she stopped.

"You're in pain," she said.

"This is the longest shift I've had since I came back and started serving rounds," Aven admitted. "I've been on my feet too long. Fa knows. He'll do something about it later."

"Or Alanar will. Or Treesi," Aria said as she took his arm. "They will argue over who gets to help you feel better."

Aven laughed. "They will. All right. Let's go slow."

They walked arm-in-arm out of the healing complex, passing a crowd of refugees in the plaza. Aven could see his cousin Marik standing in the center of them, and it looked as if he was about to take them off somewhere. Probably to the houses where they were to stay. Marik saw him and waved, and as he turned to start leading people off, Aven caught sight of Esai, Marik's lover.

"They're always together," Aria murmured. "Mannon thought that she would make a fine guard for me. But I think Marik has other ideas."

Aven smiled. "He's happy. He deserves that."

"I did not say that he didn't." Aria leaned into his arm. "Do you think they'll marry?"

"Has he taken her to Serenity yet?" Aven asked.

"No, I do not think so," Aria answered. "Oh, he has not introduced her to his mother yet?"

"When he takes her to Serenity, then it'll be so he can introduce her to Danzi. Then he'll talk to her about building a canoe."

Aria looked surprised. "Does he hold that closely to Water traditions? He always seemed to be more Earth."

Aven smiled. "He...might have talked to Fa about it," he said. "Don't tell anyone I told you that."

"How do you know?"

Aven leaned closer and whispered, "Because I might have been in the room when they talked."

"Aven!" Aria laughed. "Very well. I will say nothing. Now, there's Seventeen."

They turned toward the house, and were met at the door by Memfis, who looked very serious.

"What happened?" he asked. "Mannon came back and he's gone into his room. Not a word to me, and he won't let me in. I didn't even know the door had a lock until now. I didn't want to leave him. And I expected someone to come sooner."

"I'm surprised Del has not come already," Aria said. "Mannon was recognized by the newest refugees, and one of them tried to attack him."

Memfis' jaw dropped. "He never said a word. Was anyone hurt?"

"Only the man who tried to break the healer's peace," Aven answered. "And I put him back together again afterward."

"May I see if he'll speak to me?" Aria asked.

Memfis walked back into the house. Aven and Aria followed him until he stopped outside a closed door. He knocked gently. "Mannon?" he called. "Aria is here."

Aven heard footsteps, then the door opened. Mannon looked out at them, his face pale and drawn.

"My Heir?" he murmured. "I...I'm fine."

"You're not," Aria said. "And I don't know why no one came to see you before us. But you're not fine."

Mannon took a deep breath. He let it out and shook his head. "I'm not fine," he agreed. "I'm a threat to everyone here. To you especially. That man was ready to go through you to get to me. What's to stop them from finding out that I'm here, alone with Memfis, and attacking the house? Or going to your house, because Del is there, and the fastest way to stab me through the heart is to hurt my son? Let me go ahead. I can be gone with the tide tonight—"

"I need you here," Aria interrupted. "And I will not hear of you leaving. Not until we have a chance to talk. I need you here at the Council tonight."

Mannon's brows rose. "So I would be able to leave tomorrow?"

Aria looked thoughtful. "If you convince me that I would not need you here to help me plan, then you might be able to leave tomorrow. But you have to convince me that I will not need you here."

"And I won't be able to convince you of that without knowing the full extent of your plans," Mannon said slowly. "That makes sense." He took a deep breath and let it out, then met Aria's eyes and smiled slightly. "I'm sorry. And don't say it's not my fault. It's all of it my fault."

"I was not going to say that it was not your fault," Aria said. "As I told Afansa in the healing complex, you made your choices, and now you are trying to balance what came of those choices. You are doing what you can. But if you want to keep on doing what you can, then you cannot hide from the consequences of those choices by running back to the Palace."

Mannon looked startled for a moment, then he frowned. He opened his mouth as if he was going to say something. Then he stopped, and turned away from the door.

"That's what I'm doing, isn't it?" he said softly. "Running and hiding?"

"Perhaps it was not your intention this morning, when you first proposed leaving," Aria said. "But now? Yes, I think so. If you are at the Palace, then no one will attack me, or Del, or any of us. At least, you think that they will not."

"But that's not guaranteed," Mannon said, looking back at her. "They know I've sworn to you now. They know Del is my son. It doesn't matter if I'm here or not. Someone who wants to hurt me is going to go after him. Or you." He rubbed his hands down the front of his shirt. "If I leave, if I remove myself as a target of their hate, they might turn on you."

Aven frowned and looked at Aria. "Did you think of that? Do you think that they might?" he asked.

"I did not think anyone would try to attack someone in the healing complex," Aria said. "I think I do not know what they will do."

Mannon scowled. "I have some thinking to do. I will see you at Council. If I may be excused?"

Aria smiled. "So long as you do not brood and fret. You will make Memfis miserable if you brood and fret."

Memfis reached out and rested his hand on Mannon's shoulder. "You can do your thinking over something to eat."

Mannon looked quizzically at Memfis. "Is that your way of saying that you want something to eat?"

Memfis grinned. "Now that you mention it..."

Mannon shook his head and sighed. "I'll meet you in the kitchen. Aria, I'll walk you and Aven out."

Outside, Aven offered his arm to Aria. She took it, but didn't say anything as they walked back toward the central hub. As they turned toward Northwest, Aven cleared his throat. "My folk say that deep thinking requires deep waters. Do Airborn have any saying like that?"

"We say that the higher winds clear your mind and allow the truth to be revealed," Aria answered. "But I can't sail the high winds now. Nor can I swim deep enough."

"So you'll just have to talk to me," Aven said.

Aria smiled. "He's so different from when we first met him," she said. "On the ship in the harbor."

"I know," Aven replied. "It's hard to reconcile the two."

Aria squeezed his arm, falling silent again as they reached the turn for Northwest. "Do you think that who we're seeing now is who he was before he made his choice?"

"Who he could have been, maybe?" Aven replied. "Owyn might have more to say about that. He spent more time with Mannon. He might have a better idea."

Aria nodded. Then she yawned, and Aven chuckled.

"We'll tuck into bed when we get in. Talking to Owyn can wait until we get some rest."

They walked into the house, and Aven was surprised to see the crowd around the table. Owyn and Alanar, Del, Trey and Lady Meris all looked up in surprise.

"Is this a little Council meeting before the actual Council meeting?" Aria asked.

Owyn laughed. "No! No, this is something else entirely. Come sit. I need to show you something."

Aven glanced at Aria, and led her to a chair. He stood behind her. "If I sit, I might not get up. My hip—"

"I can feel it from here," Alanar said. "I'll take a look at it once we're done."

"What did you want to show us, Owyn?" Aria asked.

Owyn hesitated, then looked at Aven. "Say something. In water sign." Then, to Aven's surprise, he covered his eyes.

"What are you doing?" Aven asked.

"Just go ahead."

Aven looked around the table, stopping on Del. He signed, *"What is going on here?"*

"What's going on here," Owyn answered, without uncovering his eyes. "Is that I've been having heart visions."

"Owyn!" Aria gasped.

Owyn lowered his hands. "That's why we're all sitting here. Because we're figuring out what I can do and with who. Wait. Whom?" He looked at Meris. "Granna? Who or whom?"

"Whom, darling," Meris answered, smiling.

Owyn nodded. "What I can do and with whom. And we think it's limited to people I love. Really love." He colored slightly. "People I love enough to sleep with. Or...that I love enough to want to sleep with, since it works with Del."

Aven nodded slowly. "Is this because you died?"

"Apparently so," Meris answered. "Owyn is much more sensitive. I'll know more when I test him again. But for now, it appears that Owyn has started having heart visions."

"I know of them, from *The Lay of Axia's Choice.* I always thought it was a myth," Aria said. "They are real?"

"Real, but very rare. I could wish that the Smoke Dancer archives survived. If the information exists, it would be there, and

I don't know what information made it to the Palace archives. But I can hope that the Palace library has references to what we know about heart visions. We'll find out when we go north." Meris rested her hands on the table. "Now, I should go home. I was going to nap before the Council meeting. The children wore me out."

Trey got to his feet. "I'll walk you back, Lady Meris."

"Thank you, darling," Meris said. She let him help her out of her chair, and leaned on his arm.

Owyn got up and stopped them. He hugged Meris and kissed her on the cheek. Then he looked up at Trey and grinned. "You're not dumb. Karse shouldn't say that. And if you want to learn to read, I'll help."

"I'll think about it," Trey said. He leaned down and kissed Owyn gently. "Just to clear the air? I love you, too. I just never realized you loved me."

Owyn shook his head. "All right. Maybe you are a little dumb—"

"Hey!"

Owyn laughed and hugged Trey. "See you at supper. Come hungry."

"For your cooking? Always."

Trey led Meris out, and Owyn returned to his place at the table. He folded his hands and looked around. "So...that's new. And different. And really fucking weird."

Aria nodded. "Owyn, can you hear me, the way you hear Aven? And who else?"

"Right now, it's Aven, Del, Trey and Alanar. I haven't checked with Treesi, because she's asleep." Owyn looked at Aria. His eyes widened. "And...no. Aria, I don't hear you. At all."

CHAPTER SIX

A ria stared at Owyn. "You...you do not?" she stammered. "Why?"

Owyn's eyes were very wide. "I don't know," he answered. "I mean, it don't make sense." He frowned. "I love you. You...you know that, right?"

"I do know that," Aria answered. She reached past Del and took Owyn's hand, feeling the callouses on his fingers from working in the forge. "I know that you love me. And I do love you."

"I wish Granna hadn't left yet," Owyn said. "There's got to be a reason—"

"Of course there is," Alanar answered. "If you don't mind a completely unbiased viewpoint?"

"Unbiased?" Owyn asked. "How are you unbiased, love...oh. Virrik?"

Alanar smiled and tapped his temple. "Virrik. Who has a thought." He leaned his forearms on the table. "You've only been back together a month. Have either of you talked about anything that happened last winter?"

"I apologized," Aria answered, looking at Owyn. He nodded.

"We both apologized," Owyn added.

"But you haven't *talked*," Alanar stressed the word. "There's probably still a lot of emotion under the surface, and it's not going to go away just because you both said you were sorry and that you forgave each other. Those are just words. You have to deal with the emotions."

"So you are saying that Owyn cannot hear me because he is still...what? Angry at me?" Aria asked.

"I'm not!" Owyn protested, his voice spiraling up.

Alanar shook his head. "No, Owyn isn't angry. He can't stay angry for long. But he was really hurt by how you treated him. And then he hurt you, when he went off and got his ass killed. So I think that's formed a barrier between the two of you."

"You think?" Owyn asked. "Or Virrik thinks?"

"Virrik suggested it," Alanar answered. "And now that I've said it, I agree with him. You two never cleared the air between you. You were both hurt, each by the other. So there are things in the way of clear communication."

"And we need to clear that?" Owyn asked. "It...it makes sense. I think. Aria? How do we do that? Because it's not right that I can't hear you when I can hear all the other Companions. Not with me being your Fire."

"I'm not sure how we clear the air and show that we truly do forgive each other. It can't be so simple as we finally share a bed?" she asked, and was rewarded by Owyn turning bright red.

"What makes you think sharing a bed with Owyn is simple?" Alanar quipped, and Owyn went even more red.

"Fuck you," he growled. "Both. Singly, and as a pair. And not in a fun way. I'm going to go check the roast." He got up and stalked out of the room. Aria watched him disappear into the kitchen, then looked at Alanar.

"Was that because of you, or because of me?" she asked.

"Well, given his reaction, yes," Alanar answered. He sighed and shook his head, then frowned. "Shut up, Virrik. That wasn't helpful."

"What did he say?" Aven asked.

"That taking Owyn to bed would either be the best thing Aria could do, or the worst." He shrugged. "The best because it will help him to believe beyond a shadow of a doubt that you love him and forgive him."

"And how would it be the worst?" Aria asked.

"If he thinks you're doing it for the wrong reasons. Not because you love him, but because you want to make him feel better," Alanar answered. "He loves you. Completely. He would share your bed in a heartbeat. He's told me as much. But he's still not sure you want him there. And you haven't asked him."

"I thought I explained that," Aria said. "The night you married. I told you both that I did not want to put myself in your way. I wanted to give you time to be married."

Alanar nodded. "So you expected the first move to be his, when he was ready to make it. I remember."

"Does he?" Aven asked.

"We've talked about it," Alanar answered. "Especially on nights when I have an overnight shift. I told him that I don't expect him to sleep alone when I'm not there."

"He doesn't," Aven murmured. "He sleeps with Treesi."

Alanar nodded again. Then he sighed. "All Virrik can say is that the both of you still have wounds. Neither of you meant to hurt the other, but you did. Until those wounds heal, you're not going to be as close as you were. And to heal, you have to talk about it."

"Then I will go and talk to him," Aria said. She looked up at Aven. "If you would move?"

"We're not talking now." Aria turned in her chair to see Owyn had come back to stand in the doorway. "I...yeah, Virrik is right. He's right, and...and we do need to talk. But...if I talk now, I'm going to say things I don't want to. Because last winter still hurts. It hurts a lot. And until I can talk about it without hurting you with it, we're not talking."

"Would it help to talk to one of us?" Aven asked. "Me, or Del?"

"I don't know," Owyn answered. He frowned, then shook his head. "No. I don't think so. Because there's a bit of hurt in there at you, Fishie."

"Because I left you, too?" Aven asked.

"Yeah. So...just let me work it through my own head, and I'll talk to you when I'm ready to talk. When I know how to do it without losing control of it." He reached up to scratch the back of his neck, looking down at the ground. "I'll talk to Granna after she tests me. Maybe she'll have an idea. And maybe I'll dance on it." He turned back toward the kitchen.

Aria pushed awkwardly up out of her chair. "Owyn!"

He stepped toward her. Then he stopped and waited for her to cross the room. She reached out to touch his chest, her fingertips brushing the gem at the hollow of his throat.

"I am sorry," she said softly. "For everything. And whatever you have to say, it's no less than I deserve for how I treated you. When you are ready to tell me, I am ready to listen."

He covered her hand with his. "I'm sorry, too," he murmured. "When I'm ready, I know where you are." He grinned weakly. "I know where you sleep." He looked down, then drew her hand up to his mouth and kissed her palm. She trailed her fingers over his cheek, feeling the stubble where he missed a spot shaving.

"You're welcome to come join me there," she said. "I am going to bed, to sleep. Or perhaps, not sleep?"

Owyn smiled slightly. "And I have a roast in the oven to feed your Council, so...maybe don't distract me?" He nodded toward the table. "After all, none of them can cook!"

"I can so!" Aven called. "Just...not like you do."

"Yeah, well, we're not doing the many ways of eating raw fish and fermented sea oak at Council tonight," Owyn called back. He looked up at Aria and sighed. "Go get some rest. You look tired. We'll talk. And we'll clear the air. But not right now."

She nodded. Then she leaned closer and kissed him. When she drew back, he was smiling. But there was still sadness in his gold-flecked eyes.

"Go get some rest," he repeated. "I need to work on this stew." He turned and walked into the kitchen.

"He's right," Aven said from behind her. "You do need to rest."

"We both do," Aria said without turning. She walked down the hall to the bedroom and let herself in, hearing Aven's uneven step behind her. She went straight to the bed, knowing he'd close the door. As soon as she heard the click of the latch, she shuddered.

"I had no idea," she murmured. "I didn't know."

"I wonder if he knew?" Aven asked. He took her hand. "It sounds as if he didn't. Alanar saying it made him realize it."

"And that's why he was angry? Because now we both know?" Aria asked. She looked up at Aven. "He hasn't really forgiven me?"

"That's not what he said," Aven said, shaking his head. "You're both sorry. You've both forgiven each other. But there's still something that needs to come out. Like a bad wound. Sometimes, you have to lance it for it to heal all the way."

"If there's still something there, something that's keeping him from being as close to me as he is to all of you, then he has not forgiven me. And it has not healed. Not at all. He is mine...but he is not. Not completely."

Aven arched a brow. "What did the gem say?"

Aria blinked at him, confused. "What?"

"When you saw Owyn again, on the docks, when we came back. What did the gem say?" He cocked his head to the side. "What did your heart say? Is he still yours? Is he still your Fire?"

"Of course he is!" Aria protested. Then she paused. "Oh. He is, isn't he?"

Aven nodded. "You knew, the moment you saw him again, that he was still yours. I knew, the moment I saw him on the deck of that ship, that he was still ours. But you and I, we weren't the only ones Risha hurt last fall. What she did to us tore Owyn to pieces—"

"Because he's part of us," Aria finished. "And when you left him, and I turned away from him, it was salt in the wounds." She pressed her palms together, touching the tips of her fingers to her forehead. "I never meant to hurt him."

"Neither of us did, and he knows that," Aven assured her. "If you were trying to hurt him, I don't think the Mother would have given him back to you."

"Not give him back?" Aria repeated. "You mean...She wouldn't have let you bring him back?"

"Or She wouldn't have put him where I could reach him," Aven replied. "Aria, we're all here for a reason. If the Mother thought you weren't capable of doing what you needed to do, She would have shattered the bond completely when we separated." He frowned. "I...now that raises a question. If the Mother revokes Her choice, does she take the gems back?" He reached up and touched the blue Water gem at his throat. "And if She does, then why does Mannon have a gem? Yana wasn't in any shape to be Heir when she chose him."

Aria drew her wings in close and went to sit down in the low-backed chair by the window. "But her purpose was different from mine," she said as she slid her feet out of her shoes. "Perhaps her purpose was to show Mannon the way?"

Aven shrugged. "Maybe. I don't know." He shook his head. "I'm too tired for philosophy. And so are you. We wanted to sleep."

Aria smiled and stood up. She turned her back to Aven and let him undo the fastening over her wings, so she could take off the long vest that she wore. She unfastened the hooks at the back of her neck and let her loose dress fall to the ground around her feet.

"Do you want the breast-band off, too?" Aven asked, tugging his own shirt over his head.

"No, because then I'll have to put it back on," Aria answered. She looked down at herself and sighed. "I miss my feet."

Aven blinked. Then he started giggling. Giggling became whoops of laughter, hard enough that he had to sit down. Aria folded her arms and waited for him to stop, but every time he looked up at her, the giggling started again.

"You truly are tired, aren't you?" she asked, then rolled her eyes when he tipped over laughing. "Aven!"

"I'm sorry!" he wheezed. "I'm sorry." He sat up, making a visible effort to stop. "I must be more tired than I thought," he agreed. He stood up and stripped off his kilt, then held his hand out to Aria. "Come to bed, love."

They settled down into the wide bed, falling into their usual, comfortable position — Aven on his back, Aria's head cushioned on his left shoulder, her left wing spread over them both like a blanket. She yawned and cuddled as close as she could, feeling the baby tumble and kick.

Aven chuckled. "The little one is bouncy," he murmured.

"You're still not going to tell me?" Aria asked, tracing the lines of his warrior marks with her nails.

"You asked me not to, and made me promise I wouldn't, no matter how much you asked."

She sighed. It had seemed like such a good idea when she'd asked him to do that, a few days after he'd returned to her. But now? "I know what I asked, but I'm curious!"

Aven laughed. "I promised. I'm not telling."

"We'll have to choose a name."

"We'll choose one of each," Aven said. "I will tell you that there is only one baby in there. So we choose a boy's name and a girl's name. And you're supposed to be sleeping."

She felt him kiss her forehead, and smiled. She closed her eyes and let his warmth sink into her. It had been a long, exciting day, and there was still the Council to come. She needed to sleep.

Owyn was hers. She was certain of it. He just needed time. He needed to heal.

They would talk, when he was ready. And when he was ready, they'd mend whatever needed to be mended.

She just needed to be patient.

SHE'D ASKED HIM TO her bed. After so many months, she'd finally asked him.

And he'd said no. There really hadn't been a choice. Owyn knew in his bones that if he chose that path, it would end up badly. They needed to fix things first, and sex would only complicate matters. So he'd said no. Given a weak excuse.

And gone to work his frustrations out in bread dough, punching down the risen dough, shaping it into smaller round loaves, and setting them to rise a second time. He tested the roast, and decided it was cool enough to start carving into pieces for the stew. He moved it from the roasting pan to the cutting board, and got his big carving knife. Behind him, he heard soft, familiar footsteps.

"I'm sorry I overstepped," Alanar said.

"I didn't think that came from you," Owyn answered without turning. "Virrik has an acid tongue. Or would it be had?"

"He did, and I'm not sure of verb tenses when we're talking about someone who's not entirely dead. Or who might not be anything more than a broken piece of my own mind. Me talking to myself."

Owyn looked over his shoulder, seeing Alanar had gone to sit at the small table. "Still no idea which?"

"I can't tell. How can I? I'm inside it. So I either have his spirit living in my head, which means something went horribly wrong when Aven gave him back to the deep," Alanar said. "Or I am completely, irrevocably insane."

"Would you know the difference?" Owyn asked.

"I don't know. But if I am insane, I am the 'decorative, useful, and not a threat to people around' me sort of insane, so Jehan doesn't have to put that blasted backwards coat back on me." He smiled. "I don't think that there is much of a difference, really. Not in the end. Do you?"

"Not a difference that I care about, no," Owyn answered, and went back to cutting the meat into bite-sized pieces that went into the big stew-pot. Mentally, he ran through what else needed to go in — root vegetables, onions and garlic. He'd deglaze the roasting pan with the rest of the wine, and add that to the pot, too. Stew leaves, and some of the fermented fish sauce that Marik had told him was only made in Serenity.

"Well, if it was me, I'm sorry," Alanar said, breaking in to Owyn's stewing over stew. "And if it wasn't me, I'm still sorry. I didn't have to say it."

Owyn nodded. "I'm not sure it was a bad thing. I think I needed to hear it. Because now I know what it was that was stopping me from asking her." He dropped the last of the meat into the pot and picked up a towel to wipe his hands. Vegetables next. "Where's Del? He was going to help me with the vegetables."

"Not sure," Alanar admitted. "Aven and Aria went to bed, and you were in here. I think he didn't want to bother you, so he left this." He held up a slip of paper. "If I have to guess, he's gone to see his father."

Owyn went and took the paper from Alanar, reading Del's neat handwriting. *I want to see how my father is. I'll be back to help soon.*

"You're right. He's gone to see Mannon," Owyn said, putting the paper on the table. "Right. Keep me company while I peel potatoes?"

Alanar smiled. "I'd help if you trusted me with a knife."

"I can't put you back together, so just keeping me company is fine."

CHAPTER SEVEN

Del knocked on the door to Seventeen North, then tipped his head so he could hear better. He'd already knocked twice, but no one had come to the door. He hadn't expected his father to leave the house. Not after saying he was placing himself under house arrest. But either he and Memfis weren't here, or they weren't answering. Del wasn't sure which bothered him more.

He considered knocking again, then shook his head. There was no point. He'd see his father at the Council. He should head back — he'd promised to help Owyn with the cooking. He walked down the path to the street.

"I thought you didn't go anywhere alone."

Del grinned and turned to see Trey had come out of Fifteen. He waited until the guard joined him, then took out his tablet. Trey groaned.

"Small words, Del," he said. "Simple ones."

Del nodded and wrote, "*I came to see my Fa. He's not here.*"

Trey nodded. "I know. He and Memfis came over. They're in with Karse, and I think they're going to go and talk to Aleia in a bit. So I'm going down to talk to Othi. Want to come with me?"

Del shook his head and wrote, "*I'm supposed to help Owyn with cooking.*"

Trey read the tablet and nodded. "Fine. I'll go down alone, after I walk you home."

Del rolled his eyes and tucked his tablet back into his vest pocket. Now that he understood why Trey was being so protective, it wasn't quite so onerous. And he did like Trey. He felt comfortable with the guard, and enjoyed his company.

Even if he couldn't read, and didn't know water signs. He was safe. Maybe he was safe enough?

"Do you have any idea what kind of weapon you want to try?" Trey asked. "Once we start?"

Del mimed drawing a bow, then looked up at Trey.

Trey nodded. "Right. We'll try longbow and crossbow, see which works better. What else?"

Del shrugged and shook his head. Trey laughed.

"Not sure? All right, we'll try a few things. And I want to know what you've tried already. Other than spear." He studied Del for a moment. "Knives, I think. You're little and fast. A pair of long knives, maybe."

Del shuddered and shook his head, and Trey laughed again.

"Right. You want a ranged weapon, then. Something that will keep you at a distance." He nodded. "That might not be the worst idea. But we should work on close combat, too. Just in case someone gets inside your guard."

Del shrugged again, and pointed at Trey. Then he stopped and fell in behind Trey.

"Oh, you're going to stay behind me?" Trey asked, turning to walk backward. "And what happens if I go down?"

Del stopped, suddenly cold. He shook his head, hard.

Trey frowned. "Del, are you all right?" he asked.

Del pulled his tablet out of his pocket and quickly wrote, *"Don't make jokes about dying. I don't want to think about you dying."*

Trey took the tablet, his eyes narrowed as he puzzled out the words. Then he looked up. "I'm sorry. I didn't mean to upset you."

Del nodded, swallowing around the lump in his throat, tasting the bitter edges of panic for the first time in a long time. He took the tablet back, wiped it clean, and put it back into his pocket. He didn't notice Trey coming closer, and jumped in surprise when Trey put his arm around his shoulders.

"I'm sorry," Trey repeated. "Come on. I'll take you home."

Del nodded and started walking, leaning into Trey's side. When they were out on the ocean, Aven would occasionally sit with him like this, and the feeling of Trey's arm around him was very much the same — the warm, strong arm of someone Del truly liked, offering comfort and protection while not asking for anything in return.

Then Trey's arm tensed, and Del looked up.

"So," Trey said slowly. "What are we..." He paused. "Del, I'm not even sure what I'm asking. I...I'm awful at telling what people want. I never learned how. I need to be told. And, well, you...you're a Companion. And I'm married. I mean, Karse won't mind. He likes you. But...what are we?"

Del shook his head. He took a step to the side, shaking off Trey's arm, and took out his tablet. *"We're friends. I'm not looking for anything more. I'm not interested in anything more."*

Trey took the tablet and read it. "Just friends? Nothing else?"

Del nodded. He took the tablet back and wrote, *"I'm not interested in sex. I never have been. With anyone."*

Trey turned his head to read the words as Del wrote them. He grinned. "You really are like Tacen. He was like that. He hated what we had to do. If we weren't on the floor, he didn't want to be touched, ever. Even by me."

Del nodded. He looked up at Trey and smiled, then looked down and wrote, *"I've never had a brother."*

"Do you want one?" Trey asked. "A brother, I mean."

Del nodded again.

"Well, then," Trey murmured. "I've got a little brother again. I like that. Come on. Let's get you home."

They walked side-by-side toward the hub, and were just about to turn when someone called, "Excuse me?"

A woman was coming toward them. She looked familiar, but there were so many new people in Terraces that Del wasn't sure where he'd seen her before. She smiled shyly. "I'm sorry. Could you help me? I'm a little lost."

"You're new here?" Trey asked.

She nodded. "I just got here. And I've been assigned a house, but I'm all turned around. I was hoping you might know how to get to—" She paused and looked down at something in her hand. "Twenty-seven south?"

Trey blinked. "I hadn't realized that south goes that far out." He glanced at Del. "Want to take a walk? I've been down that far once or twice since we got here, exploring."

"Oh," the woman said. "Are you a refugee, too?"

Trey smiled. "From Forge. I was a guard there."

"Oh!" She looked startled. "I...I wasn't in Forge. We had a small farm, east of the Smoking Mountain."

Trey nodded. He gestured, and they started walking. As they walked, Del realized where he knew this woman from — the healing complex. Afansa.

He took his tablet out of his pocket and wrote, "*She was there when Fa was attacked at the healing complex this morning. Her name is Afansa.*" He tapped Trey on the arm and handed him the tablet.

"What's that?" Afansa asked.

"Del doesn't speak," Trey answered. He read the note, then nodded. "He says he met you this morning in the healing complex, Afansa."

She blushed. "I...yes. I was there. That's why I came to you for help, Airborn." She smiled. "I've been thinking about what the

Heir said. That he's trying. Mannon, I mean. That he's trying to fix things. I...how do you fix something so broken? How do you fix something that you've destroyed almost beyond repair?"

Trey whistled. "Well, you start by getting out of the way and letting someone who can fix it get to work. He's stepped down," he said.

"But does that mean that he's not going to have to pay for what he's done?" Afansa asked.

Trey shook his head. "Of course not. He surrendered to the Heir's judgment, whatever she decides. The only thing he asked is that if she does decide that he needs to die for what he did, that he be left alive long enough to see Risha die first."

"Who's Risha?" Afansa asked. "What did she do?"

"Tried to kill the Heir and her Water," Trey asked. He looked at Del again. "Del? Do you want me to—?" Del nodded, and Trey looked back at Afansa. "And she's the reason Del doesn't talk. He's Air. You know that. He...ah...Del had wings once. I don't know all the details. No one's told me yet, and I don't read well enough to get them all from Del. But I do know that Risha's the reason why."

Afansa went pale. "You...you had wings?"

Del nodded. He took the tablet back from Trey, wiped it, and wrote, "*I was six. She murdered my mother, and tried to kill me.*" He held the tablet out to Afansa.

"I...I don't read. At all," Afansa whispered.

Trey took the tablet, looked down at it, and whispered, "Oh, fuck, Del." He swallowed. "He says it happened when he was six. And Risha killed his mother to get to him."

"This Risha killed the Heir?" Afansa gasped. "Did she do it...no. No, Aria says that Mannon was Yana's Air."

Del swallowed and nodded. He took the tablet and started writing, his handwriting shaky. He kept his words short, so Trey could read them. "*Mannon was away. He was away a lot. Risha brought Mama and me up to the tower. Mama didn't fly. She wasn't right in the head, and she forgot how to fly.*" Dimly, he was aware that Trey had moved behind him, and was reading aloud. "*I didn't know how to fly yet. I was too little. Risha brought us up to the top of the tower, and she pushed us out.*" He shoved the tablet at Trey and walked away, wrapping his arms around his chest. A moment later, arms enclosed him from behind.

"Del, I'm sorry," Trey murmured. "I didn't know. I wouldn't have asked if I knew."

Del nodded, closing his eyes, closing out the world.

"You call your father by his name?" Afansa said. "Isn't he? Isn't Mannon your father?"

Del shook his head without opening his eyes.

"Mannon raised him," Trey added. "Adopted him. But his father was Yana's Fire. Am I remembering that right?"

Del nodded.

"And...oh, I can't. I can't do it." Del opened his eyes to see Afansa in front of him, tears running down her face. "I can't do it," she repeated.

"Can't do what?" Trey asked. He shifted, moving Del to his side, handing him the tablet, which Del slipped into his pocket. "Afansa?"

"They...they sent me because they thought you wouldn't suspect a woman. There's a bunch of them, down at the end of South. They told me they wanted you, so they could get the Usurper. So they could get their revenge." She swallowed, then raised her chin. "Aria is right. There's been enough of people working against the Heir. I won't be one of them."

Trey growled softly. "Come on," he said. "The both of you. We're going to the healing complex. And you're going to tell the Senior Healer what you just told us."

Afansa looked south. "Will they make me leave?"

"I won't let them," Trey said, his voice firm. "Because you're true to Aria. The rest of them? I don't know." He put his arm around Del, then held his hand out to Afansa. "Come with us."

DEL FOLDED HIS HANDS in his lap and tried to disappear into his chair. He wasn't sure what was happening outside Jehan's office. When they got here, Jehan had calmly listened to Trey and Afansa, nodding sagely the whole time. Then he'd ordered them to stay there, and left. Del wasn't sure if he locked the door to keep them there. It wouldn't have surprised him. He wasn't sure how long it had been. Long enough.

He thought he was safe. Safe here, and safe with Trey. Safe enough to be alone. Maybe he was safe with Trey, but he wasn't safe in Terraces. The realization hurt.

And he'd told Afansa. He'd told a *stranger*. What had he been thinking? He could see the look in Afansa's eyes now, the same look he saw from all the servants at the Palace. The same pity for the poor, broken child.

A thought occurred to him — maybe that's why he liked Trey so much. He didn't think of Del as less, because of what he'd lost. He expected Del to do the same things anyone else could do. And Trey agreed with Othi and with Aven. He thought that Del should be able to learn to fight. More, he thought he would be able to work around Del's tendency to freeze.

Maybe he was right, and his weapons master had been wrong? Maybe Del really could learn to fight for himself? Stand up for himself?

Maybe he *could* learn to fight back?

He swallowed and looked up. Trey was leaning against the desk, his arms folded over his chest, his legs crossed at the ankle. He was scowling fiercely.

"You'll curdle fresh milk with that face," Afansa murmured.

"I should be out there, helping them," Trey muttered. "I'm a guard."

"And you're guarding," she pointed out. "You're guarding him."

"And you," Trey added.

She sniffed. "I don't need guarding. I'm not a target."

Trey straightened. "You are now," he said. "You turned on them. And you turned them in. If Jehan's guards miss any of them, you'll be first on their list."

Afansa looked startled. "I..."

"*Aria will make sure that you're safe,*" Del signed. She looked at him, tracing the movements with her eyes.

"Is that...is that how you talk?" she asked. "It's like dancing. Show me again?"

Del repeated himself, then took his tablet out and wrote the same message. He handed it to Trey to read.

"Del is right," Trey said. "Aria will take care of you. And your family."

Afansa shook her head. "I don't have anyone anymore. I was married, but my man died last winter."

Trey's brows rose. "I'm sorry," he said. "You were from where? East of Forge, you said?"

"Near Sluice Creek," she answered. "Do you know it? The clay fields there were very good. We were potters, the both of us."

Trey shook his head. "I never really got out of Forge much. Karse would know."

"Guard Captain Karse?" Afansa asked. "I know that name. Do you know him?"

Trey grinned and held up his arm, revealing his bracelet. "Intimately. We've been married half a year now."

She looked from him to Del. "Oh, I...I thought you were paired."

"Nah," Trey said with a laugh. "Del's like my little brother." He moved over to perch on the arm of Del's chair. "How are you?"

Del held his hand up and waggled it, then picked up the tablet and wiped it clean. *"I'm supposed to be helping Owyn to cook."*

"He'll manage," Trey assured him. "This needed doing." He frowned. "You didn't answer the question."

There was a soft knock at the door. It opened, and Aleia came into the office. She smiled at them. "Jehan says you can come out and go home."

"Did they get them all?" Trey asked.

"Afansa, how many were supposed to be there?"

Afansa frowned slightly. "I...Jassic had two men with him when they came to me and told me they wanted me to find Del and bring him down there."

Aleia nodded. "Marik's birds saw seven. We took all seven. But Jassic wasn't one of them. So we'll need to get him, too."

"Aleia, what about Afansa?" Trey asked. "She's turned on them. That makes her a target."

Aleia turned to look at him. "You have a point. Do you have a suggestion?"

"She can come home with me," Del signed. *"Once Aria knows, she'll think of something."*

"Is...is that something I can learn to do?" Afansa whispered. "It's so pretty to watch."

Aleia smiled. "I think that can be arranged. And Del says you should go home with him. All right. Come on. You've been waiting long enough."

"I'll walk you both to the Heir's house," Trey said.

They walked around the corner and out of the healing complex, and saw the crowd in the hub. Jehan was standing with his back to them, facing a small group of people surrounded by guards.

"...you'll be given supplies, and taken through the tunnels. Do not come back to Terraces. You are not welcome here." Jehan waved one hand. "Take them out."

"Where are we supposed to go?" one of the men demanded. "This is the only safe place!"

"And we're keeping it that way," Jehan snapped back. "You attempted to waylay the Airborn Companion, with the intent of harming him. You've betrayed the Heir—"

"He's the Usurper's son!"

"He is the Airborn Companion," Jehan repeated. "Chosen by the Mother. Are you saying the Mother was wrong?" He pointed at one of the men. "Are you?" Pointed at another. "How about you?"

"No, but—"

"No," Jehan cut him off. "He is Aria's Companion. The Mother chose him. There are no buts. If you're setting yourself against him, then you're setting yourself against the Heir and against the Mother. And that's not happening in my city. Or in my tribal lands. Go back to the Fire tribe if you want. But you're not to stay in Earth tribal lands." He waved them away again, then turned. Seeing them, he came to join them.

"That's all of the ones from South," he said softly. "It should be—"

"Jassic wasn't there," Aleia interrupted. "Afansa says he organized this."

"I know. The others gave him up." Jehan nodded. "His house was empty. Marik has the birds up, searching. We'll find him." He looked at Trey. "Walk them home, Trey?"

"You didn't even need to ask me," Trey answered. He bowed slightly, then turned to Del. "Let's get you home."

They started walking, leaving Jehan and Aleia behind, heading toward the marker for Northwest. Del tucked his hands into his pockets and tried not to look over his shoulder.

Safety was just a story people told. There was no such thing as safety.

A hand slipped into his arm, and he looked to his right at Afansa.

"I'm sorry," she said. "It's all my fault. If I hadn't gotten frightened this morning, if I hadn't screamed—"

"We wouldn't know about them," Trey interrupted. "It'll be all right, Afansa."

"I saw him once, at a festival. He stopped at our shop," she said. "He bought some pottery from us. He liked the glazes, he said."

Del blinked and dug out his tablet. *"Blue and green tea bowls? With gold patterns like frost?"*

Afansa brightened when Trey slowly read the message. "Yes! That's our salt glaze."

Del smiled. *"He bought them for me. I love them. I use them all the time."*

Trey laughed. "Small world, hm?" he asked after he read the note to Afansa.

Del took the tablet and wiped it, putting it back into his pocket. As they started walking again, Del saw movement from the little pocket of a park just past Three Northwest. He touched Trey's arm and pointed, but in the moment where Trey looked at him, Jassic stepped out into the street and raised a crossbow.

Afansa screamed.

CHAPTER EIGHT

Owyn had just put the stew-pot on the stove when he heard the scream. He almost fell when the wave of panic hit him, staggering away from the stove. He shook his head, feeling his stomach roiling from the strength of it. And it wasn't him.

It was Del!

"Del?" he gasped. "Treesi, get Aven! Allie, stay here!" He grabbed his big carving knife and bolted from the kitchen. He heard Treesi scrambling behind him, but ignored her, running through the front room and out of the house. Outside, he saw a woman. She had put herself between Del and an armed man. On the ground in front of her was Trey. He wasn't moving. And the armed man was raising his crossbow...

"Hey!" Owyn shouted, running from the house. He'd never get there in time. The knife wasn't balanced for throwing. Whoever the man was, he'd shoot that woman before Owyn could stop him.

He heard something whistle past his ear, and the armed man howled and fell, dropping the crossbow and clawing at a javelin that had blossomed in his side. Owyn glanced back and saw Aven standing behind him, completely naked and with his hook swords in his hands. Behind Aven was Aria. She was wearing only her underthings, and had a handful of javelins in one hand.

"I missed," she grumbled.

"That...that was a good hit, Aria," Owyn said slowly. "He's down."

"But he's not dead," she replied. "Now Aven will have to put him back together again."

"Won't be me," Aven answered. He laid his swords on the covered bench that sat outside the house, and hurried out into the street. He knelt down next to Trey, then looked up and shouted, "Alanar! I need you out here now!"

Alanar immediately appeared in the doorway, followed by Treesi. "Who's hurt?"

"Trey."

Alanar nodded and hurried out of the house and down into the street, dropping to his knees next to Trey and Aven. Owyn bit his lip, wanting to follow. But he'd be in the way. He went instead to Del, who hadn't moved.

"Del," Owyn said gently. He could still feel the fear rolling off him. "Del, it's over." Del didn't move. He didn't blink. He was pale as milk, and as rigid as a statue. Owyn stepped closer and raised his voice. "Del!"

Del jerked, his head whipping around toward Owyn. But Owyn could tell that Del wasn't seeing him. Wasn't seeing anything. He took a shuddering breath...and collapsed.

"Fuck!" Owyn gasped. "Treesi!" He dropped his knife and fell to his knees. Was Del hurt? He didn't see any blood.

"I'm busy, Owyn!" Treesi called back.

"Fuck." Owyn tried to examine Del. No blood, but it was hard to tell. Del had curled into a tight ball.

"Is he hurt?" Owyn looked up to see the woman standing over him. "Jassic only got the one shot off. And Trey stepped in the way."

"I'm not sure what's going on," Owyn said. "Allie?"

"Busy!"

Owyn looked up, saw Alanar and Aven — who was now wearing a poorly-wrapped kilt — and Treesi, and they were all working over Trey. "Fuck," he whispered. "Oh, fuck." He looked back at the woman. "Go to the healing complex. Tell the Senior Healer we need him here now. Tell him it's an emergency." He looked over at Trey again, and felt his stomach lurch. "And tell him we need Karse. Now."

She turned and ran toward the healing complex, and Owyn turned back to Del. He could still feel the fear, which meant that Del wasn't unconscious. It itched at the inside of his head, made his stomach churn. He knew this panic, and it was enough to make him feel like screaming. Which meant...

"Oh, fuck," he breathed. "He's like me. Like I was."

"Then you know what to do?" Aria asked from behind him.

"Get him out of the street. Let me get him up." He looked up at her. "Can you take my knife?"

"If you hand it to me."

Owyn gave the knife to Aria, then got to work on getting both himself and Del up off the ground.

"It's a good thing you don't weigh much," he grunted as he got to his feet. He took another look at the healers working in the middle of the street, then forced himself to follow Aria into the house.

"His room?" she asked.

"No," Owyn answered. "Mine. Bed is bigger. He needs to know he's safe." He hesitated. "Aria, he's going to be all right? Trey? He'll be all right?"

Aria's breath caught. "I...I hope so. I think so. They're all working on him. He'll be fine." She went before him, and opened the door to the bedroom. Then she stepped out of the way and let him in. Gently, he laid Del down on the bed, bundling him up tightly in the blankets. Then he climbed onto the bed and wrapped his arms around Del.

"It's all over," he said softly, trying to believe it. Trying to stay calm. "You're safe."

The bed tipped as Aria joined him, stretching out on Del's other side. "Del, you're safe now," she said. "You're here with us. You are in Owyn's bed. We're safe."

Through the layers of blankets, Owyn could feel Del start shivering. He held on tighter. "It's safe now," he repeated. "I've got you. It's safe."

The response was a low moan, the first sound other than a laugh Owyn had ever heard from Del. "Del, it's all right. You're safe. We've got you," Owyn whispered. "It's all right." He looked at Aria. "I wonder if this is what it was like for Aven."

She frowned slightly, then blinked. "When Fandor attacked, in my grandmother's garden. You panicked like this."

Owyn nodded. "He's like me. Like I was. Worse than I was. I didn't have any problems with being alone. You know how he gets." He leaned a little harder against Del. "He's been getting better. He's been going out alone."

"Because it's safe here," Aria said. "It was safe. Until today." She looked at him. "How are you?"

Owyn frowned. He hadn't thought about it. "Worried about Trey. Three healers working on him...that means it's bad. It's really bad. And...the panic, it's kinda hard not to fall right in there with him. But I can't. I have to take care of him." Owyn sighed. "Del, we're here. Aria and me, we're here. We've got you."

He felt Del take a deep breath. Then a whisper threaded through his mind. *"Owyn?"*

"I hear you, Del," Owyn said. "I'm here. We're here. Me and Aria."

"Trey?" Del asked. *"Did I kill Trey?"*

Owyn shook his head. "No. Aven is with him. He'll be fine."

He heard a distant bang, then a raised voice, "Del!"

"Mannon's here," Owyn murmured.

"I'll go," Aria said. She started to shift off the bed.

"You might want to put some clothes on," Owyn suggested as she stood up. "So you don't shock Mannon."

Aria looked down at herself, and blushed bright red. "I went *outside* like this," she whispered.

"You were distracted, Aria. And it's a good thing you didn't stop to dress. I wasn't going to be able to stop him."

Aria nodded. She picked up a blanket and wrapped it around herself, then let herself out of the bedroom.

Owyn turned his attention back to Del. "You still with me?" he asked. "You awake in there?"

"*I'm awake.*"

Owyn heard voices outside the bedroom. There was a soft knock, and Owyn looked over his shoulder to see Mannon as he stepped inside.

"How is he?" he asked, his voice low.

"You first," Owyn said. "How's Trey?"

"They've taken him to the healing complex for observation," Mannon answered. "He'll live. There was a bit of damage. The quarrel was barbed, and the damn fool poisoned it for good measure. But Aven says Trey will take no lasting damage."

Del moaned softly, and Owyn leaned on him. "You hear that?" he asked. "He'll live. He'll be fine."

"How is he?" Mannon repeated.

"He's talking, a little," Owyn answered.

"He's *what?*"

Owyn felt Del flinch. "Keep your voice down!" he snapped. "And come around the other side of the bed. Sit. You're making my neck ache." He waited until Mannon was sitting on the foot of the bed. "Me being able to tell what Del is saying without seeing the signs? It's more than that. I can hear him even if he's not signing. And right now, he's talking to me. Well, not right at this moment, but he's already asked about Trey." He looked down at Del. "You didn't kill him. He'll be fine."

Del nodded, once, the barest movement of his head. Owyn smiled and kissed his temple.

"You take your time, love," he said. "I'll be here until you're ready to come out." He frowned. "My fa with you?" he asked Mannon. "Would you ask him to go keep an eye on the stew for tonight?"

Mannon smiled. "I'll do that. Then I want to know more about what my boy sounds like to you." He left the bedroom, and Owyn rested his forehead against Del's shoulder. Trey would be all right.

"*You were worried about him,*" Del said. "*I'm sorry. It's my fault.*"

"It wasn't your fault," Owyn answered, his voice muffled against Del's back. "You didn't shoot him. Trey was doing what Trey does. He was looking after you."

"*He said I was his new little brother. And I almost got him killed.*"

Owyn blinked. "He said that?" he asked. "Well, he likes you a lot, then. He never called me that. And you did not. It wasn't your fault. It was the fault of that idiot with the crossbow, and who the fuck was he, anyway?"

"The man who attacked me in the healing complex this morning," Mannon answered. Owyn looked over his shoulder.

"I didn't hear you come back in."

"I can be quiet when I want to be," Mannon said. He came around the bed and sat back down. "Memfis says he'll keep an eye on the stew. He's got Ambaryl in there with him. She and Rhexa arrived just as I went out."

Owyn nodded. "Just...we'll keep her away from Del, right?" he said. "Right now, I'm not sure he could take her."

Mannon nodded. He reached out and rested his hand on Del's leg. "I haven't seen him this bad in over a year. And he was doing so well!"

"When it hits, it hits hard," Owyn murmured. "Knocks the life right out of you."

"You say that with a voice of experience," Mannon said. He sounded surprised.

"Yeah, I was this bad," Owyn said. "Last time was in Lady Meris' garden, right after Aria made me hers. Fandor came after me."

"And you killed him," Mannon finished

"Nah, not that night." He frowned. "Wait, maybe it was the same night. I'm not even sure anymore. It was either that night or the next. The night he came after me in the garden, I locked up like this. And I was bad enough that Aven didn't even try to move me. He kept me in the garden and we both fell asleep. And that's when Fandor got us both."

Mannon nodded. "The night Del met Aven the first time. I remember. I didn't know it at the time, though. But Aven helped Del the same way he helped you that night." He paused. "You know Del can't be alone for long?"

"He's been doing better," Owyn said. "But yeah."

"Fandor knew that," Mannon said. "I had to meet with my men, and there was one there who had a disturbing interest in Del. I thought it best to leave him behind, so I told Fandor to let him be, and to leave someone with him. Instead, he thought it would be amusing to watch Del panic. Or so I'm given to understand. He left Del chained in his kitchen. Alone. I was surprised that he wasn't completely comatose when I got back. But he wasn't, because Aven needed him." He smiled. "I almost killed Fandor myself that night."

"And you still pardoned him," Owyn said. "Why?"

"I hoped he'd be able to bring Aria and Aven to me," Mannon answered. "I didn't realize how far gone he was in his obsession with you."

"Yeah, well, he's dead now, and good riddance." Owyn looked down at Del. His breathing had become soft and regular, and his muscles had started to relax. "You still awake in there?"

No answer, and Owyn looked back up. "I think he's asleep. So I'm going to ask you. Who the fuck did this to him?"

Mannon's face went blank. "What? The...the fall—"

"I don't think this has anything to do with the fall," Owyn interrupted. He brushed Del's hair back off his face. "When I panic, it's because of Fandor and what he did to me. What I knew he was going to do to me if he ever got his hands on me again. Del's scared to be alone. And he's scared of someone attacking him. And he's scared of fighting back." He looked up at Mannon. "Who got him alone and hurt him? Who convinced him that being alone or trying to fight back meant he was going to be hurt?"

Mannon gaped at him for a moment, and the color drained from his face. "I...I don't know. You're saying someone hurt my son? How? How could I not know?"

Owyn brushed Del's hair back again, running his fingers through the gold. "Because he didn't tell you. And who? I don't know," he said. "Someone you trusted around him? Someone who you wouldn't have looked twice at?" He frowned slightly. "Which describes a lot of people at the Palace, doesn't it?"

"Most of the staff," Mannon agreed. "But for who had closest contact? Nestor, Ambaryl. Ah...his tutor was an old Waterborn named Skela. Del doted on him. Denis, for a while—"

"How is his family?" Owyn interrupted. "I never asked."

"I don't know," Mannon answered. "I haven't been back to the Palace, nor has Nestor told me in any of his reports. Let me think. The only other person I can think of was his weapons master."

Owyn looked down at Del. "I think he mentioned that he had a weapons master, but he's never really told us about them. Just that he had one."

"From the ages of twelve to sixteen," Mannon answered. "It was part of his training. He didn't take to it. He avoided it if he could. It was the only thing he ever pushed back on—"

"And I think now you know why," Owyn said softly. "Who was the weapons master? Did I meet them?"

Mannon took a deep breath and let it out. "No, he died in his sleep when Del was sixteen. I never replaced him. There didn't seem to be a point. His name was Antavi."

Owyn nodded, studying Del's sleeping face. "I don't know what he'll tell us. But I don't think you should be there when he does. I think he won't tell us anything if you can hear." Mannon made a small, pained sound, and Owyn shook his head. "It can't be helped. He didn't tell you for a reason. He still hasn't told you for a reason, and it's been three years."

Mannon nodded. "I tried to protect him," he said softly. "I failed in that like I failed in everything else. I just...why didn't he tell me?"

"*Because he told me not to. He said no one would believe me, because I was broken. And he told me he'd hurt me worse if I tried.*"

Owyn jerked and looked down. "I thought you were asleep."

Del shook his head and opened his eyes. "*I want to sit up.*" Owyn shifted and Del sat up, holding the blanket close around him. "*Tell him it started almost a year after I started training. We were sparring, and he told me that if I lost, I'd have to pay a forfeit. I lost. I always lost. And when I lost, he'd beat me. That's how it started. Just...beatings.*"

Owyn relayed that, and Mannon went white. "That's about when you stopped wanting to swim with me. Is that why?"

Del nodded. "*I was always covered in bruises. But never where they'd show.*"

"Why didn't you tell me?" Mannon asked softly.

"*Because he said no one would believe me.*"

Owyn nodded. "Yeah, they always say that. Fandor said that, too. But he's dead, and you're not."

Del nodded. "*He's dead because Skela walked in on us, and overheard him telling me it was time to go to the next level of training.*"

Owyn snorted. "You don't even need to tell me that the next level was sex."

Del nodded. "*I was late, and Skela came looking for me. Antavi...had me bent over the railing of the salle. He was telling me what he was going to do to me, and Skela heard him. Antavi threatened us both—he'd kill the both of us if we told.*" He let the blanket shift, raised his hands. "*Skela killed him. That's why he left us. In case you found out.*"

Mannon looked startled. "I thought Antavi died in his sleep. That's what Ambaryl said."

Del shook his head. "*Skela poisoned him. And I helped.*"

CHAPTER NINE

"You...you helped?" Owyn repeated. "You helped kill that fuck?"

Del nodded slowly, and jerked in surprise when Owyn hugged him. "That's amazing. I'm proud of you."

Del stared at him, confused enough that he forgot how to use his hands. Finally, he signed. *"Proud? Of me?"*

Owyn laughed. "Yes, I'm proud of you. You took control. You said 'no more' and you took control. Remember, I've been there. The same fucking place. It took me a lot longer to be able to do that."

Del looked down at his hands. Then he shook his head. *"I didn't take control. I hated doing it. He trusted me, and I betrayed him,"* he signed.

"He betrayed you first," Mannon said. He took a deep breath. "It appears that I owe Skela a debt. Del, I am so sorry. I would have stopped him, if I'd known. I would have killed him myself."

"You realize that now that we know this, we can help you work around it so that you can learn how to fight?" Owyn said.

"Work around how?" Del asked. *"Trey says he'll teach me to shoot."*

Owyn grinned. "That's what I mean. You can't be in close-up fighting. So we keep you further back."

Del took a deep breath, feeling something tight in his chest loosen. *"Thank you. What else?"*

Owyn frowned. He looked at Mannon. "I have an idea or two. You?"

"Perhaps I shouldn't have given up on having a weapons master quite so easily," Mannon said. "Practice. Lots of practice."

"*No!*"

Owyn winced. "Well, that's interesting. Mental shouting echoes inside your skull. I could have lived without knowing that." He shook his head. "And yes. Practice until it becomes automatic. But practice against me. Or against Trey. Or Aven. One of us who you know won't hurt you." He grinned. "I'd like to see what you can do with a whip chain."

Del frowned. "*Trey says knives. He wants me to learn to use knives.*"

"Throwing knives, perhaps?" Mannon suggested. "Or a blowpipe? Treesi uses one."

Own snapped his fingers. "Javelins. Traditional Air weapon, and Aria can teach you. She's good with them."

"Oh, that would be good," Mannon agreed.

Del snapped his fingers at them. "*You're talking around me. Stop that. Talk to me.*"

Owyn grimaced. "Sorry. Look, we have options. We can try a bunch of things and see what feels good to you while Trey teaches you to shoot."

Mannon nodded, and stood up. "I'll leave you to finish getting settled. I want to go and talk to Aleia." He smiled. "I have a debt to pay, and I want to know if Skela is still around so I can." He walked around the bed and let himself out of the bedroom.

As the door clicked closed, Del looked at Owyn. "*How did you know what to do?*"

Owyn sniffed. "I told you. I've been there. I used to panic like that. Exactly like that. Ask Aven. He held me the way I held you."

Del smiled. "*I liked you holding me.*"

Owyn's answering smile didn't reach his eyes. He reached out and took Del's hand. "I have a question," he said. "What that fuck did to you...is that why—?"

"*No,*" Del answered, and saw Owyn's puzzled look. "*You heard me, didn't you?*"

"I heard you. I just don't understand. It wasn't part of it?"

"*No. I knew long before he told me he wanted me in his bed that I had no interest. Remember, I was nearly sixteen when he did that. I already knew I was different. I thought it was something else broken, but there are books in the Palace library that said no.*"

Owyn nodded. "I know sex books. Treesi collects them. She calls them pillow books."

"*No, not those!*" Del laughed. "*Although the library has those, too. I mean healing texts. They say that there are different kinds of people. Men who want women. Men who want men. Men who want both, like you and Aven. Women who want men. Women who want women. Women who want both. And there are people like me, who don't want anyone.*"

Owyn looked thoughtful. "Jehan might have those books, if you can tell me the titles. I want to read them. Or it can wait until we get to the Palace. Are you feeling up to going out to the kitchen, or do you want to stay here?"

"*I'd like to go see Trey,*" Del answered. He tugged his hand out of Owyn's and thought about walking out of the house alone. The idea made him shiver. "*Is it safe?*"

"We can go find out," Owyn answered. He got up and held his hand out. "Let's go see."

Del climbed off the bed and took Owyn's hand, following him out of the room and down the hall. There were more people in the front room than he expected — Mannon was there, talking with Aleia and Rhexa. To his surprise, Treesi was there, too, talking with Aria.

"Del!" Treesi called when she saw him, and hurried over to hug him tightly. "Are you all right? I just got back. I wanted to be sure you were all right. I need to run right back. Aven wants a report."

Del nodded and signed, "*I'm fine.*"

"Mostly fine," Owyn corrected softly.

Del smiled slightly. "*Eggshell fine,*" he added. "*Fine but fragile. I'll be better later. How's Trey?*"

Treesi's face went carefully neutral. What she called her 'Healer Treesi' expression. "He'll be fine," she answered. "He was still in healing trance when I left, and Karse was with him. Senior Healer is furious. He's going through the entire city with a fine-toothed comb, finding all of the people who came here with Jassic."

"*And Jassic?*" Del asked.

"Will live, to my regret," Aleia answered, coming over to join them. "Jehan took care of him personally. He's being held under guard tonight, and tomorrow he'll go before the tribunal. We'll see what we see then. Treesi, go on back. They'll need you."

Treesi smiled. "Right. I'm off." She hugged Del again, kissed him quickly, then went and kissed Owyn before hurrying out.

"I haven't seen what you all do for crimes yet," Owyn said. "I didn't think there were any. Not in Terraces. This is a nice place. A good place." He paused. "Well, it was, anyway. It will be again."

"From your mouth to the Mother's ears," Rhexa said. She walked over to kiss Owyn's cheek, then turned to Del. "I don't want to presume. You've had a hard day. May I hug you?" Del smiled and hugged Rhexa, hearing her laugh. "That's a yes, I suppose?"

He nodded and let her go. "*I'd like to go see Trey, if I can?*" he signed.

"We can go now," Mannon said. "I'll go with you—"

"You will not," Aleia interrupted Mannon. "You heard Jehan. You're not going anywhere without a guard. And he said he'd bring a guard with him when he was done."

Mannon scowled. Then he sighed. "Would you take him, Aleia?"

"I'd be happy to, if he wants my company." Aleia turned to Del. He nodded in response, and she smiled. "Good. We'll be back when we're back."

"I'll come with you," Rhexa said. "I should be there when Jehan decides to do whatever he's going to do. Aria, come with us? The attack was on your Companion, you should be there."

Del felt a hand on his shoulder, and turned to see Owyn standing behind him. "Keep your eyes open when you go. Want your spear?"

Del laughed and signed, "*No! I can't use it! It's stupid to carry a weapon I don't know how to use.*"

"He's right," Aleia said. "He'll be fine, Owyn. Come with me."

Del looked around. "*Do you need me for anything, Owyn?*"

Owyn looked thoughtful, then shook his head. "The stew is on the stove. The bread bowls need to go into the oven, and you can't help with that. I can't think of anything. So go on. Tell Trey I'll come by and see him in the morning."

Del nodded. He started toward the door, following Aria, Aleia and Rhexa. And at the door, he stopped. He could feel his heart hammering in his chest, hear the blood rushing in his ears. His mouth was dry.

A hand slipped into his. Aria, who smiled at him.

"I am here. You're not alone," she said softly. "We'll take the step together. Are you ready?"

Del swallowed. He nodded and looked forward. Aleia stood just outside the door, and she held her hand out to him.

"You can do it, Del. The first step is the hardest."

Del stared at her for a moment. What did she mean, the first step is the hardest? What about all the steps after that? Who said those were any easier?

He swallowed again, and took the first step, out of the house and into the sunlight. Aleia took his left hand and squeezed it. "Good. Now the next one."

For a moment, he wanted to rebel, to run back into the house and into his room, close the door behind himself and never come out again.

But Trey was in the healing complex. And he needed to see Trey, to assure himself that he hadn't killed his new-found brother.

He took the next step.

AS DEL HEADED OUT INTO the street, Owyn let out a long breath and slumped into a chair.

"Are you all right?" Mannon asked.

"I can feel him," Owyn said. "Feel his panic. And it's contagious."

"What do you mean, feel his panic?"

Owyn turned to see Memfis standing in the doorway. He smiled. "You missed it, Fa. I'm doing new tricks," he said.

"What new tricks?" Memfis asked slowly.

"Heart visions," Owyn answered.

Memfis frowned. "Heart... wait. You said *heart visions?* Meris said you were having heart visions? I thought those were just stories!"

"I know!" Owyn said. "It don't seem real. But it is. Granna says that's why I can tell what Del is saying even though I'm not looking at him. And it's not just him." He ticked names off on his fingers. "Works with Allie, with Aven, with Trey, and I haven't tested with Treesi yet." He looked up, and knew exactly what his father was thinking. The frown on his face gave it away. "And it doesn't work with Aria yet. Because we still have some dross to deal with."

Memfis' frown deepened. Then he looked thoughtful.

"That makes sense," he said. "What about Del? And panic?"

"Del panics like I do. Like I did. Like I might, if I can find the time. Even the echoes of it are making me itch." Owyn rubbed one hand over his face. "As much as I hate to say it, do you think we can convince Jehan to throw Jassic over the wall on the lowest level?"

Mannon barked with laughter. "I'd like that. But I doubt he'd do it." He looked around. "I'm here until Jehan arrives with my guard. What can I do to help?"

Owyn took a deep breath and stood up. "I need to get the bread into the oven. And...ah...you know how we've set this room up for our meetings, right? Think you can manage?"

Mannon smiled. "I can move furniture. And Memfis will happily tell me when I get something in the wrong place."

Owyn grinned. "Fine. You two do that. I'll go get back to work."

He headed down the corridor and into the kitchen, and almost ran into Ambaryl, who was standing just inside the door. He stopped short and looked at her.

"Were you listening?" he asked. "You could have come out, you know."

Ambaryl backed away from the door, shaking her head. "Oh, I'd have only been in the way," she said, turning toward the stove. "I just worry about the poor boy. If you don't mind my saying so, you're expecting far too much of him. This is all too much for him."

Owyn snorted, turning toward the stove. "He's more than capable," he said over his shoulder. "And, if you don't mind my saying so, you don't think enough of him. You need to stop treating him like a child."

"He is a child!" Ambaryl sounded indignant. "And damaged. It's unkind of you to let him believe that he can do all these things when he can't, the poor dear. You just can't expect him to—"

Owyn turned to face her. "Stop. Just stop," he said, trying to understand how those words could be coming from the woman his aunt loved enough to marry. "I heard that same sort of trash from Nestor. The poor broken child. No wonder he doesn't want to go back to the Palace. Not when you all treat him like he's an idiot."

"That's unfair—"

"No, unfair is how you refuse to give him the credit for having a brain in his head," Owyn snapped. "You know what they call him among the Water tribe? Del the Silent. And they respect the fuck out of him, because he'll steal your shirt if you're not careful, he's that good a trader." He paused. "Not that the Water tribe has shirts."

"Honestly!" Ambaryl laughed. "You expect me to believe that?"

"I'll go get Neera and have her tell you her own self," Owyn answered. "And you can call the leader of the Water tribe a liar to her face. I'll enjoy seeing her reaction." He paused. "We might need Aven after. She's got a temper, Neera does."

"I would never—!"

"You just did it to me," Owyn pointed out. His blood was starting to simmer along with the stew on the stove. "So stop. You need to stop treating Del like an idiot. He's not. He's got his scars. We all do. But he's stronger than you give him credit for being, and he's smarter than you think, and he's the Mother's own choice to hold the Air gem. So you and Nestor and everyone else who keeps treating him as a poor, broken child need to shut right the fuck up and stop undermining him."

Ambaryl's face turned red. "Is that how you talk to your elders?" she sputtered.

"If they deserve it, yeah," Owyn answered, folding his arms over his chest. "And you do. And I'll be telling the same thing to Nestor when I see him again." He stopped and frowned. "No, no, I *did* tell him that. When I was at the Palace. You all have to stop it."

Ambaryl's face went even more red, and she shook her finger at Owyn as she proclaimed, "Dyneh would have washed your mouth out with the laundry for disrespecting your elders like this!"

Owyn snorted. "Yeah, well, she's dead, so I guess we'll never know."

Ambaryl's jaw dropped. "Oh, I don't know why I expected anything better of you. If Dyneh had had the raising of you, it might have been different. But clearly you've never learned to behave yourself properly. Never learned any better, and it shows. You and that Alanar—"

"What?" Owyn snapped. "What about my Alanar?"

"Another broken one," she sniffed. "Another poor idiot encouraged to reach beyond themselves. Clearly, you have no idea—"

Simmering anger immediately boiled over. "Alanar isn't broken!" Owyn gasped. "He's a level five healer! Which, I think, is further than you got!" He scowled, looked at the door. Then he looked back at Ambaryl. "Come with me. I want to show you something."

He turned and walked out of the kitchen, heading toward the front room. He passed through without stopping to say anything to Memfis or Mannon, and headed out of the house. Outside, he stopped and waited until Ambaryl caught up with him. Then he pointed. She looked, then looked at him.

"That's my house."

"Yeah, it is," Owyn agreed. "Go there. You're not welcome here. Not anymore."

"What?" Ambaryl gasped. "You're not serious!"

"I am very serious. Now get out of my house."

Ambaryl scowled at him and folded her arms. "I'm sure Rhexa will have quite a bit to say about that."

Owyn met her scowl with one of his own. "I'm sure she will. I'm sure Jehan will, too. Especially when I tell him that you think his chosen heir is an idiot." He folded his arms over his chest. "As a matter of fact, I might need to walk up to the healing complex to have that talk with them. Or I can wait for them to come for dinner. I mean, they're welcome. Not like you." He turned and started back toward the house, and toward Memfis and Mannon, who were both standing in the door.

"You'll regret this!" Ambaryl shrilled after him.

Owyn stopped. He turned and looked back over his shoulder. "Nah," he called back. "Nah, I don't think I will."

Memfis and Mannon both stepped out of the doorway and let him in, and Mannon closed the door behind him. Memfis moved to the window and looked out.

"She's gone back to her house," he said. "Do you need to go to the healing complex?"

Owyn shook his head. "No. I'll only be in the way, and they're busy. I'll tell Auntie her new wife is a bitch later." He grimaced. "Not sure what that will do to the marriage. But I'm not sorry, either."

"We didn't hear all of it," Mannon said. "What was it that she said?"

"That Del and Alanar are both broken idiots, and that we're being unkind to let them believe that they can do things other than sit around and be pitied."

"Alanar, too?" Mannon gasped. "I never saw this. Not a sign of it."

"Yeah, I think if I hadn't made her mad, she wouldn't have shown me," Owyn answered. "I need to go get the bread into the oven. And I need to cool my head a bit."

Memfis came toward him. "Something she said?"

Owyn nodded, looking down. "She said...she said that if my real mother had raised me right, I'd think like she did. That Del and Allie were broken." He looked up at Memfis. "She wouldn't have thought that, would she? I mean...she was a healer. Dyneh was a healer. She wouldn't have thought my Allie was broken."

"I think you need to ask Rhexa that question, Mouse," Memfis said gently. He rested his hand on Owyn's shoulder. "I don't think that. I love Alanar like my own. He makes you happy, and I'm overjoyed by it."

Owyn smiled slightly. "Thanks, Fa."

"Now, go on and get finished with what you need to get done." Memfis squeezed Owyn's shoulder, then stepped back.

MANNON WATCHED SILENTLY until Owyn disappeared into the kitchen. Then he moved to stand next to Memfis.

"I keep apologizing—"

"This one isn't you," Memfis answered, keeping his voice low. "You didn't make her think that. You didn't turn her that way. It's not on you." He smiled. "But thank you."

"Now what?" Mannon asked.

"What do you mean, now what?" Memfis looked around. "We're about done here, aren't we?"

Mannon looked at the room. "Other than bringing out plates and things, yes."

"Then I think I'm going back to the house and taking a nap," Memfis answered. "You stay. Jehan will be here with your guard eventually."

Mannon nodded. "I'll pester Owyn for something to keep busy. And I'll tell him you've gone off to take a nap." He smiled as

Memfis started toward the door. "You're going the long way back? The one that detours by my brother's office?"

Memfis chuckled. "Perhaps."

CHAPTER TEN

For the entire walk from the house to the healing complex, Del clung to Aria's hand. By the time they walked through the healing complex doors, his shirt was soaked with sweat, and he was shaking. He smiled weakly at Aria as the door closed behind them, and was shocked when she hugged him.

"You did it," she said softly. "You did just fine."

Carefully, he slipped his arms around her and rested his forehead on her shoulder, being mindful of her pregnant belly. Over the past month, she'd warmed to him, but she still didn't seem entirely certain how affectionate she could be with him. She didn't want to make him uncomfortable, Aven told him. She wasn't sure where his boundaries were, and didn't want to trespass unknowingly. He appreciated the thoughtfulness. And he appreciated it more when she did things like this — impulsive affectionate gestures that told him more clearly than words that she really did want him by her side, even if she still wasn't sure just what to do with him while he was there.

She let him go, and he stepped back and looked around. Malani was at the desk, and she smiled at him as he went to the basin to wash his hands.

"I'm assuming you're here for Trey?" she asked.

"Del is," Aria answered. "Aleia, Rhexa and I are here to see Jehan. Is he in his office?"

"He's in the big meeting room. I think he was expecting you all," Malani answered. "Del, Trey is in room six. Do you need a guide?"

"I'll take him."

Del turned at the sound of Aven's voice. Aven had rewrapped his kilt properly, but the shirt he was wearing was trainee gray, and it didn't fit quite right. Aven met his eyes, leaned his walking stick against the basin and signed, "*Are you all right?*"

Del nodded. "*Mostly. I think. Owyn helped.*"

"*Owyn understands.*" Aven picked up his stick and walked past Del. He leaned down to share breath with Aria, then went to offer the same to his mother. "Fa is waiting for you in meeting room two," he said. "Alanar is with him. Treesi just went back on rounds, and I've just finished with the children. I have a minute before I need to go work on my charting. So I'll take Del to room six." He held his hand out to Del. "Trey should be waking up. I'm sure he'll want to see you. Karse is there, and...I've forgotten her name. The woman who says she was with you?"

"*Afansa,*" Del signed.

"Yes, her. She's there, too."

Del bid goodbye to the others, accepting hugs from Rhexa and Aleia, and another hug and a kiss from Aria.

"Are you sure you're all right?" Aven asked as they started down the corridor toward the patient rooms. "Afansa said that she was certain you were dead, that's how hard you dropped."

Del laughed. "*Dying and coming back is Owyn's trick. Not mine. I froze. Owyn wrapped me up tight and held me until I could think again. He said you did that to him, when he was that bad.*"

Aven nodded. "And we both fell asleep in the garden."

"*And Fandor caught you,*" Del signed. "*I heard Owyn telling my father. So it's Fandor's fault that we met the first time.*"

Aven snorted. "Never thought I'd be indebted to him for anything."

"*Nor I,*" Del agreed, and Aven laughed. Del took his hand, leaning into his arm. Aven shifted, putting his arm around Del's shoulders.

"You're really feeling all right?" he asked. "Your body says otherwise."

Del sighed. "*I'm fine now that I'm inside. Getting here...I'm surprised I made it out the door.*"

"Was it as bad as the first night after we left?" Aven asked. Del closed his eyes and shuddered at the memory, and Aven whistled. "It was that bad?"

Del shook his head. "*Not that bad. But almost.*"

"And you still made it here. Del, you're getting stronger."

"*It doesn't feel like it.*"

"A year ago, would you have risked your life to save a stranger?" Aven asked. "Would you have gotten on a canoe? Would you have walked alone through the streets of a strange city?"

Del frowned, considering each question. The answer was obvious, so he shook his head.

Aven smiled. "You're getting stronger. This is a setback. You lost a little healing. You'll get it back."

Del hesitated, then signed, "*I told Owyn why. And my father. I told them.*"

"Why..." Aven stopped and turned to face Del. "You told them? About Antavi?"

Del nodded, swallowing. "*I told them everything.*" He paused. "*Almost everything. I didn't tell them that I saw Skela while we were with your family.*"

"And?"

"Owyn says he's proud of me. And Fa says he wants to talk to Aleia, because he owes Skela a debt, and he wants to know if he's still alive."

Aven looked thoughtful. "That's not what you were expecting."

"I think that I don't really know my father as well as I thought I did. I believed Antavi when he said Fa would be angry with me." He shrugged. *"I was wrong. And Fa isn't angry."*

"That's the important part. Now, ready to see Trey?" Aven asked. Del nodded, and they started walking again, down the corridors that seemed to make no sense to Del. They weren't as logical as the corridors in the Palace.

"How do you not get lost?" he asked.

Aven chuckled. "Practice. Lots of it. And I still do, if I don't pay attention closely enough."

"Am I distracting you? I'll stop talking."

Aven smiled at him. "Del, love, you have one big thing in common with Aria and Owyn and Treesi. All three of you can distract me, just by standing next to me." He took Del's hand again. "When you're with me, I don't want to pay attention to anyone else."

Del smiled and leaned into Aven's arm again, feeling his face warming. Then he pulled his hand free. *"Is this what being in love is like? Just wanting to be with someone?"*

Aven laughed. "I think so. Be with someone. Make them happy. Be happy with them. Take care of them. Yes, I love you. All of you."

"Does it ever bother you that I'm not interested in sleeping with you?"

Aven shook his head. "No. Because if you did, you'd be doing it just to make me happy, and at the risk of making yourself miserable. Del, I like just being with you. And I want you to be happy. Which means not miserable."

Del smiled. *"Owyn said if I'm ever curious, he'll show me. I'm not sure I'm that curious."*

"If you do decide you want to know, then Owyn is probably the best of us to teach you," Aven said. "Unless you decide you want a woman's perspective first. If you want that, ask Treesi."

Del nodded, filing the information in the corner of his mind where he left things that were unlikely to ever happen, but were good to know nonetheless. He looked at the number on the door they were passing — number nine — and pointed down the hall.

Aven nodded. "Yes, we're here." He knocked on the door to room six, and opened it.

"Aven! He's finally awake," Del heard Karse say. "And fussing."

"Well, I've brought someone for him to fuss at," Aven said, and stepped inside. Del followed him, hesitating by the door. Trey was sitting up in bed. He looked pale, and he was frowning. It took Del a moment to realize that Trey was frowning at him. He swallowed and looked at Aven.

"Is he mad at me?" he signed. *"He looks like he's mad."*

Aven looked at Trey. "If you have something to say, Trey, say it," he said. "Because right now, it's looking and feeling like you're going to lash out at Del. And if that's the case, we're leaving."

Trey blinked. "I...fuck, Del. I'm not mad at you. I'm just...does it make sense if I say I'm mad near you? It's not you I'm mad at. It's what's around you."

"Because you got hurt because of me?" he signed, and Aven translated.

"Not that," Trey answered. "Because you're a fucking target, and I can't stop it. I tried, and...well, I fucked it up. So it's going to take a lot more than just me to keep you safe." He looked at Karse. "We're going, right? With them, when they leave?"

"I think that's what Aria wants," Karse answered.

"Just between us, she wants you to command her Palace Guard," Aven said. "Which means recruiting and training her Palace Guard."

Trey smiled, and the anger seemed to leak out of him. "Thought so," he said. "See?"

"Fine. You were right. You still have to ask him," Karse said, folding his arms over his chest.

Trey nodded. "Right. Del, we were talking about weapons training, right? Suppose I just volunteer to be your personal shadow?"

"*My what?*" Del signed. "*And where's Afansa?*"

Karse grinned when Aven translated. "He means your personal bodyguard," he answered. "And Afansa went to collect her things. She's going to stay with us and Meris until the troublemakers are gone."

Aven arched a brow. "You sent her alone?"

Karse sniffed. "You think I'm an idiot? Esai and Marik went with her. And then they're heading off to your place — Jehan told them that they're going to be Mannon's shadows."

"*He gets two?*" Del signed.

"Marik and Esai come as a set," Aven answered. "And I'm sure he'll share with you."

Trey sighed. "How hard is it to learn that, Aven? Signing, I mean. Can I learn it? I'm going to need to know how to sign, and how to read."

"We'll find you a tutor," Aven answered. "And...I have a few minutes to act as translator. Del, you should tell him about Antavi."

For a moment, Del couldn't remember how to use his fingers. "*What? Why?*"

"Because he's going to be teaching you, and he needs to know," Aven answered. "Just tell him what you told Owyn, and I'll translate."

So Del repeated his story. Hearing Aven speak the words aloud was somehow distancing — this was something that had happened to someone else. Not him. By the time he was done, his fingers were tired, and Trey was staring.

"I get it," he murmured. "Now I get why you freeze up." He looked at Karse. "Do you get it?"

"It's not the fighting," Karse said, nodding. "Yeah. Remember Latran?"

"He's who I was thinking of, yeah," Trey agreed.

Karse grinned and turned back to Del. "Latran was one of my trainees. Hopeless on the field. Completely hopeless. Turns out, he was hopeless because he'd been taught all the wrong way. Once I knew that, I changed up how I was teaching him, and what I was teaching him. Most of the trainees, they use short swords and knives, right? Latran would trip over his own feet, because his father beat all the wrong ways of standing and holding a sword into him." Karse nodded slowly. "Once I knew that, I put a polearm in his hands. He'd never used a pike before, never held one. Had to train him up from the very basics. Do you understand?" Del shook his head, and Karse laughed. "You didn't learn to fight, Del. You learned that weapons training meant you were going to get the shit beat out of you. So we do it a different way. What was he supposed to teach you? What weapon?"

"*Sword*," Del signed.

Karse looked thoughtful once Aven translated. "Right. No swords, then. Or knives."

"I was going to teach him to shoot," Trey volunteered.

"*Owyn says throwing knives, too*," Del added. "*Or Air javelins like Aria uses.*"

Karse nodded slowly once Aven translated. "I'll need to see what they have in their armory. And if it's something I can teach you—"

"You're going to teach him?" Aven interrupted. "I thought Trey—"

"I know more weapons than Trey, and more styles," Karse answered. "Makes sense for me to do it." He smiled. "If Del agrees?"

Del swallowed. He looked at Aven, then nodded. "*I'll do it. I don't want anyone else getting hurt because of me.*"

When Aven translated, Karse looked over at Trey. "He agrees. Do you have any objections?"

"No. Just whatever you teach him, I want to learn, too," Trey said. "We can learn together, and practice."

"We'll all go down to the armory together once you're released from care," Aven said. "Which may be in a few hours, once Fa has another look at you."

Trey blinked. Then he laughed. "I won't miss dinner!" he crowed. "See, I told you!"

Aven shook his head. "I need to go get my charts finished. Del, do you want to stay here?"

Del nodded and took his tablet out of his pocket. Karse pulled a chair over to the side of the bed, and waved at it.

"Sit," he said. "We can work on teaching this poor sot how to read."

AVEN MADE HIS SLOW way down back the corridor, leaning on his walking stick. The dull ache in his hip had turned to a sharper, stabbing pain — he wasn't sure just what he'd done, but this was definitely more than his usual level of pain from having been on his feet too long.

"You're in pain, and it's making my head hurt."

Aven stopped, smiling at his grandmother. "I can do something about the latter. I'm not sure how I managed the former. Possible when I bolted out of bed—"

"When Del was attacked in the street. I heard," Pirit said. "Come and let me look at that."

"I have to finish my charting."

Pirit frowned. "You did your charting already. This morning, when you were on rounds. You're not on rounds at the moment. What charting?"

"Not my patient," Aven answered. "I volunteered to help Fa by starting the charting for Trey, because he has to deal with the attackers. I assisted, so I can chart the basics, and Fa will finish when he's done, and add anything I miss."

Pirit nodded. "I'll come with you, then, and I'll take a look at that leg."

She followed him to the record room, and waited while he wrote up his report on Trey's injuries, the treatment, and the prognosis. He checked the details, put the file aside for Jehan then he looked up at his grandmother. "Here? Or one of the treatment rooms?"

"I'd like you lying down," Pirit said. "Let's go down to the small examination room. It's empty. Or it was when I went past it."

Aven followed his grandmother into the examination room and closed the door, then went to the bed and lay down on it, stretching out on his front. He felt the weight of her hand on the small of his back, and the warmth of her healing.

"Well, that's new," she murmured. "You've knocked the hip out of alignment. Your entire pelvis is tipped. Let me..." She shifted her hand to rest over his left hip, and pushed. Aven yelped, feeling the snap as his bones shifted. Pirit sniffed. "I don't get to do that often," she said. "I forget how awful it sounds. You're not working those muscles, Aven."

"First, what did you do?" Aven asked. "Second, what do you mean?"

"We'll start with the second," Pirit said. "The muscles that support your bones here are weakening. Which allows things to shift, because they're not getting proper support. What I did was move your hip back to where it's supposed to be. You knocked it out of place. Now, tell me what you're doing to work these muscles. Oh, and you can sit up."

Aven rolled onto his side and swung his legs over the edge of the table, shifting slightly. The shooting pain was gone — it was just sore now. "I...I'm not really, I suppose. I'm on my feet most days, but I don't think walking my rounds is doing enough work."

"You're right," Pirit said. "You need to strengthen the muscles back up. You're not using them because it hurts, which means they're not working, which means they get weaker—"

"Which means things will hurt more," Aven sighed. "Right. Suggestions?"

"Swim more," Pirit answered. "You haven't spent much time in the water since we reshaped the femoral head."

"I haven't spent any time in the water since we got here," Aven admitted. "I'll make time. Anything else?"

Pirit studied him for a moment. "Your mother told me you danced. Hook swords. She said you were very good."

Aven blinked. "I...I haven't been," he said slowly. He shook his head. "I...I wasn't sure I could anymore."

"Start." Pirit folded her arms. "Like you were starting over from the beginning. You need to rebuild the muscle structure on your back and in your belly, or that hip is going to get weaker." She frowned. "It would have been better, you know, if you hadn't vanished for four months. We'd have been able to do more."

Aven nodded. "I know. But I really didn't think I had much of a choice."

"I do understand. Now, clarify something for me. You were in bed? In the middle of the day?"

Aven's face warmed. "Napping."

"Are you often tired?" Pirit asked, and Aven realized that she wasn't asking what he thought she was.

"It's...complicated," he answered. "Aria gets tired in the middle of the day. But she won't nap, because she's too busy. Then she falls asleep in her supper. And when anyone tries to convince her to rest during the day, she'll argue with them. But if I tell her that I need to lay down, because my leg hurts, she'll join me, because—"

"Because she's taking care of you?" Pirit asked.

"Something like that," Aven said, and stood up. "Thank you, Grandmother. This feels better."

"You're welcome," she answered. She paused, then said, "I fought with your father, you know. Did he tell you? I didn't want him to go out to sea with your mother."

Aven blinked at her sudden admission. "No. I think Memfis said something once, but I don't know the details."

"I wanted him to stay at the healing center. I thought I would be able to keep him safe and hidden there. And he was a level five healer. Level fives don't leave. And then you were born, and I had another reason to want all of you to stay. My first grandchild." She paused. "He was right. I knew he was right, that there wasn't anything I could do to keep them and you safe if Mannon came hunting. But I was selfish." She cocked her head to the side. "I suppose it worked out for the best. I regret missing you growing up, and knowing you as a child. But I never had to change your clouts."

Aven blinked. "Clouts?"

Pirit looked startled. "Does the Water tribe not use...oh, of course they wouldn't!" She laughed. "You have a lot to learn, my boy."

Aven nodded. "That's a given. Start with telling me what a clout is?"

"Come and walk with me."

CHAPTER ELEVEN

The bread bowls were ready, and the stew was steaming fragrantly, scenting the entire house. The table was set, and Owyn had filled carafes with both salted and unsalted water, tea, and fruit juice. He'd even decided to teach Mannon how to make one of his favorite desserts — Honey Balls, a confection of honey-drenched fried dough.

"You've really never had these?" Owyn asked. Mannon shook his head, clumsily rolling out the last of the egg dough into long snakes, then cutting each snake into small pieces that he rolled into balls.

"I've never even seen these before," Mannon admitted. "They're traditional, you said?"

"Granna Meris used to make them for Turning," Owyn answered. "Done there?"

"Yes." Mannon brought the bowl of dough balls to Owyn, who dropped them into hot oil to fry, watching them puff and turn golden. They then went into a pan of warmed honey. Once the last of the balls were in the honey, Owyn poured the entire pan, honey and all, out into a platter.

"There." He reached over and picked up a spoon, scooping up a ball and passing it to Mannon. "Perks of being the cook," he said. "You get to check the batch."

Mannon hesitated. "I'm not fond of very sweet—"

"Just try it," Owyn urged. Mannon took the spoon and ate the ball, and his eyes got very wide.

"I thought it was going to be cloying, but it's not. It's just right." He smiled. "I think it's just right. But I think I might need another taste."

"No!" Owyn said with a laugh. "You have to wait until later, just like everyone else." He heard knocking and turned toward the door. "Someone's here." A second set of three knocks, and he smiled. "It's Del."

Mannon turned toward the door and left the kitchen, sweets forgotten. Owyn wiped his hands and followed, smiling when he saw who was with Del in the front room. Marik and Esai had arrived, as had Meris, Karse, and the woman who had been in the street with Del. And with them was...

"Trey! I wasn't expecting to see you tonight!"

Trey smiled. "They just let me go," he said. "And since we're first, I'm guessing we didn't miss dinner?"

"No, you didn't." Owyn went over and hugged Trey. "You're sure you're all right?"

"Aven said there's no lasting damage," Trey answered. "And we saw the others. They'll be here soon."

"Then we'll get the food on the table."

THE FRONT ROOM FILLED with people, and Owyn was glad he'd made three times as many bread bowls as there were invitations, and enough stew to feed a small army. In addition to the people Aria had explicitly invited, there were also Marik and Esai, who'd been assigned to act as Mannon's guards. Marik stayed close to the wide window, and kept looking outside. Owyn wondered how long he'd actually stay under the roof — it wasn't something Marik would usually do for any length of time. The newcomer, who Karse introduced as Afansa, protested that she hadn't been invited, but when Aria arrived, she insisted that Afansa stay. Aria arrived with Memfis, Jehan, Aleia and Rhexa, and for some reason Memfis looked very satisfied with himself. Aven arrived last, and with Pirit.

"I'm not staying—" Pirit started to say. She hadn't been allowed to finish; Jehan took one arm, and Aven the other, and they led her the rest of the way into the house.

Once everyone was served, Aven spoke up. "So the question on the table is when are we leaving? Mannon wants to leave tomorrow to prepare the Palace for us. Aria wants us all to go at once."

"There's something to be said for having someone go ahead, while we make arrangements for you to follow," Rhexa said. "You leaving will take three healers out of rotation. Waiting even a month will allow us to get the trainees more prepared, and rearrange the schedules."

"Waiting until the baby is born will ensure that you have all the best of everything when the time comes," Meris added. "I know you'll have three healers with you, but how many of them have attended a birth?"

"Lady Meris has a point," Aven murmured. "I haven't yet. Trees?"

"Not as attending healer, but yes," Treesi answered. "Alanar hasn't."

"They're afraid I'll miss the baby," Alanar quipped, but he didn't smile when he said it. Owyn wondered why.

"So there's something to be said for waiting," Aria said. She leaned back in her chair and took a bite of the stew soaked bread. "This is very good, Owyn."

"Thank you. Don't fill up. There are Honey Balls for dessert," Owyn replied. "So, if we stay, and Mannon goes, then who goes with him?"

"In the Palace, he's not going to need Marik and Esai," Jehan answered. "Unless they decided that they wanted to go. Ah...Mem?"

"Yeah, I'll go," Memfis answered. "I worked in the Palace for months. I can be useful."

"If you're wanting me to start your Guard, I should go, too," Karse said. "Get the training started. Go through the men already there and find the troublemakers."

"You're supposed to train Del," Trey pointed out. "And he's staying here."

Karse grumbled. "Good point. We'll figure that out, I guess."

There was a knock on the door, and it opened to reveal Aven's cousin, Othi. He arched a brow when he saw the group. "A party? And you didn't invite me?" he asked.

Aria blushed. "Council, and I should have," she admitted. "And Neera. I apologize—"

"No, no, it's fine," Othi said with a grin. "Council? What are you deciding?"

"If we're staying here while Mannon goes back to the Palace to get it ready, or if we're all going," Aven answered. He gestured to a chair. "Sit. There's salted tea."

Othi nodded and took the cup of tea that Del handed to him. He sipped it, then nodded. "If that's the question, then it's a good thing I'm here. Destria's in with news."

Mannon sat up. "I hadn't realized she'd gone out."

"She went up to the Palace, so her men could rotate out," Othi said. "She left this morning at dawn, and she just got back. We weren't expecting her until tomorrow, so we knew it was bad. Once she'd reported, I came right up here." He rested his hands on his thighs. "If you're going north, you're not going alone. You're taking a war party. Because Destria says the Palace was attacked. She came back as fast as she could to report it."

"The Palace was attacked?" Aria echoed. "Mother of us all." She paused, closed her eyes, and frowned. Then she nodded and opened her eyes. "Mannon, you'll leave first thing tomorrow. Memfis, you'll go with him? And Karse, you go, too. Take a full war party—"

Othi blushed slightly. "I...ah...I've already started picking them out. Aunt, if you'll come down and review?"

"I'll come down with you once we're done here," Aleia said. She looked at Jehan. "I should go with them as well."

Jehan sighed. "As much as I hate to agree, you're right." He leaned forward, resting his elbows on his knees. "Marik, you and Esai can go north if you wish. If you stay, then I'm assigning you to Del, at least until the day after tomorrow when we get Jassic and his lot out of here. Othi, what else did Destria say?"

Othi scowled. "We're pretty sure we know who did it. Destria says it looks like the attacks came from the sea. And she said that the ships that remained in the harbor were scuttled."

"Risha," Aria murmured. "But why attack the Palace?"

Othi shook his head. "No idea. But I can tell you that we saw nothing. No ships sailed past us going north, nothing came in from the deep waters."

"She came from the north, then," Aleia said. "She must have."

"That's Neera's thinking, too," Othi agreed. He finished his tea, and stood up. "I'll go back down and tell Neera and Destria."

Aleia stood up. "Wait for me." She leaned down and kissed Jehan, resting her forehead against his for a moment. Then she turned to Aria. "My Heir?"

"Go, and good luck," Aria said. Aleia smiled and bowed slightly. She touched Aven's arm briefly, then hurried out after Othi.

"Well, that makes that decision," Owyn said. "We'll probably be leaving sooner rather than later, yeah?"

"Why do you say that?" Alanar asked.

Owyn frowned, trying to get his thoughts in order. "Risha has to know we're not in the Palace yet," he said slowly. "On account of the Water tribe still being here and not there. So she attacked the Palace..." His frown deepened. Why would she have attacked an empty building?

"There was something there she wanted," Aven murmured. "And she wasn't willing to wait any longer to get it."

Owyn nodded. "Right. That has to be it. We need to find out what. Which means we need to go there, too."

Aria looked thoughtful. She turned to Karse. "How long, do you think, until you can secure the Palace?"

Karse coughed. "Ask me the easy questions, right?" he asked. "Ah...given enough loyal men—"

"Or a large enough war party?" Aven offered.

"Yeah, that could do it. If I have enough loyal men, I could probably secure the Palace in a day. Given that they're probably in a panic right now? I could probably secure it in an hour, given the right number of men."

Aria nodded. "Then we'll all leave together." She turned to Rhexa and Jehan. "Will that be enough time to make arrangements here?"

"We'll make it work," Rhexa said. She looked at Jehan, then turned to Pirit. "Why do I have the feeling that Jehan will be going north?"

"Because you're a very smart woman who knows my son?" Pirit answered. "You are going, Jhansri?"

Jehan scowled. "I've had my entire family together for barely a month," he grumbled. "After not knowing they were even alive for months. Of course I'm going."

Pirit smiled. "I thought as much. We'll sit down before you leave and go over what, if anything, you want me to focus on with the trainees while you're gone."

"Thank you, Mother," Jehan said. He sighed. "What would she have wanted in there? Her offices were here. Her house was here. Her personal—" He looked up when Del snapped his fingers. "What am I missing, Del?"

"She had an office and quarters at the Palace," Del signed. *"She rarely used them, though."*

"Del is right," Mannon said. "And there were records. But nothing vital that I can think of. And that doesn't answer the question of why now."

"We know why now. Because we're not there yet," Owyn said. "If she attacked when we were there, she'd never get in. She saw the opportunity, and she took it, because she must have realized she was running out of time." He looked around. "My question is, how did she know she was running out of time? How did she know we were talking about leaving Terraces...oh, fuck." The realization hit like a thrown rock. "We were talking about Mannon leaving tomorrow. At breakfast this morning. That's why. She found out that she had no time left. How?"

"Owyn, you're saying someone told her?" Jehan asked. "Someone here, in Terraces? How would they have gotten a message to her?"

"My messenger birds," Mannon said. "She's used my messenger birds before. Marik, have you noticed anything odd with the birds?"

Marik groaned. "Wraith told me this morning that there were more birds than usual flying north, and there were birds flying out over the water to the boats. I had him watching them. He didn't see where they came from, and they didn't come back. Fuck, I never thought to ask him which boats. He can't tell the difference between the canoes and the bigger ships. He's smart, but he's not that smart," He stood up. "I need to catch Aunt Aleia. They're out past the canoes, out of sight, but not out of range of the birds." He frowned and closed his eye. "It's too late in the day for Wraith to fly. I'll talk to the owls. See if they're still out there. Excuse me?" He hurried out into the night, with Esai following behind him.

"They're not," Owyn said. "I'll bet anyone that they're not still out there. Not anymore. The question though...who sent the birds? Who told them we were starting to plan to go, and that they needed to move now. Who would know there was something—" He stopped, his mouth suddenly dry as he looked at Rhexa. She went pale.

"Ambaryl," she whispered, and bolted from her chair. Owyn pelted after her, out the door and across the street. He saw her disappear into her own house, and heard her shouting, "Baryl?"

He reached the door in time to see her disappear down the corridor. He followed, ducking into the kitchen. The room was empty, except for a small, bright ball of fur that darted out from underneath the stove as he entered.

"Trinket?" Owyn whispered. He knelt and scooped up the fire-mouse. She stood on her haunches and chittered at him, then ran up his sleeve and down into his shirt pocket. He sniffed. "You know, you're the one who keeps coming back across the street," he murmured, and turned to leave the kitchen. He ran into Rhexa in the corridor.

"She's not here," she said. "I don't know where she'd have gone. She told me she wasn't coming to dinner—"

"Did she tell you why?" Owyn asked.

"Memfis told me why," Rhexa answered. "And that you'd tell me more when you had time. I wasn't going to ask. But I did tell her that I wasn't happy with how she'd treated you, Alanar and Del." She looked around. "Owyn, do you think that she sent those birds? How could she?"

"Auntie, I don't know," Owyn answered. He turned when he heard footsteps, seeing Jehan coming inside.

"She's gone?"

"Well, she's not here," Rhexa answered. "I think... check the tunnel guides. She wouldn't have gone to the ships."

"Does she ride?" Owyn asked.

"I..." Rhexa stopped. "I don't know. She didn't, but it's been so many years since she left me."

"She rides," Mannon said as he came up next to Jehan. "Not well, but she rides."

Jehan nodded. "Go back to the house," he said. "I'll head for the tunnels and make sure she doesn't leave Terraces." He grimaced. "Rhexa, I'm sorry."

Rhexa gave a weak laugh. "I should have wondered why she'd suddenly come back to me after so many years. I didn't tell you that we didn't exactly end on the best of terms. I should have asked myself why—"

"Auntie, it's not your fault," Owyn said. He put his arm around her shoulders. "Come on. Come back to the house. We'll...we'll figure something out."

He led Rhexa out of the house and back across the street. Aven and Aria were waiting outside, and Owyn could feel the question before either of them asked. He shook his head, and Aven sighed.

"Come inside, Auntie," he said. "Fa will find her."

Owyn let Aven and Aria take Rhexa into the house, then turned and headed back toward Jehan and Mannon. "Can I help?" he asked. "Is there anything I can do?"

Jehan took a deep breath. "I don't even know, Owyn," he answered. "This...I wasn't expecting anything like this."

"What, that Mannon's people aren't loyal to him?" Owyn asked, looking at Mannon.

"This one is surprising," Mannon agreed. "And that Ambaryl is loyal to Risha is even more surprising. She was rarely at the Palace. She was here. I wanted her here, away from Del."

Jehan nodded. "So who else was Risha talking to, under your nose? Was it only Ambaryl?"

Mannon shook his head. "Let me know what you find out. I'm going to go and apologize to Rhexa." He sighed again. "I do it so much these days. I think I'm getting rather good at it." He walked back into the house.

Jehan patted Owyn on the back. "Come with me. Let's go get the tunnel guides on alert."

Owyn followed him up the street and past the healing complex. Up the stairs to the next terrace, turning toward the closest tunnel. Halfway there, they were hailed by one of the tunnel guides.

"Senior Healer? I was coming to find you," she called. "We didn't think you'd have sent someone out this late in the day. But we've got someone at the stables with orders for a cart—"

"Orders?" Jehan repeated. "In my hand?"

"Looks an awful lot like it, but the wording is strange. Raffi is keeping her busy while I came for you."

Jehan nodded. "Keep her there. I'm on my way. She is not to be allowed to leave Terraces."

"Yes, sir," Anniki said. She nodded, and trotted off. Jehan turned to Owyn.

"Go back to the house," he said. "Tell Karse I want him at the stables. Then...you stay there. Make sure Trey doesn't follow. He's not ready for a fight yet."

"You think she'll fight?" Owyn asked.

"I think she's cornered," Jehan answered. "Which means I don't know what she'll do. Go on, run."

Owyn nodded and ran off down the stairs, retracing their steps. It didn't surprise him that Karse was pacing outside the house. What did surprise him was that Aven was with him.

"Karse, Jehan wants you at the stables," Owyn said. "Just you. Trey needs to stay here."

Karse nodded. "Right. Stables are north, yeah? Can you show me?"

"I'm supposed to stay here and make sure that Trey doesn't follow you," Owyn answered. "Ah..." He frowned. "Aven, who can we send?"

Aven turned toward the house. "Memfis doesn't know Terraces. Mannon doesn't know, and he couldn't go alone, even if he did know. Not sending Alanar or Treesi. Or Del. Rhexa is in a state right now, and Lady Meris is with her. I don't know my way around yet." He turned back. "I'll sit on Trey. You go."

Owyn nodded. "Right." He turned toward Karse. "Let's go."

They hurried through streets that were growing darker, until they reached the mouth of the tunnels that led to the stables. Jehan was waiting there, and arched a brow when he saw Owyn.

"Karse didn't know the way," Owyn answered. "And I'm the only one who could bring him. Aven is with Trey."

Jehan nodded and turned toward the tunnel mouth. "Then let's go." He started forward, and Karse and Owyn fell in behind him. All at once, Owyn was aware that he was unarmed.

"If it comes to a fight," Karse murmured. "You stay back."

"Not arguing," Owyn answered. "But...you've met Ambaryl. Do you think she will?"

"I've no idea," Karse answered. "So be ready."

Owyn nodded, feeling his skin crawling as they passed through the narrow part of the tunnels. Close spaces were harder, ever since the box...no, he needed to focus. He swallowed and started walking a little faster.

The tunnels opened up into the stable area, and Owyn saw Ambaryl, waving a paper at one of the grooms.

"I tell you, I need this cart right now!"

"Ambaryl!" Jehan shouted.

The woman turned, all color draining from her face. She covered her mouth with one hand, going even more pale as she swallowed. She lowered her hand and said, "I...Senior Healer."

"Where are you going, Ambaryl?" Jehan asked.

She looked down, and her shoulders slumped. "Nowhere. Nowhere at all. Not now."

Jehan nodded. "I'm glad we're in agreement. Come with me. I think you have quite a bit to tell me."

Ambaryl folded her hands in front of her. "I won't be telling you anything," she answered. "It's already too late."

Jehan frowned. "Too late?"

Ambaryl shook her head. "Yes. It's too late." She looked past Jehan to Owyn. "Tell your aunt that I'm sorry."

"You need to tell her that yourself," Owyn said. "You need to explain to her why you broke her heart."

Ambaryl took two steps forward, then crumpled to the ground. Jehan dove toward her, dropping to his knees and turning her onto her back. Her face was turning blue.

"What the fuck?" Owyn gasped. "What...what did she do?"

"Poison," Jehan snapped. "When she covered her mouth. Owyn, go back to the house. I need all the healers. Now!"

Owyn turned and ran

CHAPTER TWELVE

Owyn paced back and forth across the front room. The large room felt empty, even though Aria and Del were still sitting on the long couch near the windows. Trey had taken Meris and Afansa home, while Memfis and Mannon had walked Rhexa across to her house and hadn't yet come back.

"What do you think she knew?" Aria asked.

Owyn shook his head. "No idea. Something she was willing to die to keep secret," he answered. "I can't even imagine what was that important."

Del looked up. He was sitting with his knees drawn to his chest, his arms wrapped around them. It made him look very small. He shook his head, and lowered it again, resting his forehead on his arms. Aria moved to sit next to him, putting her arm around his shoulders.

"This is hard for you," she said.

"*She helped raise me,*" Del signed, raising his head. "*After Mama died, Ambaryl took care of me. I didn't...she doesn't like me much. Not anymore. I know that. But I don't want her to die.*"

"She likes you just fine," Owyn said. He moved over to join them on the long couch, sitting on Del's other side. "She just doesn't think you have a brain in your head."

Del snorted and signed, "*That's not liking me. She thinks I'm a pretty idiot, and she hates that I push back. She doesn't think I can do anything on my own.*"

"She thinks the same about Alanar," Owyn said, lowering his voice. "Do not tell him that."

Del grinned. "*Like I could.*" The smile faded, and he looked out the window. "*How long do you think they'll take?*"

"It takes as long as it takes," Owyn answered. "I used to hate when Mem would tell me that. But it's true. You can't rush."

"Someone is outside," Aria said, a moment before there was a knock on the door. The door opened, and Mannon, Memfis and Rhexa came in together.

"We searched everything," Rhexa said. "There's nothing untoward anywhere in the house. There are no papers, nothing that tells me why she did this."

"Auntie," Owyn said slowly. "She asked me to tell you that she was sorry."

Rhexa sniffed. "Because sorry makes everything better?" she asked. "Because it makes up for her betraying me? Betraying me again?" She turned away, her hands pressed to her face. Mannon came up behind her and rested his hands on her shoulders. To Owyn's surprise, she turned to him and stepped into his embrace. Owyn glanced at Del, who looked just as surprised. Mannon scowled at the both of them as he put his arms around Rhexa; Owyn took the hint and stayed silent.

"You said betrayed again," Mannon murmured. "You were partners before?"

"You didn't know?" Rhexa asked. "Oh, no, I suppose you wouldn't know. You weren't here yet when she got here. And I suppose she never talked about me."

"We never really talked," Mannon said as he shook his head, and led Rhexa to a chair. Owyn could feel his eyebrows climbing toward the top of his scalp, and turned away before they flew off to hit the ceiling. Aria met his gaze and smiled, then yawned.

"You should go to sleep," Owyn said. "It's late."

"I want to wait for Aven," Aria said. "I want to know what's happening. Perhaps you could make some tea?"

Owyn nodded. "I'll go put the kettle on," he said, and stood up. "And there are Honey Balls. We never got to dessert."

Aria hummed. "Yes, please. I'd forgotten that you made them. That would be lovely."

Owyn walked off toward the kitchen, filling the kettle and putting it on the stove to boil. He scooped tea leaves into the big teapot, then brought the platter of Honey Balls out to the front room. He busied himself with filling bowls until he heard the kettle whistling, then went back into the kitchen, filled the teapot, and brought it back out to the main room. There was still no sign of the healers. That was good, wasn't it? If they were taking so long, they had to be still working. He set the teapot down and went to the window, looking out into the night. Memfis came up behind him, clearly visible in the dark glass.

"They're taking a long time," Owyn said softly. "That's good, right?"

"It might be," Memfis answered, his voice equally quiet. "I wanted to tell you—"

"I know you went to Rhexa, if that's what you're confessing," Owyn said. "It's fine. I'd have told her about Ambaryl myself, when I had time."

"I didn't want her to get to Rhexa first and tell her some wild lies," Memfis said. "She's your only blood family. I didn't want there to be a war between you."

Owyn smiled. "Thanks, Fa."

Memfis rested his hand on Owyn's shoulder. "None of this makes sense. What would Risha have hidden in the Palace? Especially since she was never there?"

Owyn shook his head. "Knowing her? Probably information about people she tortured to death. How-to manuals, some shit like that."

"That's macabre, Mouse."

"I know," Owyn answered. He took a deep breath. "Let me go pour the tea. Want some?"

"Serve the others first," Memfis said, and stepped back. Owyn nodded. He went back to the table and started to fill cups. He felt someone at his elbow, and looked over his shoulder to see Del.

"Can I help?"

Owyn nodded. "Take this one to Aria?" he said. He took two other cups, and carried them over to Mannon and Rhexa. Rhexa looked up and smiled.

"Thank you, Owyn," she said, taking a cup. She handed it to Mannon, then took the other. "I'm sorry."

"Auntie, you didn't do anything to be sorry for," Owyn said. He crouched to sit on his heels, then grinned. "Except having horrible taste in women. You can be sorry for that."

Rhexa looked startled, then laughed hard enough that Mannon reached over and took her teacup away before it spilled. "I do apologize for that," she said, when it was clear that she could breathe again. "I hadn't realized it was quite so poor, though. But then, I have a sample set of one."

"Sample set of one?" Mannon repeated. "What does...oh." He coughed, and his face turned bright red. "I...I apologize. For bringing a viper into your house."

Rhexa shook her head. "It wasn't your doing that brought her back here. That was Risha. It wasn't you that made her stay. That was my own doing. And...it wasn't you that betrayed us. That was one hundred percent Ambaryl." She took her tea back from Mannon and looked toward the door. "They're taking a very long time."

"Is that good, or bad?" Mannon asked.

"Yes," Owyn answered. "One of those."

Mannon snorted. "That's...well, it's truthful, if not entirely helpful."

Owyn grinned and stood up. "Yeah. We don't know. Want some of the Honey Balls?"

"Please," Mannon answered. He stood up. "Let me help. You've been on your feet all day getting this ready. Go and sit."

Owyn started to turn, then froze as someone knocked on the door. No one moved or said anything. The door opened, and Treesi came inside. Aven. Alanar. Then Jehan. Jehan looked at the younger healers, then stepped forward, and Owyn knew what he was going to say before he started speaking.

So did Rhexa. She stood up and met Jehan's gaze. "She's dead, isn't she?"

Jehan took a deep breath and let it out. "Yes. We tried...pretty much everything."

"What was it?" Owyn asked. "What the fuck did she take?"

Jehan shook his head. "I don't know. I've never seen anything like it. Nor has my mother. It's...I have no idea what that was. Mother is going to look through the archives, see if she can find anything." He closed his eyes, and Owyn could see how tired he was. All of the healers looked tired. And Aven...

Aven stood between Alanar and Treesi. His shoulders were slumped, and he didn't look up. Owyn glanced at Aria, saw that she'd noticed. She got to her feet and started toward Aven. Alanar cocked his head to the side, and stepped between Aria and Aven.

"Aria." Alanar said her name, and she stopped. "This...we're borrowing Aven tonight. It's..." He turned toward Aven and Treesi, then back toward Aria. "It's a healer thing."

Aria looked startled. "I...is Aven all right?" she asked. "Alanar?"

"No," Aven answered. His voice sounded small and strangled. "No, I...I'm not."

"Allie, take him on, and I'll explain," Treesi said.

Alanar nodded. He put his arm around Aven's shoulders and turned him, guiding him down the hall. As he disappeared, Owyn realized that his husband hadn't said a word to him.

"What is this, Treesi?" Aria asked. She joined Owyn, taking his hand.

Treesi nodded. "Aven lost his first patient tonight," she answered. "And...he's not taking it well. He—" She stopped and looked at Jehan. "Can I tell them this?"

Jehan nodded. "You can tell them."

Treesi hesitated, then said, "He tried to go deep into the healing meld. To bring her back the way he brought back Owyn. And it didn't work." She paused again. "And we had to pull him back. He went too far in."

"It's a mistake that very strong healers sometimes make, before they learn their limits," Jehan added. "It's something he should have been warned about in training. But when I was teaching him, he wasn't nearly as strong a healer as he is now. And Risha...well, the less said about her, the better. She had no business teaching someone stronger than she was. She clearly didn't know the risks."

"Know what risks?" Owyn asked. "What would have happened?"

Jehan swallowed. "If a healer goes too far in trying to save a terminal patient...they risk following the patient."

"We didn't know," Treesi said. "None of us. It was Pirit who saw it happening. She saw his heart skip—"

"What?" Aria gasped.

"He's fine," Treesi hurried to add. "Pirit saw it, and she pulled him back. It didn't hurt him. But now...added to the loss of his first patient is the guilt. He thinks he should have done more."

She looked over her shoulder, down the hall. "It's custom for established healers to help a new healer mourn when they lose their first patient. Right now, that's me and Allie. So we'll be keeping him tonight."

"Will he be all right?" Aria asked.

"Physically, he's fine. I mean, except for the awful headache that Pirit said she was leaving him as a lesson. And which Allie is probably already taking care of." Treesi closed her eyes. "It's hard to lose a patient. To lose your first patient. And it really doesn't get any easier with your second. Or third. We're healers. We're supposed to stop people from hurting. From dying. But we fail. And we mourn." She opened her eyes. "I should go." She looked down the hall, then back at Owyn. "Owyn, Allie...he's sort of distracted right now. He was the senior training partner, and it was his responsibility to look out for me and for Aven. So he's sort of blaming himself for not warning Aven."

"Did he even know?" Owyn asked. "You just said that Risha didn't tell you."

Treesi rolled her eyes. "You know him. He thinks he should have known, even though Risha never taught us about it." She shook her head. "So I need to hurry up and keep them from guilting at each other. Tomorrow, he'll be all guilty at you for ignoring you. But now you know why."

Owyn nodded, relaxing slightly. Oddly enough, Treesi's explanation did help. "I understand. Tell him I knew who I was marrying when I said yes, and he's not allowed to feel guilty. He has work to do. I'll be all right."

Aria rested her hand on Owyn's shoulder. "He'll be with me," she added.

Owyn looked at her. "You're sure? I mean...I can sleep on the couch or something—" He kept turned toward the couch, and his breath caught.

Unnoticed and ignored, Del had returned to the couch, to his former position — sitting with his knees drawn up, his arms wrapped around them. His head was bowed, and his shoulders were shaking.

"Del," Owyn whispered, and moved for the couch. Mannon got there first, dropping down next to Del and pulling him into a tight embrace, rocking gently as Del sobbed into his shirt.

"I...I didn't notice," Owyn whispered. "I didn't—"

"You were distracted," Aria said gently. "By Aven, and by Alanar. You were focused on them."

"I still..." Now that he was paying attention, Del's grief stung, like salt in an open wound. He started toward the couch, only to be brought up short by Jehan stepped in the way.

"Let him be," Jehan said softly. "Let Mannon take care of him first."

"But—"

"Owyn, Mannon knows what he needs right now." Jehan took a deep breath, and Owyn realized just how shaken the older man really was. Before he could say anything, Jehan shook his head. "I...I should go." He paused and looked around. "Aleia isn't back?"

"No," Aria answered. "Is there anything you need? She was your patient, too."

Jehan nodded. "I...yes. I...this isn't for you, though. Thank you." He frowned and looked around. "Memfis, do you have plans tonight?"

"I'm thinking I do now," Memfis answered. He put his arm around Jehan's shoulders. "Come on, old man. You can talk to me." He led Jehan toward the door, and the both of them went out into the night.

Aria watched the door close, then took a deep breath and left Owyn's side. She picked up a napkin, then went to the couch. She sat down on Del's other side, but didn't touch him. She folded her hands and said nothing. Owyn hesitated for a moment, then followed her lead, coming to sit on the floor at Del's feet. Mannon looked at Aria, then down at Owyn. He nodded gently, then closed his eyes and sighed, his breath ruffling Del's hair.

Eventually, Del's sobs eased. He sat up, scrubbing at his face with one hand. Aria held the napkin out to him, and he smiled weakly as he took it.

"Mannon, we should let them get some rest," Rhexa said gently. "I'll walk you home."

Mannon looked up at her, then back at Del. "Will you be all right?"

Del nodded. He mopped his face with the napkin, blew his nose, then nodded again.

Mannon arched a brow. "Are you sure? You can always come home with me tonight—" He paused, then looked up. "Did Jehan take Memfis to his house or ours?"

"Oh," Rhexa murmured. "I'm not sure. Perhaps...come on. Let's leave Owyn and Aria to take care of Del, and we'll go find out."

Mannon hesitated, turning as Del poked him in the arm.

"*Go home,*" Del signed. "*I'll be fine with Aria and Owyn.*"

"Are you sure?" Mannon repeated.

Del nodded, and waved toward the door. When Mannon didn't move, he waved again, more emphatically.

Owyn chuckled. "I think he's throwing you out," he said. "Politely, but...go home."

Mannon laughed. "All right. I'll come see you in the morning." He stood up and stretched. "Good night."

Rhexa led him out, and Del flopped back on the couch. Owyn reached out and took the sodden napkin from him, getting to his feet and taking it to throw in the basket with other soiled linens. When he came back to the couch, Aria and Del were both standing, waiting for him.

"Del will be with us tonight," Aria said. "If you don't mind?"

"Why should I mind?" Owyn asked. He reached out and took Del's hand. "We'll be here for you. And if you want to talk, we can talk. If you need to cry more, you can cry more."

Del smiled. "*I'm tired. It's been a long day. I want to sleep.*"

"It has been a long day," Aria agreed. "We'll see what the dawn brings. Come to bed, the both of you."

"I need to clean up a bit," Owyn said. "Go get ready, and I'll be in soon."

Aria smiled and kissed him, then led Del out of the front room and down the hall. Owyn tidied up, taking empty bowls and cups into the kitchen, setting dirty dishes to soak and covering the last of the honey balls with a cloth. He hoped they'd still be edible in the morning — he'd never had leftovers to deal with before. He took one last turn around the front room to see if he'd missed anything, then blew out the lamps. He stopped in the kitchen, pausing to put a small pile of tear nuts underneath the stove for Trinket. Then he banked the fire, blew out the lamps, and headed on to Aria's bedroom. From down the hall, he heard voices — he could pick out Alanar's voice, but he couldn't hear what they were saying. For a moment, he thought about going and listening at the door, then decided against it. There were three healers in that room — they'd know he was there. And besides, this was healer business. If there was anything he needed to know, Alanar would tell him tomorrow.

He knocked on Aria's door, and it opened. Del peered out at him, then stepped back to let Owyn in. Owyn stepped inside, closed the door behind him, then leaned in and kissed Del on the cheek. Aria, he saw, was sitting on the bed.

"You're comfortable with this?" he asked softly. "With sleeping with us tonight?"

Del nodded, and his mental voice was tentative in Owyn's inner ear. *"Aria just asked me the same thing. I think I need to not be alone tonight."*

Owyn smiled. "Then you won't be." He stepped back and tugged his shirt off. "Aria, how undressed do you want us?" he asked.

"Whatever makes you comfortable," she answered. "And if you wouldn't mind? I need help with my boots."

"I can do that," Del signed. He went and knelt in front of Aria, and started working on the laces. He set the boots side by side under the bed, then rocked back to sit and take off his own boots. They undressed in silence, Del lowered the lamp, and they all climbed into the bed. They ended up with Owyn on his back in the middle. Aria was on his left, and Del on his right, both of them with their heads pillowed on his shoulders. Owyn kissed Aria's forehead, then turned and kissed the top of Del's head. There was a soft, sleepy mumble of pleasure from Del, barely a whisper to Owyn's inner ear.

"Shouldn't Del be in the middle?" Owyn asked. "So that we can both hold him?"

"I like this." Del's mental voice already sounded half-asleep. *"And the baby makes me nervous. If I move wrong, I might hurt them."*

Owyn chuckled, and Aria ran her nails over his chest. "What did he say?"

"That he likes lying like this, and he's afraid of rolling over onto the baby."

Aria giggled. "I like that. Good night, my loves."

CHAPTER
THIRTEEN

Aven sat on the edge of the bed and tried to ignore Alanar and Treesi. They moved around him, circling like hang-on fish around sharks. He tried to ignore them, until Treesi's voice cut through his mental fog.

"My first was a boy named Agate. He was ten, and he had been kicked by a horse," she said softly. The bed rocked as she crawled up behind him. "It was when I came here. I was still a basic student, and we didn't have a senior healer with us on that trip, because the healing center where I trained in the mountains couldn't spare anyone to come with me. Agate was the son of the caravan leader. I did...everything I could think of. But it wasn't enough."

The bed shifted again as Alanar sat down next to Aven. "My first was actually two patients," he said. "It was the only time I attended a pregnant woman. And she's the reason I don't attend pregnant women. It's not that they don't trust me. It's that I don't trust myself. I missed something. I missed something badly. Calline had a seizure, so bad that it destroyed her brain. I missed what was causing it, and I couldn't stop it. I couldn't save her. Or the baby. The baby was born too soon..." He trailed off. "Maybe I shouldn't be telling this story. Just...I'm not going to be attending Aria. At all."

"Calline was another healer," Treesi added. "A year behind us. Virrik liked her. A lot. We weren't ever sure if the baby was his. I don't think any of us wanted to know. But he learned everything he could about attending a pregnant woman after she died." She paused. "Allie, did you ever ask yourself if Risha let her get that bad on purpose?"

Alanar coughed. "Not yet, I hadn't!" he answered. "Fuck, Trees..." He took Aven's hand. "You're always going to remember your first failure, Aven. It happens to all of us. Every healer has a story like this." He took a long breath, let it out. "Your father...he probably has dozens of stories like this. He served as a healer in the Palace when they had mountain fever."

"He never told me about that," Aven said. "He never warned me."

"As your first teacher, he should have. And I should have warned you," Alanar said. "I was your senior training partner. I should have warned you about what it's like to lose your first patient." He grimaced. "I wish I'd known to warn you about going in too deep. That was new for me, too."

"It doesn't matter," Treesi murmured, gently tugging at Aven's shirt. He helped her peel it up over his head, then let his head fall forward when she started massaging his shoulders. "Even if we had warned you, even if Risha had told you, or your father, the warning doesn't sink in. Not until it's real. You always think it won't happen to you. You're better than that. You're more careful. And then...you're not."

"We all go through it," Alanar added. "All of us."

Aven sighed, feeling the tension starting to leave his shoulders under Treesi's ministrations. "I could have brought her back," he murmured. "I did it with Owyn—"

"The Mother sent Owyn back to us," Treesi said. "You said that yourself. It was different. You can't compare it. Owyn was needed, and the Mother gave him back to you. Ambaryl—"

"Aven, she wanted to die," Alanar said. "She made her choice."

"But now we don't know anything—" Aven protested, looking up. The rest of his words died on his lips as he realized that he was the only one on the bed wearing any clothing. "What...?"

"We're taking you to bed," Treesi said softly, wrapping her arms around him. "To show you that life is for the living. To help you process. To help you grieve."

"It's a custom for healers," Alanar said. "If you don't object?"

"I don't...I think I'd have liked to be asked first," Aven stammered. He turned slightly, shifting and putting his arm around Treesi. "And...does Owyn know?"

"He knows," Treesi said. "I told him. Oh, Allie, he says you're not allowed to feel guilty for taking care of Aven, because he understands."

Alanar smiled. "I married a smart man," he said. "Now, Aven, if you've any objections at all, we won't do this. But this is a healer custom, after losing a patient. I'm sure your father is..." he paused. "Maybe I should stop there."

"Yes, you should definitely stop there!" Aven said. He dragged his fingers through his hair, then looked at Treesi. She smiled at him, then stretched up to kiss him. He heard Alanar chuckle softly.

"Is that a yes?" he asked, running his hand up Aven's leg, slipping underneath the kilt.

Aven drew back from Treesi and turned toward Alanar. "That's a let me get undressed." He felt Treesi's hands on his shoulders, pulling him back and down onto the bed, as Alanar shifted to move over him.

Alanar grinned broadly, reminding Aven of a shark. "Now where's the fun in that?"

OWYN WOKE UP WHEN HE heard the distant knocking. He was on his side, with Aria pressed up against his back, her wing curled over him. Del was curled against his chest, his arm draped over Owyn's side, underneath Aria's wing. Owyn blinked, then grumbled and closed his eyes. He was warm and comfortable, and had not had nearly enough sleep. Whoever it was could come back later.

The knocking became pounding, and Owyn swore silently, and started to try and get out from between Del and Aria without waking either of them. He nudged Del over, and carefully shifted down the bed so he could climb over the footboard. He grabbed his trousers and tugged them on, then looked back at the bed to see that Del had shifted closer to Aria, and she'd covered him with her wing. He smiled slightly, then headed out of the bedroom.

Once he reached the front room, he could hear someone calling his name, "Owyn?" The door started to open before Owyn reached it, and he froze and reached for a whip chain that wasn't there. The door opened to reveal Memfis, with Jehan right behind him. Owyn relaxed slightly, until he realized that the both of them looked worried.

"What is it?" Owyn asked. "And keep your voices down. Everyone else is still asleep."

Memfis looked startled. "It's hours past when you're usually up."

"Yeah, well, I'm not usually up most of the night worrying about a traitor. So?"

"Did Mannon stay here last night?" Jehan asked. "He never came home."

Owyn blinked. Blinked again. "How did you...no, never mind." He paused and scrubbed one hand over his face. "Right. I remember now. You went off for healer things, the same way Allie and Treesi took Aven off. Ummm...Mannon. Rhexa said she was going to walk him home. So he didn't go out alone, like you all told him not to do, and so that they could see if you were there." He pointed at Jehan. "We didn't know which house you headed off to when you left here. So...since you were in Mem's bed last night, the first place I'd look for Mannon is across the street?" He looked up at Memfis, saw the shocked look on his face. "What?"

"Mannon...and Rhexa?" Jehan said slowly. "I...well." He tapped Memfis' arm. "Let's go wake up Rhexa."

"Why?" Owyn asked. "It's still early, isn't it?"

"Because Mannon has to leave today," Memfis answered. "To go back to the Palace."

Owyn nodded. "Right. Look, I'm not even a little bit awake yet. Let me go fire the stove and make some tea." He shook his head, trying to clear it. "Del took Ambaryl dying hard. So we didn't go to bed until a while after you left. He and Aria are still asleep. And I'm not sure what's going on in my room, but I haven't heard anything since last night." He paused, wondering if Alanar had shown Aven any of his favorite tricks.

"So we need to head across the street." Memfis turned toward the open door, then laughed. "Or...not. You were right, Mouse. Here they come."

A moment later, Mannon and Rhexa came inside.

"Good morning," Mannon said. "How's Del?"

"Still asleep, last I checked," Owyn answered. "Only reason I'm up is someone...no. Sometwo got themselves all worked up over nothing."

"We didn't know it was nothing," Jehan protested. "And we don't know if we got all of Jassic's cohorts yet."

"Oh, was I the nothing?" Mannon asked. "But I left a note telling you where I was spending the night."

Memfis turned to look at him. "You did? Where?"

"On the kitchen table," Mannon answered. "Where you sit every morning when I make breakfast. As a matter of fact, I even put it into your favorite teacup."

Jehan started laughing, and Memfis looked positively embarrassed. Mannon looked at him, then at Jehan. "You never went to look? You just...what? Assumed the absolute worst? That I was dead in a park somewhere?"

"You're a trouble magnet!" Jehan answered. "Of course we assumed the worst!"

"Well, unless you think my guest room is the worst, you wasted all that worry for nothing. And woke Owyn up for no good reason." Rhexa folded her arms. "Gentlemen?"

Memfis sighed. "I'm sorry, Mouse."

"So am I," Jehan added. "We'll let you go back to bed. Mannon, you're leaving today. Do you need anything from me?"

"Walk back to the house with me, and we'll see if I do," Mannon answered. "Owyn, tell Del that I'll see him before I go, will you?"

Owyn started to nod, then heard the footstep behind him. He turned to see Del standing in the doorway, wearing only his trousers.

"*I heard voices,*" Del mumbled in Owyn's mind. Then he blinked and smiled, signing, "*Fa! Good morning!*"

"Good morning," Mannon answered. "How are you this morning?"

"*Not awake,*" Del answered. "*And better, I think. What's going to happen to Ambaryl?*"

Jehan cleared his throat, and looked at Rhexa. "Did she have any specific wishes?" he asked. "Or rites?"

"Not that she told me," Rhexa answered. "There really isn't anything special about the rites from our home village. The catacombs here will be just fine."

"Catacombs?" Owyn asked.

"Tunnels, deep under Terraces, and back under the mountain where it's dry," Rhexa answered. "I won't go into specifics, but that's where the dead are entombed. Well, our dead, here in Terraces."

Del nodded. *"When will that happen? We leave today, don't we? Will it happen before we leave? Can it happen today?"*

"Auntie, Del wants to know if it will happen before we leave?" Owyn asked.

Rhexa nodded. "Jehan?"

"Tomorrow," Jehan answered slowly. He nodded. "Yes, I think we can have all the preparations done by tomorrow."

"Then we should wait a day?" Mannon asked. "Witness the rites, then go on to the Palace?"

"We'll discuss it with Aria when she wakes up," Jehan answered. "In the meantime, let's proceed like you were leaving with the late tide. If you're ready and then you don't go, you're still ready. If you're not ready...well...." He turned to Owyn and smiled. "I am sorry for waking you unnecessarily. We'll let you go back to bed."

Owyn nodded. "I don't think I can at this point. I'm awake now. But thank you. Apology accepted. Out, all of you."

They left, laughing and apologizing. Owyn closed the door behind them and leaned on it, tipping his head back to thump against the wood.

"What happened?"

Owyn snorted. "This is convenient. I don't have to open my eyes to know what you said. Mem and Jehan woke up this morning and your fa wasn't there, and they lost their fucking minds. Thought he'd been attacked or something. So they came here to see if he'd slept on our couch last night."

"Where was he?"

Owyn looked at Del and grinned. "Across the street."

Del's eyes widened. *"With Rhexa?"*

"In her guest room, she says." Owyn locked over his shoulder. "Which...I don't remember her having a guest room."

"*Oh!*"

Owyn looked back at Del, nodding. "Yeah. Oh. Come on. Let's go make some tea. Unless you want to go back to bed?"

"*Can we make breakfast?*"

"Sure. We can make breakfast. We'll make something nice to wake the others up with." He smiled and held his hand out Del. "I liked having you in the bed with us last night."

Del blushed slightly. "*I liked being there.*"

"You can do it more often, if you want," Owyn said. "Now, let me teach you to make griddle cakes. We have enough of everything for those. Oh, and I can teach you how to rake out the stove and get the fire up. That's first."

SOMETHING SMELLED GOOD.

The bed was odd. It was softer than Aven remembered. The position was strange — he was on his left side. He didn't usually sleep on his left side. And he couldn't move. He blinked, realized that his hands were tucked behind his back.

No, his hands were *tied* behind his back, and his ankles were tied together. The memory of the previous night came back in a rush — somewhere in the middle of the night, mellowed by some number of orgasms, Aven had agreed to let Alanar show him something new. Now Aven knew why the bed was strange. It wasn't his bed. He was still with Alanar and Treesi. Caught between Alanar and Treesi, at the moment, and the both of them were still asleep. Treesi was pressed against his chest, and Alanar was against his back, Aven's hands pressed tight against Alanar's stomach. Aven shifted, but there was no give in the soft, flat cords that Alanar had used. He wasn't going anywhere.

And oddly enough, the thought didn't bother him. He was safe with Alanar and Treesi. And the memories of the previous night weren't as painful as they had been. Looking back at it now, he knew that he hadn't made any mistakes. He hadn't killed Ambaryl. He just hadn't been able to save her from herself. He could live with that. He sighed, and closed his eyes again. Maybe he could go back to sleep....

A warm hand ran up his side, then down over his stomach.

"Did you know the texture of your skin changes?" Alanar said, his voice rumbling in Aven's ear. "I can tell where your tattoos start. I could probably trace them."

"That would be interesting," Aven answered, keeping his voice low. He turned his head. "Do I get untied?"

Alanar chuckled, his hand roaming lower, until Aven gasped. "Maybe. Or maybe I'll just play with you some more." He growled softly into Aven's ear, then nipped the lobe. Aven heard Treesi laugh.

"You two!" she giggled. "You're as bad with him as you are with Owyn!"

"Oh, I think they'd both agree I'm very, very good," Alanar replied. He laughed again. "I smell something. Is it morning, Trees?"

"It's morning. And it smells like Owyn is making breakfast."

There was a light tapping at the door. Aven twisted to look over his shoulder as Aria came into the bedroom.

"Owyn and Del have made griddle cakes," she said. "I heard your voices, so I knew you were awake." She smiled. "Did you have a good night? Are you feeling better?"

"Yes, I did," Aven answered. "And yes, I am."

"And Aven has learned that he rather enjoys something new," Alanar added. He shifted, rolling to sit up on the edge of the bed; Aven yelped as he tipped onto his back. Aria looked at him curiously. Then her eyes widened.

"Aven, why are you lying like that?"

Aven shifted slightly, his eyes on Aria. He felt warm, and wondered if he was blushing. "Because I can't move?" he answered.

"Can't..." Aria looked up at Alanar. "Why can't he move? What have you done?"

Alanar grinned and stood up. "Griddle cakes are best hot. I'll let Aven explain, and we'll leave you two to explore. Treesi, where's my robe?"

Treesi giggled. "Oh, we can't stay and watch?" She leaned over Aven and kissed him, then rolled off the bed and picked up her own robe. She put it on, and carried Alanar's around the bed to him. He put it on, took Treesi's arm, and the two of them left. Aria moved closer to the bed.

"Why can't you move?" she asked again. She sat down on the edge of the bed. "Are you all right?"

"I'm fine," Aven answered. "I'm...is there something better than fine?"

Aria laughed. "Are they that good in bed together? I know Treesi is wonderful, but—" She stopped. "And why can't you move?"

"Because Alanar likes to tie his partner up," Aven answered. He shifted slightly. "He asked me, and I said yes."

Aria's eyes widened. "You're teasing me."

"I am not!" Aven laughed. "It makes things...I'm not sure. More intense, maybe. I wasn't really analyzing what was happening when it was happening." He shifted again, and saw the speculative look on Aria's face.

"And you like this?" she murmured, reaching out and running her hand down Aven's chest, letting it rest on his stomach. He shivered, his breath catching in his throat, and she laughed. "I see. Is this something you want to explore with me?"

Aven swallowed and tried to remember how to talk. "I...I'm willing. If you want—"

Aria smiled at him and shifted closer. "I want."

CHAPTER FOURTEEN

Del looked over his shoulder and smiled as Aven and Aria came into the front room and joined them at the table. Aven took his usual seat next to Del; he seemed to be moving slower than usual. But his smile was warm.

"*How are you feeling this morning?*" Del signed.

"Better," Aven answered. "Not as raw. I can live with it, I think. I don't like it. But I can live with it." He reached for the serving plate and what was left of the griddle cakes; Owyn looked startled, reaching out to catch Aven's hand.

"Allie," Owyn said. "You marked him." He ran his fingers over a dark spot on Aven's wrist. "Sloppy."

"I'm fine, Mouse," Aven said.

"And that might have been me," Aria added.

"Not when it's that dark," Owyn said. "This has had time to color. It happened a few hours ago. This was Allie." Owyn let go of Aven's hand. "Allie, you do something about that."

"Of course," Alanar said with a smile. "Aven, give me your hand."

As Aven reached out and let Alanar take his hand, Aria cleared her throat. "Alanar, I will want to talk to you—"

Alanar nodded, closing his eyes. "Just a moment, Aria. Aven, I am sorry. Owyn is right. This was me. I was sloppy. This shouldn't have happened." He released Aven's hand. "There. All better."

"Thank you," Aven said. "Are these for us?" he asked, gesturing to the plate. When Owyn nodded, Aven split the remaining between his plate and Aria's.

"They're cold by now," Owyn said. "Sorry. I'd have put them into the warming oven if I'd known you were going to...well...if I'd known." He looked at Alanar and Treesi. "You could have told me, you know."

Treesi giggled. "How were we supposed to know how long they were going to take?"

Aven snorted, and Aria turned pink. She looked down at her plate. Then she looked at Treesi and said, "Clearly, you have not been paying attention, my Earth." Alanar and Owyn both burst out laughing.

Treesi stuck her tongue out at Aria, then laughed. "I yield," she declared. "Now, what are we doing today?"

"A good question," Aria said. "What are we doing today?"

"Well, there's a question on the table," Owyn said. "You eat, I'll talk." He poured another cup of tea for himself, then poured one for Aria. "Aven, your fa was here this morning, and Mem. Seems they woke up and found that Mannon hadn't come home last night. And, them being them, they panicked."

Aven chewed and swallowed. "My fa? Panicked? I...that must have been interesting."

"Where was Mannon?" Aria asked. "He wasn't here, was he?"

"No," Owyn answered, drawing the sound out. "No, he was across the street."

"Across the street?" Treesi repeated. "From them?"

Owyn grinned and pointed over his shoulder, toward the front window. "Across the street from us."

Alanar sputtered. "He was with Rhexa?"

"In her guest room," Owyn said. "You know, the one she doesn't have?" He shrugged, picking up his teacup. "And I tell you, if at the end of this, he decides he's going to ask my aunt for something more? I'm good with that." He sipped his tea, then put the cup down. "Now, part of that conversation this morning was what rites were going to happen for Ambaryl. Mannon wants to know if he can wait a day to leave, so he can be here for it."

"What should we expect?" Aven asked. "What do they do with the dead in the Earth tribe?"

Alanar cocked his head to the side. "In the Earth tribe in general, or here in Terraces? It's different."

"Both," Aria answered. "I don't know what's done anywhere outside of the mountains. Or I didn't, until recently."

Alanar nodded. "Usually, bodies are buried. We're given back to the earth that bore us. Here in Terraces, though, there's no place for a burying ground. So there are caves, deep under the mountains, where everything is dry. The dead are laid to rest there." He smiled slightly. "Which is going to be interesting when it's my turn."

Aria coughed. "I...yes, that would be interesting."

"*Why?*" Del signed. "*What are the Air rites? I never looked, and I don't remember what was done with my mother.*"

"Del asked about the Air rites," Aven translated. "And I'm curious, too. We've never discussed this. You all know about Water, don't you?" He looked around the table, then continued. "Fire is...I suppose giving the body to the volcano is out, since the Smoking Mountain is unsafe now?"

"That's only special cases," Owyn said. "Usually, it's just a regular funeral pyre. And the Smoking Mountain was never safe."

"Which begs the question of why live there," Treesi teased. "All right. Aria, what are the Air rites? I don't know that either."

Aria looked thoughtful. "Sky burial," she answered. "Which...it's very different."

"It involves shadow-hawks, like Wraith," Alanar said. "Since our lore says that our wings came from the shadow-hawk."

"Wait, how does burial work with birds?" Owyn asked. "I mean, Marik says Wraith will eat carrion. So won't they..." He stopped. "Oh. Oh, that's...really?"

Aven put down his teacup. "Air burial...is being eaten? But...how does the Mother know you're you, then?"

"We're laid out under the sky for Her to find," Aria answered. "The bodies are watched over for three days, while their flock celebrates their life. Then they're left for the shadow-hawks."

"So it's not like feeding someone you don't like to sharks, and having the Mother only find shark shit," Owyn said slowly. "All right. I can see the difference. Allie, you'd better leave good instructions on how you want them to deal with you."

"Sky burial, and what the hawks leave gets buried in the ground," Alanar answered. "It's already written down."

Owyn blinked. "Should I have known that?"

"Probably," Alanar answered. "I just didn't think of telling you. I've no intention of anyone actually needing that information for a long time."

"We'll need that information," Aria said. "For the records, in the Palace. So things are done properly when the time comes. Which will hopefully be a very long time in the future. Now, Ambaryl is being buried in the mountain?"

"Yes," Owyn answered. "And Del and Mannon wanted to know if we should wait and leave after, so we can be here for it."

Aria nodded slowly. She sipped her tea, then folded a griddlecake into quarters and spooned some jam onto it. She ate a bite, then nodded again. "Yes, we should stay and witness. I'll speak to Jehan about holding the ceremony at such a time that we can leave directly after. Now, we need to start preparing to follow. What do we need to do so we can leave? Besides pack?"

"Schedules will need to be rearranged at the healing complex," Aven answered. "And Owyn will have to hand off his work with Rhexa."

"We're not going by boat, are we?" Treesi asked. "I don't like boats."

"You can go by canoe, with Othi," Aven offered, and Treesi blushed.

"I'm not sure that would be any better," she murmured. "Although it would certainly be more distracting. Is it just me, or is Othi's flirting trying to shift into courting?"

Del frowned slightly. "*Is there a difference?*" he signed.

Treesi frowned slightly. "Is there a difference? Is that what you said?" When Del nodded, she smiled. "I'm learning! And yes, there's a difference. Flirting...that doesn't mean much. It's just in fun. Courting, though...he's serious. He wants more than just being fun. Flirting is temporary. Courting is...well, it's more. And I'm not sure I can give him more. Not and be true to myself and my responsibilities to all of you."

Aven sighed. "Have you told him that? He's a reasonable person. He'll understand if you tell him that you're not sure if you can give him what he wants." He paused. "If you were free to do so, would you? If you didn't have responsibilities to us?"

"I don't know?" Treesi sounded confused. "I mean...I didn't think I'd ever be with just one person. Healers...well, they don't do that, usually. And he wants...he wants forever. I never thought about forever. Not with one person."

"You wouldn't be with one person," Alanar said. "You'd be like Owyn. He's married to me, but he's still a Companion, and no one expects him not to be. And I'm still a healer. If I need to be with a patient, Owyn understands that."

"I'm not sure Othi will," Treesi said softly. "And I really don't want to hurt him."

"Then you're going to need to talk to him," Aria said. "I think he may surprise you, Treesi."

Treesi nodded. "I'll find the time," she said. "I'll make the time." She sighed and looked down at her plate. "Who has rounds today?"

Aven frowned and looked at Alanar. "I don't remember if we were given a schedule. But I was a bit out of my head last night."

Alanar closed his eyes for a moment. Then he shook his head. "No, we weren't. That's...we should walk over to the healing center. Find out if we missed something, see what we need to do to be ready to leave." He stood up. "I'll go wash up. Treesi?"

"I'll be along in a moment," Treesi said. "You go ahead."

"Want help?" Owyn asked.

Alanar smiled. "From you? Always."

Owyn grinned in response and followed Alanar out of the front room.

Aria finished her griddlecake and looked around. "Aven, you and Treesi should go and get ready. I will clean up," she said. "And then...Del, will you come with me and Owyn to speak to Rhexa about our leaving?"

Del smiled and nodded. He reached for his tablet, then realized he wasn't wearing his vest. He slowly signed, *"I'd be happy to help you."*

Aria took his hand. "I'll learn them all someday," she said with a smile. "For now, I think you said yes?"

Del nodded, making Aria laugh. "Good. I am learning." She let go of his hand and stood up, then laughed and pressed one hand to her belly.

"Swimming in spirals?" Aven asked.

"Or flying," Aria answered. "I can't tell. But yes." She looked down and smiled gently, then looked back at Aven. "You should go and get ready."

Aven got up, but instead of following Treesi back to the bedrooms, he walked around the table to Aria. He pulled her close and rested his forehead against hers, breathing with her for a long moment before kissing her gently.

She tipped her head back and smiled. "Go get ready," she repeated.

Aven laughed and headed down the corridor to the bedrooms.

Aria watched him go, then turned to Del. "Let's get cleaned up."

LEAVING THE HOUSE WAS easier than it had been the day before. Owyn stayed on Del's left, and Aria on his right, and having them there made Del feel almost normal. Almost safe. He looked up at the sky, at the high, slate-gray clouds, and concentrated on Owyn.

"*It's a good thing Fa isn't leaving today. It's going to rain.*"

Owyn looked up. "Think you're right," he agreed. "This time of year, it'll be a good, long, soaking rain, too."

Aria glanced at them, then looked up. "You think it will rain? It does not smell of rain. Not yet."

Del turned so that he was walking backwards to face them, signing, "*It's going to. Just not for hours yet.*"

Aria chuckled. "I never did ask. You are part Air, like I am, and Alanar. How is your Air sense?"

Del shrugged. "*I don't bump into things in the dark, and I'm a good dancer.*"

"You dance?" Owyn asked. "I should show you how to use the whip chain."

"*I don't even know what that is,*" Del admitted. "*But I don't know many weapons.*"

"This is a Fire weapon, and using it is very much like dancing," Aria answered. "And Owyn is very good with one."

"When we're done, and before Trey takes you off to start showing you things, I'll take you down to the lowest terrace and show you."

"It may be raining by that time. So perhaps you should go down to the armory with them," Aria suggested.

Owyn hesitated, then shook his head. "Ah...no. I...no."

Aria took Owyn's arm and stopped. "Owyn?"

"I..." Owyn took a deep, shaky breath. "Aven and I changed places. Now he's fine in the caves, and I'm not. Not for long, anyway. I can get through to the stables, if I have to. But I don't like being in the caves for too long. They start closing in."

Aria stared at him, her eyes wide. "This is new."

Owyn nodded. "Since Teva. I didn't tell you all about that. You didn't need to know. But...yeah, since Teva."

"Oh, Owyn," Aria breathed. "I had no idea."

"Because I didn't tell you," Owyn said. "I didn't tell anyone. Not anyone. Alanar doesn't even know, and he's been there for the nightmares." He stopped and closed his eyes. "I need to stop. Or I'm not going to be any good to you, and we have work to do."

Del moved without hesitation, closing the space between them and hugging Owyn as tightly as he could. He felt Owyn laugh.

"You don't weigh enough for that to do much," Owyn murmured into his hair. Arms closed around Del. "But it's good. Thank you."

Del felt Owyn kiss the top of his head, and the arms around him loosened. He stepped back, watching Owyn intently. His face was pale, and there were shadows in his eyes.

"Take a deep breath," Aria said. "Do you want to go back to the house and wash your face? You could meet us."

"I...yeah. Mem will notice if I go in looking like this. I'll catch you up." He took another deep breath, then nodded. "I'll catch up," he repeated, and turned to go back to the house.

Del fell in next to Aria as they started walking again. She took his hand and squeezed his fingers.

"When we get to the Palace," she said. "You're going to have to show me where everything is. And we'll have to help Treesi so she doesn't get lost all the time."

Del looked at her, then gestured with his free hand for her to keep going. She smiled and added, "Treesi has trouble with rights and lefts, and with reading. Her mind reverses the directions and the letters. No one told you that?"

Del shook his head, tugging his hand free from hers and taking his tablet from his pocket. *"Is that why she reads so slowly?"*

Aria read the tablet and nodded. "Yes, exactly. She's already worried about getting lost in the Palace."

Del nodded, wiping the tablet clean and writing, *"I'll help her. It will help that we'll all be in the same suite."*

"We will?"

Del nodded. *"The Heir's Suite. There's a big sitting room, and the Heir's rooms, and the rooms for each of the Companions. It takes up part of one wing, and is across from the Firstborn's Suite."* He grinned as he wrote the words. *"I wasn't supposed to be in there. But since I wasn't supposed to be there, Ambaryl would never look for me there, so I could play alone for hours."*

Aria read the tablet, then asked, "Do you like being alone?"

Del shrugged. *"I'm used to being alone,"* he wrote. *"The children in the Palace who played with me before were afraid of me after. Because my wings were gone, and because I didn't talk. So I got used to playing by myself. Or just being with Fa."* He smiled. *"He taught me to read, and to write. He taught me to play Wolves and Sheep, and Gammon, and Gambit. Do you play Gambit?"*

"I don't even know what Gambit is," Aria answered. "Will you show me?"

Del nodded. He wiped the tablet and wrote, "*You should ask Fa. He's very good.*"

"I'll do that. In what spare time, I'm not sure, but I'll do that." Aria took the tablet and closed it, and slipped it into Del's pocket. Then she took his hand again. "Do you mind, not being alone anymore?"

Del shook his head and leaned gently into her arm, hearing her laugh.

"I think that's a no," she said. "Will you share my bed again tonight, Del?"

Del stopped walking, then hurried to start again when Aria didn't stop. She looked at him and smiled. "I've confused you?"

Del nodded, then shook his head, making her laugh.

"You want to know why?"

Del nodded again, still stunned. She wanted him in her bed?

She ran her thumb over his fingers. "Because I woke up this morning, and I knew you'd been there, and it felt right. You are part of me, as much as any of the others. You are mine, my Air. And it doesn't matter to me if we never share our bodies. I'm just happy to have you share my bed. Just be with me."

Del stopped, and this time Aria stopped as well. He stepped in front of her, facing her. She smiled and met his eyes, and her brows rose in surprise when he leaned forward and kissed her gently on the lips.

"Well," she said as they started walking again. "I think that's a yes." Del nodded, and she laughed. "Good."

CHAPTER FIFTEEN

Owyn took a deep breath and knocked on the door to the house Mannon and Memfis shared.

"Come in, Mouse!" he heard Memfis call. He opened the door and went in, seeing them all sitting crowded around the small dining table.

"We should be doing this at our house," Owyn said. "We have more room."

"We're fine, Owyn," Rhexa said. "Pull a chair up. We're making lists."

Owyn had to go into the kitchen to find an empty chair, and he dragged it into the front room and sat down next to Del, who had a stack of paper, a dip pen and an ink pot in front of him. "What have you all decided so far?" Owyn asked, tipping his head so he could read one of the pages.

"To start with," Jehan said. "We can do the burial rites either tonight at sunset or tomorrow at dawn. If we do them tonight, you'll have more time tomorrow to get ready to leave."

"And if you just pack what you need to take with you immediately, I can take care of packing everything else and send it by cart," Rhexa added. "So you won't have to waste too much time packing."

Aria nodded slowly. "Who would you send?" she asked.

"I'm not sure yet," Rhexa answered. "But they'll go with guards."

"Have you all talked to Granna yet?" Owyn asked. "I don't think she'll want to stay behind."

Memfis frowned slightly. "I'll go next door and see if they'll join us."

"Tell them to bring chairs," Mannon said, not looking up from what he was writing. "We only have one left."

Memfis chuckled and got up, walking out of the house. When he returned, Meris was on his arm, and Karse and Trey were behind him, carrying chairs.

"What's this Memfis is saying? We're leaving when?" Karse asked.

"Tomorrow, and we are all leaving at once," Aria answered. "You said you could secure the Palace in an hour? You're going to prove it."

Karse coughed. "But no pressure, right? Not at all." He set his chair down and sat, dragging his fingers through his hair as he stared at the floor. "Yeah, all right. Given the men and women Othi introduced me to last night? Yeah, I can secure the Palace in an hour. Maybe two, if we go slow. But you're sure you want to go north now, Aria?"

"I think that we must," Aria answered. "We need to secure the Palace, the throne, and my rule, before Risha does anything else. We must find out what she was looking for in the Palace and if she found it. And from the Palace, it won't be a long trip to the Temple."

"You can't go straight there. You have to make the Progress," Mannon said.

"And once we do, we'll see what we find there," Jehan murmured. "Remember Aleia's theory."

"I do remember," Aria said. "And if there is no Crown at the Temple, if my father is still alive, then we see what we need to do then." She looked thoughtful. "There was no connection between Risha and the Palace healers, was there? Rhexa?"

"None," Rhexa answered. "She was a trainee at the healing center when–" She stopped and bit her lip. "Twenty-five years ago," she finished.

"When I attacked the Palace," Mannon said softly. "You don't need to prevaricate. We all know what I did."

Rhexa sighed. "I know. But I don't need to rub salt in the wound." She rested her hand on his arm. "Regardless, Risha was nowhere near the Palace when it happened. Pirit said that none of the healers who were in the Palace on that day ever went on to teach at the healing center, so Risha wouldn't have had contact with them as a student or trainee. And she herself was a full healer when she was assigned to the Palace, as the only healer in the Palace."

"Del was...three or four, I think," Mannon mused. "So call it fifteen or sixteen years ago. Rhexa came to replace our previous healer. Who she never met, I don't believe." He looked over at Jehan. "Healer Waran?"

"Waran?" Jehan whistled. "He was your Palace Healer? When I was training, he was already old enough to remember Axia taking her first steps."

"He was our second or third in two years, I think. Healers didn't like to stay at the Palace. I can't think why," Mannon said with a wry laugh. "I think Pirit assigned him to me out of spite. But he was a good man, and I liked him. I think the only reason that Yana survived to choose me was because of him. He died in his sleep and I had him buried with honors on the Palace grounds. Then I sent word to the healing center for a replacement healer."

"And got Risha," Owyn said. He nodded. "So she couldn't have known if any of the other healers had been up to something, because she never actually talked to any of them?"

"But there are records," Rhexa said. "You know, maybe I should come with you," she added, turning toward Mannon. "I'm more familiar with healer records than any of the healers making this trip. I should be able to find something—"

Jehan cleared his throat. "I'm going, Rhexa," he said gently. "I need you here."

Rhexa blushed slightly. "Oh. Yes. You said that."

Jehan nodded. "I'll go through the healer records, see if I can find anything. But all of those records were duplicated here, and Mother's gone through them. There was nothing there out of the ordinary."

"Assuming that everything was copied accurately," Memfis added, pacing behind Jehan.

Jehan looked up and nodded. "Assuming that everything was copied accurately. That's what I'll be looking for."

Aria nodded, then turned toward Meris, who was sitting in Memfis' chair. "Grandmother, will you come with us, or do you want to stay here?" she asked. "I will understand if you want to stay here. So many of the Fire tribe are here now, and they look to you—"

"They can look a little further, then," Meris said. "I'm coming with you, my dear. There's a great-great grandchild in my future, and I'm rather looking forward to meeting them." She sighed. "And it will be good to see the Palace again. I haven't been inside since the day I left, when we took Riga to the Temple for the last time. I never went back."

There was a long silence, then Jehan gestured to Del. "Let me see your notes, Del," he said. Del passed the papers to him, and Jehan read through them, nodding slowly. "I'll need to make certain the schedules for rounds are taken care of—"

"Alanar, Aven and Treesi went to look into that," Owyn said. "Since they none of them were sure what their schedules were today."

"They don't have schedules today," Jehan replied. He reached for Del's pen and another sheet of paper, making his own list. "Aria, burial tonight or tomorrow?"

"We'll do it tonight," Aria answered. "Then sail tomorrow morning. Will that be enough time for us all to prepare?" She looked at the window. "And will the rain that Del says is coming hamper any of the preparations?"

Jehan looked over his shoulder at the window, then shook his head. "No, it shouldn't."

Rhexa looked at the window, then at Del. "It's going to rain?"

Del nodded, signing, "*In a few hours.*"

"How do you know?"

Del frowned. He looked at Aria, then at Mannon. Then he shrugged.

Mannon laughed. "He's always known," he said. "I'm not sure if it's an Air talent, or just Del."

"It may be Air," Aria said. "We are more sensitive to air pressure and currents. We have to be. But it is not something I can do. Nor can Alanar, I do not think."

"I think we're done here," Jehan said. "Burial tonight, and we all leave tomorrow. Aria, you and your Companions should prepare whatever you're taking with you. Rhexa, will you need Owyn?"

"Please," Rhexa said. "I'll need notes on the projects you're working on, so that I can hand them off."

Owyn nodded. "I'll come with you to your office and get that taken care of now." He drummed his fingers on the table. "I was supposed to show Del my whip chain, but we can do that once things are packed."

"*I don't really have anything to pack,*" Del signed. "*What can I do to help somewhere else?*"

"Come down to the docks with me? I need to talk to Othi about tomorrow," Karse suggested. "And then you can show me how to find the armory, so we can see what you can do."

THERE WERE FOUR OF them when they made their way to the armory — Othi decided to accompany them.

"Trying to get any kind of weapon into Del's hand was like sailing against the tide," he said as they walked through the tunnels. "I want to see if you can do what I couldn't. And what you end up doing."

Karse snorted. "He didn't tell you?"

"Tell me what?" Othi looked at Del. "What didn't you tell me?"

Del sighed. He started signing, "*Why I freeze. I know why.*" He repeated the story, signing quickly, and watched the color drain from Othi's face. "*That's it. That's why. I just never told anyone before yesterday. Except for Aven. He knows.*"

Othi arched a brow and signed back, "*Do they know?*"

"*Yes.*"

Othi nodded, and asked out loud, "All right, then. I'm assuming that he still needs to pay for this? Do I get to kill him, or is that Aven's job?"

Karse and Trey both laughed, and Del smiled and shook his head. "*I already killed him.*"

Othi gaped at him for a moment. "You? You killed someone? You're pulling my tail, Del!"

"*I did have help, from Skela. Don't tell them that he's alive. I haven't told my father that yet.*"

Othi nodded and signed. "*What did you do?*"

"*Poisoned him.*"

Othi grinned. "Good."

"So, knowing that, we can work around it," Karse said. "I just want to see what we have to work with. And there are a couple of things that Owyn wants to show Del, but he's busy."

"Like what?" Othi asked.

"*Whip chain,*" Del signed. "*Aria says it's a traditional Fire weapon.*"

Othi looked puzzled. "Whip chain? I don't know that one."

"Length of chain, about ten feet long," Karse said. "Handle at one end, blade at the other. And Owyn is really good with one."

Othi nodded slowly. "Sounds like a really long falling star. Which isn't a weapon we use anymore. That's old. Really old. I don't think there are a lot of people that dance it anymore." He frowned. "Maybe Neera knows."

"Might be interesting to compare them," Trey said. "If we can find someone who knows it."

Othi grinned. "I'll ask around. And I want to see what Owyn can do. I've seen him dance—"

"Where?" Trey asked.

"The Floating City," Othi answered. "He went hunting visions. Danced with Aven's hook swords. It's not all that different from how we dance, but we don't fall down at the end."

They entered the large bubble cavern that had been Pirit's base for the years when she'd been in hiding, raising an army against Mannon. The armory was a large building set against the cavern wall, with a fenced practice field in front of it. Karse stopped outside the armory and looked Del up and down.

"No swords," he said. "Nothing that even resembles a sword. So no long knives either. That leaves us ranged weapons and polearms." He looked inside the armory. "Right. I see long bow, crossbow...you said javelins, yeah?"

Del nodded, and Karse gestured to Trey. They both entered the armory, and when they came out, Trey was carrying a crossbow and a bundle of quarrels. Karse had a longbow in one hand, and something that looked like someone had combined a sword and a staff — the pole was taller than Del, and it ended with a short sword blade.

"This might be an option," he said. "Del, take this."

Del took the pole and looked up at it, then at Karse, arching a brow. Karse grinned. "It's a swordstaff," he said. "Meant for fighting against a mounted opponent, but you can use it like a staff. Take it to the practice yard and I'll show you."

Del looked up at the blade again, then followed Karse as they walked. "I want you to learn close-in fighting, too," Karse said over his shoulder. "Dirty fighting. The sort of thing you need to know to keep yourself alive until help comes. They've got some good weapons for that in there, too."

Del nodded slowly, wondering just what he'd gotten himself into. Trey nudged his arm. "It's all right," he said softly. "You'll be fine."

Del met his eyes and made a face. They stopped at the practice field, and Karse leaned the longbow against the rail and took the swordstaff from Del. He walked into the field and stood in the middle of the space, running his hands up and down the pole, hefting it, swinging it slightly so that the blade cut a line in the sand. All at once, he lunged, sweeping the blade wide. He turned, snapping the staff around and lunging again, stabbing an invisible foe. He jerked the staff back — pulling it free from his opponent, Del realized — and cut diagonally, down one way, up the other. Lunged again, this time with the butt of the staff forward. He stopped, stood straight, and nodded.

"Very nice."

Del jumped at the unexpected voice behind him, turning to see Aleia had come up to join them. She smiled at him.

"I'm assuming that this is for you?" she asked. Del nodded. She looked at him thoughtfully, then shook her head. "Karse, he doesn't have the mass to use that effectively."

Karse looked up. "When did you get here?"

"Halfway through," Aleia answered. "The swordstaff is a good weapon, but not for Del. He needs light and fast."

"Aunt Aleia, do we know anyone who still dances falling star?" Othi asked.

Aleia frowned. "I haven't seen anyone dance that in years. But I was only ever at the larger gatherings. Why?"

"Wanted to know how much like a whip chain it was," Othi answered. He rested his hand on Del's shoulder. "We need something light and fast. Owyn is going to show Del whip chain, but maybe he could learn to dance with falling stars?"

Aleia looked thoughtful. Then she nodded. "I'll ask."

Trey coughed. "Dancing? I thought we were talking about fighting." he asked.

"It's both," Aleia answered. "Or did you not realize that most of Water's dances are war dances?"

"I never thought of it," Trey admitted.

"I like that swordstaff," Karse said as he came out of the practice field. "I might talk to Pirit about keeping it. Del, we need to get you set up with an arm-guard and a glove. Come to the armory with me. Then...where do we go to practice archery?"

OWYN LEANED BACK IN his chair and closed his eyes, rubbing his hand over his face. "I think that's everything, Auntie," he said as he opened his eyes.

Rhexa looked over the papers spread out on her desk and nodded. "I think you're right. And if you aren't, I'll muddle through." She looked up at him and smiled. "I'm going to miss you."

Owyn sighed. "I'm going to miss you, too. It's going to be really weird, not having you right across the street. But it's not far, and I'm not worried about going by ship anymore. I can come see you." He grinned. "And you can come see us. Ah...Auntie?"

Rhexa met his eyes. "You're going to ask me about last night?"

"Well...."

"I'm not answering," Rhexa said. She collected the papers into a pile, tapped them neatly together, and put them into her desk. "Quite frankly, Owyn Jaxis, it's none of your business."

Owyn sat up. "Looking out for my favorite auntie—"

"I'm your only auntie."

"So? Favorite only auntie." Owyn spread his arms. "Why shouldn't I be looking after you?"

Rhexa smiled. "I appreciate that you do. But it's still none of your business." She laughed and stood up. "You should see your face."

"Nah, I know what I look like." Owyn got up and walked over to the door. "I'd rather look at Allie. Or Aria, or Del. Someone prettier." He opened the door, and they walked side by side through the healing complex. Owyn looked over at his aunt. "You'll be all right, when I'm gone? Since...ah...well..."

"Since Ambaryl is dead?" Rhexa asked. "Honestly, Owyn? I'm not sure how I feel. She said yes. We exchanged pledge bracelets. And...I don't think any of it was real. I think she was lying to me the entire time she was here. And I was too stupid to notice."

"You weren't stupid!" Owyn protested. "You loved her. She was the stupid one, not to see what she had. She threw it all away."

Rhexa sighed. "Maybe, but it doesn't make me feel any better. I should have realized—"

"You said something about it not being the first time," Owyn said. "She...what happened?"

Rhexa sniffed. "What I told you? About me going into administration, and Ambaryl going off—"

"And ending up in the Palace? Yeah, what about it?"

"I didn't tell you that she ended up in the Palace by leaving me and running off with my best friend." Rhexa glanced at Owyn. "He was a guard with the regular trading caravan, and she left with him. Just left — no note or anything. I didn't find out what happened to her until Raist came back to Terraces and told me that she'd left him."

"That's all kinds of fucked up, Auntie," Owyn said. "Why'd you let her back in?"

"The real reason? I had too much to drink that night, and I made a very bad choice." Rhexa snorted. "I'm not allowed to drink that much wine ever again. Remember that."

Owyn nodded. "Right. You and Mem both. No wine. I'll make sure whoever ends up taking care of the lot of us at the Palace knows that."

Rhexa took his arm. "I am going to miss you so much," she repeated. "But you're going to do amazing things. Dyneh and Huris would be so proud of you." She paused. "I'm proud of you."

Owyn smiled, slipping his arm free so he could put it around Rhexa's shoulders. "That means more to me, you know. I don't remember them. But I know you. It means more to me to have you proud of me."

"Just promise me that you'll be careful."

"I promise."

CHAPTER SIXTEEN

The rain rolled in from the ocean and settled over Terraces in soft, gray showers. They started just as Karse and Trey delivered Del home, his arms loaded with bundles of arrows, an unstrung longbow, and a quiver. Trey carried a crossbow, several bundles of quarrels, and a bag. Del wasn't sure what was in the bag — Karse had just told him to bring it when they went north. It made interesting clanking noises when it banged against Trey's leg.

Karse knocked three times, then opened the door so that Del could enter. He went inside, putting his armload down on the couch. Trey followed him, putting his burden down on another part of the couch.

"Del?" Aven came into the front room from the bedrooms. "There you are. We were wondering where you'd gotten to. Hello, Karse, Trey." He stopped, seeing the weapons on the couch. One brow rose. "I thought tonight was a funeral. Not an invasion."

Del grinned as Karse and Trey both laughed. "This is for training," Karse answered. "We worked a little with a longbow today. Not bad for a first time."

"*I hit the target once,*" Del signed. "*Barely. How is that not bad?*"

Karse looked at him, then at Aven. "You're going to have to teach me this."

"We'll start tomorrow," Aven said. "He says he only hit the target once. Barely."

"Right. He hit the target," Karse said. "Trey? How long did it take you to do that well with a longbow?"

Trey huffed softly. "Gonna make me say it?"

"Trey..."

"Ten days, and I took the skin off my left arm. Twice," Trey grumbled.

"He wouldn't listen when I told him he was standing wrong," Karse added. "Del, you listen, you have good posture, and you know how to stand already. You're going to be fantastic with a longbow. We'll try a crossbow when we're settled into the Palace. And I want to see you with Owyn's whip chain—"

"What?" Aven interrupted.

"*Owyn was going to show me,*" Del signed. "*And Othi said something about falling stars, and how they might be similar. Your mother said she'd have to find someone who knew how to dance them.*"

Aven shook his head. "I don't know what they are, so hopefully, Ama will find someone. I'm curious to know, too. Now, we need to get ready to go. Karse, Trey, are you coming?"

"We can be there, yeah," Karse answered. "If you want us."

"*I think Owyn might appreciate having you there,*" Del signed.

"Then we'll need to go change," Trey said. "We're all over sand from the practice yards."

Karse nodded, and he and Trey left. Once they were gone, Aven walked over to look at the collection of weapons. He whistled softly. "This is impressive. And you're comfortable with these?" He looked over at Del.

"*I think so. The longbow felt good, once I was used to it. Karse says I might be sore in the morning, across the chest and in the shoulders.*"

"What's in the bag?"

Del shook his head. "*I don't know. Karse just told me to bring it with us when we leave. He wants me to learn what he calls dirty fighting, though. Maybe it's for that?*"

"Karse is going to teach you to fight dirty?" Owyn asked as he walked into the front room. He was wearing a deep red shirt that Del had never seen before, with dark trousers. He smiled as he joined them. "How was weapons practice?"

"*I hit the target shooting a longbow,*" Del answered. "*Sort of.*"

"What does sort of mean?" Owyn asked.

"*The target is mounted on a bale of hay,*" Del answered. "*I hit the hay right at the edge of the target.*"

Owyn nodded. "Not bad. That's better than I did with a crossbow. First time I tried, the arrow went straight up, and Marik laughed himself sick." He grinned, then gestured to the corridor. "Aria and Treesi are almost ready. Alanar is just finishing washing up, so the bathing room is yours next, Del."

DEL WAS THE LAST ONE out into the front room. He remembered people wearing white when his mother died, so he'd chosen a white shirt, but he didn't have white trousers. He opted for gray instead, and his usual vest over the top. He'd expected the others to be in white, too. But only Aria was. Alanar and Treesi both wore clothing of somber, dark brown, and Owyn was in his red. How had he missed that each tribe had their own colors for mourning?

Aven's clothes looked the same as usual, but there was something on his cheek — a single cut. A mourning stripe. Del remembered Aven explaining it to him after they'd gotten to his family canoes. On the face for a man, on the arm for a woman, to show respect for the dead. Did Water not dress for mourning the way the other tribes did?

"Are you ready, Del?" Treesi asked.

He nodded and came out to join them. "*What are we doing now? What's the custom here?*"

Aven nodded. "I was just about to ask. Treesi, Alanar, what's the custom here? Where do we go?"

"The healing center," Alanar answered. "We'll follow the body from there to the burial caves."

Del looked sideways at Owyn. *"Will you be all right?"* he thought. Owyn glanced at him and nodded slightly. Del stepped closer and took his hand.

Owyn smiled, then cleared his throat. "All right. So clearly, brown is the Earth funeral color. White is Air?"

Aria nodded. "White is Air, yes. I'm surprised that there is no color for Water."

"Water doesn't have a color," Aven replied, and it took a moment before Del realized that he was saying two things at once. Aven tapped his cheek. "Men show their mourning here. Women on the shoulder."

"You didn't have to." Rhexa said from the doorway. She took down the hood of her rain cloak. "Aven, you didn't have to cut yourself. Not for her."

"I didn't do it for her. This is for you. Sometimes, the best you can say about someone is that they're dead. But we still honor the loss to their survivors." Aven walked over to Rhexa and took her hand, raising it to kiss her palm. "Fa calls Owyn the son of his heart. I think that makes you the aunt of mine. Our aunt. All of us."

Rhexa's jaw dropped. "I...you're adopting me? All of you?"

"We had not discussed it," Aria answered. "Not formally. But I do think Aven is right. You treat us all as your own. That means that you are ours." She looked around. "Are we agreed?"

A chorus of agreement went up, with Del adding his silent assent. Rhexa looked around at them, and tears started to well in her eyes. "Oh, you had to do this to me right before you leave?" she cried. "It's hard enough as it is to let you go!"

Aven pulled her into an embrace, and Owyn dropped Del's hand to go join him. Treesi joined, and Del just barely beat Aria into the group hug.

"Am I allowed in?" Alanar asked.

"Of course you are!" Aria answered. "You are part of us as well." Alanar smiled and stepped close behind Del, pressing against him as he wrapped his arms around the group.

Del wasn't sure who started giggling first, but it spread like flame through kindling, and when Jehan and Aleia entered, it was to find all of them laughing. Jehan stared at them for a moment.

"Odd way to start a funeral," he said slowly. The laughter, which had been starting to die off, flared again. Aleia smiled, covering her mouth with her hand.

"What's funny?" Mannon asked, coming inside and taking down his wet hood. Memfis followed him in, and chuckled.

"Sounds like stress release," Memfis said. "Best to get it out of the way now."

"True," Aleia agreed. "Who else is joining us?"

"Mother will be leading the ceremony," Jehan answered. "It's usually the duty of the Senior Healer, but I've never done one. She's in the caverns now, preparing. We saw Karse and Trey, and they'll meet us at the healing center. Katrin says she'll be there. Marik and Esai. I think Neera and Othi are coming, too. Lady Meris asked to be excused tonight, given the hour we'll need to be leaving."

"Grandmother is home alone?' Aria asked.

"No, Afansa is with her," Memfis said. "She seems to have appointed herself Lady Meris' attendant. And she's being sweet enough about it that Meris can't bring herself to tell her to stop."

Mannon nodded. "She's actually rather nice."

Del waved to get his father's attention, then signed, "*She's the potter who made the blue tea bowls you gave me. That's how she knew you.*"

Mannon looked surprised. "I wondered how she was so certain!"

Jehan shook his head and looked out the door. "I hope you all have rain cloaks. It's soaking in well, but we'll all be drenched by the time we get inside."

"Will we have to go out again?" Owyn asked. "I'll get the cloaks." He disappeared down the corridor, coming back a moment later with an armload. "All right. Treesi, this is yours." He passed them out, running out of cloaks before he ran out of people. "Aven, what are you wearing?"

Aven blinked. "You expected me to wear something? To *not* get wet?"

"I...right. That's a silly question, isn't it?" Owyn turned to Del. "We cleaned yours, but I never got around to patching it. It still has a hole in it."

Del shrugged. "*I'll be fine,*" he signed. "*It's just water.*"

Owyn headed back down the corridor. He came back with Del's cloak and his own. Del took his and put it on, remembering the last time he'd worn it. The night his world had changed for the second time.

This was definitely a change for the better. He drew his hood up and looked around.

"Are we all ready?" Jehan asked. "Let's go."

THE STREETS WERE EMPTY, the rain keeping everyone inside. They walked in silence to the healing complex, where Malani told them that Pirit had taken the others on with her. Their first stop was Jehan's office, where they left their cloaks. From there, they walked through the administration side, using corridors that Owyn was certain he'd never been down before. They seemed to slant downward, and between one step and the next, change from a man-made corridor to a long cave tunnel.

"Have we been this way?" he asked Alanar.

"No, we only use these tunnels in emergencies," Alanar answered. "In big storms, this is where we bring patients to shelter. There's a cavern down below. And below that is the morgue."

Owyn swallowed and took his husband's hand. Mistake. Alanar turned sharply toward him.

"What's wrong? Your heart is racing."

Owyn swallowed again. "I'm...not dealing well with closed-in places," he said softly. "Not anymore."

"You didn't tell me," Alanar said softly. "What happened?"

Owyn shook his head, then sighed. "Allie, I can't do this now. I need to be all right for my aunt. So I can't tell you. I'll fall to pieces."

Alanar nodded. "Will you tell me later? And will you tell me why you didn't tell me?"

"I will tell you everything later," Owyn said. "Umm...not tonight. Tonight we need to sleep, and if I tell you, I won't. Tomorrow."

"That's fair. I'm here, love. You're safe."

Owyn squeezed Alanar's hand. "Just keep telling me that, will you?" He looked down the corridor. "How big are these caves where we're going?" he asked, raising his voice.

"The shelter cave is very large," Treesi answered. "It has to be — there's always the chance that we might have everyone in Terraces in there. The burial caves are smaller, and long."

"We won't be going down those tunnels, though," Jehan added. "The actual ceremony is at the mouth of the burial tunnels."

Owyn nodded slowly. "I should be all right," he said softly, his voice pitched for Alanar's ears alone. "If the caves are big, I should be all right."

They kept walking, and the tunnel opened up, revealing a cavern similar to the one where Pirit had sheltered. There were torches burning against the sides of the cave, and in tall fire-pots that seemed to mark their route. Jehan led the way toward where Owyn could see a group waiting. It was easy to pick Othi out of the group — there was no one else in Terraces who was quite so massive. As they got closer, they could see Neera standing next to her brother, with Katrin and the guards ranging around them. Karse nodded to them as they approached, and stepped forward to bow to Rhexa.

"You honor us," he said gravely. "For allowing us to join you. I'm not sure what's appropriate for Earth, but in Fire, we say 'may the flame of their memory never die.'" He paused, then frowned. "And I'm not sure if that's appropriate in any case."

"Perhaps not," Rhexa replied. "But thank you." She looked around. "Thank you all."

Neera stepped forward and bowed. "May the Mother judge her wisely and well," she said. Behind her, Othi thumped one fist against his chest, hard enough that Owyn heard distant, faint echoes from the high cave ceiling.

"Are we all here?" Pirit asked, coming forward. She was dressed in a multitude of shades of brown, and her usually tightly-braided hair hung loose around her shoulder in silver-gray waves.

"We're all here," Jehan answered.

"Then let us begin." Pirit turned and led them toward a dark opening in the cavern. A cave mouth. There was a bier set before the cave, and on the bier, a body draped in brown linen.

Owyn heard Rhexa moan softly, and Alanar squeezed his hand. "You should be with her," he murmured.

"We should be with her," Owyn corrected, and led Alanar forward so that they stood behind Rhexa. He reached out to touch her shoulder, and she covered his hand with hers. Behind him,

Owyn heard movement, and looked back to see that the others had arranged themselves in some sort of order. Behind him were Aria and the Companions, along with Jehan, Katrin and Marik. Behind them were Mannon and Memfis, Karse and Trey, Esai, Neera, Othi and Aleia. He wondered at how they were standing, then heard a chime and turned back around. Pirit had walked to stand by the bier, and as she turned to face them, Owyn heard the chime again.

"Mother of us all," Pirit raised her voice as the chimes died away. "We surrender to Your arms a daughter of Earth. Ambaryl, daughter of Rylan, daughter of Amira, of the line of Mika. We return her to the Earth, and so send her to face You, to lay her heart open that You may see the moments of her life and pass judgment. If her blessings outweigh her faults, then we ask that You welcome her back to the Earth that bore us. If her faults are too great, and the harms that she caused too many, then allow her to pass from Your memory, and be forgotten." She lowered her head for a moment, then raised it once more and asked, "Are there any who wish to speak for the dead?"

Speak for the dead? Owyn looked at Alanar, wondering what that meant. Did that mean they would be down here for much longer? Owyn glanced up at the high ceiling — the cave was large, but it still felt as if the ceiling was starting to get closer. Starting to close in around him.

"Wyn?" Alanar whispered.

"I'm fine," Owyn lied. He knew Alanar would know he was lying. But as close as she was, Rhexa would be able to hear him clearly.

"I'll speak for her," Rhexa said. She stepped forward and turned to face them. Her face was pale. "Ambaryl and I...we grew up together. We loved each other for a long time. I loved her even when it was really clear that she didn't love me. She...she took care of people. She arranged things, organized things. She told me once that making things easier for other people was what made her happy. That taking care of people was how she showed them that she cared." She smiled slightly. "Like a certain nephew of mine."

Owyn snorted softly. "I never betrayed the people I was taking care of," he whispered, and heard Alanar's soft murmur of agreement.

Rhexa paused, and Owyn wondered if she'd heard him. She took a deep breath and continued, "I don't know where she went wrong. How she went wrong. I don't know what she was doing, or why. But...I can be certain of one thing. She did what she did because she was trying to take care of...someone. I don't know if that will make a difference in the end." She stopped and turned to Pirit, bowing slightly. Then she returned to her place.

Behind Owyn, he heard movement. Then Del appeared on his right, followed by Aven. Del walked forward and bowed to Pirit, then turned and looked at them.

"I'm ready," Aven said.

Del licked his lips and started signing, and Aven started translating, "*After my mother died, Ambaryl was my mother, as much as she could be. She took care of me until I recovered. She helped me heal, and mourn. She tried to help me learn to live without my wings, but she didn't know what it was to have them. But she tried. Half the time, she didn't know what to do with me, though. Fa said once that watching her try to mother me was like watching a hen taking care of a duck.*" There was a ripple of laughter, and Del smiled slightly. He flexed his fingers, and started signing again. "*I don't know why she decided I was broken. I think it was her that got the rest of the Palace servants to think it. But she started treating me like I'd lost my wits and not my voice. I know she wanted the best for me, but she thought I was stupid, and I couldn't show her otherwise, no matter what I did. She meant well, I know. But...she didn't know what to do with me, and I think at the end, she loved me, but she didn't like me very much. She never really accepted who I am, because I wasn't who she thought I should be. And because I wouldn't let her smother me."* He looked back over his shoulder, then audibly sighed. *"I'm still going to miss her."* He looked at Aven and nodded, then turned and bowed to Pirit again. He started back to his place, but Rhexa stopped him.

"Thank you," she said. Del smiled and kissed her cheek, then returned to his place behind Owyn.

Pirit stepped forward. "Will anyone else speak for the dead?" she asked. When no one answered, she nodded. "So be it. Let her be consigned to the Earth, and may the Mother judge her." She turned her back to them, and the chime rang again. As the sound died away, Alanar touched Owyn's arm.

"That's it," he said. "We can go."

Owyn nodded and turned, meeting Aven's eyes as he did. Aven looked at him, and immediately stepped forward.

"What's wrong?" he whispered. "You've gone pale."

"He's been pale," Alanar said. "He'll be fine once we're out in the air."

Aven nodded and took Owyn's other hand. "Come on." He snorted. "You're learning my tricks, and that's not a good thing."

"Yeah, but they're not yours anymore," Owyn answered. "They're mine. And it's still not a good thing. Can we go?"

CHAPTER
SEVENTEEN

O wyn closed his eyes and breathed in deeply, letting the salt sea air tickle the back of his throat. Amazing, how much he enjoyed the sea now that he wasn't terrified of it. He rested his hands on the ship's rail and took another deep breath, trying not to yawn.

"You didn't sleep last night, did you?"

Owyn didn't turn, feeling Aven come up behind him, his arms framing Owyn's on the rail. "Not so you'd notice, no."

"When were you going to tell me something was wrong? Tell any of us?"

Owyn tipped his head back against Aven's shoulder. "When I could tell you without screaming?" he answered. "I think I'm there. And...I should tell everyone, shouldn't I?"

"Considering that I've already been trying to get the information out of Alanar? And you haven't even told him?" Aven answered with a laugh. "Yes. Although...does Aria know? She didn't seem surprised at all that you were upset in the caves last night, or in the tunnels down to the dock this morning."

"She doesn't know all of it. No one knows all of it. But she and Del...she suggested I take Del down to the armory to show him the whip chain. And the idea of going through the tunnels set me off. They saw it. But they don't know why." He turned in the circle of

Aven's arms. "Where is everyone? If I don't do this now, it's not happening."

Aven frowned. "We don't have any privacy," he said. "Lady Meris and Afansa are in the captain's cabin with Aria and Treesi and Alanar. And Alanar is swearing he's not moving until we've docked. Did you know he wouldn't be able to tell where he was on a ship?"

"I didn't, no," Owyn answered. "It makes sense. But we didn't know before."

Aven nodded. "Del is with Captain Destria," he added. "Do you want Memfis with us when you tell us? We'd have to wait anyway if you do."

Owyn thought about it for a moment, then took a long breath. "I don't know. I mean, I don't know if he needs to know all the details. The basics, yeah. But not everything," he answered. "But that means I don't want to say it around Granna Meris, either. Or Afansa, since I don't really know her. How long before we get there?"

Aven frowned and looked around. "Come with me," he said, moving away from the rail. They walked to the front of the ship, and Aven looked down at the water. Owyn tried to figure out what he was looking at, but none of it made sense to him.

"You're supposed to teach me how to navigate, remember?"

Aven grinned. "Right now? I'm just judging how fast we're going. It's a good wind. We'll be there in an hour. Maybe less."

Owyn nodded. "I can wait if you can." He looked around at the canoes that sailed with them, a fleet of them that extended as far as he could see. There were more Water under the waves, he knew. "Aven, why aren't you out there?" he asked. "On a canoe, or in the water?"

"I thought maybe we'd go on my canoe," Aven answered. "But Aria wasn't comfortable with it. Her balance is off with the baby.

And she said Treesi gets sick, so it wasn't fair to ask her." He looked longingly down at the water. "And I thought about swimming, but I'm not fast enough to keep up with the fleet anymore."

"Oh, fuck, Aven," Owyn breathed. "I'm sorry."

Aven shook his head. "I can change. I can still swim. She tried to take that from me and failed. And someday, she'll pay for it." He shrugged. "Speed...seems like a small price to pay."

"You shouldn't have had to pay it at all," Owyn insisted. "Where's your walking stick, anyway?"

"Neither should you," Aven replied. "She hurt you, too."

Owyn shook his head. "Nah, what happened to me was Teva. She...she actually wouldn't let him do worse than he did."

"And if it wasn't for her, he wouldn't have had you at all," Aven pointed out. "It's all her, and the price she ll pay...well, she'll repay it in full. Eventually. And to answer your question, I left it in the cabin. I'm fine right now."

"From your mouth to the Mother's ears," Owyn murmured. "About her paying, I mean. An hour...that means the war party is hitting the Palace now, isn't it?"

Aven nodded. "That's about right, yes. If they haven't already hit it." He glanced at Owyn. "Worried about Memfis?"

Owyn thought about it for a moment. "No. Karse and Trey will look out for him, and your mother. They'll keep him from doing something stupid. I mean, really, Mannon won't let him fart without being at his elbow, so he'll be fine. I don't like that he's gone and put himself out there, but he'll be all right." He leaned his arms on the rail and looked down at the water. "You worried about your cousin?"

"A little. Othi has a hard head," Aven answered. He leaned on the rail next to Owyn. "He'll listen to Ama, though. I think he's scared of her."

"Think they'll be done by the time we get there?" Owyn asked. "Karse said he could take the Palace in an hour, given enough men."

"We'll find out in an hour," Aven answered. "Let's go see how everyone is doing."

SOMEONE KNOCKED ON the door. Aria felt a finger trail over her cheek and opened her eyes. She was leaning against Aven, dozing with her head on his shoulder, and she sat up as Destria came into the crowded cabin. "Captain?" Aria said. "Do we have a signal?"

"We do indeed. And a welcoming party on the dock. Permission to take us in?"

Aria smiled. "Please do. And thank you."

Destria bowed and closed the door, and Aria rolled her neck and sighed, then took the Diadem from the table next to her and put it on. "I'm ready. I think. Someone should wake up Owyn," she said, looking over at the bed where Owyn was snoring softly. "I want us all to enter the Palace together."

"I'll wake him," Alanar said. He shifted around in his place on the edge of the bed, leaned down, and kissed Owyn. Owyn jumped, then sighed and reached up to run his fingers through Alanar's hair.

"Time to wake up, Owyn," Treesi said. "We're here."

"Well, we're almost here," Aven added. "We're docking. That will take a few minutes."

Owyn let Alanar go and rolled onto his side. "Did they win?"

"Destria says there's a signal and a welcoming party, so I think so," Aven answered.

Owyn grinned and sat up, folding his legs and taking Alanar's hand. He looked around and frowned. "Where's Granna?"

"She went out," Treesi answered. "She said she wanted to see the Palace. Del's with her, and Afansa."

"We should go out and join them." Aven stood up, taking his walking stick with one hand, then offering his other hand to Aria. She smiled and took it, letting him help her to her feet and steady her when the ship bobbed beneath them. She sighed, then laughed.

"My balance will never be the same," she said. "I never had a problem standing on the canoe!"

"You didn't have a passenger when we were on the canoe," Aven pointed out. "You'll find your balance again." He looked around, then asked, "Aria, it hasn't even been a year yet, has it?"

"Since you first found me?" Aria asked. She shook her head. "No. So much has happened, and it's not even been a year." They walked out of the cabin, with Owyn and Treesi leading Alanar behind them. "We're not finished yet. There is still so much to do."

"I don't think we'll be finished until we're sent to the Mother," Owyn called. "No one ever said this would be easy, right?"

Aria looked at Aven, who shook his head. "No, no one ever did. But it's worth it."

"Completely," Aria agreed.

They walked toward the prow of the ship, where they could see Meris and Afansa. Afansa turned and smiled at them.

"It's so beautiful!" she said. "I've never seen any place so beautiful!"

Aria smiled and looked at the Palace. She'd only ever seen it at a distance before, when they were on their way to Terraces. From a distance, it had glowed in the sunlight like snow on a mountain top. Up close? The white stone walls soared high overhead, and she wondered how such a thing had ever been built.

"It is," she murmured. "It is very beautiful."

"We were supposed to have been born here," Aven said. "Memfis said that, remember?"

Aria nodded. Then she took Aven's hand and rested it on her belly. "Our baby will be born here."

He looked at her and smiled, then leaned down and kissed her cheek.

"Once we dock, I'll want to hear from the guard before I let you disembark," Destria said as she came toward them. "It looks like Karse's second is waiting for us. And the big Water warrior."

"Othi," Aven supplied. "Trey and Othi."

Destria nodded. "They're both on the docks. I imagine that means Karse and the War Leader are in the Palace proper. Once we hear from Trey that it's safe, then you can go ashore. I'll have your baggage sent up."

"Thank you, Captain," Aria said.

"Do you need any help, Captain?" Aven asked.

Destria smiled. "My crew know their jobs, Waterborn. But I thank you." She bowed slightly and walked away, shouting orders. The crew swarmed around Aria and the Companions, and they moved to the bow of the ship to be out of the way.

"Look, there's Trey! And Othi!" Treesi waved, and Othi waved back. Then he handed something to Trey and dove off the dock.

Aven looked over the side of the ship. "I don't know what he's planning," he said. "But he's not going to be able to reach to get up here. We'll have to lower a rope."

"Maybe he's just going to escort us in?" Owyn suggested. He peered over the rail. "I don't see him. Shouldn't he be here already?"

"He should," Aven agreed. "Unless..." He looked over the rail again, then grabbed Owyn and pulled him back from the rail just as Aria heard a splash from below. A moment later, hands grabbed the rail, and Othi pulled himself up until he was resting on his elbows. He grinned, and Aven burst out laughing.

"You're insane!" he told his cousin. "Owyn, help me get him over the rail."

Othi made a rude noise and started to lever himself up and over the rail. Then his hand slipped. For a heartbeat, they just saw the shock on his face, then he tumbled back down into the water with a splash. Aria joined the others at the rail, looking down as the now red-faced Othi surfaced again.

"Go back to the dock!" Treesi called. "We'll be there soon."

Othi grinned and vanished under the water, only to reappear at the dock where he succeeded in getting out of the water on the first try.

Aven shook his head and sighed. "Treesi, you're going to have to put him out of his misery before he does something really stupid."

"Put him out of his misery?" Meris asked. "Oh, is the young warrior interested in Treesi?"

"Yes, Granna," Owyn answered. "And that wasn't really stupid? Aven?"

"No, that was Othi showing off." Aven grinned. "I did the same thing for you two, remember? In the cove?"

Aria smiled. "Were you showing off when you did that?"

Aven blushed slightly. "A little," he admitted. "It's...ah..." His blush deepened. "It's a courting display." He swallowed. Then he laughed. "I don't know why I'm embarrassed. Breaching like that shows off the strength of your tail. And your hips."

"Oh?" Treesi said. Then her eyes widened. "Oh." She looked toward the dock. "Could...could you do that jump?"

"Before? Probably. But I'm smaller than Othi. I was faster, and I could launch myself higher because I didn't have as much to launch." Aven grimaced. "Now? It's lucky you all love me. And weren't given a choice."

"Aven!" Aria gasped. "Don't say that!"

"Yeah, Fishie," Owyn agreed. "There's more to love than how good you are at pounding someone into the mattress. You all taught me that."

Aria moved to Aven's side and slid her arm around his back. He draped his arm over her shoulders and hugged her to his side. "I know," he said. "But still...it chafes. I'm still not used to it."

"I understand that," Alanar said from his place at the bow. "And it takes time to come to terms with the loss. Del will tell you that, too." He put his hand on Del's shoulder. "Am I right?" Del nodded, and Alanar smiled. "There, you see? I'm right!"

Aven's lips twitched. "You know what he answered from feeling his muscles move, didn't you?"

Alanar laughed. "You know my tricks. Yes. Now, someone tell me what I just missed."

Owyn went to his husband and tugged his head down to kiss him. "Othi is showing off for Trees," he said. "And he must have gone down to the bottom of the harbor, because he came up out of the water like an arrow and grabbed onto the side of the ship. Slipped and fell back in."

"What, no one had a net?" Alanar asked. Then he whistled. "Virrik is impressed. He says he wouldn't have been able to do that."

"Well, Othi couldn't either," Owyn said. "Tell Virrik to hush. We're docking."

The ship drew up to the dock, and ropes were tossed down to waiting workers, who quickly secured the lines. The gangplank was laid, and Trey and Othi both walked up to the rail.

"What was it?" Trey asked Othi, just loud enough that Aria could hear him.

"Permission—"

"Oh, right," Trey interrupted. He turned toward Destria. "Permission to come aboard?"

"Granted, Commander," Destria answered. "What's the word?"

Trey looked startled. "Commander?"

"You're second to the Guard Captain, aren't you?" Destria asked, sounding amused. "That makes you Commander. Now, what's the word?"

"The Palace is secure," Trey answered. "Wasn't hard."

"It's also a mess," Othi added. "Aunt Aleia says we're going to be cleaning for a while."

"That's true in many ways," Aria said. "If the Palace is secure, then we can enter?"

Trey smiled and bowed. "My Heir, it would be my honor to escort you to your rightful home."

ARIA WENT FIRST, WITH Trey on her left, and Othi on her right. Behind her were her Companions, all four in a row. Behind them was Alanar, with Meris on one arm, and Afansa on the other. Aria suspected that they were guiding him, at least until they were on solid ground again. Then he would act as their escort.

At the end of the dock, Aleia was waiting, with Karse and Mannon. As Aria reached them, they bowed as one.

"Oh, do not!" Aria gasped. "Aleia, you are not to bow to me!"

"You're my Heir," Aleia said as she straightened. "I want to. The Palace is secure, my Heir. Will you enter?"

"Thank you, War Leader," Aria answered, trying to regain her composure. It was harder than usual in the face of where they were. This was happening. It was actually happening. "I will."

Karse went on ahead of them as they started off the dock. Aleia took Trey's place on Aria's left, and Mannon took Othi's place on her right, and they walked up the wide paved path to the wall, where Aria could see dark streaks marring the white stone. Scorch marks? It seemed likely, but how? Through the open gates, she could see a crowd of people, surrounded by Water warriors. Memfis was with the Waterborn, and Jehan. Both were beaming.

"Who are all of those people?" she asked softly.

"The Palace staff," Mannon answered. "They've assembled to witness. And...well, we're not sure yet which of them were in league with Risha. If any. So best to have them all in one place."

Aria nodded. Then she straightened, turning to look at Mannon. "Do I look...Heir-ish?"

Mannon blinked. "Heir-ish?" he repeated. "Owyn is rubbing off on you. You look magnificent, Aria."

She smiled. She looked forward and drew herself up, flaring her wings slightly as she passed through the archway and into the Palace courtyard. As she entered, she heard Karse's voice.

"Hail the Heir! Aria, daughter of Milon, chosen by the Mother!"

In response, Jehan, Memfis and all of the warriors shouted as one: "Aria!"

Aria walked further into the courtyard, seeing the faces of the Palace staff. The disbelief on some. The shock on others. And on a few faces, the tears of joy.

"Thank you," she said, pitching her voice to carry. "Thank you for welcoming me home."

She wasn't prepared for the second cheer, the one that started among the servants and spread to nearly everyone in the courtyard.

She wasn't prepared for Mannon, who stepped forward as the cheers died away, and dropped to his knees in front of her.

"My Heir," he announced, his voice ringing off the walls. "Accept my abdication. And my surrender to your judgment for my crimes against Adavar."

CHAPTER EIGHTEEN

Aria stared in stunned silence down at Mannon. Then she nodded, trying to think.

"I accept, both your abdication and your surrender," she said. "Captain Karse, attend." She waited until Karse joined them. "Who managed the Palace in Mannon's absence?"

"The Steward, Nestor," Karse answered. "But he was killed in the attacks. By all accounts, by Risha herself."

Aria frowned. "That...complicates things," she murmured. "It means I will have to research the laws, and that will take time. So, until I know what must be done, take Mannon into custody. He is to be confined to his chambers—"

"My Heir, there's a dungeon—"

"I said his chambers," Aria repeated, glaring at Karse. "Do not interrupt me. I know what I'm saying. In the past month, Mannon has risked his life for me, and for the people I love. He has served me and mine well. I would have him held in comfort while my Companions and I deliberate his fate." She gestured. "Take him away."

Karse bowed slightly, then helped Mannon to his feet and led him off. Aria turned to her Companions. Del looked horrified, and she moved closer to him.

"I have no intention of starting my rule anointed in your father's blood," she said softly. "If there is any way to avoid it, I will. But I'll need your help."

Del nodded slowly. Then he looked at Owyn.

"He says he's read the laws," Owyn said. "He'll show you the books. And he doesn't think that there is a way to avoid it."

"He's right," Aleia said softly. "Aria, don't make promises you can't keep."

"We will find a way," Aria insisted. "Now, I need to go and meet my people, and find out if they really are my people." She turned back to face the group of servants, smiled, and walked toward them.

"Do you know who I am?" she said as she stopped in front of them.

A woman stepped forward. She was holding the hands of two young girls, and an older boy was at her shoulder. She looked tired and frightened. "You're the Heir. Mannon said you would be coming. That he'd be stepping down when you did. We weren't sure it was true."

Aria nodded. "After all these years? I'd be skeptical myself. And I wasn't entirely certain that we'd get here. It's been a very strange year."

The two little girls giggled, and Aria laughed. "Are these your daughters?"

"Yes, my Heir," the woman said. "This is Ami, and this is Zia." She held up each girl's hand as she named them. Then she turned to the boy. "And this is my son, Danir."

Aria smiled at the children, then turned back to their mother. "And your name is?"

"Lexi."

The answer came from behind Aria, and she turned to see that Alanar had walked closer. "Lexi, I am so sorry," he said. "Aria, her husband was with us when we were attacked on the road."

"I told you that was Healer Alanar," Ami whispered.

"But his hair is all gone!" Zia protested.

Alanar laughed. "It is me," he said. "And you two still sound exactly the same. How am I ever supposed to tell you apart? Lexi, do you mind if I take Ami and Zia off, so you can talk without distraction?"

Lexi looked down at her daughters. "Mind the Healer now," she said. "Be good and listen to him."

The girls ran off, each of them catching one of Alanar's hands, and he led them away. Aria could hear the both of them chattering at once as she turned back to Lexi. "I am sorry about your husband," Aria said. "Was he a guard?"

Lexi looked startled. "No!" she gasped. "No, Denis was a valet. He was assigned to serve your Fireborn and Healer Alanar, and when the healer got sick, he volunteered to help care for him on the road. And he never came home." She sighed. "He was wonderful at taking care of people, and he was completely unable to care for himself. He couldn't hold a knife without cutting himself." She shook her head. "Thank you. Now, since Ambaryl left us, I'm acting housekeeper."

Aria nodded. "Very good. Would you introduce me to the others?"

Lexi blinked. "You don't want to go to your suite?" she asked. "The staff can wait—"

"I'd like to meet them first," Aria answered. "Before I take possession of the Palace, I need to know that everyone within it is willing to serve me and no other."

Lexi's eyes widened. "You know?" she gasped. "Well, I can tell you this. When Risha attacked, I'm fairly certain that she either took or killed everyone who was part of her secrets. I don't think there's anyone left who knew everything that she knew."

"Do you at least know a little?" Aria asked. Lexi smiled.

"Servants always know more than a little. And secrets aren't always as secret as they want you to think. I probably know more than I should. And I'll happily tell you everything once you're settled." She folded her hands over her stomach. "Now, I don't like to keep you standing here, my Heir. Everyone standing in the courtyard served Mannon because he was a good master to us. We will serve you because you are our Heir."

"And I hope to be a good mistress to you," Aria added. "But you're going to have to help me." She looked at the collected faces. "I've never had servants before. I don't have the faintest idea what to do with most of you!"

A ripple of laughter, and Lexi smiled. "That's what you need a housekeeper for," she said. "And we'll need to appoint a steward. For now, let me show you and your Companions to your suite."

"You should meet them first," Aria said. She turned. "Aven Waterborn, son of my father's Companions Jehan and Aleia. Owyn Fireborn, whom you've met. Son of Dyneh, Huris and Memfis. Treesi Earthborn, daughter of..." She paused. "Treesi, how do I not know this?"

"You never asked!" Treesi said with a laugh. "Daughter of Gisa and Elan."

"And you already know my Del," she finished. "Del Airborn, son of Yana and Delandri. And Mannon." Del's brilliant smile warmed her, and she turned back to Lexi. "My Companions, may I present Lexi, our housekeeper?"

Lexi had been bowing to each Companion in turn. When Aria named Del, she stopped, looking stunned. "Del? Our Del? Is your Airborn?"

"The Mother chose him," Aria said softly, watching as Del's face went blank. Aven rested his hand on Del's shoulder.

"But—"

"That's something that will stop right now," Aria said. "The Mother chose Del to be at my side. She sent him to me, knowing how valuable he would be to me. How skilled he is, and how intelligent. He has no voice, but that doesn't mean he cannot be heard. Or that his words have any less value than yours." She raised her voice slightly. "I've heard that there were some among you who treated him as less, who called him broken. You have looked but you have not seen him. I made the same mistake. I ask you not to do the same."

She heard the footstep next to her, and turned to see Del had joined her. Aven stood behind his left shoulder, and Owyn behind his right. Del looked at her, then gestured toward the crowd. Aria nodded.

"Please. You know them better than I."

Del nodded, and started signing. Aria stepped back as Aven started to translate.

"*Some of you have known me since before Risha did this to me. Some of you remember my mother, and how she was addled. You assumed that because I was hurt, I was like her. You were wrong. The Water tribe, they call me Del the Silent, and none of the traders dares to try and cheat me. They found out that I'd catch them. Just because my voice comes through my fingers doesn't mean my brains are broken. It just means that I'm different.*"

"Is...are those Del's words?" Lexi asked. "Is your Aven translating Del's words?"

"Did none of you ever learn Water signs?" Aria asked. "Did you not know what Del was learning?"

"Not...Mannon told us, but...but Ambaryl thought it just...well, she never thought Skela was actually teaching him anything. She told us it was all play. Like dancing." She covered her mouth with one hand. "Oh, Mother. I should never have listened to her."

Del snorted. "*No, you shouldn't have.*"

Aven translated, then he coughed. "Del, that's rude."

Del scowled at him.

"He's more than earned the right to be rude," Lexi said quickly. "Now, how hard is it to learn those hand gestures?"

"It will take time," Aven answered. "Or Del can tell you what he has to say by writing it. If you can read." He smiled, a crooked, almost arrogant grin. It was a look Aria had never seen on his face before, and she didn't like it. "Can you?"

Lexi's eyes narrowed. "I am an upper servant in the Palace. Of course I can read. And keep accounts," she said, her voice tart. "And I can run the entire Palace, even though I rarely got the chance before Ambaryl left us." She paused, then looked at Aven. Her jaw dropped. "You...you just did to me what we were doing to Del."

"And you didn't like it, did you?" Aven asked. He smiled, his normal, lovely smile.

"Not at all," Lexi answered. She folded her arms over her chest. "Well. We have a lot of unlearning to do. And a lot of learning to fill the gaps. Del, I apologize."

Del smiled and bowed slightly. Lexi bowed in return, and turned around. "Well, you all know your duties," she said, raising her voice. "Let's get back to them." She turned back to Aria. "My Heir, if you'll follow me, I'll show you to your suite."

"Aria?"

Aria turned to see Jehan coming toward her. "Yes?"

"There's one thing you need to do before you see your rooms. You should do it first."

"Oh!" Lexi gasped. "Oh, of course. Where are my wits? Yes, you have to take formal possession of the Palace."

Aria glanced at Jehan. "And...how do I do that?" she asked.

"This way," Lexi said. "Ami, Zia! Bring Healer Alanar to the Hall!"

LEXI LED THEM THROUGH corridors marred with dark scorch marks and gouged wood and tile.

"Is this all recent damage?" Jehan asked.

"I'm afraid so. Once the dust had settled and we'd dealt with the dead, we started trying to clean it up," Lexi answered. "But with half the staff gone, we didn't have time to finish before you arrived. Not while keeping up with the daily chores of keeping the Palace running. Once we have a new steward, we'll be able to bring in more servants. Until then, we've been making due." She shook her head. "I have to say, when all the armed men came rushing in, I thought Risha was back to finish the rest of us."

"Lexi, do you know why she attacked?" Aven asked. He paused, leaning on his walking stick. "It was honestly the last thing we expected to hear."

"I don't know all of it," Lexi answered. "She showed up here, bold as you please. And when Nestor went to meet her, she killed him. Then her men overran the Palace. They brought all of us out to the practice yards and kept us there while Risha did...whatever she did inside. There was something here that she and Ambaryl and Nestor kept secret between them. She was dealing with that, I think. Then they separated us, brought the others to the front courtyard where we met you. We never saw the others alive again." She looked back at Aven. "I think the ones that she took away were the ones who knew why she was here. They were the ones who answered to Nestor, who worked most closely with him. And most of them were older, had served in the Palace longer."

"Nestor started serving in the Palace when Riga was Heir," Owyn said. "He told me that. Said he'd seen four Firstborn with his own eyes."

"He knew every inch of this Palace," Lexi agreed. "Every nook and cranny and hidden passage—"

"Hidden passages?" Aven interrupted.

Lexi nodded. "There are passages for the servants, so that we aren't in the way," she answered. "But there are other passages, too. The Palace is old. Things have changed and changed again over time. There are corridors that were walled off, and rooms that were closed off. I'm not sure anyone knows all of what's hidden behind the walls."

Behind her, Aria heard Owyn's voice. "You do?" She looked back to see Del was blushing.

"Del?"

"He says he knows," Owyn said.

Del grinned and started signing, and Owyn translated, "*I used to explore. Mostly to hide from Ambaryl. I would pretend I was exploring a world no one had ever seen before. I even made maps. Until Nestor caught me at it and told Fa. They told me it wasn't safe. Nestor said some of those corridors were closed off because of damage.*"

"That doesn't make sense," Alanar said. "Why close them off if you're still going to live here? Why not just fix them?"

Lexi shook her head. "I don't know. Most of those changes were done before I came into service here. The only thing that's been closed off since was the Heir's Tower, and that was ages ago."

"Ages?" Owyn repeated. "Wait. Where's Mem?"

"Back here," Memfis called. "And that's not what I was told. Mannon said it was damaged in the storms last autumn."

"Oh, no. It's been closed far longer than that. Since Yana died," Lexi said. She stopped and turned around, and her eyes widened when she saw Memfis coming toward her. "You...Mother of us all, I didn't really look at you before. Memfis, what happened?"

Memfis looked down at himself and the pinned-up sleeve where his arm used to be. "Do you know what a Widowmaker snake is?"

"And you *lived*?" Lexi shrilled.

Memfis smiled slightly. "It was Mannon. He wouldn't let me die, Lexi. He dragged me on his back for days. Until we reached the healers."

Lexi looked stunned. She swallowed, then looked at Aria. "And...will you take that into account when you judge him, My Heir."

"It's one of the reasons why he is in his room, and not in the dungeon," Aria answered. "And he will be kept in comfort, with all of his needs met, until I know enough to pass a fair judgment."

"Aria?" Owyn asked. "Del wants to know if he can visit his fa."

Aria nodded. "Of course he can. And I need to visit as well. I seem to remember that I'm supposed to ask him to teach me to play Gambit?"

Del beamed at her.

They started walking again, and Aria tried to keep track of the turns and the corridors. Glancing back, she saw that Treesi was clinging to Aven's free hand.

"Lexi," Aria said softly. "My Earth has trouble with directions. How can we help her?"

"Trouble with directions? Meaning...she can't tell right from left? And she reverses her letters when she reads?"

Aria nodded and said, "Yes. How did you know?"

Lexi smiled in response. "She's like my Danir. I'll say one good thing about Risha — she knew how to help him." She looked back for a moment. "Oh, that must be it! She said she had a healer trainee who had the same problem. Is your Earth a healer? She must be."

"She is, and Treesi is probably who Risha was speaking of."

Lexi nodded. "Then I'll assign Danir to help her. He's long since learned how to find his way around. Living in the Palace can be confusing for anyone. New servants always get lost. We'll help her. All of you, until you get your bearings." She turned left down a corridor, and stopped in front of a set of double doors. "Now, you asked what you needed to do to take possession of the Palace?" she asked. Then she opened the doors, revealing a large room dominated by a round table. There were five chairs, each marked with a sigil. She recognized four of the sigils as belonging to each of the tribes. The last chair bore the same blazon as the banner that Jehan had described to Aria in Terraces, that they had sewed and flown when they had sent Destria's ship out to the approaching canoes. The seats would have made the points of a star — the Heir's place at the top, with Water at the left, and Air at the right. To the right of Air was Earth, and Fire was on Water's left.

"I was wondering why you took us this way," Jehan said from the back of the group as they entered.

"I thought we'd start here," Lexi called back. "Now, this is the Little Council chamber. This is where the Heir and their Companions come together. The Greater Council chambers are through that door." She pointed to a door to their right. "That's where the Firstborn meets with their Companions. There's another entrance to that room further down the corridor, past where we came in." She walked around the table to a large door that faced the Heir's place, opened it, then turned and smiled. "And this is the Hall. This is where the Firstborn sits in state, and meets with the people." She bowed to Aria. "My Heir, will you take your place in the Hall? And, seeing as we have no Firstborn, will you take the Palace?"

Aria heard the thump of Aven's walking stick behind her. Then he was on her right, offering his arm. "My Heir?"

She blinked at him, then looked to see that the others were behind her. Owyn smiled. "He was first. It's his place to walk you the rest of the way. We'll follow."

Aria swallowed. Then she took Aven's arm and let him lead her around the table and through the door into the Hall. Her mother had described this place to her once. The Hall had been filled with light and music and laughter and love. The Hall was silent now, but the sunlight streamed through the colored glass of the high arched windows and turned the floating motes of dust to gold. There were two daises at the end of the Hall. The higher of the two was centered on the soaring windows, the lower was offset and to Aria's left. There were five chairs on each — the chairs on the lower dais were carved with the same sigils that were on the chairs in the Little Council. The chairs on the higher, central dais had no carved sigils — instead, the backs of four of the chairs were crowned with insets of colored glass pieced together to depict the sigils of their respective tribes. The last chair, the center chair, bore a simple circle of golden glass.

"Will you take your place, my Heir?" Lexi asked again.

"I will take my place," Aria answered. "The Heir's place. Until I visit the Temple, the Firstborn's place is my father's." She looked at Aven, who nodded his agreement and started walking, bringing her up the lower dais stairs to the Heir's seat. Her Companions followed, each to their places — Del to Air's place, Treesi to Earth's. Owyn stopped at Fire and she felt their eyes on her as Aven stopped next to the Heir's seat. He released her hand, stepped back, and bowed.

"Stop that," she whispered. He straightened and grinned. Then he leaned in and kissed her before going to his own seat at her left.

Aria rested her hand on the back of the chair, feeling the wood warm under her palm. She swallowed and looked out into the Hall, seeing Jehan and Memfis. Half hidden behind Memfis was Aleia, and behind her were Meris, Alanar, and Afansa.

"We've all gone through so much to get here," she said, her quiet voice sounding like a shout in the stillness of the room. "But we are here." She took a deep breath. Then she sat down and rested her hands on the arms of the chair, waiting until her Companions were all seated before saying, "Lexi, as Heir to the Firstborn, and in the absence of my father, I take possession of the Palace."

CHAPTER NINETEEN

The Heir's suite was larger than their house in Terraces. It had a large, central sitting room that contained several couches, padded chairs, and a long table with chairs around it. There were six doors opening off the room. Five of the doors were marked with sigils, and opened into smaller, private sitting rooms, with an interior door that led to a bedroom. Each room boasted a bed that Owyn declared was large enough for a small orgy. They also each had a small, personal bathing room, while the sixth, unmarked door off the main room was a communal bathing room.

"This feels...excessive," Treesi said, coming out through the door that bore the Earth sigil. "It's...I could get lost without ever leaving the suite!"

Jehan snorted. "I think we all said that, when we came here the first time. The only one who was used to this was Milon." He grinned and sat down on one of the couches. Aleia joined him, and he put his arm around her as he looked around. "It still looks the same. I'm amazed that it all looks the same."

"Mannon was very insistent that things in here be kept the same, at least as much as was possible," Lexi said. "Now, your baggage has been brought up. Do you want help with unpacking?"

"Nah, I think we're good," Owyn answered. "We're none of us used to being waited on." He settled onto another couch with

Alanar. "This suite is really big. Is the other one as big? The Firstborn's?"

Lexi smiled. "It's larger," she answered. "Now, if you're not comfortable all living together here, there are other options. I seem to remember Milon and his Companions kept rooms with a little more distance between them?"

Jehan chuckled. "We weren't immediately as close as you all are," he said. "When we first arrived, we had rooms up on the next floor. We had a little more space, and a lot more time to get comfortable with each other. In the five years we were together, we only ever came into this room to spend time with Milon." He tipped his head back. "Mem, were you here or upstairs?"

"I was here." Memfis answered. "Owyn, your room was mine once. And Liara was here, too, but she'd only just moved to the Air suite before she took her season. As I remember it, it was you and Guppy who were still up in our initial rooms?"

"We were, but we were going to move into the Companion rooms here when Liara came back, remember?" Aleia said to Jehan. "We were ready." She looked around and shook her head. "It seems like a lifetime ago."

"It was a lifetime ago," Memfis agreed. "Now? Now this is their place." He gestured, looking around the room, finally stopping when he was facing Aria.

Aria smiled from her seat in a single chair. She had her head resting on one hand, and she looked around to see that Aven had come back out of the room that was marked with the Water sigil.

"There's a salt water pool in the bedroom," he said, taking a chair next to Aria's. "A bed and a pool deep enough to sleep in! How did they manage that?"

"Fire ingenuity," Memfis answered. "Or so I'm told. There are a number of bedrooms in the Palace that have them. Aleia, yours did, didn't it?"

"If you mean the Water suite one flight up? It still does. And it's still hers, if she wants it," Lexi said. "I hadn't assigned you rooms yet, but if that was your room before—"

"No," Aleia said. She sat up straight and turned to face Lexi. "I won't have that room again. It's where we were—" She stopped and closed her eyes, and Jehan put his hand on her shoulder.

"Oh," Lexi breathed. "Oh, of course. That was...incredibly insensitive of me. I apologize."

"Wait," Aria said, sitting up. "This is where they were attacked? My father? In this room? And Firstborn Tirine was murdered right across the corridor? And you expect us to sleep in these rooms?"

"Actually, Milon and I weren't in here when the attacks came," Memfis said. He looked down, fidgeting ever so slightly. "I...look, there are a lot of rooms in this palace. And a lot of beds that no one uses. And..."

Jehan coughed, his eyes wide and his cheeks red. "Wait. He used the 'every bed in the Palace' line on you, too?"

"That sounds like a challenge," Owyn muttered in a singsong voice, just loud enough for everyone to hear him.

Alanar snorted his amusement. "Or a goal."

Memfis coughed, and stammered slightly when he answered, "Yes. Something like that. Every bed in the Palace. So we weren't here. We were..." he frowned. "Where were we? Ah...the Amber room, I think. Which is two floors up, and closer to the outer walls. And Milon...he left me there asleep. There was a note, in case I woke up and found him gone — he was going to surprise me with breakfast. He was in the corridor when he was attacked. I woke up when I heard the fighting."

"So that's how you got him to our room so quickly!" Aleia said. "I'd always wondered — it never made sense for you to have brought him upstairs, but I never had a chance to ask. Then it just wasn't important anymore."

"I was bringing him downstairs," Memfis said. "I never knew how Mannon's men found us—"

"I...think I can answer that," Lexi said slowly. "Now, I was only a maid at the time, but I do remember the housekeeper making notes on which of the rooms were going to need to be turned out. It always struck me as being odd, because it seemed random, and they were rooms that I was certain weren't being used. It was usually a night that there were no guests, and it always seemed to amuse her."

"Because of course he'd warn the servants they'd need to change the linens when we were done," Memfis murmured. "Of course he would. That...that was just Milon. And I remember the board that Galia had that showed which rooms were occupied—"

"I still use it," Lexi said. "And yes, she would have marked that you were using the Amber room that night."

Memfis nodded. "That explains that, finally. So, to go back to your question, Aria, no. We weren't in here that night."

"And all of the furnishings that were in the Firstborn's suite were taken and burned," Lexi added. "Everything, down to the draperies and the carpets. The rooms were stripped to the bare stones and everything was rebuilt. There's not a scrap of anything in that suite that was there on the night of the attack."

Memfis gaped at her. "When did that happen?"

Lexi smiled sadly. "When Yana came," she answered. "When she looked at Mannon and called him her Air. He ordered the rooms completely renewed for her. It was a massive undertaking. It took years. And...well, she never saw it complete. He finished it in her memory."

"*I think I remember that work being done. I didn't know why, though. Is that why it always felt like no one ever lived there?*" Del signed. Once Aven translated, Lexi nodded.

"I imagine so. It's quite...unlived in." Lexi looked over her shoulder at the door. "It always gave me the shivers, actually. I thought it felt like it was waiting for someone." She looked back at Aria. "Waiting for you, perhaps?"

"It will have to keep waiting, at least a little longer," Aria answered.

Lexi smiled. "The entire Palace has been waiting for you. Now, I've duties to see to. My Heir, will you dine here, or in the dining room?"

Aria looked around, studying the faces of her Companions. "Here, I think," she said. "Today has been an event. Where is my grandmother?"

"Lady Meris and her maid have been given the suite reserved for the Council leader of the Fire Tribe," Lexi answered. "I understand that she is the Council leader, correct?"

"Right now, she is the entire Council," Memfis answered.

"Well, then, she's definitely in the right suite," Lexi said. "Now, I'll be back with your meal. Oh, and I'll bring Danir, so you can properly meet him. Del, do you want to supervise having your room moved?" When Del nodded, she bowed slightly. "Very good. My Heir, if I may?"

Aria wasn't sure what permission she was looking for, but Aleia answered for her. "You're dismissed, Lexi. Thank you."

Lexi straightened and looked at Aria, who nodded. "Yes, thank you," she repeated. "I didn't know that's what you were waiting for. I will learn."

Lexi smiled. "We'll all learn. I'll bring your meal as soon as it's ready." She bowed again, then left.

Aria closed her eyes and took a deep breath. "And now...what?" she asked aloud.

"That's a good question," Owyn said. "Now what do we do?"

"Who is Danir?" Treesi asked.

"Lexi's son," Aria answered. "He's going to be in charge of making sure that none of us gets lost in the Palace."

"He'll be working with me forever," Treesi moaned. She moved over to the couch where Owyn and Alanar sat and plopped down on Alanar's other side, leaning against him. "I'm already so lost!"

"Back to the question," Aven said. "What do we do now? What do we have to do?"

"Find out what Risha was doing here when she attacked," Owyn answered. "First thing to do there is look at Nestor's records."

"We need to figure out a way to not have to execute Mannon," Alanar added. "Which means going through the laws to find a loophole."

"We need to go into the mountains, to the Temple," Aven said. "We need to know if the Crown is there."

"And if it isn't, we need to find my father," Aria said. She sighed. "How are we going to accomplish that? Any of that?"

"We had some ideas," Owyn said slowly. "We were making plans, Mannon and I, back when we were here in the early spring. There were notes. Mine are gone, but..." he groaned. "Nestor had his copies. Fuck. Risha probably knows everything we were planning for you!"

"Which was?" Jehan asked.

"A progress," Owyn answered. He frowned. "You know, I think it was Nestor who suggested that. I'd never heard of one before. He had to explain it to me. So maybe it wasn't a good idea at all."

"What's a progress?" Aria asked.

"The Progress." Memfis corrected. "It isn't a suggestion. It's required. It's the journey that the Heir makes, when they go in search of their Companions. It's supposed to emulate the journey Axia took when she first found hers. There's a set path. You travel from the Palace, south through Earth to Fire, then east through Fire lands. Back north through the foothills and up to the mountains to the Solstice village and the Temple. Then back to the Palace."

"Where's Water in that?" Aven asked.

"First, usually," Aleia answered. "The trip starts with a sea voyage, out to the Floating City. But since the entire Water tribe is in the harbor, I think just going down to the beach will fulfill that part."

Aria nodded slowly, considering. "That will take...months, will it not?"

"Milon's took nearly a year, but that's because the weather was bad that year and we were stuck in Forge for most of the winter because of the rains." She cocked her head to the side. "I hadn't thought of that in years. But Milon's progress was backwards. There was so much rain that we couldn't go the traditional route because of flooding. We went to the Solstice village first instead of last. Then south to the healing center, and then on to Forge."

Aria looked at Aven. "We...don't have a year. This baby is supposed to be born here. In the Palace."

Aven licked his lips and narrowed his eyes. "If we're back by Summer Solstice, they will be."

"Or it can wait until after the baby is born," Jehan added. "Because once you start a Progress, you can't turn back. It's a bad omen. Even deviating from the route is bad – Milon's progress was supposed to be cursed. So perhaps we should wait."

"Or we could just not worry about it and go anyway," Memfis suggested. "We'll have three healers with us—"

"Four," Jehan corrected.

"Four?" Aleia turned toward her husband. "You're Senior Healer. You can't just go handing off your responsibilities for most of a year!"

"Are you going?" Jehan asked.

Aleia frowned. "I'm not Clan Mother—"

"Are you going?" Jehan repeated.

"I thought I might—"

"Then I'm going," Jehan said. "I've had my fill of living without you, of not even knowing if you were alive or dead. I'm not doing that again. Mother knows what to do."

"Your mother is going to lay into you like she was beating the chaff out of the entire harvest if you lay this at her feet," Aleia snapped. "And don't expect me to stand in her way."

"Don't think I was asking you to," Jehan snapped back. Then he sighed. "We'll discuss it later? Alone?" He reached out and took Aleia's hand. "I don't want to be alone again, Leia. I can't."

Aleia smiled slightly. She leaned toward him and rested her forehead against his. "We'll talk," she said softly.

"So..." Aven said slowly, drawing it out. "A progress. And that will do...what? Other than take us back on the road again?"

"Well, other than the ritual part, the idea is that the people need to see Aria. They need to know that they have an Heir again, and they need to know that Mannon is out of power," Owyn answered. "They need to see us, too. They need to know who is speaking for them. The Water tribe all knows you, Fishie, but Earth needs to see Treesi. Fire needs to see me. And when we get to the mountains and the Solstice village, Air needs to see Del."

"Could we go to the Temple first?" Aria asked. "And then make the Progress? If this is to choose my Companions...I've already done that."

"You still need to follow the path and in the right order." Memfis answered.

"*What about Fa?*" Del signed.

"Aria, Del said—"

"Thank you, Aven. I understood. And as important as the Progress is, what we need to do first is here," Aria said. She closed her eyes and ran one finger down the bridge of her nose, flexing her wings as she thought. "Everything else can wait. All of it will wait until we answer this. How can I avoid having to execute Mannon?" She opened her eyes and looked around the room. "Is there anyone here who cannot say that he's changed? That he's shown himself true to Yana's memory, and to me?"

"It's still hard to forget that it was his order that destroyed all our lives," Aleia said. "But now? He might as well be a different man."

"There's something else to consider," Owyn said. "I don't remember who thought of this, if it was me, or if it was Nestor. I think it was me. But if you kill him, the people who followed him are going to rise up in his name." He leaned forward and rested his elbows on his knees, his hands clasped. "You have to keep him alive, and you have to keep him visible. Which means no locking him away in a tower for the rest of his life, either. People will think you killed him and are lying about it."

Aria groaned. "How? If the law says that I have no options, how do I do otherwise? It was violating the laws that got us here in the first place! What do I do?" She heard snapping, and turned to see Del was trying to get her attention. "Del?"

Del smiled. "*You get creative,*" he signed. Then he stood up. "*I'm going to get the law texts. I'll be back.*"

WHEN DEL RETURNED, he was carrying three thick books in his arms. He brought them to the table and set them down with a heavy thump. Then he took one and flipped it open, turning pages until he found what he wanted. He tapped the passage, then gestured for Owyn to join him. Owyn leaned over the book and read aloud.

"*...the word of the Mother's Chosen, called the Firstborn, shall be considered law, and none shall say otherwise. To act against the*

Firstborn is to act against the Mother, and shall be condemned."
He turned the page. "There's no penalty here, though. No
punishment."

Del reached across the table and pulled another book close,
opening it and turning pages as Owyn looked over his shoulder. He
pointed, and Owyn read again, "*...and in the most dire of cases, let
the mal...*what's that word?"

"*Malfeasant,*" Del's voice answered in his mind. "*It means the
person who did the bad things.*"

"That's a word? Really?" Del nodded, and Owyn continued.
"*Let the malfeasant be sent to the Mother for judgment, and let their
name be forgotten by Her for all time.* That means execution, don't
it?"

"Del, where are you going with this?" Aleia asked. "The law is
clear—"

"Oh," Aria breathed. "Oh, I think I know. Del, come with me.
Bring the books, please. Aleia, would you join us?" She led them
into her room, closing the door behind them.

Owyn looked around, feeling lost. "Right, so how do we get
creative with being told outright that we have to execute him?
Because that's what that book said. It said send him to the Mother."

"Del seems to have an idea," Memfis said. "And he's more
familiar with the laws than the rest of you. And possibly than we
are, and we had the Companion training."

Owyn scowled and pushed away from the table. He walked
over to Aria's door and stood there for a moment, his eyes closed,
listening. He couldn't hear anything, so he shook his head and
walked back to the couch.

"Can't hear," he said in a low voice. "Allie, you try."

"Should you be trying to listen to them?" Treesi asked.

"Maybe not, but it's a survival instinct," Owyn answered. "You listen at doors, and you learn things. You live longer. And maybe, someone you care about lives longer."

Alanar stood up, but didn't move. "I'm not sure where I am in this room. Where am I going?"

Owyn led him to the door to Aria's room, then walked over to stand next to Aven's chair. "What are you thinking?"

"That I don't know enough," Aven answered. "That none of us know enough. Except for Del. We none of us have that Companions training. You never did pass that on to us, Fa," Aven pointed out.

"When did I have the time?" Jehan asked.

Aven grinned. "I know. But we need to learn that, and we need to learn fast."

Alanar leaned against the wall and tucked his chin, closing his eyes. He frowned. "Aleia's giggling."

"Giggling?" Aven repeated. "I...don't think I've ever heard Ama giggle before. Fa?"

Owyn looked over at Jehan, and saw matching looks of horror on both Jehan and Memfis' faces. "What's wrong with Aleia giggling?" he asked.

"It means to hold on, she's taking us into a storm," Jehan answered.

"In non-Water terms? Someone in there came up with an insane idea, and she likes it. A lot. Aleia giggling is the definition of a crackpot plan."

"But they always worked," Jehan said.

Memfis frowned slightly. "True. They did always work. The more she giggled, the better they worked."

Alanar straightened and walked back to the couch, sitting down just as the door opened. Aria looked out. "How do I send for Lexi?"

"There should be a blue bell rope," Owyn answered. "Blue for service, green for kitchen, red for guard."

"Oh, thank you. I should have Karse here, too." She closed the door again.

"She's not going to tell us, is she?" Owyn said. "How...I mean, I thought we were going to decide this. Not just her."

"I think she's working out her plans," Aven answered. "She'll tell us when she needs us to check the lines."

A few minutes later, there was a knock at the door. Lexi came in, looking curious. With her was a boy that Owyn recognized from the courtyard. "The bell in the Heir's sitting room—"

"Aria's up to something," Owyn answered. "And she wants you. She wants Karse, too."

Lexi nodded and turned to the boy. "Danir, go find Captain Karse. Tell him the Heir wants him and bring him right back here. No dawdling."

"Yes, Mama," Danir answered. He left at a run. Lexi passed through the sitting room and knocked on Aria's door, then disappeared inside. A few minutes later, the scene was repeated when Karse arrived. Alanar returned to his spot by the door.

"There's more giggling in there," he said softly. "I can't tell who, though."

"This is either going to be really good, or really scary," Jehan muttered.

"Or really, scarily good?" Owyn asked, and laughed at the sour look that Jehan shot at him. "Well, it's an option!"

The door opened, and Alanar jumped in surprise. Aria looked out, saw him, and smiled.

"You couldn't hear, Owyn?" she asked.

"Ah...no," Owyn answered. "And Allie's ears are better than mine. So what's the plan?"

Aria stepped out of the room and went to the table, sitting down at the head. "I'll tell you over our meal. Lexi? You may serve whenever you're ready. And tea, please. A lot of it. We've a long night ahead of us."

CHAPTER TWENTY

Riders went out at dawn to announce to anyone within easy traveling distance that the new Heir had taken control of the Palace, and that Mannon had surrendered to her will. The Heir had decreed that she would make his fate known just past midday. All were welcome to attend.

As Aria had said, it had been a long night. They'd discussed her proposal until late, bringing in Lady Meris when Memfis had suggested it. Meris had listened and had offered her advice, and they'd changed and rearranged details until Del could no longer think of ways to subvert their plans. Only then did Aria declare them finished.

"Are you going to tell him?" Meris asked.

"No," Aria answered. "Not until it's done. I don't want it to seem as if it was all an act. Let him hear his fate when everyone else does."

Meris nodded. "It's an interesting idea." She smiled. "I can't wait to see how it plays out."

Now, an hour past midday, Aria stood in front of the looking glass in her bedroom, with Lexi fussing at the skirts of the gold-shot white silk gown which had been altered overnight to fit Aria.

"This looks as if it was made for me," Aria murmured. "Am I ready?

"You are as ready as I think I can make you," Lexi said. She looked in the mirror to meet Aria's eyes. "Will it work?"

"I hope so," Aria answered. She went to the dressing table, picking up the Diadem and putting it on. "Shall we?"

Lexi opened the door, and Aria walked through her sitting room and out into the main room. Her Companions were all there, waiting, and the look on Aven's face when he saw her made her breath catch.

"You look amazing," he breathed. "That...Aria, you're beautiful."

She felt her face grow warm, and looked down at the gown. "I'm pleased you like it. I'm very happy with it."

"He's right," Owyn said. "That looks like it was made for you. It's perfect." He smiled. "You're perfect."

Aria laughed softly and pressed her hands to her cheeks. "I'm going to burst into flames if I blush any harder. You all look wonderful." She looked at each of them — Aven was wearing a dark kilt that somehow made his tattoos look darker, and an open vest in a deep purple.

"I've never seen you wear purple," she said. "It is a wonderful color on you."

"It's a sacred color," Aven said. He looked down at the vest. "Ama gave it to me this morning. She says that it's a color that only the Waterborn Companion is allowed to wear."

Aria smiled. "Then it's a good thing it looks wonderful on you." She turned to look at Owyn. "I've never seen you in solid black before. You wear every other color."

"Apparently, our parents decided they needed to dress us proper," Owyn answered. "Mem says that the Fireborn Companion wears ash black and orange." He held out his arm so that Aria could see the orange decorative stitching at the wrists of his long sleeves. "For the fire at the heart of the world."

"Jehan was in charge of me," Treesi said. She turned in a circle, showing off the intricately cut vest that looked like leaves, each a slightly different shade of green, which she wore over a gown of darker green. "I'm not sure how they did this in one night!"

"They didn't," Jehan said from the doorway. "That was mine. And Owyn's shirt was Mem's." He stepped into the room and closed the door behind him. "Lexi said they'd packed away all the things we left behind. That included all of the ritual wear. I'm glad the vest fits you."

Treesi stared at him, shocked. "This was *yours*?"

He smiled. "Wear it well, Treesi."

Aria smiled as Treesi ran to hug Jehan, and turned to her last Companion. Del wore blue — his shirt was the bright blue of a summer sky, his trousers the darker blue of twilight. Over them, he wore a long vest that was the soft dark gray of a storm cloud. He looked at her, but didn't smile.

"You're nervous," she said.

"*What if it doesn't work?*" he signed.

"It will work," Owyn assured him. "It has to work."

"It will work," Aria echoed Owyn's words. "Remember, the text says that the word of the Firstborn is considered law." She looked at Jehan. "Don't say it."

"I wasn't going to. You know already." Jehan sighed. "I want it to work, too. Now, I'm going down to the Hall. Danir is outside to escort you. Alanar, will you come with me?"

"If you'll lead," Alanar said. He was dressed in the black shirt, trousers and vest that he'd worn to marry Owyn, and he smoothed his vest as he stood up. "I have no idea where I'm going in this place."

"You'll learn," Jehan said. He took Alanar's arm, and looked around at the rest of them. He smiled, pride shining in his eyes. "We'll see you in the Hall. Remember the order."

"We'll remember," Aria said. "And I may not abide by it. Now go."

Jehan grinned and led Alanar out of the room. Before he closed the door, Danir slipped inside. He tucked his hands behind his back and shifted from one foot to the other. "Mama?"

"You know what to do, Danir," Lexi said. "You'll do just fine."

"And what is it that you have to do?" Aven asked.

Danir drew himself up a little. "I'm to take you to the Hall. We're going to the Little Council room first."

"Thank you, Danir," Aria said, feeling something very much like relief. "I wouldn't have known how to find it again."

Danir grinned. "That's what Mama said you might say," he said. "If you're ready?"

He led them out of the suite and down the halls, running his fingers along the trim on the walls, and stopping at each turning before continuing on. At one turning, he looked back at Aria. "Mama said that your Earth is like me, too. And that when you weren't busy, I might talk to her?"

Treesi looked over at him. "I am?"

Danir nodded. "You get your letters backwards, Mama says. And directions. She said that I could help you learn how to find your way around the Palace, and you might be able to help me learn more about...well...everything."

Treesi laughed. "I will happily make that deal," she said. "We'll talk more later."

"Yes, Healer," he said, and stopped in front of a door that Aria thought she recognized. He opened it to reveal the Little Council room. They filed inside, and once the door was closed, Aria turned and looked at Lexi.

"Is Karse ready?"

"I'll go and see," Lexi said. She left the room, going through the door that led to the Hall. A few minutes later, she came back. "Yes,

My Heir. Everyone is ready. The Hall is...rather full," Lexi said. "I think there are entire communities who came to see what you were going to do."

"Well, that's convenient," Owyn said. "We can skip those communities when we go on progress."

"Owyn—" Aven rumbled softly.

"I know. First things first," Owyn smiled and looked around. "We're here. We're really here. We're really doing this." He closed his eyes and visibly shivered. "I...it don't feel real, does it? I keep thinking I'm going to wake up in my bed back in Forge, and none of this year will have happened." He frowned. "I don't want to wake up. Even with everything that's happened, I wouldn't have missed any of this. So don't nobody pinch me."

Aven laughed and moved to stand behind Owyn, wrapping his arms around Owyn's shoulders. "We're not dreaming, Mouse. This is real. This is what we've been working toward. We did it."

"We're not finished yet," Aria said. She looked at the door. "We're only just starting. Now, are we all ready?" She turned to look at Treesi and Del. "How are you both?"

Del shrugged slightly. "*Still nervous,*" he signed. "*I wasn't expecting a full Hall.*"

"We're doing just what we talked about?" Treesi asked.

"Exactly the way we discussed," Aria agreed. She looked at the door again and drew herself up. "Now, shall we?"

Aven straightened, but not before he kissed Owyn's cheek. He went back to Aria's side, and held his hand out, palm down. She rested her hand on top of it, then nodded.

"Lexi, we're ready."

Lexi beamed at them for a moment, then went out into the Hall, taking Danir with her. A moment later, they heard a bell tolling, a deep, almost rumbling peal. The door to the Hall opened again, and Aven led Aria out.

There was a moment as they crossed the threshold. A moment of silence, where it seemed as if everyone in the Hall had all taken a breath and held it, all at the same time. Aria had to fight the urge to look around, to try and count just how many people were staring at her. At them. Behind her, Owyn would be in the center, escorting Treesi and Del as Aven was escorting her. They crossed the wide Hall, and heard not a cough, not a sneeze. There was nothing but the weight of the hopes of so many people. Aria glanced up at Aven, found him looking at her and smiling. She smiled back, raised her chin a little, and relaxed her wings. This was what she'd been born to do — to bear the weight of all those hopes.

They slowly walked up the dais stairs, and Aven brought her to the central chair. He bowed over her hand, then kissed her fingers. Then he backed away, toward the Water place at her left. Just past him, Owyn was already standing in front of the chair marked with the Fire sigil, while Del led Treesi behind the other chairs to their places on Aria's right. Once they stood in their places, Aria turned to face the Hall. For a moment, all she saw was the sea of people facing her. Staring at her. She stared back, noticing that there was a table set before the dais, just as they'd discussed. On the table was a balance, and two baskets — one filled with white stones, the other with black..

"When Firstborn Tirine was murdered," she said, her voice carrying clearly in the silent Hall. "Smoke Dancers throughout the Fire Tribe asked a question. How might balance be restored? How might the Usurper be overthrown? And the answer came to each of them in the same vision. It came to be known as the Vision of the Dove. Balance would be restored when came the dove, the water-cat, the flame, the flower, and the broken feather." She paused, then looked to her left, and to her right. "Now we are here. I am Aria, daughter of Milon, daughter of Liara, of the line of Liara of old."

"I am Aven, son of Aleia, son of Jehan, of the line of Abin," Aven announced.

"Owyn Jaxis," Owyn's voice rang out. "Son of Dyneh, son of Huris. Adopted son of Memfis, of the line of Nerris."

"Treesi, daughter of Gisa. Daughter of Elan, of the line of Mika."

Treesi's voice died away, and Aria turned to Del, and saw him start to sign. "*Del*," Aria translated. "*Son of Yana, son of Delandri, of the line of Liara of old.*" She paused, seeing him continue. "*Adopted son of Mannon.*"

She turned back to face the crowd of people, some of whom had shocked looks on their faces. "We have been chosen by the Mother. And now we are here." She reached back, touched her chair with her hand, and sat, resting her hands easily on the arms. "Now, we have work to do. Please, all of you, bear witness." She waited until her Companions were seated, then raised her voice. "Bring him!"

The doors at the back of the Hall opened. Down the central aisle marched Karse and Trey, both dressed in spotless uniforms. Between them, they escorted Mannon, and Aria heard a sharp intake of breath from her right.

Mannon was in chains.

"I didn't order that," she whispered. "Del—" She looked at him, saw him nod.

"He says it was probably Mannon's own idea," Owyn whispered from Aria's other side. "Just go with it. Keep to the plan."

Aria nodded and sat up, facing forward as Karse and Trey brought Mannon to the foot of the dais. He stood, with his head bowed, and said nothing.

"Go on, then. State your name," Karse said. Mannon nodded.

"Mannon," he said. "Son of Elcam. Son of Falla."

"Mannon, you have surrendered to be judged for your crimes against the Mother and against Adavar," Aria said. "Tell us those crimes."

Mannon looked up, and blinked. He smiled slightly. "You look beautiful," he said. "You all do."

"Mannon," Aria prompted, and the people closest to the dais laughed. Mannon's face turned red.

"I defied the Mother," he said, his voice shaking. "I was stupid, and stubborn, and I defied the Mother. I am responsible for...well, just about every bad thing that's happened over the last twenty-five years." He took a deep breath, then let it out. "Do I have to be more specific?"

"No, I do not think so," Aria answered. She looked up. "Mannon's deeds must be weighed, both the good and the bad." She rose, and walked down the steps of the dais to the table. She picked a black stone up out of one of two baskets and set it onto one side of the balance. "For the murder of Firstborn Tirine," she said.

She picked up another stone, set it with the first. "For defying the Mother."

A third stone. "And for the destruction of the Mother's temple." She stepped back, folding her hands over her stomach as she raised her voice "Who will add to this? Who will speak against Mannon?"

She turned, and walked back up the dais stairs — Aven met her halfway up and brought her back to her chair. She sat, and waited, until Aleia walked forward. As she moved in front of Mannon, his face crumpled.

"For Milon and Liara," she said, and added two more black stones to the balance. She walked back to join Jehan, Memfis and Alanar, passing Meris on the way. Meris took another black stone and set it into the balance.

"For corrupting the Council of Forge, and giving the Fire tribe to men such as Fandor, who preyed on the innocent," she announced. Mannon closed his eyes and nodded.

Movement to Aria's right, and Treesi walked down the steps to the balance. She dropped two stones into place, and the soft *plink-plink* as they fell was as loud as a drum. "For the destruction of the Healing Centers," she said. "And for Risha."

Mannon flinched. "Add another one for her," he said, his voice clear. "I should have strangled her when I found out the truth about Yana. I never should have let her live."

Treesi turned, looking surprised. Aria nodded, and Treesi turned back, adding another stone. She returned to her seat, and for a long moment, no one else moved.

"Does anyone else wish to speak against Mannon?" Aria asked, and was answered by silence. "There is no one else who will speak to the ill?" When no one else came forward, Aria nodded. "Will anyone speak for him? Who will name the good this man has done?"

"I will," Memfis' voice rang out. He walked over to the balance and took four white stones from the other basket. "You could have left me to die," he said. "I was bitten by a Widowmaker snake, and that doesn't mean anything but death. You wouldn't let me die. You carried me for four days, to get me to a healer." The stones hit the balance one at the time, and Memfis walked back to his place, only to return to the balance with Alanar.

"You could have let me die, too," Alanar said. "I was dying from ague, and dying from the arrow wound. Anyone else would have given up on me. You didn't. You brought me back to Terraces. You saved my life." He held one hand out, and Memfis handed him a white stone, guiding him to place it with the others.

Once they were gone, Aria looked out into the crowd again. "Who else will speak to the good?" she called.

What followed was a parade of local farmers, of tradesmen, of servants, all of them speaking of Mannon's generosity to those under his care, of his hard-work. Of the love they had for him. They knew what he'd done. Each of them admitted it. Each of them placed a white stone. And each of them ignored the black stones in the other basket.

Then Del rose. He looked across the dais, and Aven stood up. They walked down the dais together, and Aven nodded.

"I'm ready."

Del nodded, and started signing, and Aven started translating. "*Mannon raised me as his own son. He loved me, and he loved my mother. And after Risha murdered my mother, and did this to me, he took care of me, and he gave me everything I could ever have needed. He pushed me to do for myself, and he helped me learn to speak the only way I can.*" He glanced at Aven, then looked back at the crowd. "*He never treated me as less, because I can't speak. He treated me as his.*" He stepped back and licked his lips, then shook his head, taking a white stone from the nearly-empty basket and putting it on the heavier side of the balance. The other end of the balance, the lighter end, still only held nine stones. He turned, and walked back to his place. Aven remained where he was, and Aria rose, walking down the stairs to join him.

"I will speak," she said, taking the last few white stones from the basket. "Over the past month, this man has risked his life for me, and for my family. He refused his place in the lifeboat that would have taken him away from Forge and the Smoking Mountain, so that Senior Healer Jehan would be safe. He saved the life of Memfis, who is father of my heart. He served as Air Companion to Yana, and served her faithfully until her death. He serves her still, and he has sworn to serve me as well as he served her."

"Better than I served her," Mannon murmured. "I failed her. I won't fail you."

"He has cared for me and for each of my Companions as if we were his own children, and he has sworn his loyalty to me," Aria continued, and she slowly dropped the stones from her fingers into the heavier side of the balance, which threatened to spill white stones onto the floor. Then she spread her hands. "Can anyone here deny that the good he has done far outweighs the evil? That he has spent years trying to undo the damage that he caused?" She looked around, heard nothing, and continued. "And yet, the damage was done, and must be answered for. You surrendered to my will, Mannon, son of Elcam. Are you ready to hear my judgment?"

Mannon slowly lowered himself to his knees. "I'm ready."

Aria nodded. "It is the will of the Heir that the deeds of Mannon be written into our history as a warning to future generations that the Mother's will is not to be questioned. It is by Her choice that the Firstborn is enthroned. We must abide by that choice. Let it be written that as punishment for his crimes, the name of Mannon passed from the Mother's memory, and was forgotten."

Silence, broken only by a slight, hitching breath. "Thank you," the prisoner murmured in a cracking voice. "I will abide."

Aria turned to Aven, who looked like he was trying not to laugh. She nodded, and asked him, "What did we have to do next?"

He cleared his throat. "You needed to appoint a steward, My Heir," he answered.

"Yes, of course." She turned back to the kneeling man. "You, there." He looked up sharply, and Aria cocked her head to the side. "I seem to have forgotten your name," she said. "Who are you?"

A torrent of emotions washed over his face. Confusion. Disbelief. Astonishment. Then awareness that shifted quickly into joy.

"My Heir," he answered. "I am your Steward, if you'll have me as such."

Aria smiled. "Rise, Steward, and attend."

CHAPTER
TWENTY-ONE

Aria called for an hour's recess so that her new steward could be properly attired for his position. She took the time to tour the Hall on Aven's arm, learning about the people who had come to see them. She could see Owyn and Treesi on occasion when the crowds parted enough to see across the room but there were so many people that it didn't happen often. As they went, she saw Othi and Neera, who had joined Jehan and Aleia near the wall. Karse and Trey were talking with Memfis, and Trey waved when he saw Aria looking at them. Aria smiled, but didn't wave back, turning her attention to an older woman who came up and bowed.

"Thank you," the woman said. "You could have just killed him. We know you could have. We all know what he did, who he was...but we've seen him change over the years. He tries so hard to care for us—"

Aria smiled. "The very last thing I wanted to do was to start my reign in blood," she said. "It would be a horrible omen. And he's tried so hard to care for me and for mine over the past month. In truth, I've grown fond of him."

"In truth, we all have, my Heir," the woman nodded. "And when is the little one due?"

Aria looked up at Aven. "Mid to late summer, or thereabouts," he answered.

Aria could almost hear the woman counting backward. She looked up at Aven again and arched a brow. He nodded.

"A storm child?" the woman finally asked. "And...I heard your bloodlines. A child of all four tribes, and a storm child. They'll do wonders, this one."

"A storm child," Aven repeated. "Is that...I'm sorry, is that an Earth thing?"

The woman laughed. "It's an old midwife thing, my dear. According to the lore, a child conceived in the height of a storm will carry part of the storm with them throughout their life."

"I've never heard that before," Aven said. "I wonder if Fa knows it."

"Not likely," the woman said with a laugh. "This is women's lore. To be honest, I shouldn't be telling you!"

Aven smiled broadly. "Telling me what?" he asked. Then he leaned down and kissed Aria's cheek. "If you want to talk more about this, I'll step away."

"No, you've more things to do, and more important things, than entertaining me," the woman answered. "No, I'll come back up once you've had a chance to settle in, and we'll have a nice long visit. My home village isn't more than an hour away, and Lexi knows me. I was here when she bore her girls." She smiled. "My name is Zarai, and I think I've seen all the babies born in the Palace for the past twenty years, including your Del." She looked around. "Where is Del, by the by?"

"I think he went out with Steward," Aven answered.

"And that's going to be confusing, isn't it?" Zarai asked. "Steward. He's going to need to readopt the boy, isn't he?"

"We'll swim those currents when we reach them," Aven answered. He looked up and straightened. "They're back."

"Oh?" Aria turned, saw Del escorting Man— no. No, until he chose a new name, he was Steward. Steward wore the livery of the

Palace, and he looked more at ease than he had even in Terraces. He stopped just out of reach of Aria and bowed deeply.

"My Heir," he said.

"Steward," Aria replied with a smile. "We've been waiting for you." She turned back to Zarai. "We've work to do now."

"And you'll do marvelously," Zarai answered. "Especially with our new Steward at your elbow." She patted Steward on the arm. "Now, I'll come up and visit with you in a few days. I'm sure your healers know more about healing than I do, but I wager I know more about delivering babies than any of them."

"That's not a wager I'll take," Aven told her, making her laugh. "Will I be allowed to listen? Or will it be more women's lore? I've read about attending a pregnant woman, but I haven't had any practical experience yet. I want to learn what I need to know."

"Ah, so it's a teacher you want? Of course, my boy. Of course. Now, go make us all proud." Zarai shooed them away.

"I like her," Aven said as they started back to the dais.

"Zarai is a good woman," Steward said. "She's a gifted midwife, and she'd have made an excellent healer, if she'd had the gift. Or so every healer in the Palace has ever said. And she has excellent taste."

"How so?" Aria asked.

"She absolutely despised Risha," Steward answered, his face expressionless. But there was mirth in his eyes. Aria rolled her eyes and laughed. He smiled. Then he sobered quickly. "Aria—"

"If you're going to thank me," Aria said, pitching her voice low. "Please wait until we're in private? I suspect that we'll both be in tears by the end of it, and I won't cry in front of my people. Not today."

He smiled. "As you wish, my Heir."

"You're going to need a name," Aven said. "We can't keep calling you Steward. That's not a name. That's a job."

"I'm happy with just being Steward for now," Steward answered. "And if that's the only name I have for the rest of my days? It's more than I was expecting. I didn't expect to have any days after this—"

"I thought we were waiting for privacy?" Aria murmured. They stopped at the dais steps, and she turned, seeing Owyn and Treesi coming toward them. "Now...go do steward things."

Steward snorted. "Owyn really is rubbing off on you," he said. He bowed, and walked over to where Lexi stood near the sidewall. Owyn and Treesi joined them, and Owyn grinned, reaching out and tugging Del close so he could put his arm around Del's shoulders.

"There's not a single person we talked to who objects to what we did here today. Not one," he said. He looked over his shoulder and smiled. "We did a good thing."

"And we're going to do more good things," Treesi said. "What good thing are we doing next?"

"We're going to learn something," Aria answered. She offered her hand to Aven, and let him lead her back up the stairs. As they took their seats, the Hall fell quiet. Aria rested her hands on the arms of her chair, and raised her voice.

"One of the last things that the Usurper did before he abdicated, and before his name was forgotten, was to outlaw the Healer Risha, once Senior Healer of the Earth tribe," she said, her voice carrying through the Hall. "Her crimes against the Water and Air tribes have been abhorrent, and close-felt. We may never have an accurate accounting of how many she murdered from Water, in her attempts to break the cycle of change. Nor do we yet know how many Air she mutilated—" She paused, her throat closing as the horror rose in her. She remembered waking, unable to move, Risha telling her in detail what she was planning before leaving her alone. She closed her eyes, and reached to her left, and felt Aven's hand closing around hers. "By...by taking their wings. These are things she would have done to me, and to my Water." She heard the gasp of horror from the assembly, and opened her eyes again to look at Aven. Aven squeezed her fingers, then leaned over the arm of his chair to kiss her hand. She smiled at him, then looked back at the people before her. "It has only been a few days since Risha attacked this Palace, since she killed many of the servants. We want to know why. And we want to find her, so that she may face the Mother's justice. So I ask you, is there anyone who may know anything? Why would Risha attack the Palace?"

People started talking to each other, a buzz that rose and fell with emotion and emphasis. Aria looked to her left — Aven had gone stone-faced, while Owyn was leaning forward, one elbow resting on his knee. To her right, Treesi had one hand on Del's arm, leaning across the space between them. Aria arched a brow, and Treesi smiled and shook her head.

"My Heir?"

Aria turned, and blinked in surprise at the boy standing in front of the dais. "Danir?"

"You...you wanted to know if we knew anything," the boy said, fidgeting where he stood. "One of the people who disappeared when Risha attacked was a friend of mine. We never found his body. I don't know what happened to him. He...he told me—" He swallowed, looked toward the wall where his mother stood. "Am I gonna be in trouble?"

"No, my dear," Aria answered gently. "What do you want to tell me?"

He relaxed slightly, although he kept his hands clasped. "Gregor, he was a junior guard. And he told me once that she wanted him to get into the Heir's Tower. That there was something she wanted him to find and bring out of there. But he never got inside. I think she killed him for it."

Aria took a moment to gather her thoughts, then raised her voice. "Steward?"

"I heard him," Steward answered. "And I have honestly no idea what she'd have been looking for. The Tower was sealed when Yana died."

"She must have believed what you told Mem, about the Tower being undermined in the storm," Owyn said. "She had to get whatever it was out of there before it fell in."

Aria nodded. "Danir, do you know what Gregor was supposed to be looking for?" she asked.

He shook his head. "All he told me was that it was a box. He didn't tell me anything else." He frowned. "He said that she wanted him to find a special box. But he didn't describe it or anything. And he said he shouldn't even have told me that much." His eyes widened, and he turned to look at his mother. "She'd have killed me if she knew I knew!" he gasped. "Mama—"

Lexi was at his side in an instant, wrapping her arms around her son. "You're safe, love," she murmured into his hair, just loud enough for Aria to hear. "She can't get you now."

"Oh, she won't get near him."

Aria looked up to see that Othi had come forward. He looked unusually serious. He met Aria's eyes, then gestured toward Danir. She nodded, and Othi turned toward Lexi and Danir. He went to one knee next to them, which put him on eye level with the boy.

"Danir, is it?" Othi said. "I'm Othi. You might have seen me this morning, or yesterday—"

"It's kind of hard to miss you, sir," Danir answered. Othi grinned, and the people closest to them giggled.

"You don't have to sir at me. I'm not a sir. I'm just Othi." He nodded toward the dais. "Aven, he's my cousin. He'll tell you. I'm not all that formal when I don't have to be." He paused. "And I'm not going to let that woman get to you. Understand?" He pointed to where Karse was standing. "Captain Karse over there, and Trey, and me, and all of the other guards, we're going to keep you safe." He looked up at Lexi. "Mother Lexi, is there any reason your son can't train with us? We'll be training Del, too, and they're about the same size—"

A rude noise sounded from Aria's right, and Owyn made a strangled noise and squeaked, "Where did you learn *that*?"

Aria looked at Owyn, saw his red face, and gasped. "Del! What did you *say*?"

For a few minutes, the entire Hall was full of laughter. When it died down, Othi looked up at Lexi again.

"Well?"

"I...don't think there's a reason to say no," Lexi said. "If he wants to learn. Danir?"

"Train?" Danir gasped. "To fight? The old guard captain said I couldn't learn until I was sixteen! He said I was too young."

"Sixteen? That old?" Othi turned. "Ven, when did you start?"

"You expect me to remember that far back?" Aven asked. "I was...five? Six? Ask my mother."

"Four," Aleia called. "He was four."

Othi nodded and turned back to Danir. "See? We start young," he said. "Out in the deep. That's our way. Now, I can't make you little again, to start learning like that. I mean...well, you are little. Compared to me, everybody is little. I mean I can't make you younger. But I can still teach you. If you want to learn?"

Danir stared at him for a moment, then threw himself at Othi and hugged him fiercely. Othi laughed, hugging the boy back. Then he stood up, and Danir clung to him, giggling.

"Oops," Othi said, winking at Aria. "Got a barnacle."

More giggling, and Othi started to carry Danir off to the side of the room.

"A moment, Othi?" Steward called. "Danir, is there anything else you can tell us about what Risha wanted?"

Othi put Danir down, and the boy smoothed the front of his tunic and looked up at Steward seriously. "No, sir. Just she wanted a special box, and that it was in the Tower. That's all."

Steward nodded, and Othi and Danir walked to the side of the room. He turned to Aria. "My Heir," he said slowly. "As much as it pains me to ask this, may I have permission to open the Heir's Tower and search?"

"Not alone," Aria answered. "I won't ask that of you."

"I want to help," Memfis called. "I've been studying that tower for nearly half a year. I want to see the inside. Again. It's been a long time."

"I'm going in, too," Jehan added. "I've been in there before, too. Milon had an observatory at the top."

"Aria?"

Aria turned to look at Owyn. "Yes, my Fire?"

"Not me. Del wants to go."

Aria turned to look at Del. "You want to go into the Tower?"

Del nodded, his face pale. *I want to help.*

"You're not going in there alone," Owyn said. "I'll go with him, Aria."

"If you're both sure," Aria answered. "Steward, will that be enough?"

"Ah…" Steward breathed. He folded his arms and looked at Memfis. Then he nodded. "Should be," he answered. "When?"

"No time like now," Memfis suggested. "My Heir, are we done?"

Aria looked at Aven and Owyn, then at Treesi and Del. "We've stood in judgment on the Usurper. We're starting to see what we can find for answers. Am I forgetting anything?"

"Nestor's records," Owyn said. "And preparing for the progress."

"Ah, yes," Aria nodded. "Steward, Nestor's office is your office now, and I want a full accounting of his records. I want you to know everything that he knew. And I want you to find everything that he hid."

"As you wish, my Heir. If I might borrow Owyn for that? I understand he helped his aunt in Terraces in a similar manner."

"Owyn?" Aria turned to him.

"I'm not sure how much help I'll be, but I'll try," Owyn answered.

"My Heir, the office has been locked since Nestor died," Lexi called out. She took a ring of keys from her belt, went through them, and took one off. She brought it to Steward. "This is yours now."

"Thank you," he said. He slipped the key into his pocket, then turned and smiled at Owyn. "And I'll be glad of your help. And...the Progress? Immediately, or in the fall? Have you decided?"

"As soon as it can be arranged," Aria answered.

Steward bowed. "I'll start making plans. Once I have something more detailed than leave and come back, I'll bring it to you for review."

Aria smiled. "I look forward to seeing it," she said. "Is there anything else?"

"I thought of something," Treesi said. "There's supposed to be a small healing center inside the Palace walls. Aven, you and I should get that cleaned up and running again."

"Do I get to help?" Alanar called.

Aria laughed. "Of course you get to help, Healer Alanar," she answered. She turned back to face her people. "Thank you all for coming, especially on such short notice. When you return to your homes, please tell anyone who could not be here that the Heir has taken control of the Palace, and that we will be working to set things right. And if any of you hear news of Risha or her whereabouts, I want to know." She stood up, hearing her Companions getting to their feet around her. And as they all rose, a cheer rose with them, loud enough that Aria took a step back, her wings flaring wide. Then she heard what they were shouting.

Aria! Aria! Aria!

THE DOOR BETWEEN THE Hall and the Little Council room closed, and Owyn pounced on Aven and hugged him. "We did it!"

Aven laughed and wrapped his arms around Owyn. "Aria did it."

"No, Owyn's right," Aria corrected. She walked around the table to the Heir's seat and sat down. "We did it."

Aven smiled and reached out, tugging Treesi into the hug. "I don't think we could have if you weren't so perfect, love."

Aria smiled and looked around. Del had gone to the far side of the room, and was staring intently at the wall. She looked at the others, then got up and slowly walked over to join him.

"Del?" Del looked up at her. He wasn't smiling, and his face was still too pale. She rested her hand on his shoulder, and he turned and threw his arms around her. "Oh, Del," she murmured, and hugged him, bringing her wings in close to shield him from whatever was haunting him.

"You don't have to go in there," Owyn said from behind Aria. "I can do it."

Del shook his head and stepped back far enough to raise his hands. "*It's not that.*"

"Then what?" Aven asked. He came around Aria. "Del, what's wrong?"

Del looked at them and swallowed. "*I know what she was looking for. I think I know. And I'm not sure, but now I think it was the real reason she killed my mother.*"

"Del!" Aria gasped. "What was it?"

"*A fancy box. Like Danir said. I saw it. We saw it when we were in the tower. It was on a shelf up high. Too high for Mama to reach. I didn't see what was in it. I don't know if Mama knew what it was.*"

"And that's why you want to go in?" Owyn asked. "For answers?"

Del nodded.

There was a knock on the door, and Steward slipped into the room. His eyes widened when he saw them clustered around Del.

"Is something wrong?"

"Del might know what we're looking for in the tower," Owyn answered.

"What?" Steward came closer. "Del? Is there something that you didn't tell me?"

"*Only because I didn't realize it was important,*" Del answered. "*I was six. How was I supposed to know it was important? It was when Risha took us to the top of the tower. I guess to the observatory Jehan mentioned. She was showing me how far you can see, and Mama was wandering. You know how she would flit from place to place. You called her a butterfly.*"

Steward smiled. "I didn't think you'd remember that."

"*She was doing that, and she found something. She got really excited. She said it was hers, and she wanted it. It was a box on a high shelf, and she couldn't reach it. She kept pointing and saying it was hers, and when Risha wouldn't get it for her, Mama said she was going to go and find someone to get it down.*" Del stopped. "*That's when Risha pushed me.*"

"Mother of us all," Treesi breathed.

"And then you sealed the tower," Owyn said. "And whatever it was got locked up inside where Risha couldn't reach it." He rested his hand on Del's shoulder, and looked at Steward. "Let's go find it."

"Let's go change first," Treesi said. "We're all wearing nice clothes. We shouldn't get them mucked up, and there's how many years' worth of dust in that tower?"

"Thirteen," Steward answered. "Nearly fourteen." He nodded. "I'll go tell Memfis and Jehan we're going now. Owyn? Del?"

"What are we going to be doing?" Aven asked.

Aria looked thoughtful. Then she turned to Steward. "Would you mind if we collected Nestor's records? Before anyone else gets into the office? Now that it's been announced that we're going to be going through them, if there's anyone left who answers to Risha, they might try to get them first. But if we move them to our suite—"

"I don't mind in the slightest," Steward said. He took the key from his pocket and passed it to Aria.

She took it and handed it to Aven, then looked around. "We have things to learn. Let's go."

CHAPTER
TWENTY-TWO

Owyn and Del stood in the courtyard, and Owyn tipped his head back to look up at the tower. "You don't have to go in there," he said softly.

"*I want to go in. I want to know.*"

Owyn nodded. "I understand. And...you're welcome to spend the night with us. With me and Allie. I don't think you'd sleep if you were alone." Del looked quizzically at him, and Owyn chuckled. "Just for sleep," he added. "I figure, you'd feel safer if you were in the middle, and you weren't comfortable with being in the middle with Aria."

Del smiled. "*We'll see how I feel when we're done. You may be right.*" He looked over his shoulder. "*Here they come. And they remembered lanterns.*"

Owyn turned to see Steward, Memfis and Jehan coming toward them. "I already asked Del if he was sure he wanted to go in," he said. "So you don't have to ask."

"Saved me a step, then," Steward said. "Where's Alanar?"

"He said he was going to start arranging the healing center," Owyn said. "Which I'm not sure how he's going to do it, unless he gets help from someone. He's having trouble finding his way around. How are we doing this?"

"Start at the top?" Memfis suggested. "Work our way down? That's where Del said he saw the box, after all. I doubt Risha had time to move it—" He paused and coughed, looking sidelong at Steward.

Steward just snorted. He handed a lantern to Owyn. "I keep thinking I'm through with the pain. It's been so many years. I keep thinking I should be through it. Then I look at this damned tower and...no."

"Are you sure you want to go in?" Jehan asked as he passed a lantern to Del. "We can go. You can stay here."

"I need answers, Jehan," Steward said. He frowned slightly. "I need to go in there. I should have done it years ago." He went into his pocket and took out a heavy key, turning it over in his hands for a moment before looking up at the tower again. "Let's go."

The door hinges screamed in protest as Steward dragged the door open. They entered in a single file, and Owyn immediately sneezed. "That's what fourteen years of dust looks like," he said as he rubbed the back of his hand over his nose. "It's like a carpet."

"Start at the top, you said," Jehan said. He gestured with his lantern. "The stairs are there. Let's go."

Steward led the way up the stairs, with Del and Owyn in the rear. The stairs spiraled around the outside wall of the tower, with landings every so often. On each landing, there were grimy windows on the left, and a door on the right. Owyn counted an incredible fifteen doors before Steward stopped. To rest, Owyn thought, until he heard Jehan's voice.

"What is it?" Jehan asked.

"The door is open," Steward answered. "I thought everything was sealed in here. That shouldn't be open." He looked down the stairs at them. "Look now, or on the way down? This is the last level before we get to the observatory."

Memfis scowled and peered into the room. "There's no one here. Looks like a broken window. Maybe the wind?"

"The doors all open inward," Jehan said. "Steward, you take the boys up. Mem, we'll check this room."

"The boys?" Owyn repeated. "Really?"

Jehan looked at him and smiled. "Sons of my heart? Of course you're my boys. As much as Aven is my boy."

"Me, too?" Del signed.

"Yes. You, too," Jehan said with a laugh, and Del grinned.

"All right, let's keep going. I'd forgotten how many stairs to the top." Steward started up the stairs again, with Del and Owyn following on his heels. At the top, the stairs opened up into a round room that took up the entire top level. There were eight large windows evenly spaced around the room, with bookcases in between them. A table and chairs were in the center of the room, all covered with a fine layer of dust.

"Not as much dust up here," Owyn said. "That's odd."

"Del? Where was the box?" Steward asked.

Del frowned and walked over to one of the bookcases. He pointed to an empty spot on the shelf. *"It was there."*

"Oh, fuck," Owyn breathed. "Someone got here first?"

"Or someone moved it," Steward said. "Let's search."

Owyn nodded, and moved to the left, to another bookcase. Dusty books. Scrolls. Dry inkwells and moth-eaten quill pens. And a dusty figure that Owyn had to rub against his shirt sleeve to see properly. It was a doll, roughly carved from wood, and painted in a crude approximation of the Palace guard livery. He looked at it, then held it up. "Del?"

Del turned to look at him, and the look of shock on his face told Owyn that if he found nothing else today, it didn't matter. He'd found a lost treasure. Del came over and took the toy soldier from Owyn, running his fingers over the surface. He smiled. Then he hugged it to his chest.

"So, that's yours?" Owyn asked.

"*Fa made him for me,*" Del answered in Owyn's mind. "*His name is Captain. I thought I'd lost him.*"

"Fa...you made this?" Owyn looked around to see that Steward was kneeling, looking underneath the table. "You carved this?"

"Carved...carved what?" Steward looked up, and his eyes widened. "Mother of us all! Is that Captain? Where did you find him?"

"On the shelf here," Owyn answered and pointed.

Del looked up and smiled. He tucked the soldier under his arm, and signed, "*I had him with me when we came up here. I never saw him again. I thought he was gone!*"

"I remember how upset you were, and it took me days to realize why. And I never could make another that you'd accept as Captain." Steward shook his head. "Well, if the box being missing wasn't enough to confirm that someone was here, Captain is. Someone was definitely in here after I sealed the tower. Because Captain was not on that shelf. I'm sure of that. I came up here and I searched for him."

"So...someone put him where he'd be found, and moved the box," Owyn said. He looked around. "Someone who knew you were looking for him. But you never came back after the first time you looked?"

"I only looked once," Steward confirmed. "I couldn't make myself come up here again."

Owyn nodded. "Who else had access to that key?"

Steward frowned, crossing his arms over his chest and tucking his chin. Owyn saw movement, and looked to see that Jehan and Memfis had come up the stairs. Jehan arched a brow, and Owyn nodded.

"I thought I held the only key," Steward said slowly. "But I wonder...Nestor's predecessor might have had a key. Which means Nestor had a key, and he kept it from me."

"If Nestor had a key, and he was working with Risha, why couldn't she get into the Tower to find the box?" Memfis asked.

"Because it's not where Del saw it," Owyn answered. "It's been moved."

Jehan frowned. "The room downstairs was ransacked. Thoroughly. I'll bet that the others were the same. I wonder...do you think she was in here? And couldn't find it?" He looked around. "She became Senior Healer how long ago?"

"Four years," Owyn answered. "Almost five."

Jehan nodded. "So...four or five years ago, she lost her access to the Tower." He looked around. "There's not as much dust in here. Or in the room below."

"Five years of dust, instead of fourteen?" Memfis said. "That makes sense."

"So..." Owyn walked to the table and looked around at the dusty shelves. "I don't think Risha knew what was in that box either. Not when Yana pointed it out. Or she wouldn't have been trying to find it later. She'd have taken it then." He looked up at the shelf and frowned, then walked over to it, stretching up to try and reach the shelf. He could just barely touch it with his fingertips. He turned around to face the others. "How tall was Yana?"

Steward frowned. "She was tiny," he said. "You're a full head taller than she was. Treesi is taller than Yana was."

Owyn looked up again. "And Risha is shorter than me, too." He nodded. "Right. Nestor might have been tall enough to get that shelf. I don't know about the person who was steward before him. His uncle, wasn't it?"

"He told you that? Yes. Ankem was taller than I am," Memfis said. "That shelf would have been easily within his reach."

Owyn nodded again. He looked up at the shelf, letting his thoughts range and seethe like storm clouds. He heard Steward start to say something, heard Memfis silence him. What would a tall man have hidden here? And when?

"Del?" he called. "Can you remember that day? Really well?"

He heard Del coming up next to him, and looked to see Del signing, "*I think so. Why?*"

"Was the box dusty?"

Del hummed softly. "*I don't remember. I couldn't see the shelf really well.*"

"Del was a small child," Steward offered.

Owyn nodded, then grabbed a chair. He dragged it back to the shelf and stepped up on it. Now he could see the back of the shelf, and the heavy layer of dust that outlined where a box once had been.

"Mouse, what are you thinking?"

"That Risha definitely had no idea what was up here. And that it had been up here a long time." He jumped down off the chair and moved it back. "The dust up there is thicker than it was downstairs. I'm guessing that no one has really cleaned up here—"

"In twenty-five years," Jehan finished in a soft voice. "That box was there from before?"

"It was something Milon put there?" Memfis asked. "He...he wasn't that tall."

"Nah, I don't think so," Owyn said. "It was put there by someone who didn't think anyone would look here." He considered the shelf again, then shook his head. "I don't think there's any reason to search the rest of the rooms. They've been tossed already. But what they wanted, it was moved already." He nodded back to the shelf. "There's dust where it was. Maybe about as much dust as was on Captain. Whoever put Captain on the shelf moved the box at the same time." He looked over at Del, at the toy soldier in his hands. "I don't know yet. Let's go see if the others have found anything."

LEXI UNLOCKED THE HEAVY door and stepped out of the way. "No one has been inside since the attack," she said.

"Are you certain?" Aven asked.

"As much as I can be," Lexi answered. "Until I gave the key to Man...to Steward, the only key was on my ring, which stays with me."

Aria let Aven go into the room first, and she and Treesi followed him once he nodded. It was a large office, larger than Rhexa's office back in Terraces. Two tall bookcases. A desk and chair. A table. A chalkboard on one wall, covered in cramped handwriting. A shorter bookcase under it, with each shelf full of flat boxes filled with papers. The boxes were labeled in the same cramped handwriting: Housekeeping. Guard. Stable. Kitchens. Healing Center. Home Farm. Harbor.

"The current records and ledgers are here, on the top shelves," Lexi said, gesturing to one shelf. "And last year is on the bottom shelves. At Turning, we start new books for the new year, and move the oldest set to the archives. Will we need to get those?"

"I think that depends on what we find here," Aria said. "We might. But I don't know yet." She looked around. "I'm not even sure where to start."

"This year's records," Treesi said. "And the boxes...Lexi, these are current notes, aren't they?" When Lexi nodded, Treesi laughed. "He used the same system that Rhexa does."

"Do you know what to look for?" Aven asked. "I know I don't."

"Honestly, we might want to ask Rhexa to come," Treesi said slowly. "I'm not going to be much help — not with handwritten records. Owyn will be better at this, but there might need to be a full audit of the records, and that will take time." She went to the shorter bookcase and started looking through papers. Aria watched her, but for some reason, she kept looking at the chalkboard. She wasn't sure why — there wasn't anything interesting about it. There were notes about livery needed for the new pages. The palace needed to trade for millet, and the Home Farm had put in a request for breeding stock.

"Aria," Aven said, and she dragged her attention from the board to look at him. "What's wrong? You have the oddest look on your face."

"I...I'm not certain," Aria answered. She looked back at the chalkboard. "There's something about it. The chalkboard. Something—"

There was no warning before the world fell away, and the vision hit. All at once, Aria was alone in the room. She saw a tall man come in, carrying a large box that Aria knew in her bones contained something important. He locked the door behind him, then went to the chalkboard. He reached up to the top of it, and did something; there was a click, and the board swung away from the wall...

Aria drew in a sharp breath, and looked up at Aven, who was holding her by both arms. "There's something behind the board!"

Then her legs gave out under her, and only Aven's hands on her arms kept her from falling. He scooped her up in his arms, and carried her to the chair. Treesi came to crouch on the other side of the chair, taking Aria's hand.

"Lexi, we're going to need something for Aria to eat," she said without looking away from her. "And something to drink. Please."

"Is she all right?" Lexi asked.

"I'm fine," Aria said. "Just...I'm fine."

"You had a vision, didn't you?" Aven asked. "You went down the same way Owyn did on the beach."

"I did not!" Aria protested. "I did not faint!"

Aven smiled at her. "Good thing you didn't," he said. "Or I'd be taking you back to the suite and putting you to bed. Now, you said there's something behind the board?"

Aria nodded. "It swings open. There's a catch." She pointed. "Up at the top, on the right."

Aven walked around the desk and over to the board. He reached up, fumbling at the top of the board. "How tall was the person who designed this?" he grumbled. "I think...there—" There was a click, and Aven stepped back and pulled the chalkboard forward.

"What's in there?" Treesi asked.

Aven disappeared behind the board. "A...there's a space back here. A box? And books. A lot of books."

"Bring them out," Aria said. She sat up straight in her chair. "That's what we're looking for."

A moment later, Aven reappeared, carrying a large box in his arms. He brought it to the desk, put it down, and went back behind the board, coming back with three large books with green leather covers.

"There are nine more of them in there." Aven set the books down next to the box. "Aria, these need to come to our suite."

Aria nodded. The books were important, but she couldn't take her eyes off that box. "Lexi, we'll need servants—"

"No," Aven said. "No one touches these that we can't vouch for." He frowned. "Lexi, go and find Othi, please? Ask him to bring three warriors."

"And I'll fetch something for Aria to eat while I'm gone," Lexi said. "Here, or in your suite?"

"In the suite, please. And lock this door until you have Othi?" Aven turned to Treesi. "Trees, the box isn't heavy, just big. Will you carry it?"

Treesi nodded and looked at the box. "It's locked."

"We'll let Del play with it," Aven said. "He's good with locks." He came back around the desk, and before Aria realized what he was doing, she was in his arms.

"Aven!" she laughed. "Put me down! I can walk!"

He looked at her. Then he grinned. "No. Lexi, would you open the door?"

OWYN SAW THE BOX ON the table the minute he opened the suite door. "That...Del, is that it?"

Del moved past him and nodded. "*Where did you find it?*" He looked up. "*And is that sweet rice? Is there any left?*"

"There's plenty," Aven said. "And cut fruit, and some really nice marinated fish. And this is the fancy box you said that you saw in the tower? How did it get here?"

"*Where did you find it?*" Del signed again. He walked over to the table, looked at the box, and signed, "*And what's in it?*"

"I think I know what was in it," Aria said. "But it's locked. Aven said you might be able to open it. Where are the others? Steward and Memfis and Jehan?"

"Coming," Owyn answered. "So we can wait until they get here."

The next several minutes were chaotic, as Othi arrived with three Water warriors, each of them with an armload of books, the four of them making the room seem very cramped as they came in to leave the books on the table. As they left, they passed Steward, who arrived with Memfis and Jehan on his heels.

"Is that the box? You found it?" Steward gasped. "Where?"

"Your new office," Aria answered. "There is a hidden place behind the chalkboard."

"Mem, Aria had a vision," Aven added.

"Aria—" Steward gaped at Aven for a moment, then turned to Aria. "You're a Smoke Dancer?"

"A completely untrained Smoke Dancer," Aria answered. "I've only ever had four visions. My waking vision, the vision of the dove, the one that sent me to the Temple, and this one."

"And she went down like Owyn on the beach," Aven added.

"Aven..." There was a definite tone of warning in Aria's voice, and Aven leaned over and kissed her. She scowled at him, then sighed. "You are terrible."

"And I love you very much," Aven replied. "So we found this, and the books."

Memfis came closer to look at the box and the books. "Aria, what was the vision?" he asked.

"A very tall man, who came into the office, locked the door, and put the box into the space behind the board," Aria answered.

"Very tall...that would have been Ankem. He was steward before Nestor, and he was Nestor's uncle. Nestor trained under him. There really never was any question that Nestor would follow him." Steward looked at the books. "And these?"

"They were in the space with the box," Treesi answered. "Can we open the box now?"

"Del, do you think you can pick the lock?" Aven asked. Del went to the box, looking at it. Then he nodded and went into his room. He came back a few minutes later with what looked like long, thin needles.

"Del, where did you learn to pick locks?" Steward asked as he watched over Del's shoulder. Del snorted, but didn't stop what he was doing. Steward looked at Owyn. "He didn't answer, did he?"

"I don't think he wants you to know," Owyn said. "I don't care where he learned it. I just want him to show me how to do it."

Owyn heard something snap. Then Del whistled, and dropped two halves of one of his needles onto the table. Next to them, he laid the open lock. He glanced at Owyn, then turned the box and pushed it across to Aria.

"You want me to open it?" Aria asked. "Del, your answers are in here."

Del pushed the box closer to Aria, and she reached out and pulled it to her, her fingers tingling with certainty. Yes, she knew why Yana wanted this box. She stood up so that she could better see, licked her lips, then unfastened the catch and opened the lid. She nodded.

"I thought as much. It's empty."

CHAPTER TWENTY-THREE

"Empty?" Owyn came around the table and looked into the box. Aria reached into the box and touched the lining. It was cream colored velvet, and thickly padded. There were marks in the velvet where something had pressed into it, but there was nothing there now. Treesi joined him, looking closely at the inside of the box, saying nothing. Del stepped back to give them room, then sat down, picking up the wooden figure he'd been carrying when he came in.

"It was still locked," Aven said. "The box was locked, and hidden away in a locked compartment. How could it be empty?"

"Someone beat us to it?" Jehan suggested. "At least they didn't take the books. We might learn something there."

"No, I know what was in here," Aria said. "I...Treesi, would you get the Diadem for me? It's in my bedroom. I put it away after the ceremony in the Hall."

"Of course," Treesi answered. She kissed Aria, then hurried off to Aria's room. She came back a moment later holding the Diadem in her hands. She handed it to Aria, who turned it, then put it into the box.

It fit perfectly into the indentations in the velvet.

"That's why the box was empty," Aria said. "

"Because it held the Diadem?" Treesi said. "But—"

"We never found it," Steward said, his voice quiet. "We found Milon, and we searched for the Diadem. But it wasn't with him, and it wasn't anywhere we looked."

"You didn't find it? He left it here, in his room," Memfis said. "When we went up to the Amber room."

"It wasn't here when we went looking," Steward said. "I never knew what happened to it, until Yana came forward as Heir. And we never found it after the last battle. Given her head wound, I thought it might have been destroyed."

"So...someone got there first, and took it," Owyn said. "And...put it in a locked box, and hid it in the Tower." He looked at the others. "So how did it get out of the box?"

"Yana," Jehan answered. "There was an Heir at the Temple. The Diadem had to be there for her to find. The Mother took it."

"But it left enough of itself behind that Yana recognized the box as having held it," Aria said. "I understand. I felt it, too. I knew the moment I saw the box in the vision that it was important. And I knew once I touched it why."

"You mean...the Diadem disappeared out of the box, and reappeared in the Temple?" Owyn asked, sounding incredulous. "Really? That really happens? It's not just a story people tell?"

"The Crown does it," Steward said. "Jehan, you weren't here when Elcam died. You didn't see it. I did. They laid him out in state in the Hall, with the Crown on his chest. And...when they rang the final bell, the Crown vanished. The next time I saw it was when Tirine took it up at the Temple. She wore the Diadem into the Crypt and came out with the Crown. When I went into the Crypt, there was no sign of the Diadem, and believe me, I looked. So I imagine the Diadem did the same thing the Crown did. The Mother took it when it was time to give it to the right person."

"But...the Diadem was in that box long enough for it to make marks in the velvet. It shouldn't have been. It should have gone back to the Mother when Milon—" Jehan stopped, turned to Memfis. "Mother of us all..."

"He is still alive," Memfis breathed. "Aleia was right. That's the proof. He didn't die when we left him, or when the healers tended to him here in the Palace. If he'd died, the Diadem would have gone back to the Mother immediately. It wouldn't have been in the box long enough to leave marks. It must have been there until Yana went to the Temple."

Aria shivered, cold to her core. Milon had survived. Her father had survived the attacks on the Palace. But what had happened to him? "What is in the books?"

Steward opened one of the books and frowned. "Journals. This...I think this might be Ankem's handwriting." He picked one up and turned the pages. "Hrm...these were from Tirine's reign. Or this one is." He flipped pages, and his eyes widened. "This...this..." he stammered. He looked up, his face gone suddenly pale. "This was the journal he was keeping when the attack...when..." He shook his head and looked down again, reading aloud, "*The unthinkable has happened. Our Lady is dead. Our Palace is overrun. There are armed men in our halls, and Elcam's bastard has claimed the throne. We cannot fight him. All we can do is protect what we hold and pray the Mother delivers us.*" He turned pages, read more. "*There is nothing that can be done. Mannon has entrenched himself into the Palace, and to overthrow him will take more than can be given at this time. We will continue as we have been, and we will hope and pray, and the healers will continue to work. Perhaps the Mother will be merciful.*" He looked up. "I have no idea what this is talking about. I can't think that the healers were caring for anyone—"

"That you knew of," Jehan said. "The Palace healer twenty-five years ago was Agisti. Am I remembering correctly?"

Steward frowned, then nodded. "Yes, it was Agisti. Then Anilis. Then Waran."

"And where are their records?" Jehan asked.

"In the archives," Steward answered. "We can bring them out, cross-reference them with these—

"I don't think we need to," Owyn said slowly. He'd picked up another of the books, and was looking at it. "This is Nestor's book, I think. Steward, isn't this Nestor's handwriting?"

Steward came around and looked. "Yes, that is."

Owyn nodded. "Listen to this. *An ague is ravaging the Palace, and the timing could not have been worse. Waran is dead, and we have no healer who is sworn to protect the secret. I have brought Galia's assistant into the fold. She has healing training, and may be able to help until Waran's replacement is appointed. To think, all these years may be for naught, laid to waste by a simple ague.*" He looked up at Steward. "You said Risha got here when Del was little. So this record is about sixteen years ago."

"And Galia's assistant? That was Ambaryl," Steward said.

"The people who died when Risha attacked were the people who knew what this was about," Aria said. She rested her hands on the tabletop. "And...she attacked because he was here. My father was here, in the Palace, the entire time." She closed her eyes. "That's why Risha attacked. That's what she wanted here. And that's why she killed the people who knew. Risha has my father."

"Aria," Memfis' voice was strangled, and he slumped heavily into a chair. "No. No...I looked. I *looked*! I wanted to know...I had to know what was done...if they burned...I never saw anything. Not a fucking thing!" He rubbed his hand over his face. "I...he's alive. He's *alive*...and I..." He closed his eyes. "I can't even go look."

"I can," Owyn said. He put the book down and came around the table, resting his hand on Memfis' shoulder. "I will. Once we're done here."

"There's no way," Steward said weakly. "There's no possible way they could have kept him hidden under my nose. Not for twenty-five years! I've been over every inch of this Palace. I know corners of this building that Nestor didn't know!"

Owyn cleared his throat. "Del wants to know if you know all the hidden passages," he said. "Because he thinks maybe that's why Nestor told him to stop exploring them."

Steward turned and looked at them, his face going pale. "I...Mother of us all. I...Del, you had maps. Where are they?"

Del looked at his door, then back at them. "*I need to go to my old room. I haven't had time to go pack and bring things over. Aven, come with me?*"

"If you want me to," Aven said. He stood up and winced. "I need to listen to my grandmother," he grumbled.

"What did Mother say?"

"She told me that I needed to start dancing again, to build up the muscles that support my hip," Aven answered. "And I should swim more."

"You have a whole harbor to do it in," Steward said. "And there are passages that take you right down to the water. I'll show you later."

Aven nodded his thanks, and he and Del walked out of the suite. Aria laced her fingers together and pressed her forefingers to her lips, thinking.

"Nestor thought Del was broken," she said softly. "And...Ambaryl did as well. He was injured, therefore he was unfit."

"I'm glad you waited until he was gone to say that," Owyn muttered.

Aria nodded. "Those attitudes...suppose that they were not the first to think that? Suppose they learned it here, from others? Ankem was Nestor's uncle, you said. Did he feel the same way?" She reached for the book that Steward had read from. "*There is nothing that can be done. Mannon has entrenched himself into the Palace, and to overthrow him will take more than can be given at this time. We will continue as we have been, and we will hope and pray, and the healers will continue to work. Perhaps the Mother will be merciful,"* she read again. "Is anyone else reading this the way I am? They pinned their hopes on Milon rising up against Mannon, but he could not, and the reason was something that the healers needed to work on. And that made Ankem pray for the Mother's mercy." She looked up. "What does this tell you?"

Jehan leaned forward. "That Milon's life was saved, but he wasn't healed entirely. Something...the attack damaged him somehow." He reached out and rested his hand on Memfis'. "That's how they kept him locked away. He couldn't fight back."

"You can stop now," Memfis growled. "You can just stop." He tugged his hand out from underneath Jehan's and rubbed it over his face. "I shouldn't have left him."

"He gave you an order, Mem," Jehan said.

"I should have told him to stuff his order," Memfis snapped. "I shouldn't have left him. I should have sent you and Aleia out through the servant passage, and I should have stayed with him." He swallowed and looked up. "Where are your blades, Mouse?"

"In my room. I'll get them," Owyn answered. He squeezed Memfis' shoulder, then left the room. He came back a moment later carrying his smoke blades, with the bag that held his book slung over his shoulder. "Now, Fa?"

"If you don't mind," Memfis said, and got to his feet.

Owyn nodded. "Treesi, if Allie comes back while I'm gone, make him rest, will you?"

"Are we going to do anything else here?" Treesi asked. "Because I can go help him with the healing center, if you don't need me anymore."

Aria looked at the book and nodded. "Do that," she said. "I think I'll be spending the rest of the afternoon reading." She smiled up at Steward. "Will you hand one of those books to me?"

OWYN FOLLOWED MEMFIS out into the courtyard, wondering where they were going. Memfis didn't seem to be in the mood to answer questions, so Owyn just followed as they turned left around the Palace. He'd find out where they were going when they got there.

"I hope they've kept it maintained," he heard Memfis mutter. It seemed like enough of an invitation.

"Kept what maintained?" he asked. "Where are we going?"

"There's always a Smoke Dancer at the Firstborn's side," Memfis answered. "So, there's a dancing floor. But I have no idea if they've maintained it."

"Mem?"

Owyn turned at the sound of Aleia's voice. She looked puzzled. "Where are you going?" she asked as she caught up with them. "You look like something is chasing you. What's wrong?"

Memfis scowled. Then his shoulders slumped. "The dancing floor. Guppy, he's alive. You were right. He's alive."

"He...Milon?" Aleia stepped back, closed her eyes. "How do you know?"

"It's a long story, Mamaleia," Owyn said. "But I told Mem I'd dance for him, to try and get some answers."

She looked at him, one brow raised. "What did you call me?"

Owyn felt his face warm. "Ah...you told me I could call you Mama. Remember? And...well...sometimes things just come out when I'm not paying attention."

"Mamaleia," she repeated. "It's a mouthful." She smiled. "I like it. Can I come with you?"

Owyn looked at Memfis. "Mem?"

"It's up to you, Mouse."

"Well, I don't mind. Where are we going?"

Memfis started walking again, and Aleia fell in next to Owyn. "How did you find this out?"

"The servants kept records. Hidden records, and Aria found them in Nestor's office. And found the box they'd put the Diadem in until the Mother swiped it back."

Both brows rose this time. "They did what?"

Owyn snorted. "We'll show you. Everything is up in the suite. Is that...oh, that's nice."

Memfis stopped by a low fence that surrounded a round, flat green area. He turned and looked at Owyn. "This is the dancing floor."

Owyn nodded and took his bag off his shoulder. Memfis took the bag as Owyn set down his blades and sat down on a bench to take off his shoes. He lined them up beneath the bench, picked up his blades, and entered the dancing floor. The ground was cold under his bare feet, and didn't feel like grass.

"What is this?" he asked, bouncing a little in place. "It's not grass. It's spongy."

"Moss," Aleia answered. "The groundskeeper used to say you couldn't kill it, no matter how often you danced on it." She smiled slightly. "This is where I was teaching Milon to use hook swords."

"So Aven can dance here?" Owyn looked down. "I'll tell him. He said Pirit wants him to start dancing again. All right. Let's see what I can see." He took a deep breath, feeling his skin tingle. Oh, this was going to be a strong one. Second breath, and his hair stood on end. Third breath, and he started to move...

The vision hit him like a club, hard enough that he couldn't breathe, and knew he was falling. At the same moment, he knew he couldn't move, that there was something tight around his wrists, around his upper body. He couldn't see, couldn't scream.

But he could hear.

Risha laughing. Creaking...wood? Yes, he remembered now. The ship timbers had creaked, just like that. He heard wind, and seabirds.

"Who's there? I feel you!"

It was a voice he didn't know, but it was clear in his mind, as clear as when he heard Del, or Trey, or Aven. *"Who are you?"*

"I...I have no name. Not anymore. I was forgotten."

"Who were you, then?"

A long pause. *"Milon. I was Milon."*

Owyn shuddered. *"You still are Milon. No one forgot you. And we're going to find you. We're coming. Where are you?"*

A wry laugh. *"I haven't the faintest idea. A ship, I think. It moves like a ship. Other than that? I don't know. Who is we? Who are you?"*

"Owyn. Owyn Fireborn. Son of Memfis. Adopted son."

"Mem? My Mem? They told me he was dead! They told me none of my Companions survived!"

"We were all told that you were dead," Owyn answered. *"So we're even that way."*

"And...you are Fireborn. Like he was. That means there's an Heir?"

"Your daughter is Heir. Her name is Aria, and she wants to meet you. So don't die until we find you." Owyn paused. *"How can you be talking to me like this?"*

"Talking to yourself?"

It was Risha's voice, and the slap that followed threw Owyn out of the vision. He pushed himself up onto his hands and knees, then groaned and wrapped his arms around his head.

"Owyn?" Memfis sounded terrified, but Owyn couldn't remember how to talk, how to tell his father he was fine.

Then again, he wasn't fine. He tried to push himself up again, and his gorge rose in protest; he vomited all over the moss carpet.

"Vision shock," he heard Memfis say. "He's going into vision shock. He...he never did this. Not even when he was first learning. Aleia, we need to get him inside! We need Meris...and Jehan. He'll know what to do."

He heard Aleia shouting, her voice fading. Felt Memfis' hand, cold on the back of his neck. Tried to remember how to put words together.

"Mem—" he croaked.

"Don't talk, Owyn," Memfis said. "Just be still. Do you remember our early lessons? About vision shock? You'll be all right. Help is coming."

"Found...found him," Owyn sputtered. "Talk...talked to him."

"You...you *what*? No. No, you be still. You'll tell me later. You are going to tell me later."

Owyn would have nodded, but he wasn't sure his head would stay in place if he did. It felt too big, and like it was going to either fall off or float away. No, floating away was more likely. He definitely felt floaty.

Floaty...couldn't be good.

"Fa," Owyn mumbled. "Don't...don't let me float away."

He heard shouting coming closer.

Maybe Alanar would catch him before he floated away.

ARIA LOOKED UP FROM the journal she was reading and flexed her shoulders and her wings, hearing the muscles pop. Aven and Del were at the other end of the table, and Del was bent over a stack of blank paper, drawing something. They'd returned from Del's room empty-handed, and Aven had said something about a burned box that had made Steward swear violently. Aria wasn't sure what it was about, and wasn't going to ask just yet — she didn't want to upset either Del or Steward without good reason. It would wait until she could talk to Aven alone. She reached for her cup, and jumped when the door burst open, hard enough to hit the wall and bounce back into Trey.

"Senior Healer," he gasped. "You have to come. It's Owyn—"

Jehan dropped the journal he was reading and jumped to his feet. "What? What happened? He was going to dance—"

"Memfis says it's vision shock," Trey answered. "And you need to come. They're in the infirmary. Lady Meris is on her way there."

"Vision shock? What's vision shock?" Aven asked, straightening. Jehan turned and looked at him.

"I'll explain on the way. Come with me," he said. "Fast."

Aven's eyes widened, and he followed Jehan toward the door, breaking into an uneven run as they left. Aria got to her feet and looked at Steward.

"Please tell me you know what vision shock is?"

He shook his head. "Something to do with being a Smoke Dancer, I assume. They keep their secrets close."

Aria nodded. "Then tell me you know where they are going."

"That I can answer," Steward said, and offered his arm. "This way, my Heir."

CHAPTER
TWENTY-FOUR

A ria hurried through the halls between Steward and Del.
"What was this about a box?" she asked. They both
seemed distracted enough that it felt safe to bring it up.

Del sighed. He started signing, paused, then started again, this
time with Steward translating, "*It was my treasure box. All of the
maps I made were in there, and I kept it under my bed. Fa helped me
build it, and I painted it. But it was gone when we got there. And
Aven found burned pieces of it in my fireplace, and some of the things
that were inside of it that wouldn't burn were in the ashes.*"

"Oh!" Aria breathed. "Oh, Del. Did Nestor know you'd made
the maps?"

"*Nestor taught me to make maps,*" Del answered. He snorted.
"*I showed them to him. He knew. He really did think I was an idiot,
though. I don't* need *the maps. I remember every turn. But Aven
asked me to redo them, so that everyone else would know.*"

"And that's what you were drawing?" Aria asked. "I'd
wondered, but I didn't want to interrupt. May I ask what else was
in the box?"

"*Flowers my mother gave to me, and pretty rocks,*" Del answered.
"*Pictures she drew. A lock of her hair.*" He shook his head. "*I don't
understand why they'd burn the entire box when all they wanted was
the maps.*"

"Because they're heartless," Aria said. "And cruel. And...and I don't know. That was so senseless. I am sorry, Del."

Del smiled and took her hand. She squeezed his fingers, then turned back to Steward. "You do not know what vision shock is?"

"That was the first time I'd ever heard the words," Steward answered. "We'll find out."

She nodded again. "Where are we going?"

"The healing center is on the first level, in the back of the Palace, near the kitchens. There's a healer garden back there, near the kitchen garden." He guided her down another corridor, toward a set of double doors marked with the Healer sigil. He knocked, then opened the door.

"Can we come in?" he called.

"If you stay out of the way," Jehan called back. "Stay with Memfis."

Steward led them into a large, airy room with wide windows that looked out into what Aria guessed was the healing garden. There were long, low couches along the walls, and another door that led down a wide corridor with doors on either side. Standing at that door was Memfis, and standing in front of him, her fists planted on her hips, was Treesi.

"You're not going in until the Senior Healer says you can," she said, and Aria could tell that she'd already said those words, probably more than once.

"Meris is in there—"

"You yourself said that Lady Meris knows more about this than you do," Treesi said. "Now please go sit down. Jehan says it won't take long to put him right, but he needs me in there to do it." She looked past him and nodded at Aria. "You can explain to Aria what happened, and wait for Aleia to come back."

"Memfis," Aria said. "Please, come and sit with me. Explain. What happened to Owyn? He was going to dance and catch visions."

"He did," Memfis said. He turned toward her, and Treesi slipped away and into one of the rooms. "He did, and..." He stopped and closed his eyes. "Milon was a strong Smoke Dancer. That's why it didn't surprise me all that much to learn you were."

Aria nodded, and took Memfis' hand, leading him to one of the couches. They sat down, and Steward sat down on Memfis' other side.

"Owyn danced," Aria said. "What did he see? And what is vision shock?"

"Vision shock...it's something you see most often in novice Dancers," Memfis said slowly. "Ones who have learned how to dance the smoke, but not how to completely surrender themselves to the visions. The vision controls you, you don't control it. Remember that, Aria." He paused. "If a Dancer tries to break a vision, a headache is the mildest reaction they can expect. An extreme reaction...that's vision shock."

Aria frowned. "When Owyn danced for us the first time, when he had his vision where he saw Del, you said something about what happens if a Smoke Dancer does not anchor themselves after they have a vision. That they might lose their place in the real world—"

Memfis shook his head. "It's not the same thing. That's another risk a Smoke Dancer faces. This..." He took a deep breath. "Seeking visions requires balance and control. It takes a lot of control to be able to give up control to the vision. Does that make sense to you?" Memfis waited until Aria nodded before he continued. "Vision shock...the body is so thrown out of balance that it starts to shut down. I've never seen it in a fully trained Smoke Dancer. And Owyn has never experienced it, not ever, as a novice."

"Memfis, you're saying this could have killed him?" Steward asked slowly. "Mother of us all, what did he *see*?"

Memfis looked up, and his face looked drawn, his eyes haunted. "He didn't tell me much. But...he said...he said he talked to Milon."

Aria turned and stared at him. "He talked to my father?"

Memfis nodded. "He'll tell us more, once he's well." He let his head fall again. "Milon was a strong dancer. Stronger than I was. Meris always told him he'd have to be careful."

"Can strong Smoke Dancers do that?" Steward asked. "Talk to each other in visions? Or is this part of the heart visions?"

Memfis shook his head. "I don't know. I've never heard of this before. But Owyn...he isn't any kind of Smoke Dancer that I recognize. Not anymore. He's something else."

Del sat down on the floor in front of them, and raised his hands. "*Because he died and came back?*"

Memfis shrugged. "I can't even imagine. But all of you, you're all something else. Something more." Del snorted, and Memfis smiled and shook his head. "You are. All of you are. You have to be." He looked up, and Aria turned to see Meris standing in the door.

"Grandmother?" Aria said. "How is he?"

"He'll be fine," Meris said. "He's asleep now, and Alanar is with him."

"Meris, do you know what happened?" Memfis asked. "He's never had vision shock before. He's always been so controlled—"

"It wasn't his fault," Meris said. "He told me, before he fell asleep. He told me he shared his mind with Milon. That my Milon is alive." She stopped, and smiled slightly. "He told me that he promised Milon that you'd find him. And he told me that Risha slapped Milon, and he thinks that was what severed the link."

Memfis sat up. "She did what?"

"He'll tell you all about it when he wakes up." Meris sat down next to Aria. "It's odd, though. I asked him what he saw. And he says he didn't see anything. Just heard. That's not like Owyn at all. He doesn't have aural visions."

Memfis shook his head. "No, his visions have always been visual. And visceral. He feels his visions intensely."

"Which may be why he felt the blow, and why it caused him to snap out of the vision," Meris said. She sighed. "He will be fine. Alanar is with him, and Aven."

"Where's Aleia?" Memfis asked. "She was here. I missed her leaving."

Meris raised a brow. "You missed that? She says she'll be back when she's back, but by now, I think half the Water tribe is getting ready to sail. Risha has Milon on board a ship. There's no place on the sea they'll be able to hide for long."

"They've been hiding at sea for months," Steward grumbled. "But then, Aleia wasn't looking for her then, was she?"

Aria found herself smiling. "I think Risha should be very afraid."

"I wouldn't count on her being caught until we see her in a net," Aven said from the doorway. He leaned against the wall and folded his arms over his chest. "And even then, I'll wait until I see her head in a basket before I count this as being done."

"That's bloodthirsty," Jehan said as he joined his son. "You're in pain, aren't you?"

Aven snorted. "I'm awake, aren't I?"

"Aven..."

Aven closed his eyes. "Sorry, Fa. Yes. I shouldn't have run. I know it's not going to feel good when I do. But I had to. You needed me. Owyn needed me." He shook his head. "I hate her, Fa. For what she did to me. To Aria and Owyn...and Alanar and Del."

Jehan sighed and rested his hand on Aven's shoulder. "I know, Ven. I know. Do you want me to work on your hip?"

Aven shook his head. "I—"

"Am going to listen to your father," Aria said. Aven whipped around to look at her.

"Aria—"

She got up and walked over to him, standing close enough that she could rest her hands on the waist of his kilt. "I don't like seeing you in pain, Aven. And there's nothing I can do to make it any better." She met his eyes, wondering if she could ever count the gold flecks in them. If they'd ever have the time for her to try. "Except order you to let your father do what he can."

He took a deep breath, let it out, then smiled slightly. "You're ordering me to take care of myself?"

She nodded. "Yes, my Water. Because I love you."

He shifted, and she stepped into his embrace, resting her cheek on his shoulder, wishing she could take away the pain and anger she could feel rolling off of him. He sighed, and his arms around her tightened.

"Let me go and take care of myself," he murmured into her ear. "Go back to the suite and rest. You're tired. You barely slept last night."

She chuckled. "I have reading to do."

Aven's arms grew tighter. "I can order you to take care of yourself, too."

She pulled back and rested her forehead against his, feeling his breath warm on her skin. "You can certainly try," she said and he laughed. He kissed her gently on the lips, then let her go.

"Go back and rest," he repeated. "I'll be there when I— Othi?"

Aria turned, seeing the big Water warrior in the doorway. "I...am I interrupting?" he asked.

"What is it, Othi?" Jehan asked.

Othi, to Aria's surprise, blushed. "I...I was looking for Treesi. If she's available?"

Jehan shook his head. "She's with a patient."

Othi nodded. "Aunt Aleia said she might be. But...well, I'm leaving with the warriors. We're going hunting. And...I wanted to see Treesi before I left. I only have a few minutes, though. Would you tell her I stopped to see her?"

"Othi?" Aven said. "What is it?" He looked over his shoulder, down the corridor, and he tensed. "Oh. Really?"

Othi's blush deepened. "Ummm...yeah. But...you know...it's her course. And...and I don't know her course. And I don't have time to find out." He looked down. "Just...tell her I stopped to see her? I really need to go."

Jehan nodded. "I'll tell her."

Othi smiled slightly, and Aria realized that he was much younger than she'd originally thought. "Thank you, Uncle. Aven..." He frowned, then signed something. Aven's eyes widened, and he signed back, his movements sharp, and too fast for Aria to translate. Othi's response was short, and Aven sighed and nodded. Othi smiled, and Aria recognized his final sign — thank you. Then he turned and left.

"What did he say?" Aria asked, looking up at Aven. "He was signing too fast. What did he say?"

Aven shook his head. Then Steward cleared his throat.

"That young man doesn't expect to come back," he said softly. "He asked Aven to take care of Treesi for him if he goes back to the deep."

Aven's jaw dropped. "That was a private conversation!"

"Then you shouldn't have had it where three other people could understand it," Steward said. "Jehan, go get Treesi and send her after him. Give the boy something to fight for."

Jehan smiled slightly. "When did you become a romantic?"

"When the reason for my life opened her eyes and called me hers," Steward answered. "And I've missed it every day for years now. Go get her."

Jehan turned, raising his voice as he did, "Treesi!"

She appeared in the doorway almost immediately. "Is something wrong?"

"Treesi, you need to go down to the harbor," Jehan said. "Othi is leaving, and you need to go say goodbye. You need to catch him before he leaves."

"Leaves?" she repeated. "Is he going with Aleia?" She frowned. "Why do I need to go say goodbye? He'll be back in a few days."

"He'll appreciate seeing you before he leaves," Aven said.

"And you going down there will give him a little something more to fight for," Steward added. "Go on."

Treesi looked back down the hall. "But Owyn—"

"We'll stay with Owyn," Jehan said. "Go say goodbye to Othi."

"Trees," Aven said softly. "Othi is counted as a warrior, but he's never been in a real battle before yesterday. And from what they tell me, it wasn't really a battle taking the Palace. It was more a relief to the servants here that someone who wouldn't hurt them was taking control. So he's done mock-battles, but he's never fought for real." He looked at the door that led out of the healing center. "He's scared."

Treesi went pale under her freckles. "He's afraid he isn't coming back, isn't he?" she whispered. "And...he came...how do I get to the harbor? Quickly? Can someone take me so I don't get lost?"

Del got to his feet and held out his hand. Treesi smiled, and the two of them hurried out of the healing center.

TREESI FOLLOWED DEL down corridors that she knew she'd never have found on her own, out of the Palace, and through a small gate in the curtain wall. The gate let them out onto a path that followed the cliff line and took them to a long stairway that led down toward the harbor.

"This is the fastest way?" Treesi asked.

Del nodded.

"Are you coming with me?"

He shook his head and held up one finger.

Treesi frowned. "Oh, there's only one way to go?"

Del nodded again, then made shooing motions with his hands. Treesi laughed, kissing him on the cheek, then hurried down the stairs. It felt as if there were thousands of them, but at last she reached the bottom, and a long, white sand beach. There were canoes pulled up out of the water, and men and women hurrying this way and that. She didn't see Othi anywhere.

"Treesi?"

Treesi turned, and saw Neera coming toward her from one of the canoes. She looked worried.

"Is something wrong?" Neera asked. Her eyes widened. "Is Owyn all right? Aunt Aleia said he was sick...or something. I didn't follow it."

"Owyn is fine. Will be fine," Treesi said. "He was asleep when I left, and Alanar is with him. I was looking for Othi. He came up to the Palace, and I missed him. I was hoping I didn't miss him again? Have they gone?"

"Not yet," Neera said. "Come with me." She took Treesi's hand and led her down the beach and around a large promontory of rock. On the other side, Treesi could see the harbor, the docks and the vast number of canoes. And, on the docks, she saw Othi standing with Aleia.

"Othi!" Neera shouted. Othi and Aleia both turned, and Othi's jaw dropped. He hurried back down the dock to meet them.

"You...you came down?" he stammered. "You...you came here? Is...is Owyn all right?" He paled. "He is all right, isn't he?"

"He's fine," Treesi said. "I came to see you. They told me I missed you."

His eyes widened, and to Treesi's surprise, he blushed. The stammer grew worse. "Me? You...you came to see me? You came down here? For me?"

Next to him, Aleia chuckled. "I need to go up and say goodbye to Jehan, and check on my boys before we leave," she said. "You have a few minutes. Why don't you take a walk?"

"A walk?" Othi repeated. "Oh. Oh, yes. A walk." He turned to Treesi. "Will you walk with me?"

Treesi smiled up at him. "That's why I came down here."

His blush deepened, and he held his hand out. Treesi took it, and they walked off the dock and back down the beach. He led her back the way she'd come, past the canoes and the stairs. The rock wall curved out in front of them, and there was a spill of rocks near the water's edge. Othi stopped there, and drew Treesi down to sit with him on one of the sun-warmed rocks.

"Thank you for coming down," he said softly. "I didn't think I'd see you before I left. I know you were busy."

"I'm sorry I missed you," Treesi said. "Othi—"

"Can I ask you something? Without...without offending you?" he blurted. "I don't know how to do this right, and Neera won't do it for me, even though she's older and Clan Mother and everything. And I know my mother would never have allowed it. So I don't know what I'm doing and Neera says I have to sail these waters on my own. Which...I think she'd getting back at me for teasing her about being sweet on Del." He stopped. Swallowed audibly, then took Treesi's hand. "I know you're bound to Aria. You're her Earthborn. But...she let Owyn have his husband. And I was wondering...well, hoping, really...that you...you might build a canoe? With me?" He bit his lip, then added, "Please?"

"I don't know anything about building a canoe, Othi," Treesi said. "And...I can't go out on the deep. I get sick—"

"And your place is here. With Aria. I know that. I'm...I'm willing to stay. On land. I like Karse, and he'll have me as a guard. So I can be a guard here. If it means I'll get to be with you, I'll stay and be a guard. And I know you have to be with Aria, and with the other Companions, and I'm fine with that." He paused. "I mean, I think I'm fine with that. I mean...I know I won't be the only man in your life, the only person in your life. I just want to be one of them."

Treesi laced her fingers with his, hearing her heart pounding in her ears. "I never thought I'd ever be with just one person. Ever. I'm a healer. I was raised by healers. It's not something we do," she said. "My parents love each other, but they never married. Not like Jehan and Aleia, or Owyn and Allie." She looked up at him, at his dark eyes. "I'm not sure what we are, Othi. Or what we'll be. But I want to find out."

His eyes widened. So did his grin. "Is that a yes?"

"That's a 'you have to come back so we can see what we'll be together'," Treesi answered. She wasn't expecting Othi to whoop and jump to his feet, and the next thing she knew, she was in his arms, spinning through the air as he whirled in circles. She clung to him, equal parts elated and alarmed.

"Othi! I'll get sick!" she yelped. "Othi, stop it!"

"I'm not going to let you get sick," Othi said. He stopped spinning. He also didn't put Treesi down, holding her tightly to his chest. He grinned at her. "I like this."

"I know something you might like better, but you have to put me down."

He arched a brow. "Not sure," he told her. "Letting you go? Not liking that at all." He set her on her feet, and she led him back to the rocks.

"Sit down."

He looked curious, but sat back down on the rock. She smiled, then joined him, straddling his lap and putting her arms back around his neck. He laughed and wrapped his arms around her again.

"You're right," he said. "I do like this."

"You'll like this better," she murmured. Then she kissed him. He tensed — was he really that surprised? Then his arms tightened around her, and he kissed her back hard enough that the sounds of wind and water were completely drowned out by the roar of the blood rushing in her ears. Someone moaned, and she wasn't sure if it was her, or Othi, or both of them at once.

They broke the kiss, but she didn't move, her forehead resting against his. Breathing with him, the way she would with Aven. It felt right.

"You're right," he murmured. "I like that much better."

She smiled and closed her eyes, running her fingers through the tight curls of his hair. "You'll have to come back for the rest."

He chuckled, a warm sound that made Treesi shiver. She wanted to hear that sound with her ear against his chest. "Oh, I'll be back," he said. "And then...we'll see what we are."

CHAPTER
TWENTY-FIVE

"We don't have to go back yet," Alanar said. "We could spend the night in the healing center."

Owyn leaned into Alanar's arm. "Now why would I do that?" he asked, turning his head to look up at his husband. The movement immediately made him feel dizzy, and he grimaced. "You're going to be right next to me all night. And Aven and Treesi are right across the way. How would being in the healing center be any better?"

"You're not all right," Alanar said. He shifted, sliding his arm around Owyn's back.

"Dizzy," Owyn said. "Off-balance. I don't like it. I thought Jehan said I was fine?"

"He said you will be fine," Alanar corrected. "We just need to take care of you. And you can't push yourself. You're going to rest, and eat, and sleep. And we'll see how you feel in the morning."

"And if I still feel like this?" Owyn asked. "Turn here."

Alanar turned, and Owyn saw the doors to the Heir's suite ahead of them. "If you still feel like this after breakfast tomorrow, then we'll examine you again and see what we're missing. And if we can't figure it out, then you and I will take a sail out to Terraces and we'll let Pirit examine you."

Owyn sighed. "I'm sorry I'm a troublemaker, Allie."

"You're worth it," Alanar said. "Now, we're here, aren't we?"

"You're getting better at this," Owyn said. "Yes." He reached out and opened the door. The only person he saw in the room was Steward, who looked up from the book he was reading as the door opened.

"Owyn!" He sounded elated, and he got up and hurried toward the door. As he reached them, his eyes widened. "Oh, Owyn, you need to be sitting."

Owyn laughed, hating how weak it sounded. "I know. I'll be sitting a lot for the next day or two, I think."

"Or longer," Alanar muttered from next to him.

Steward stepped back and let them into the room. Owyn went to one of the padded chairs and sank into it. "I can't wait for the room to stop moving," he grumbled.

"Stop..." Steward turned to Alanar. "Should he be out of the healing center?"

"There are three healers in this room!" Owyn groaned. "How is being bored in the healing center any better for me? I mean, I can be bored right here!"

"Actually, there's only one healer in this room," Steward corrected. "And that's only because Alanar is here."

"Where are Aven and Treesi?" Alanar asked. "I thought they'd be here. Jehan let Aven go before Owyn woke up."

Steward sat down in the chair facing Owyn. "Treesi hasn't yet come back from seeing Othi off with the Water tribe warriors. Del was starting to get worried, because the canoes left a while ago, so he and Aven went down to see where she is, in case she was lost. And I think Aven was going to swim while he was down at the water, to help ease his hip."

"And where's Aria?"

"With Memfis and Lady Meris. She says that since she can't learn to dance until after she has the baby, she wants to learn all the theory she can now. So they're off having lessons, and she's having her evening meal with them. I told them that I'd go through the journals. Which meant staying here, since Aria doesn't want them to leave this room."

"Can I help with that?" Owyn asked. "I can read. And...if there's something to eat, I wouldn't say no. Especially since it's late enough for Aria to be having an evening meal."

"Something light," Alanar added.

Steward smiled. "I'll ring for Lexi, and I'll bring a book to you. I'm taking notes on anything I think might be useful, too. Now that we know that they're talking about Milon, things are much more clear." He walked away.

Owyn had to fight the urge to turn and look at him. It would only make his head spin. He closed his eyes instead. That helped.

"You could go to bed," Alanar suggested. "I mean...we could go to bed. You need to sleep."

"I already slept. If I sleep more, I'll wake up in an hour and be awake all night," Owyn replied without opening his eyes. "And not in a fun way. Not that there's anything fun about this. I...this is worse than being sick. When I was really sick, I didn't know I how sick I was—"

"When you had the ague, you mean?" Alanar asked. "And you met Trey?"

"Yeah," Owyn answered. "I was out of my head, and I didn't really know how sick I was. And I haven't been that sick since." He took a deep breath and let it out. "I don't like this at all. And I'm never ever going to tease Treesi about being seasick. Ever. I'm landsick."

He heard Steward laugh, and opened his eyes to see that he had come back with one of the books. "I've always heard that called mirligoes," he said, handing the book to Owyn. "And I'm told that spiceroot helps. I rang for Lexi."

Alanar blinked. "I haven't heard that before. Either that word, or that spiceroot helps."

"I like spiceroot," Owyn said. "We have spiceroot cookies at Turning. I didn't make them this year. I should have. I'll have to make them, when I have a kitchen again." He opened the book and started to read. Only to stop and close the book, then close his eyes again. "The words are dancing. Everything on the page is dancing." He growled softly. "This is going to be a long day or two."

"Man..." Alanar started. Then he stopped. "Steward. That's right. Steward, would you get a blanket? I think Owyn is going to have something to eat, then rest right here in the chair."

"Allie!"

"Or we could go back to the healing center," Alanar added. "It's one or the other, love."

Owyn took a deep breath. "Mirligoes? Is that what you called this? It sounds like how I feel. Mirligoes round and round like a wagon wheel. Can't walk a straight line after."

Steward laughed. "Yes, it does sound like it feels. It's wretched."

"You've had this?" Owyn opened his eyes.

"Something very like it. I got water in my ears a few years back, and it went stagnant. I couldn't keep my balance or keep food down for days," Steward answered. "I looked like I was seven nights drunk, and I stayed that way until Risha got here." He frowned. "Must have been two years ago. Maybe three. Del would know." He turned and looked at the table. "He's finished the maps, by the way."

"Maps?" Owyn said. "What maps?"

"The maps of the secret passages," Steward answered. "Let me get that blanket." He walked away, and again, Owyn had to fight to keep from looking after him. He hadn't realized how often he did that.

"I thought he had maps," he called.

"Oh, you weren't here when we found out." Steward came back with a folded blanket. He shook it out and spread it over Owyn, then went to sit down. "You knew that Del made maps of the hidden passages that he'd explored as a boy. He and Aven went to get them, and found that someone — Nestor, probably — had burned them, and the box that he kept them in. Along with his last mementos of his mother." He paused. "I don't think I ever realized that Del's memory is as good as it is. I know he remembers everything he's ever read. But he's redrawn all the maps from memory, so that we can search and see if you can find where they kept Milon prisoner."

"What do we hope to learn?" Alanar asked.

Steward leaned back in his chair and crossed one leg over the other. "I'm not sure. Aria wants the answers, but she didn't tell me why before she went off with Memfis and Meris. It may be just so that we have a more complete picture of what happened. Or there may be more answers hidden away. Memfis said that Milon used to keep journals, so maybe we'll find those."

Owyn closed his eyes, listening to Steward and Alanar talk about histories and possibilities. The blanket was warm and soft, and he was starting to feel just as warm and soft, drifting into a half-slumber. He heard Lexi come in, heard Steward asking for an invalid's meal, and for spiceroot tea. He briefly thought about protesting — he wasn't an invalid! But it was too much effort to open his eyes. So he just listened, letting his mind wander, until he smelled seawater a heartbeat before warm lips pressed against his, and a brief, warm wave washed over him. He opened his eyes as Aven straightened. He was, Owyn noticed, wet.

"Went swimming?" Owyn asked.

"After Treesi and Del came back in. Melody wanted to play, and I needed to work the hip. How are you feeling?"

Owyn snorted. He rolled his shoulders, feeling the muscles pop. "Better. Like you didn't know that, though. I felt you checking."

Aven grinned. "Yes, but I wanted to hear you say it."

Owyn sat up and looked around. His head didn't feel like it was going to fall off, so that was better. Steward was sitting at the table with Memfis and Aria, both of them bent over books.

"Where's everyone else?" he asked.

"Del went to bed, and so did Treesi," Aven answered. "I just sent Alanar to bed, and I'll go get him. I'll go get all of them; we all want to know what you saw, if you're up to telling us."

"I should tell you all at once, shouldn't I?" Owyn asked. "Since I scared the absolute fuck out of everyone."

"You did," Aria said without looking up from her book. "And you should." She raised her head and smiled. "Owyn, I need for you to break this new habit of yours, please?"

"New habit?" Owyn looked up at Aven, who shrugged. "Which new habit?" he asked, looking back at Aria.

"This new trying to die habit. It's tiresome."

Owyn grinned. "It's not my idea!" he protested. "It's never been my idea. I plan to live forever. Other people...they keep not liking that plan."

Aria laughed. "I like that plan."

"So do I," Aven agreed. He offered his hand to Owyn. "Come to the table?"

Owyn took his hand, and let himself be pulled up out of the chair and into Aven's arms. He leaned against Aven's chest and wrapped his arms around him, not worrying about the damp seeping into his trousers from Aven's wet kilt.

"You know I still love you, Fishie," he murmured. "Don't you?"

Aven's arms closed around. "I never doubted that you love me, Mouse," he said. "You do need to stop scaring me, though." Owyn nodded, and Aven yelped. "And you need to shave again. You're scratchy."

"Maybe I'll just grow a beard," Owyn said as they walked over to the table. "It'll save time." He sat down next to Memfis, who slid a teacup in front of him.

"Drink that," Memfis said. "Then eat something. Then we'll talk."

"I want my book," Owyn said. He sipped the tea, which was sweet and spicy and warm. When Aven put a bowl in front of him, he ate it, not even sure what it was.

"This is good."

"Sweet rice," Steward said. "Del loves it. And it's fairly light, so it shouldn't upset your stomach."

"I'll go change," Aven said. "Then I'll get your book." He squeezed Owyn's shoulder and left the table, disappearing into his own room.

"How do you feel?" Memfis asked.

"Not so much like a kite," Owyn answered. "More...anchored. And eating is helping. But eating always helps."

"There's some cut fruit, too," Steward said. "Berries are very good with the sweet rice."

Owyn nodded. He set his cup down and tried not to yawn. "What did you learn from the books?" he asked.

"What did you learn when you spoke to my father?" Aria asked in response. Owyn grinned.

"If I'm going to tell the story, I should tell it to everyone. Which means we need Alanar and Treesi here. And Del—" He stopped talking as arms encircled him from behind. Del leaned over the back of his chair and kissed his cheek. Then he took the chair next to Owyn and poured a cup of tea for himself.

"If I may excuse myself?" Steward said. "I promised Lady Meris that I'd tell her when you woke up. And I want to see if I can find Karse, if he's still awake. I just realized that the guards were supposed to start drilling this afternoon, but I think half of them went out with Aleia." He stood up, bowed slightly, then left the room.

"When are you starting your training?" Owyn asked, turning to Del. "Do you know?"

"*I saw Trey when we came back in. He says we'll start tomorrow, me and Danir,*" Del signed. "*But I don't know in what yet. Or if I'll be awake for it.*"

"Treesi will be out in a moment. She was asleep. And Del stole my chair," Aven grumbled as he came back to the table. He put Owyn's book down, and set a charcoal vine on top of it. "Alanar is coming, too."

"You come sit with me, Aven" Aria said. "It's a better angle to keep watch."

"But too far to touch," Aven pointed out. Once he was sitting, he reached for a pitcher set off to one side and poured the contents into a cup. He sipped it, then looked at the piles of books and papers. "What do we know?"

"They're almost writing in code," Memfis said. "We're having to interpret everything, and there's no way to know if we're right."

"Ankem knew what he was writing about, and it did not matter that no one else would know. No one else was supposed to read these," Aria added. "I have his books. Memfis has Nestor's. When we are done, we will trade. But Ankem seemed to be very disappointed that Milon did not immediately rise and channel the wrath of the Mother to smite the Usurper." She touched the pile of papers. "He kept notes on the lies he told Milon. So he could remember them, I suppose."

"Aren't we supposed to wait?" Owyn asked.

"Alanar and Treesi were here when we learned this," Aria answered. "You were asleep." She grinned. "And snoring."

Owyn blinked. "Snoring? I snore?" He looked around the table. "I snore? Allie never said I snore. Neither did Treesi."

"Because you don't, usually," Aven said. "At least, not when I've been there to hear." He frowned. "I don't think. It might not have been enough to wake me up, though."

"The night we stole him back from Fandor," Aria said. "He did snore, at least a little. But you were asleep, too."

"Oh?" Aven frowned. "It might have been the drugs, then, and how heavily you were asleep. Because you were very deeply asleep here."

"Really?"

Aven smiled. "When I woke you? That wasn't the first kiss," he said. "And I wasn't the only one kissing you. You slept through Treesi and Del coming back, them both going to bed, me coming back, and Alanar going to bed." He looked at Memfis. "That's what you told me, isn't it? About Treesi and Del?"

Memfis nudged his shoulder against Owyn's. "It was impressive. Usually, I could wake you just by stepping on the singing stair. But this...you slept through practically everything."

"How long was I asleep?" Owyn asked. "I'm not even sure what time it is now. It was past midday when we had court. It was...probably coming on supper when Mem and I went out and I fell over. What time is it now?"

"The guard just called the midnight watch," Alanar said as he came into the room. He yawned as he came around the table, and Owyn would have stood up if Del and Memfis both hadn't grabbed him and held him in his chair.

"*You stay sitting!*" Del sounded unusually sharp in Owyn's mind, enough that Owyn winced.

"You don't have to yell at me," he said, and Del's eyes widened.

"Who yelled?" Treesi asked as she came around the table. She leaned down and kissed Owyn, then looked at Del. "Oh. Did Del yell?" She paused. "What does Del yelling sound like? To you, I mean?"

"It's echoey, in my head," Owyn answered. "And don't nobody say nothing about it echoes because there's nothing in there!"

Alanar snickered. "Now you're in my head."

"Too fucking crowded in your head, love," Owyn said. He tipped his head back. "Memfis on one side, Del on the other. Gonna sit in my lap?"

"I'll move," Memfis said. "Alanar, sit."

"May I have some of that tea?" Alanar asked as he took Memfis' place. Treesi went around the table to sit next to Aven.

Owyn passed a cup to Alanar, then opened his book. He turned to a blank page, picked up the charcoal...then put it down.

"Mouse?" Aven asked.

"I didn't see anything," Owyn said. "So there's nothing to draw. I...Aven, can you pass that pen over?" Aven passed the pen and the inkwell, and Owyn started to write. The creaking of the wood. The sound of the wind and birds—

"They were close enough to land that I could hear birds," he said without looking up.

"That'll make it easier for Ama," Aven murmured. "I hope."

Own nodded and kept writing. The feeling of restriction on his wrists. Around his chest. And...the pen fell from his fingers, leaving splotches of ink on the page. "Oh," he breathed. "Oh, fuck. I think...I think I know what they're talking about. Ankem, and Nestor. About why they never did anything with Milon when they had him. Why they gave up on him. I think I know." He looked up, looking around for Memfis. "Mem, when you were attacked, when he was hurt...how was he hurt? What did they do?"

"Why?" Memfis asked. "What did you see?"

"Not see," Owyn corrected. "Feel. And...not feel." He licked his lips. "I was feeling what he felt. There were ropes...or...or straps.

Something around his wrists. Around his chest. But there wasn't anything below the waist. Because I couldn't feel anything below the waist." He swallowed and looked at Memfis again. "He was stabbed in the back, wasn't he?"

Memfis went ashen. "He...yes." He sank into the armchair where Owyn had been sleeping. "I...yes."

CHAPTER
TWENTY-SIX

Jehan stared at them. "No," he said, resting his hands on the tabletop. "No, that's not possible. He was hurt, yes. But there was nothing wrong with his spine!"

Owyn rubbed his hand over his face. He had slept again, but it hadn't helped as much as he'd hoped it would. He still felt off-balance, and wanted to go back to bed. But Memfis had arrived early, asking him to explain what he'd experienced to Jehan. So Owyn was awake, and the Senior Healer had joined them for breakfast in the Heir's suite. "There wasn't anything wrong when you left him," he said. "But you don't know what happened after you were gone."

"How badly was he hurt, Jehan?" Memfis asked. "I know he was all over blood. I was covered in his blood. But I never asked you—"

Jehan closed his eyes and visibly shuddered. "I'm not sure I'd have told you," he said hesitantly. "Not then." He took a deep breath. Then he opened his eyes. "Maybe not now. Where is everyone?"

"Del ate early and went off for weapons training," Owyn answered. "Alanar and Treesi are with Lexi, seeing what needs to be done to properly supply the healing center, and Aria went off to watch Aven dance, then they're meeting with Steward to go over...something. I don't know. And you're avoiding the question."

Jehan snorted. "A bit, yeah," he admitted. "Fine. Milon...whoever stabbed him did a piss-poor job of it. They came in too low to kill him right off. They did...a lot of damage, though. Without a better healer, he was going to die no matter what I did. He—" He paused. "Can I just say that there was no damage to the spine?" he asked. "The blade entered too far to the left." He paused again. Then he shook his head. "That's all I'll say, Mem."

"Jehan—"

"If I say more, you'll have nightmares, and I need to sleep."

Owyn blinked and looked at his father. "Oh?"

"Out from under my bed, Mouse. And besides, this shouldn't be news to you," Memfis grumbled. He snorted. "Fine. It wasn't the attack that did it. What did?"

"We won't know that until we find where they hid him," Owyn said. "Steward said you told him that Milon kept journals. Maybe we'll find them when we find where they kept him. From what it sounded like, Risha hit here hard and fast." He looked at Memfis for confirmation; Memfis nodded.

"From what Lexi said, the entire attack took practically no time at all. Risha's own people let her into the Palace, and they weren't expecting her to turn on them. The servants who didn't know were herded into the practice yard—"

"Which is out of sight of the harbor and the main courtyard," Jehan murmured.

Memfis nodded. "Which is a good thing, in a way. The Palace staff who were killed were cut down in the main courtyard. Lexi said they could hear the screaming."

"The kids must have been terrified," Owyn murmured. "I'd have been terrified. But between guarding the practice yard and...well, what was happening in the courtyard, there wasn't a lot of time for them to get into the Palace, get to Milon, and get him out again." Again he looked at Memfis, who frowned. Then he nodded.

"So there's a good chance that when we find where they were hiding Milon, there will be information there." Jehan nodded. "When do we start looking?"

Owyn shrugged and picked up his now-cold cup of tea. "Not sure," he admitted. "Aven, Alanar and Treesi jumped on me with all six feet when I said I was fine to help with the searching. I don't want to be left out of helping. But I'm not steady enough. Not yet." He closed his eyes and took a deep breath, then sipped the tea. "This is really fucking awful."

Jehan smiled and held his hand out. "Give me your hand."

Owyn reached across the table and clasped Jehan's hand. Warmth chased up his arm, and he closed his eyes and let Jehan work. His ears popped, one right after the other, hard enough to make him wince.

"That should help with the dizziness," Jehan said. "There was uneven pressure in your ears. And you need to eat something."

"I just did," Owyn protested, opening his eyes. "You saw me. I ate like I've never seen food before."

"And your body still thinks you're starving." He frowned. "Mem, Smoke Dancers burn through food faster than others, don't they? Am I remembering that correctly?" Memfis nodded, and Jehan turned back to Owyn. "Have your clothes started getting looser?"

Owyn blinked. "I...yes. I...I eat like a horse, and my trousers aren't getting any tighter. They're too big. Alanar says my ribs are sticking out."

"Because you're burning through it faster than you did before," Jehan said. "You need to eat more." He frowned. "I wonder if that's why things hit you so hard last night?"

"You think he went into vision shock because he was already unanchored going into the vision?" Memfis turned and stared at Owyn. "That...I'll have to talk to Meris. We don't know enough about heart visions, but if it has the same effect on the body as dancing—"

Owyn drained the last of his tea and reached for a piece of bread. He leaned back in his chair and took a bite, thinking. "It makes sense," he said once he'd swallowed. "I'm having heart visions, you said. All the time. I hear Del and Aven and Treesi and Allie and Trey all the time. And at some point, I'll have Aria in my head, too. If bodies work like forges, you have to feed the flame. I'm trying to run too hot a fire without enough fuel. Right?"

"Say rather without the right fuel," Jehan said. "Come to the healing center with me. We'll figure out what your new diet should be. Less bread and sweets, more meat, I think. More things that will stay with you longer."

Owyn set down the bread he'd been eating. "I like bread," he grumbled. "But...sounds like I need less kindling and more coal?"

Jehan chuckled. "Something like that." He looked at the tabletop. "Is there anything else? Anything else you felt, or noticed?"

Owyn thought about it. Then he frowned. "I asked him who he was. And he told me he didn't have a name. That he'd been forgotten. And he said that they'd told him all of you were dead. I told him that you thought he was dead, so we were even. And I told him who I was, and that we were going to find him." He licked his lips. "It might be worth it to try again—"

"No!" Both men chorused in unison.

Owyn burst out laughing. "I didn't say right now!" he protested. "I don't think I could, even if I wanted to." He leaned back in his chair, considering the remains of their breakfast. He reached over and picked up a boiled egg, then leaned back again.

"No, I mean once I get this under control. Once I'm steady, I want to try again. Especially if you think it will help." He paused. "Well? Will it?" He bit into the egg, waiting for an answer.

Jehan took a deep breath. "It might," he admitted. "We don't know. And we can have all the healers out on the dancing floor. Just in case."

Memfis scowled. "I still don't like it. It's too risky."

"We can't not take risks, though," Owyn replied. "If we weren't going to take risks, we'd still be in Forge." He frowned. "No...no, we wouldn't. Because Forge isn't there anymore. We have to take risks. We don't have a choice. Just being here is a risk we had to take." He rested his hand on Memfis' arm. "If we don't take the risks, then what else is going to blow up?"

There was a knock on the door, and Meris came in, followed by Afansa. "We came to see how Owyn is doing," Meris said. "No, Owyn, don't get up!"

Owyn snorted. "If I don't get up, I can't get a proper hug," he grumbled. He steadied himself on the back of Memfis' chair, then went to Meris and hugged her as tightly as he dared, feeling her lips brush against his cheek.

"My darling boy," she murmured. "Go and sit before you fall down."

"If I do fall down, it was totally worth it," he said as he turned back to his chair. He swayed slightly, but gathered himself as he felt a hand on his arm. He smiled at Afansa. "Thank you. I'm good." He sat down, then smiled at Meris. "I just want you to know that it was totally worth it."

Meris laughed and came around the table to sit next to Jehan. "Do we know anything?"

"Meris, is having heart visions like dancing?" Memfis asked. "We think that Owyn might have gone into vision shock because he was already drained from the constant heart visions."

Meris looked thoughtful. "That's an interesting theory," she said. "I'm not certain. We know so little about heart visions, and of that, some of it is only tales. I'll have to see what of our references were duplicated here. Then research will take time. I honestly don't remember if there is anything." She looked at Afansa. "Do you read, my dear?"

Afansa shook her head. "No, my lady."

"Afansa." There was a fond note in Meris' voice, and a slight hint of warning.

Afansa smiled. "No, Meris," she corrected. "I'll remember eventually."

Meris laughed as she took Afansa's hand. "I know this is all new to you. But we're all doing new things. And now...I think you'll be adding another. You're going to learn to read, to write, and to cipher."

Afansa looked puzzled. "I can cipher. I was a merchant. I can use an abacus, and I know the exchanges for changing Fire casts to Earth talents. I'm not entirely ignorant. I know that much."

"That's more than I know," Owyn said. "I never could remember how many talents to a cast."

"One cast is three talents and four grains," Afansa answered immediately. "And there are twelve grains to a talent, and twenty-five coppers in a cast."

Owyn blinked at her. "See, that's something I could never remember. But then, I didn't know how many coppers were in a cast until I was as tall as I am now. Which was when I first saw a cast."

Afansa looked puzzled. "How could you not know that? You were in Forge, weren't you? Didn't you go to your District school?"

Owyn looked down at his hands and licked his lips. "I...didn't go to school," he said quietly. "I was a street rat."

"Oh," Afansa murmured. She nodded. "I understand."

"Do you?" Owyn asked.

She smiled. "My mother was the village whore," she said. "So I understand completely. I always wanted to go to school. But we didn't have one in my village, and the Loremaster wouldn't allow me to go with the other children to the next village. He said I would be a bad influence, and I shouldn't put on airs." She sniffed. "Righteous old stick, he was."

Meris sighed. "We had a good number of righteous old sticks in the Fire tribe," she said. "But now, you've no need to worry about them. Either of you." She patted Afansa's hand. "Now, we'll need to arrange lessons. I'll speak to Lexi. Would you object to lessons with her daughters?"

"To learn to read? I'd study with fire mice!"

Owyn laughed. "I did study with fire mice!" he told her. "I read to them, out loud. It helped to be reading to someone who couldn't laugh when I made mistakes." He paused. "I don't think Trinket laughed, anyway."

"You have a fire mouse? As a pet?" Afansa asked. "I didn't think you could tame them!"

"I do, and I don't. I mean, she's not here," Owyn answered. "Not yet. She stayed behind in Terraces with my aunt when we came here. I didn't want her to get lost in the Palace, especially since we still have work to do. Once we're settled, then I'll bring her." He grinned. "And maybe reading to them helps tame them?"

"All right," Jehan said. "We have some work to do. Owyn, come to the healing center with me. We'll figure out your new diet."

"Meris, I'll come to the library with you and Afansa," Memfis said. "We'll start on the research."

AVEN LOWERED HIS SWORDS, feeling the quivering in his muscles that said he'd done too much. Or maybe, that he hadn't been doing enough. "I used to be able to dance longer," he grumbled, limping over to the fence that surrounded the dancing floor. Aria was sitting on a bench outside the fence; she smiled at him as he came off the floor, and handed a flask to him.

"Salted tea," she said. "I asked a servant for it when they came past."

"Thank you," Aven said. He leaned down and kissed her, then opened the flask and took a long drink.

"You dance very well," Aria said. She sipped her own tea. "And it is very much like how Owyn danced. But you're faster."

"You should see when there's a group," Aven said. He drank more of his tea and put his swords back into their case. "When Othi comes back, I'll ask him and some of our side cousins and demonstrate."

"Side cousins?" Aria asked. "What's a side cousin? Air doesn't have that."

Aven sat down next to her on the bench. "You know Water traces bloodline through the mother line. So our blood relations come from our mothers and their sisters, and their mother and her sisters. Arana was my grandmother. Her children are Ama, my aunt Jisa, and their brother, my uncle Tamir. He married into a different canoe, and he became part of his wife's family. They have six children, and those are my side cousins. Neera and Othi are my blood cousins."

Aria looked at him, frowning. "That's very confusing."

Aven shrugged and finished his tea. "That's how we do it," he said. "I think it's less confusing then how Fire does it. Were you there when Owyn explained how they trace lineage?"

"I don't remember," Aria said. "How do they do it? Through the mother line, or the father?"

"I'm not sure. Father line, I think. And Owyn says they don't usually marry the way they do in Earth. Him and Alanar, and Karse and Trey, they're unusual. Owyn says that in Fire, when you have children, the Loremaster records it in the *Book of Silver*. And if you want to have children, your bloodlines have to be researched so they can tell if you're too closely related to your partner. He said it could take weeks."

"Weeks? That's ridiculous!"

"That's Fire's way," Aven said. Then he studied Aria's expression for a moment, the narrowed eyes and stubborn jut of her chin. "And you're not going to change it."

"How did you know what I was thinking?"

"At this point? I know you. Outlawing slavery, the way we talked about? That's one thing. Changing how they record their bloodlines? That's entirely different. No, you're not going to push the entire Fire tribe to rebel."

"And they would not rebel when we outlaw slavery?" Aria asked.

Aven smiled. "They might push back. But that's not the same thing. If you try to change how they trace their lineage, that's going to change their identity, and the core beliefs about how the world works. We can't do that."

Aria frowned slightly. "But...I—"

"Would you tell Air that they needed to count their bloodlines through the mother line?"

"No!" Aria gasped, sounding shocked at the notion. Then she blinked, looked at Aven, and started laughing. "You've made your point."

"Good." Aven stood up and held his hand out to Aria. "Let's go see the guards drill. I want to see how Del is faring." He helped her to her feet, stealing a kiss as she laughed. He picked up his swordcase, and they started walking.

The guard barracks and the practice yards were behind the Palace, past the healer's garden and the kitchens. Aven could hear the sounds of practice before he could see them. Then they came around a corner and could see the crowd — men and women in livery, Water warriors in kilts and vests, and Karse, who clearly was trying to be everywhere.

"We'll need to adjust the livery," Aria murmured. "So our Water warriors will be comfortable wearing it."

Aven nodded. "That shouldn't take much adjusting. Do you see Del?"

"Not yet," Aria answered. They went closer, and Aven heard someone call their names. He turned to see Trey, waving.

"If you're looking for Del, he's over here," he called.

Aven touched Aria's arm, and they headed toward Trey. He waved again, and started walking away from them toward another fenced area. It was an archery range, and Del was standing at the line, holding a longbow. As they watched, he drew and released, and the arrow flew off to thump solidly into the target. Next to him, Danir had a similar, smaller bow.

"You'd never know he'd never done this before a week ago," Trey said as they reached him. "He's a natural. And we tried him on throwing spikes, too. He's going to be even better."

"Have you tried javelins?" Aria asked. Trey shook his head.

"Not yet," he answered. "We don't want to overwhelm him." He looked at the pair of archers, then back at the Palace. "I heard about Owyn. I just haven't had the time to go and see him. How is he?"

"More stable, this morning. But still unbalanced," Aven answered. "Fa is with him."

Trey nodded. "That's good. He'll be able to put things right." He turned as a man in livery came trotting toward them. "What is it, Hilah?"

"Captain wants you, Commander," Hilah said. "Over by the water butts."

Trey looked around. "And he didn't bellow? That's odd. Right. I'll be back in a minute." He looked at the archers again. "Del, once you finish that quiver, change over to crossbow. Danir, once you're done with yours, you're done. Your mother doesn't want you to push too hard your first day."

"Do I have to be done?" Danir protested. "This is fun!"

"I'll teach you to fletch arrows," Trey answered. "And to braid a bowstring. But it'll be enough shooting today. You'll feel it tomorrow."

Del lowered his bow and turned to look at Trey, smiling when he saw Aven and Aria. He nodded, looking down at the quiver stuck into the ground at his feet. He held up his gloved hand, fingers spread.

"Five more arrows?" Trey asked. "Good. You're doing really well."

Del grinned and reached down for another arrow. Trey nodded and turned back to Aven and Aria. "Stay and watch?"

"If we won't be in the way," Aria answered.

"No, you're fine. Aria, you shoot, don't you? If you want to take a turn, feel free."

Aria smiled. "Tomorrow, perhaps. I didn't bring my crossbow down."

Trey nodded, and trotted off across the practice yard, disappearing into the crowd. Hilah smiled and bowed.

"My Heir, it's an honor," he said. He glanced at the archery range. "Del is quite good. I wasn't aware that he knew how to shoot."

"He's only just started," Aria said.

Hilah nodded. He moved closer, standing just behind Aven and on his left. Aven felt something poke him in the ribs. He winced at the sudden, sharp pain, wondering if he'd been stung by an insect. But as he started to turn, Hilah grabbed his arm.

"I wouldn't, Fish," the guard said, his voice low. "If you move or shout, she dies."

CHAPTER
TWENTY-SEVEN

"What?" Aria turned toward them, and her eyes widened.

"And if you do anything, you both die," Hilah continued. "Now, do you see the archer over that way? In the corner, by the arch?"

Aven nodded slowly. "I see him."

"He has orders to kill the both of you if either of you tries to call for help. And he'll kill her first. So you're both going to be quiet, and we're going to walk that way, and through the arch." HIlah pushed Aven forward. "Drop the swordcase and walk."

The pain in Aven's side increased when he hesitated, and he winced and dropped the case. It landed with a thump, and Aven saw Del turn toward them. He looked puzzled for a moment, then laid down his longbow and turned to pick up his crossbow.

"Walk," Hilah said. "The both of you."

"What are you doing, Hilah?" Aria asked as they started walking.

"My lady says that she needs to finish what she started," Hilah answered. "She said she was closer than she'd ever been to breaking the cycle, and she wants another go at it."

Aven shuddered. "No."

"You don't get a say, Fish," Hilah said. "Maybe once you're human. But animals don't get a choice. Or a throne."

Aven swallowed, trying to think. Once they reached the outcropping of the wall, they wouldn't be able to be seen from the practice yard anymore. No one would know where they'd gone. "*Owyn, can you hear me?*" he tried to reach Owyn's mind, but had no idea if he'd be heard at this distance. "*Owyn, we're in trouble! Risha has men in the guard!*"

"Let Aria go," he said. "I'll go with you, if you let her go."

"Aven!"

"No," Hilah snapped. "Stop that. I was told to bring both of you. And if you don't stop yammering, I'll just let him kill you. Bringing your heads is an option."

"You know that my guard will kill you," Aria said in a low voice.

"You'll die first," Hilah answered. He sounded almost cheerful about it.

Aven could feel blood running down his side, and tried to think of something he could do. They were passing the wall, and were almost to the archway. If he went for Hilah, the archer would kill Aria — they were so close that there was no way he could miss. If Aven tried to get between the archer and Aria, Hilah would gut him, and Aria would still die. He stumbled, suddenly dizzy, and the pain in his side increased. Aven gasped, and Hilah swore, his fingers digging into Aven's arm.

"Just keep walking," he snapped.

"Stop hurting him!"

Hilah growled, but before he could say anything, there was a commotion behind them. Aven heard Karse's voice, and suddenly understood what Trey meant about the bellow.

"Aven!"

Hilah swore again. "Keep going!" he snapped, and pushed Aven forward. Aven stumbled again as another wave of dizziness washed over him. He heard something snap, heard someone cry out. Aven struggled to regain his balance, and saw the archer in front of them fall, a quarrel embedded in his chest. Hilah froze. Aven didn't — he spun, striking with the heel of his hand, driving it into Hilah's nose and snapping his head back. Hilah fell, dropping the bloody knife; Aven scooped it up and kicked the groaning Hilah onto his back, dropping his knee into the middle of Hilah's chest. He heard something crack, and Hilah howled in pain.

Good.

"Aven, don't kill him," Aria's voice pierced his rage. He didn't look up, pressing the point of the knife underneath Hilah's chin.

"My Heir?" Aven didn't move the knife. "He was going to kill you. I'm just returning the sentiment."

"We need to know what he knows," Aria said. She rested her hand on his shoulder. "I want him to live, my Water. For the moment."

Aven scowled. Then he raised his head, hearing Karse shouting his name again. The guard captain appeared around the corner, with Steward on his heels. Behind them were Jehan and Owyn.

"Report!" Karse snapped.

Hilah opened his mouth, and yowled when Aven poked him with the knife. "He didn't mean you," Aven snapped, looking down at the guard. "Aria?"

"He was taking us to Risha," Aria answered. "Who wants another attempt to kill my Water. There was another guard, an archer. He would have killed us both if we'd tried to call for help."

"Oh, fuck that!" Owyn breathed. "She left spies?"

"So that's why Del killed one of the guards?"

Aven jerked up at the sound of Trey's voice. He was standing next to Owyn, and Del was on his other side. "Del? Del shot the guard?" Aven stammered.

Del looked down at the crossbow that he was still carrying, then looked at Owyn.

"He saw you drop your swordcase," Owyn said. "You wouldn't do that unless there was something wrong. You would never do that to your swords. So he knew something was wrong." He frowned. "He said he saw blood. How badly are you hurt?"

"I don't know," Aven answered. "I know I'm bleeding, but I'm not sure how deep the wound is. Karse, my Heir wants him alive. Would you take him?"

"With pleasure," Karse growled. He looked back. "I need restraints!"

Aven didn't move or take the knife away from Hilah's throat until Karse came over to stand next to him, carrying a pair of heavy manacles. He cocked his head to the side and looked down. "Aven, should he be turning that color?"

Aven looked down, then rested his free hand on Hilah's chest. "Oh," he murmured. "I broke his ribs and punctured his lung. Fa—"

"I've got him," Jehan said. He turned. "I need a stretcher and four volunteers!" he shouted, then turned back to Aven. "You follow me. I want Alanar to look at your side."

"Yes, Fa," Aven said. He took the knife from Hilah's throat and handed it to Karse, then got to his feet. His head spun, and he swayed, feeling Aria grab his arm.

"Don't fall," she said. "I can't catch you if you fall."

"I'm fine," he said. "Just a little dizzy." He turned and pulled her into his arms. "Are you all right?"

"I was frightened," she said. "The idea of her hurting you again...she almost killed you before. If she had us again, had you again..." Her arms slipped around him, carefully avoiding his side. "Now, though, I'm not frightened. I am angry."

Aven nodded, closing his eyes and holding her. He wasn't sure if his shaking was from the aftermath of the fight, or from blood loss. Either way...

"I think I need to sit down," he said.

"Come lean on me."

Aven turned and saw that Steward had come up behind him. "Uncle," he said. "Thank you."

Steward looked startled, then smiled. "Well, we'll just say that's from the blood loss, hm?" he said. "I don't think you're thinking clearly." He slid his arm around Aven's back. "There's a bench on the other side of the wall. Then I'll see what I can do for that side while we wait for a healer."

"I'm not addled," Aven protested, leaning on Steward and letting himself be helped around to the bench. He sat down gratefully, then raised his arm so Steward could see the wound. "You are my uncle."

"He was your uncle," Steward murmured. "The one whose name was forgotten. He was your father's brother. I am..." He paused, then continued in a sad voice. "I'm no one."

"You're our uncle," Owyn said, his voice firm. "We're adopting you. Aria, tell him."

"I don't think I have to," Aria said. "You've done it quite well. And Del says you are his father. Odd that he's been adopted twice, isn't it?"

Steward looked up from his work. "Aria, my dear, there should be a basket, with bandaging and salves, over on the rack there. I'll need that and some water."

Del waved his hand, then handed the crossbow to Owyn and trotted off with Trey following him. They were back a moment later, with the basket and a bucket of water.

"I pulled that from the water butts myself," Trey said. "And we were all drinking from the water butts, so the water is safe." He set the bucket down next to Aven's feet. "Aven, I'm sorry."

"You had no idea he was a spy," Aven said, looking away and trying to ignore the stinging pain that accompanied whatever Steward was doing to him. "He was a Palace guard, wasn't he?"

"Yes," Trey said. "And once Karse gets back, I think we'll be having a good long talk with the other Palace guard who survived."

"Might want to make sure none of them slip off while you're busy," Owyn said softly. Trey looked at him, then nodded.

"Good point. I'll go talk to the Water warriors. We'll get the old guards confined to quarters under guard." He turned and bowed slightly to Aria, then headed off, shouting orders.

"He doesn't have Karse's bellow yet," Steward murmured. "But he'll get there. A roll of that bandaging, please, Aria? Thank you." He wound the bandages tightly around Aven's midsection, and tied them off. "That'll do, until we get Alanar or Treesi out here."

"I can go to them," Aven protested.

"You're not moving until a healer gets here," Steward said firmly. "You have no idea how pale you are right now."

Aven blinked. "I didn't think I'd lost that much blood."

"Uncle, he wasn't poisoned, was he?" Owyn asked. "Was that blade poisoned?"

Aven shook his head, then winced. "No, it couldn't be. I cut Hilah with it. There wasn't any poison in his blood when I checked to see why he was turning blue." He frowned slightly. "Not poisoned. No."

"Then why are you acting drunk?" Steward looked up, his eyes wide. "Del? You know the fastest way to the healing center. We need a healer now."

Del took off running. Owyn came closer and knelt down on the ground at Aven's feet. "Don't you go trying to die, Fishie. Just because I keep doing it doesn't mean you get to do it, too."

"Dying is on the list of things I'm not doing today," Aven replied. He closed his eyes, feeling suddenly tired, and oddly cold. "It's at the very top."

"Aven?" Aria said. He felt her hand on his shoulder, burning like a brand. "Aven, what is it?"

Aven swallowed. His throat felt dry. "I think...I think Del needs to hurry. I don't feel right."

"Aven!" Steward's voice was sharp, and Aven forced his eyes open and shook his head before turning to look at him.

"Uncle?"

"You stay with us, boy. Your mother will murder me twice if anything happens to you."

"I'll be fine once someone comes," Aven said slowly.

"He's slurring," Owyn gasped. "He...we need salt water. A lot of it!"

"Had...had tea."

"Mother of us all," Aria whispered. "It wasn't the blade that was poisoned. It was the tea!"

"Aven," Steward called his name. Hands on the side of his face, turning his head. Someone patting his cheek. "Aven, you stay awake. Aven, listen to me. Stay awake. Where's the blasted healer?"

AVEN WOKE UP AT THE bottom of a salt water pool, with no memory of how he'd gotten there. He recognized the tiles, though — this was the pool in his bedroom. How had he gotten here? He circled, then surfaced, wiping water from his eyes and looking around. The light coming through the windows cast long, purple shadows, and Owyn was sleeping on his bed. Aven leaned his arms on the edge of the pool and slapped the surface of the water with his tail. The sound was enough to wake Owyn, who jerked awake, then rolled to look at him.

"Wasn't expecting you to wake up before morning," he said. "How do you feel?"

Aven shrugged and started to lift himself out of the pool so he could start the change. Owyn coughed and sat up.

"No, you stay in the water. Your father says so. He says it'll help flush the rest of the poisons out of your blood." He swung his legs over the edge of the bed. "Remember, you don't have to talk, or sign. Just think it. I'll hear you."

Aven lowered himself back into the water, deep enough to keep his gills submerged. *"Did you hear me before?"*

"Heard you, and then I heard your father swear when I told him what you told me." Owyn grinned. "Did you know that when he really gets going, he could hold his own on Tannery Row in any of the taverns, and probably teach the drovers a thing or six? I should have been taking notes."

"My *father?*"

"Yes, your father." Owyn got up and walked over to sit on the floor next to the pool. "How are you feeling?"

"Better," Aven answered. *"What did they give me? And was it on the knife or in the tea?"*

"It was something in the tea," Owyn answered. "Jehan told me what, but I don't remember. He'll tell you when he comes to see you. Which will be later. He's busy right now."

"With Hilah?" Aven asked. *"Or did I kill him?"*

Owyn shook his head. "No, Hilah's alive. He's in the dungeons. And...let me see. You slept through most of the day. So, what you've missed. All the Palace guard who were here when we got here are under arrest, and each of them gets to have a lovely sit down with Steward, your father, Allie, and Aria, who is furious. I don't think I've ever seen her this angry, and she's scary right now."

"Aria? Scary?"

"I don't think her wings have gone down since we carried you inside," Owyn said. "She had to go through a couple of doors sideways. She looks...menacing. Yeah, that's the word. When they're done with the guard, then they're going on to the Palace servants, and Lexi will be part of that. She's just as mad, but she don't have the wings to show it. She did say something about sharpening a cleaver while she talked to her people, though."

"*Now you're teasing me.*"

Owyn laughed. "I am not, I promise!"

Aven smiled and ducked under the water again. When he surfaced, he asked, "*Who poisoned me?*" A thought occurred to him, and he rose up a little higher. "*Owyn, they didn't try to poison Aria, too? She had tea when I did. Just not salted tea.*"

"No, there was nothing in her tea," Owyn answered. "And Jehan says there's no signs of anything in her blood. He had Alanar check while he worked on you, then he checked again when Allie asked him to."

Aven shook his head, hearing water spray from his hair. "*That doesn't make sense,*" he said. "*Why try to kill me right before trying to kidnap me?*"

Owyn frowned and shook his head. "It only makes sense if you think it's two different people behind it," he answered. "You know how to truth-tell?"

"*I read about it. I haven't tried it.*"

"Allie is good at it," Owyn said. "Hilah didn't know about the poison. Or the tea. He was as surprised as we were. And angry."

"*Why angry? He wanted me dead, too.*"

"He didn't want you immediately dead. He wanted you dead later," Owyn corrected. "So, that's where Aria and Allie are. Del is doing something with his maps, and I think we're going to start searching tomorrow. Treesi is on duty in the healing center. And I'm here with you." He smiled. "Is the water cold?"

Aven looked down, then back at Owyn. "*No,*" he answered. Then he smiled, thinking. There was something Owyn had said to him once, out on the canoe. But it hadn't been safe to actually try it. Not in deep water. Here, though? "*Want to come in?*"

Owyn laughed and tugged his shirt up over his head. "I haven't had time to just be with you in...I think we were still out on the canoe." He stood up and started to unfasten his trousers. Aven nodded and pushed off from the wall, watching Owyn strip.

"*You've lost weight.*"

Owyn grimaced. "Apparently, it's the heart visions. Granna and Mem are going through the archives, trying to find more information. But she thinks that having heart visions are like smoke dancing. I'm having visions all the time, and it's burning a lot of energy. So that's what happened yesterday, and why I fell over so bad. Jehan says I need to eat more. I have a list, and Lexi has it, too." He walked over to the edge of the pool. "How deep is it?"

"*I won't let you go under,*" Aven answered. "*And it's maybe as deep as the hot spring.*"

"The one in Forge, in the bath?" Owyn sat down on the edge of the pool and slipped into the water — it came up to his chest. Aven smiled and swam around him, and Owyn laughed.

"*There's a bench. You should sit.*" Aven said. He led Owyn to the bench and let him sit, then joined him for a moment. "*Are you feeling better now?*"

"Me?" Owyn asked. "Feeling a bit like I'm being fattened up for market, but yeah. I really do need the extra fuel." He chuckled. "I'm under orders to keep food with me at all times. Nuts are best, Jehan says. So Trinket is going to love me."

"*Trinket already loves you.*" Aven slid his arm around Owyn, tugging him close. Owyn sighed and rested his head on Aven's shoulder.

"It's not easy, being a Companion," he said softly. "Being Aria's Companion."

Aven nodded. *"We never thought it would be. I'm not even sure either of us thought we'd ever get this far."*

"We had good reason," Owyn pointed out, turning his head so his nose brushed against Aven's cheek. "We've had people trying to kill us since...well, since before we even met." He sighed slightly, then twisted, so that he was straddling Aven's tail. "But we're alive, and they're not."

"Most of them aren't," Aven corrected.

"We can fix that," Owyn said, his voice firm. "We will fix that. And then everything is going to be fine. And we'll have kids, and everything will be all happy. Right?" He looked over his shoulder at the door. "Boy or girl?" he asked, turning back to Aven. Aven arched a brow, and Owyn smiled. "Is Aria having a boy or a girl? You know. I know you know."

Aven shook his head. *"Not telling. I promised her I wouldn't."*

Owyn sighed. "Well, I had to ask. I just...I really can't wait to find out. And I'm terrified to find out. I've never been around little babies before. I don't know what to do!"

"Me either. But we'll learn." Aven smiled and changed the subject. *"Do you remember, back on the canoe, you said it must be very useful to have gills?"*

Owyn looked thoughtful. "I...I don't remember. Did I?"

"You did," Aven said. *"And I agree."* He gently moved Owyn off of his tail and back onto the bench, then slipped underneath the water. He made one lap of the pool, then swam up in front of Owyn and ran his hands up Owyn's legs.

"Aven, what are you— *Aven*!"

CHAPTER
TWENTY-EIGHT

O wyn was surprised to find himself the first person awake
when he came out of Aven's room in the morning. Aven was
still stretched out on the bottom of the pool, still deeply asleep.
Owyn pulled the bell rope, then went to his own door, passing
through the sitting room to the bedroom door. He peered inside,
wondering how many lumps he'd find in the bed.

Two. Alanar hadn't slept alone. Good. He closed the door
softly and turned, going back out to the main room. He thought
about waiting in one of the overstuffed chairs, but the papers on
the table caught his eye. There were pages of maps, the drawings
running from one page to the next in long, elaborate corridors.
Owyn whistled as he studied them.

"This is going to take days," he murmured. He cocked his head
to the side, studying the maps. "I wonder what it would take to
open all this back up?" Then he frowned. "I wonder how well-lit it
is."

A soft knock, and the door opened; Lexi came in. She smiled
when she saw him.

"Good morning," she said. "Only one awake?"

"Seems like it," Owyn answered. "What can we do about
breakfast?" He looked around. "I'm...sort of used to being the one
who cooks it. It'll take me a while to get used to being served."

"You cook?" Lexi asked. "If you want to start coming down to the kitchens, I'll let them know—"

"I don't want to be in the way," Owyn protested. "I just...I miss it."

"Then you come down, and you can help. You wouldn't be the first Companion to do it. Or Firstborn, for that matter," Lexi said with a laugh. "I seem to remember Tirine sneaking down to the kitchens in the middle of the night to make herself coddled eggs when she couldn't sleep."

Owyn grinned. "Well, if the staff is used to it. What's a coddled egg?"

"Similar to poached eggs, but cooked with cream and cheese." Lexi nodded. "Now, I have your new diet, so I'll prepare that, and plenty of it. Should I choose for the others the way I have been, or do they have any preferences?"

"Aven likes fermented sea oak, if you have any. Del likes it, too," Owyn answered. "And there's a tea blend that Aria really likes, but I don't know if it's something they only have in Terraces."

"What's in it?"

Owyn sat down, thinking. "Ah...I'm not even sure. It's called Terraces Red, and it smells wonderful. Treesi would know what's in it, but she's still asleep."

Lexi nodded. "I'll see if we have any in our stores. What else?"

Owyn smiled. "Coddled eggs? Those sounded really good."

"And coddled eggs," Lexi agreed. "I'm supervising the cooking myself, so I'll be back with breakfast."

"Thank you." Owyn looked at the papers again. "Lexi, look at these?"

She came over and her brows rose. "Oh. These are very good."

"Del did them. They're—"

"The servant corridors," Lexi finished. "I know." She tapped one of the pages. "This is the section that runs down to the dock below the Palace. We use it to bring up supplies."

"How well-lit are they?"

"The ones that we use regularly? Very — there are lamps every six feet or so, and there are a half dozen older pages who are assigned to keep them filled and the wicks trimmed." She looked over the rest of the pages. "But I only know some of these corridors. The rest? I have no idea what the lighting is like." She looked at Owyn. "Sit down. I'll go get the breakfast started, and I'll send Danir up with something to tide you over until things are ready. You're looking pale."

"Am I?" Owyn sat down. "I was starting to think I was feeling pale."

"Sit," Lexi repeated. Then she left, and Owyn picked up the closest of the maps.

"If I were the Firstborn, where would they hide me?" he murmured, and frowned. "How do these fit into the layout of the Palace? We need floor plans for the entire Palace."

"*Those are in the library,*" Del said, sounding sleepy. Owyn looked up and started to turn, then realized that Del was standing in front of him. He hadn't come out of his own room — he'd come out of Owyn and Alanar's.

"Good morning," Owyn said. "You spent the night with Allie?"

"*He asked me to,*" Del answered. "*He didn't want to be alone, and Treesi is with Aria.*" He rubbed one hand over his face, then looked startled. "*You don't mind, do you? I wouldn't have said yes if I thought it would bother you!*"

Owyn shook his head. "It doesn't bother me. I'm glad you took care of him. I just...did he..." He frowned. "I didn't think you were interested—"

Del smiled. *"We didn't have sex. He didn't even ask. He just wanted the company."* He came over to the table. *"Why do you want the Palace floor plans?"*

"Trying to get a sense of scale," Owyn answered. "I—" He stopped when someone knocked on the door. The door opened, and Steward came in, followed by Danir and two servants carrying large trays.

"Good morning," he said. "Lexi asked me to escort Danir and the servants."

"Something to tide me over, she said," Owyn said. "This...this is a lot of tiding."

Steward laughed. "We'll need the table. Del, would you put your maps in order?"

Del collected the pages and put them aside, and the servants put out various plates and bowls. Cut fruit and cheese, some kind of sausage, a bowl of fermented sea oak, and several large pitchers. Bowls and spoons and plates. Danir set the table, poured what turned out to be fruit juice into a cup, and put it in front of Owyn. Then he looked up at Steward.

"That's fine, Danir," Steward said. "Thank you. Now, Lexi says that the rest will be ready shortly. Why don't you go and help her?" Danir nodded and he and the servants left. When the door closed, Steward asked, "Owyn, how's Aven?"

"Still asleep," Owyn answered. "But he woke up late yesterday. He seems to be fine." He grinned, remembering the previous night. "None the worse for wear, I think."

Steward nodded. "Good."

Del snapped his fingers, and signed quickly to Steward, who looked surprised. "I can bring copies, of course. All of them?" When Del nodded, he asked, "Why?"

"If this is about the floor plans of the Palace, I wanted to see how the hidden passages related to what's actually here. I need to see where they are in relation to everything else, so I have an idea where to look," Owyn answered. He glanced at Del, then back at Steward. "We might need to draw on them."

"That probably won't be the worst idea," Steward replied. "Especially since we don't want any more secrets. I know you both draw with a good hand, so I definitely have no objections. I'll bring them and you can work on them after you eat. Or I can set them up in the library and you can work there?"

Owyn considered it. "The library has bigger tables, and more room. We won't have to move when it's time to eat, or if we have other work to do. Just...how do we secure things when we're not there? I don't want things to end up in the fireplace again."

Steward folded his arms over his chest and tucked his chin, and Owyn served himself some of the fruit and cheese while he waited. Finally, Steward said, "I'll lock them in my office, if I have to. Or we can bring them back here."

Owyn nodded, and heard a door open. He turned and saw Treesi coming out of Aria's room, rubbing sleep out of her eyes. She smiled.

"Good morning. Oh, there's food already? Am I late?"

"No, I'm early," Owyn said. "I can't get used to not being up first, even if I'm not cooking. Lexi says I can come play in her kitchen, though." He grinned as Treesi laughed, then heard another door open behind him. He assumed it was Aria, until a hand settled on his shoulder, slid down his chest and up his throat. Owyn looked up — he didn't have much choice as Aven caught his chin, then claimed his mouth. The kiss went on for days, and wasn't nearly long enough, and Owyn had to bite down on a whimper when Aven finally let him go.

Aven smiled as he sat down next to Owyn. "Good morning."

Owyn coughed. "Good morning," he replied, and heard his own voice crack. Thankfully, everyone else seemed to ignore it. "You...you're getting better at that."

Aven chuckled. "I don't know. I think I need more practice."

"Practice doing what?"

Owyn and Aven both looked up — Aria was standing behind them.

"What are you practicing?" she asked.

"Kissing," Owyn answered. "Aven's getting better at it."

Aria smiled. "Are you? Let me see." She leaned over the low back of the chair and kissed Aven. It didn't seem to last as long as the one Owyn had gotten, but he couldn't be sure. He wasn't inside it, after all. Aria hummed as she straightened. "Yes, I do think I agree. But I need a comparison." And she leaned over the back of Owyn's chair.

Aria had been practicing, too, and Owyn was almost certain that time stopped entirely. This time, he did whimper when she moved away, and she giggled slightly as she stood up.

"I think you've both improved quite a lot," she declared.

"Do I get a turn?" Treesi demanded. "Because I think I need to catch up."

"Of course you get a turn," Aven answered. He held his hand out to Treesi, and when she took it, he pulled her into his lap. She giggled and kissed him.

"*May I have a kiss, too?*"

Del's voice was hesitant, almost shy, and Owyn looked around to see him standing near the table, still holding his maps. He was blushing, and biting his lower lip.

"Of course you can!" Owyn answered, and held his hand out. Del put the maps down on a side table and came closer. He took Owyn's hand and blushed harder. Owyn glanced at Treesi, then tugged Del closer. "You can sit with me, if you want. You don't have to be shy about asking."

Del nodded, and slipped into Owyn's lap. He shifted slightly, then buried his face in Owyn's neck. Owyn put his arms around Del.

"It's all right," he said softly. "You can want this. You can want to be close, even if you don't want to do anything else."

Del nodded, not raising his head. When he finally did look up, he bit his lip again, then kissed Owyn gently on the lips. He frowned, then shook his head.

"*That's not how Aven kissed you,*" he said. "*Or Aria. But I don't know how to do that.*"

"You kiss me the way you kiss me," Owyn said. "Don't worry about how anyone else does things. Your kisses are just as special." He smiled and tightened his arms around Del. "You're just as special."

Del sighed softly and rested his head on Owyn's shoulder. Then he sighed again and closed his eyes, and Owyn looked up to see that Aria was behind him, combing her fingers through Del's hair.

Lexi arrived with more servants carrying trays, and the table was laden with breakfast. Owyn reluctantly released Del, then pushed his chair away from the table.

"I should check on Alanar," he said. "It's not like him to sleep this late." He walked around the table to the room he shared with his husband. He knocked gently on the bedroom door before letting himself in. "Allie?"

Alanar was sprawled on his back in the middle of the bed, the sheet drawn up to his waist. Owyn couldn't tell if he was asleep or not, so he went closer and sat down on the edge of the bed, reaching out to run his hand down Alanar's bare chest. "Allie, it's time for breakfast."

Alanar took a long breath, and reached up to wrap his hand around Owyn's wrist. He tugged Owyn further onto the bed.

"Look what I caught," he murmured, his voice still thick with sleep. "Allie's spark."

Owyn blinked. "What? Allie, since when do you call me that?"

Alanar chuckled. "He's still asleep. I get to be the one up front for a change."

"You..." Owyn paused. There was something different about his voice. It took Owyn a minute to realize that Alanar was speaking with the same sort of cadence that Aven had. A Water accent. "Oh. Virrik? You...you haven't done this before." He tugged against Alanar's hand, his mind racing. He knew his husband claimed to have his dead lover sharing his mind, had shared what Virrik was telling him, but this was the first time Virrik had spoken to others. "Come on. Breakfast is ready, and there's fermented sea oak. If Allie stays asleep long enough, you can have some."

Alanar laughed. "He'll never forgive me. I made him try some once. He said he was still tasting it a week later."

Owyn grinned. "He told me that story. Virrik...how come you're talking? Like this, I mean. You haven't done this before."

Alanar shrugged. "I wanted to see if having someone else using the body would mean things would work differently. I wanted to see if I could see you. But his eyes don't work, no matter who is behind them." He frowned slightly. "Your heart is racing. But you're not aroused. Am I scaring you?"

Owyn coughed. "Umm...a little, yeah."

"I don't want to scare you," Alanar said, and let Owyn's wrist go. "You make Allie happy. You're good to him."

Owyn sat up and rubbed his wrist. "I love him."

"I know," Alanar said, and raised his left hand. The pledge bracelet shone in the dim light. "He'd never have asked you for permanence if there'd been any doubt in him that you loved him.

That's not the healer's way. And you'd never have put this on his wrist if you didn't love him. That's not Fire's way. And it's not your way."

Owyn reached out with his left hand, taking Alanar's. "I love him," he repeated. "I wish I'd had the chance to know you. But I promise I'll keep making him happy."

Alanar smiled. "You make us both happy, you know. I like how he feels when he's with you."

"Good. Now, there's breakfast, and it's getting cold."

Alanar nodded. "Then I'll let him wake up. It was nice to talk with you, Owyn."

Owyn licked his lips. "It was nice to meet you, Virrik. Just...don't do that again?"

Alanar laughed. Then he went limp. It was only for a moment, but that moment was enough to frighten Owyn to his bones. Then Alanar yawned and opened his eyes.

"Good morning," he mumbled. "Am I late for breakfast?" He frowned. "Your heart is racing. What's wrong?"

"I don't know," Owyn answered slowly. "Allie...what would you say if I told you I'd just had a whole conversation with Virrik?"

Alanar started to laugh. "Really, Wyn?"

"Really. Like...really, really. It was...fuck, Allie, it wasn't you in there!"

Alanar sobered immediately and propped himself up on his elbows. "You're not joking?"

"Love, I wish I was."

"I..." Alanar frowned and sat up. "So, does that mean that I'm really insane, or really not alone in my head?"

Owyn sighed. "I don't know," he said. "I think we need to ask Jehan that."

Alanar nodded. "You're right. Let me get up. I'll come meet you at the table. Go eat. You need to eat." He ran his fingers through his short hair. "Wyn...don't say anything to the others? I want to talk to Jehan first."

Owyn swallowed. "I'm not sure I'll be able to hide it, Allie," he said. "Aven and Aria, they'll notice."

"Right. Of course they will. They know you." Alanar grimaced. "Stay here, then. Let me get dressed. Then I'll come out with you. You still need to eat, though, so I guess we'll have to tell them first."

"They're all at the table. And Steward, he's out there, too."

Owyn watched as Alanar shifted off the bed. He was getting better about moving around their room, now that he knew where things were, and what each obstacle actually was. His Air sense, Owyn had learned, told him there were things around him, but the knowledge of what those things were came from practice. In the new rooms, he was having to remap his entire world. But he was learning, and he made his way to the clothes press, took some things out, and brought them to the bed.

"Do I have a shirt and trousers?" he asked. "I think some of the pins fell out."

"I'll check later," Owyn said. "And yes."

"Do they match?"

Owyn grinned. "They match. You're fine."

Alanar nodded and turned, heading into the bathing room. When the door closed, Owyn took a deep breath. He wasn't sure what this meant, but he didn't think any of it was good. He just wasn't sure how it was bad, either. He didn't think Virrik would hurt anyone. But he hadn't thought Allie was capable of hurting anyone, either. Not until he'd gone insane thinking Owyn was dead, and attacked Treesi.

No, he was better now.

If better included having your dead lover in your head.

Owyn sighed and took another deep breath as Alanar came out of the bathing room. He picked up the shirt and asked, "So how is Aven? Did he stay in the pool last night, like Jehan said he should?"

"He did," Owyn answered. "And he's fine this morning."

Alanar grinned. "Did you stay in the pool?"

"No," Owyn laughed. "I slept in the bed."

"You spent some time in the pool," Alanar said as he pulled the shirt over his head. "I heard you."

Owyn laughed. "Were you listening at doors again, love?"

Alanar looked indignant, which was impressive for a man wearing no trousers. "I was not! I was coming to check on my patient. Jehan says that verdiscent salt poisoning can be nasty in Waterborn."

"That's what it was!" Owyn said. "I couldn't remember. I've never heard of it before."

Alanar nodded. "Jehan should be coming to see him. He wanted to talk to Aven about it." He sat down to pull on his trousers, then stood up to adjust them. He buttoned them, and ran his hands down his chest. "I'm ready. I think I'm ready."

Owyn walked around the bed and rested his hands on Alanar's waist. "You know I love you, right?"

Alanar smiled. "Of course I know." He clicked his fingernail against his pledge bracelet. "You'd never have made this for me if you didn't." He kissed Owyn, running his hands up Owyn's arms to frame his face. "Now let's go. I can hear your stomach growling."

CHAPTER
TWENTY-NINE

O wyn took Alanar's hand and led him out of the bedroom. The table was laden with food, and Lexi and the servants were gone. Del had claimed the chair next to Aven, so Owyn brought Alanar to the empty seats on their side of the table.

"You didn't finish this, Owyn," Aven said, and pushed Owyn's unfinished fruit and cheese across the table. "There's tea, and Lexi said that the smaller plate of coddled eggs is all yours. And that I'm not to eat them, because there's cheese in them. There are boiled eggs for me." He cocked his head to the side. "What's wrong?"

Owyn laughed. "Told you," he said softly to Alanar. He pulled the smaller plate of coddled eggs over to him. "There's six of these. She expects me to eat six eggs?"

"She expects you to eat until you're full. And yes, you were right. They know you too well," Alanar said. "Eat, and I'll explain what I can." He folded his hands and rested them on the table. "Apparently, Virrik had a conversation with Owyn this morning, and I wasn't there."

"What?" Treesi yelped. "Allie...how?"

Alanar shook his head. "I don't know. I...I don't know what it means. I mean...either I'm imagining he's in my head, and I'm talking to myself, or he's actually there and I'm two people in one skull. I don't know which of them this is pointing to. Once we eat, I want to talk to Jehan. Who needs to talk to you anyway, Aven."

Aven had leaned forward, and was resting his chin in his hand, his eyes narrowed. It took Owyn a moment to realize what he was doing. "Aven, are you...are you examining him from over there?"

Aven smiled. "Am I being obvious?"

"If you stared any harder, you'd burn holes in his shirt," Owyn answered.

"Don't do that. I like this shirt. It feels good." Alanar turned toward Owyn. "Would you load a plate for me? Please? I smell porridge."

"Tell us more?" Aria asked. She filled a bowl with porridge and passed it to Aven, who handed it to Owyn. "What happened?"

"Not...not a whole lot," Owyn answered. He prepared the porridge the way Alanar liked it, then put it in front of his husband. "Spoon on your left. Fruit?"

"Yes, please. And some of those eggs with the cheese in them."

Owyn continued as he made the plate. "I thought Allie was asleep. I touched him, and he grabbed my wrist. He...Virrik, he said he wanted to see if Allie's body would work differently because he was the one using it. He wanted to see if he could see me." He glanced at Alanar. "He didn't."

"That's not a shock," Alanar muttered. "The nerves behind my eyes are dead. He knew that."

"We talked," Owyn continued. "I invited him to breakfast, told him we had sea oak—"

"Oh, he wouldn't!" Alanar sputtered.

"He said you wouldn't forgive him if he got up and ate some. He...he said I made him happy, because I made you happy. And when he realized he was scaring the actual fuck out of me, he left."

"And that's when I woke up?" Alanar asked. He sighed. "I...I really need to talk to Jehan." He ate some of the porridge, then swore softly. "I am not going to let them put that coat back on me.

I'm not." He turned toward Owyn. "Wyn, don't let them lock me up alone in that room again."

"Do you want me to go find Jehan?"

Owyn jerked. He had forgotten that Steward was at the table. "Ah...please? And...fuck." He turned back to the others. "What are we supposed to be doing today?"

"Searching. I want answers," Aria answered. "And starting to plan the progress. But searching first."

"Then we'll need the floor plans so we can lay Del's maps out on them," Aven said.

Steward nodded and stood up. "I'll bring those back once I find Jehan." He bowed slightly and left. Aven closed his eyes and sighed, rubbing his hands over his face.

"This is...I don't even know what this is," he said. "Treesi, have you ever heard of anything like this? You have more book-learning than I do."

Treesi closed her eyes and frowned slightly. Then she shook her head. "No...and yes. I mean, I've heard of people losing their wits and thinking that they were hearing voices, or that they were other people. But I'm not sure this is the same."

"And how do we tell?" Alanar asked. "I mean, am I insane? I...I don't feel insane. But how would I know?" He reached out toward Owyn, his hand shaking. Owyn took it between his own.

"It'll be all right, Allie," he said. "I'm not going to let them lock you up or take you away." He glanced at Aria, and she nodded.

"I won't allow it, Alanar," she said. "You are mine, as much as Owyn. I won't let anyone take you or hurt you."

Alanar shivered. "And if I try to hurt someone again?"

"I'm not letting you do that," Owyn said. He squeezed Alanar's fingers. "I won't let you hurt anyone. And I won't let anyone hurt you. And I'll do a better job of it this time."

Alanar snorted. "That wasn't your fault, love." He raised Owyn's hand to his lips and kissed his knuckles, then let go of his hand. "Eat, Owyn."

"You eat, too." Owyn turned back to his eggs and studied them for a moment — the coddled eggs looked like poached eggs, each in a cup just big enough to hold it. "These look interesting. How do you eat them?"

"With a spoon?" Aven asked. "Tell me how they are."

Owyn grinned and picked up a spoon, digging into the first egg. The yolk was still soft, but not messy, and he scooped the first bite into his mouth. Whatever cheese the cook had used in it was smooth and tangy, and somehow didn't overpower the egg. "Oh," he mumbled. "Oh, this is good. This is really good. Allie—"

"Once I'm done with the porridge," Alanar said. "Don't worry about me. Eat."

Owyn turned back to his plate and the eggs. Between bites of egg, he finished the small plate of fruit and cheese, and managed to keep himself to a single piece of bread. He looked longingly at the porridge before going back for another egg.

All six little cups on his plate were empty.

He blinked, then looked around. "What happened to my eggs?"

"You ate them," Aven said, sounding both amused and impressed. "All of them. I'm not sure where you put them. I don't think I could eat six eggs."

"No, I..." Owyn looked down, and realized something. "I'm full."

"After six eggs? I should hope so!" Treesi said.

"No..." Owyn leaned back in his chair. "That's...look, when you spend your growing years on the streets, and you're always hungry, you get used to it. Hungry doesn't mean the same thing to me that it means to other people. I was always hungry when I was little, so hungry was just...normal for me. So when I say I'm hungry, I'm really sort of reminding myself that I should eat. That I can eat, whenever I want. And right now? I'm full." He looked at the cups again, thinking. "You know, I think that I've been hungry for days, the same way I used to be when I was on the streets. Maybe longer than days. I just didn't notice."

"I thought we'd broken you of that habit a long time ago."

Owyn looked up and smiled. Memfis was standing in the doorway, and Owyn could see Jehan behind him. "Mem!"

"You used to have to be reminded to eat," Memfis continued. "I used to have to give you permission to eat, and leave plates where you would find them, so you would be reminded when I wasn't there to remind you." He came into the room, and Jehan closed the door behind them.

"Steward said he needed to get something, and he'd be along soon," Jehan said. "Now, am I understanding this correctly? You can't tell when you're hungry?"

Owyn frowned. "Ah...that's not quite it," he said slowly. "I mean...huh, how do I explain this?" He drummed his fingers on the table. "When you get hungry, what do you do?"

Jehan looked puzzled. "I get something to eat."

"Because you know that 'hungry' means you have to eat," Owyn said. "You learned that, and I bet you never had to worry about where your next meal came from. None of you did. When I was growing up, hungry was...was like breathing. It was just there. It was something my stomach did, and I couldn't stop it, like I couldn't stop breathing. I ate when I could, but I never stopped being hungry." He shrugged. "I thought I'd never have to worry about my next meal ever again. But it hasn't been long enough for me to learn that always being hungry isn't normal."

"I'll remind you," Alanar said, reaching over and taking Owyn's hand. "I didn't realize, or I'd have started doing it sooner."

"It wasn't a problem before," Owyn said. He leaned back in his chair. "I just need to remember to eat more, and more often. And now I'm not sure if I should eat any more or not."

"Don't," Memfis warned. "Not yet. In an hour, maybe. If you eat now, you'll purge."

"Do you feel better?" Aven asked.

"What, you can't tell?" Owyn grinned as Aven balled up a napkin and threw it at him. "Yes, I feel better. But really, you can't tell?"

"I couldn't tell you were starving to death under my nose," Aven answered. "I don't think any of us noticed."

"Probably because it was gradual," Jehan said. "As the heart visions grew stronger, the draw on his body also increased." He frowned slightly. "I need to talk to Meris. I need to know what to watch for when we finally go off on progress."

"And we have to do that?" Treesi asked. "We have to go traipsing out over all of Adavar?"

"Not all," Aria corrected. "Just the path that Axia once walked. And not over the water, because almost everyone who lives there is already here." She sipped her tea. "And yes. It's required. And it's necessary. Can you think of a better way to reach everyone, to let them know that we are here? And to search for my father?"

"Risha is on the deep—" Aven started.

"She won't stay there. She can't stay there," Aria interrupted. "There is no one on the deep who will help her, and Aleia is hunting her. She has to come on land. The question is where?"

Del snapped his fingers, then signed, "*North. There's nothing south for her. South is Terraces and ashes*"

"He's right," Jehan said. "When Steward gets here, we'll see about sending patrols north to start scouting." He turned in his chair as the door opened. Steward came in with his arms filled with rolls of paper. He stopped and looked around.

"I missed something?"

"A discussion that can happen once we are finished, and while Del transfers his maps to the floor plans," Aria answered. "Sit and have something to eat. There is plenty."

"Fa, what came of the questioning?" Aven asked. "Who is trying to kill me? Is it Risha?"

"No. No connection to Risha at all," Jehan answered. "It was an exceptionally eager and very young serving girl who doesn't know the difference between sea salt and verdiscent salt."

"Verdiscent salt?" Aven repeated. "The salt we use to make green dyes for tapestry?"

Jehan nodded. "Remember your lessons? Why don't we make green taipa to wear?"

Aven looked thoughtful. "Because..." he stopped, his eyes wide. "Because the green dye is poisonous, and absorbs through the skin."

"And to get the green dye, you mix verdiscent salt with—"

"Brown seaweed extract," Aven answered. "Which...Fa, what am I missing? We don't have brown seaweed extract here, do we?"

"No, but the same compound in brown seaweed that extracts the green dye can be found in that tea you're drinking," Jehan said, pointing to the teacup. "Tannin."

"Mother of us all," Treesi breathed. "If it's that poisonous, why do they even have that in the kitchens?"

Steward coughed. "Laundry," he said. "The laundresses use it to take oil stains out of cloth. At least, that's what Lexi tells me. It shouldn't have been in the scullery, but apparently someone left a jar there after using it to clean linens."

Aven looked down at his tea, then back at his father. "You're saying this was an accident?"

Jehan nodded. "It was an accident. A serving girl who wanted to make her pretty Heir and her very pretty Water happy. She is very sorry, and is very worried that you'll put her out."

Aria reached out and rested her hand on Aven's arm. "What are you thinking? This should be yours to say."

"I'm not sure," Aven said. "I...it was an accident, but even an accident could have killed me." He looked around the table. "What should I do?"

Owyn laced his fingers together and rested his elbows on the table. "What does the law say?"

Del grimaced. "*You won't like the answer.*"

Owyn groaned. "I was afraid you'd say that. Right. What can we do?"

"It was an accident," Treesi said. "Why does anything need to be done?"

Steward sighed and put the rolls of paper down on a chair. "Normally, a mistake of this magnitude would lead to her being dismissed. But I hesitate to do that — her work here supports her younger siblings. They're Palace fosterlings."

Aven groaned. "Uncle!" He rubbed his hand over his face. "How many siblings? And how old is she?"

Steward took a seat and folded his hands on the table. "She's fifteen. And there are three. Nine-year-old boy, five-year-old boy, and a three-year-old girl." He smiled. "They've been here a little under a year. She marched up to the gates as bold as you please, with the little ones in tow, and told me that I was giving her a job."

"And their parents?" Aria asked. "Are they alone?"

"They are," Steward answered. "Their mother died when the youngest was born, and their father died when his fishing boat sank last year."

Aven closed his eyes and groaned again. "Wonderful. We can't put her out. I don't even want to know what the law says, if Del says we won't like the answer. But I have to do something. What do I do?"

"Assign her to you," Alanar answered. "She's now your assistant in the healing center. Her punishment is that she needs to learn how not to kill people by accident."

Aven sat up. "Can I do that?" he asked. "Uncle, can I do that?"

Aria laughed. "I say you can do that," she said. "I like it. Uncle, what is her name?"

Jehan looked up at Steward. "Since when are you everyone's uncle?"

"Yesterday," Steward answered. "They all decided yesterday, and I wasn't given a say in the matter." He smiled. "Not that I'm objecting. Now, her name is Gathi, and I will tell her that her punishment is that she is to attend Healer Aven when he is in the healing center, so that she learns not to make this kind of mistake ever again."

"I'll meet her later," Aven added. "If she's quick, she might make a good healing assistant by the time we go on this progress. Perhaps she might even benefit from going to Terraces for more training." He looked at Aria. "What do you think?"

Aria nodded. "Good. Very good. Now, Steward, tell me about the guard. What else did Hilah have to say? Was there anything of use?"

Steward shook his head. He gestured to a cup, and Aven reached out and picked it up, filling it from one of the pitchers. "I don't think that's salted," he said as he passed it to him.

"Salted tea doesn't bother me," Steward said. "My grandmother was Water."

Aven blinked and looked at his father. "You might be part Water? You never told me that!"

Jehan shrugged. "I've never been entirely sure of anything other than Earth. And honestly, a drop more Water in your veins? Doesn't seem to be important. Now, the guard. Steward?"

Steward took another sip of tea and put his cup down. "There were five guards left who still answered to Risha. They were left behind with instructions to bring the Heir and her Water to Risha by any means necessary. There was a meeting place set, and a signal. We're sending a squadron of guards to the meeting place and they'll give the signal. We'll see what happens."

"Which guards are you sending?" Owyn asked.

"Trey picked them himself, and he'll be leading them," Steward answered. "There wasn't much else that Hilah could tell us. He doesn't know where Risha went, except for what Del just suggested — she has a hiding place somewhere north. He's never been there, but he knows it exists."

"That's something," Owyn said. He reached out and picked up another piece of cheese, broke it in half, and ate a piece. "What else?"

"None of the other guards knew even that much," Alanar answered. "They all answered to Hilah and to the guard that Del killed."

"So we really don't know much more than what we already were thinking?" Owyn asked. He ate the other half of his cheese and leaned back in his chair, smiling as Alanar rested his hand on the back of his neck. He closed his eyes and sighed, then chuckled when he felt warmth. "I'm fine, love."

"I'll be the judge of that."

Owyn laughed, tipping his head back. "And?"

"You're fine." Alanar started stroking Owyn's neck with his fingertips. "What are we doing now?"

"Well, I have an assistant to start training," Aven said. "And you, me and Treesi should go and finish preparing the healing center. Gathi can help with that."

"I need to talk to Jehan," Alanar said. Jehan arched a brow, but said nothing.

"And Del and I need to map the tunnels out onto the floor plans," Owyn added. "Mem, you want to help?"

"I'm supposed to meet Lady Meris in the library again this morning," Memfis said. "As a matter of fact, I should be there now."

"Aria, I have paperwork to go over with you," Steward said. "And we need to start planning the progress. In addition, Owyn suggested a census, and I think that's a good idea."

Aria paled. "I know nothing of planning such things," she said. "I have never done such things."

"I'd be very surprised if you had," Steward said with a smile. "You're going to learn. There is a great deal you need to learn. So let's start with this."

CHAPTER THIRTY

There was a knock on the door, which opened to reveal Lexi. She came into the suite and bowed slightly. "My Heir, several wagons just arrived from Terraces. They're led by a young man named Marik, and one of our guards?"

"Oh, Marik and Esai?" Aria said. "They were to bring the rest of our things."

"They're trustworthy?" Lexi asked.

"Marik is my sister's son," Jehan said. "And Esai is true to the Heir. They're safe."

"Very good," Lexi said. "I'll order the wagons unloaded, and the boxes brought here."

"And bring Marik and Esai to the Heir's office, Lexi," Steward said. "I'm sure they'll want to see Aria."

"Very good," Lexi repeated. "And I'll have them assigned rooms."

"Room, I think," Jehan murmured. "No, wait. Marik won't stay inside. I..." He looked at Steward. "I don't have any ideas."

"I remember. Caves are fine. Houses aren't." Steward frowned. "Ah...Lexi, the mews. Are they still closed off?"

"The mews? They haven't been used in years!" Lexi protested.

"I know. Do you think they can be cleaned out and arranged for Marik and Esai, before dark? The falconer's quarters are attached, and I think Marik will be comfortable there. And it will let his birds be nearby. If you see a very large bird hanging around, it's with Marik."

"Oh?" Lexi smiled. "I'll arrange things." She bowed again and left.

"Thank you. And...I have an office?" Aria asked. "Where?"

"When you're done eating, I'll show you. It's a very nice office. Overlooks the cliffs and the sea."

Aria nodded. "I'm finished. Shall we get to work?" She stood up, setting her napkin on the table, then leaned down and kissed Aven. She made her way around the table to each of the Companions, then stopped at Steward's chair. "And we can talk about sending patrols north."

"Oh?" Steward stood up and offered his arm. "In addition to the guards that are going with Trey?"

"Yes. I'll tell you as we go." Aria took Steward's arm, and they left the room, Memfis following in their wake.

Jehan turned toward Alanar. "What did you need to talk about?"

Alanar took a deep breath. "First, tell me the truth. That coat that you had me wear when I was out of my head. It's still in Terraces, isn't it?"

"Now I'm terrified," Jehan said. "Yes. Why?"

"Because Virrik had a conversation with Owyn this morning, and I wasn't part of it."

"Had a conver—" Jehan stopped. He looked at Owyn, then at Alanar. "Tell me."

"I thought Allie was still asleep. I went in to get him for breakfast, and he grabbed my wrist. Told me he wanted to see if Allie's body would work different since there was someone else behind the eyes." He thought about the conversation. "His voice was different. He had a Water accent. And when he realized he was scaring me, he left."

Jehan whistled, then rubbed his hand over his face. "This is new and different. I've never heard of something like this." He looked thoughtful. "And I seem to be saying that quite a lot around you."

"Me?" Alanar asked. "Or us?"

"Collective you," Jehan answered. "I realize that these are extraordinary circumstances. But every time I think I'm getting used to it, the Mother finds a new way to work through you. Again, collective you."

"Fa?" Aven said.

Jehan smiled at him. "Aven, when I assessed your healing ability out on the deep, what did I say you were?"

"Level two," Aven answered.

"That's all?" Treesi blurted.

"That's all," Jehan answered. "Then we went south, and things happened. And the next time I saw you, you weren't just a level five, you were a natural five. But when I tested you the first time, you weren't."

"That's not possible," Alanar said. He frowned slightly. "At least, I didn't think it was possible. You either are a natural five, or you're not."

"Exactly," Jehan said. "Training might raise you one level. Two, if you're very good. There's no way that simple training would elevate someone to a natural five." He took a deep breath. "Unless there was help."

"You're saying the Mother pushed me to be more than I was," Aven said. "That...Fa, I'm not sure if I should be insulted or not."

"You needed to be more, to save my life. To save my life twice," Owyn said. "I'm not complaining that she shoved you into deeper waters." He frowned. "She did it to me, too. The heart visions. She put that on me."

"And she let you come back from the dead," Alanar added. "Don't forget that."

"As if I could," Owyn said. He grinned. "And now Alanar is two people, and he's not crack-pot insane."

"We're still not sure of that," Alanar said.

"No, I'm sure now," Owyn replied. "Because you weren't you. You were him, and it was different enough that it was kind of scary." He frowned, then pointed at his husband. "Virrik, don't you dare try that when we're alone in bed."

Alanar burst into laughter. "I don't think he could. I was asleep, after all. I don't think he could take control when I'm awake."

"Yeah, let's not find out," Owyn grumbled, and turned to see Jehan studying the table with rapt fascination. Across from Owyn, Aven was making a study of the inside of his teacup, and Del looked as if he was going to burst into flames. "Oh. Sorry. That was a bit much."

"Just a bit," Aven said. He picked up his tea and drained it, then shook his head. "The Mother is taking a very active role in this. Why didn't She before? She could have." He frowned. "Couldn't She?"

"When She had the right tools," Owyn said. "What about Del, and Treesi?"

Jehan looked over at where Del and Treesi were sitting. He smiled, then shrugged. "I honestly have no idea. Nor will I pretend to know the mind of the Mother. But She definitely has the right tools to work with now."

"Speaking of work, we have some," Treesi said. "So we should get to it." She stood up and walked around the table, stopping to kiss Owyn as she passed him. "Try not to push too hard today."

Owyn smiled up at her. "I'll be good. I'm going to be here with Del, drawing." He reached out and picked up another little egg cup. "And eating."

The servants arrived to clear the table as the healers left. Owyn explained to them what he and Del were going to be doing in the suite, and they cleared the food and the dishes from the long table and left. By the time Owyn and Del had moved chairs and spread out the floor plans, Lexi returned with more servants, and they turned a piece of furniture against one wall into a long array of nibble food and drinks.

"What's all this?" Owyn asked.

"You need to eat," Lexi said. "The Senior Healer's orders. So there's to be something here at all times. Everything here will stay without spoiling for most of a day." She wiped her hands on her apron and came to look at the long table and the floor plans. "Do you need any supplies for this?"

Owyn looked at Del, who signed, *"We'll need vine charcoal, pens and ink, and colored drawing chalk."*

Owyn relayed the list to Lexi, who nodded. "I'll bring everything right away."

Once she was gone, Owyn walked around, picking up small, heavy items that he used to weigh down the curling corners of the paper. "All right," he said. "Where do we start?"

"We need the chalk first. I need to color the different types of corridor." Del laid one of his smaller maps down and pointed. *"This one is a servant passage. There's almost always someone here. But this one—"* He tapped the paper. *"This one is a relic from a rebuild. No one uses it."*

Owyn nodded. "So one color will tell us where there's nothing to hide, because the servants would notice if something was there?"

"Blue, I think," Del answered without looking up. *"Green for where we need to look. And we'll find new corridors as we go, I think. We'll need to mark those on the maps so we can come back to them later."*

Owyn whistled softly. "Just tell me which is which." He looked down. "Which maps are we marking?"

"*The smaller ones we'll draw and give to everyone so that they don't get lost as we search.*" He looked up and grinned. "*I fell asleep thinking of this. About how we were going to search. Because there wasn't much else to do — I can't talk to Alanar. He's very sweet, but he can't read the signs, and he can't hear me.*" He shrugged. "*The next time I share a bed with him, I want you there so we all can talk.*"

"Well, the next time you share a bed with him, I'll make sure to be there," Owyn said. "Now, I have some vine charcoal. I'll go get it, and we can get started."

"HEALER AVEN?"

Aven heard his name, but he was shoulders deep in a cabinet, trying to reach the last three jars at the very back. "Just a moment," he called. He grabbed one of the jars and held it out blindly. "Take this, would you? Put it on the table."

Someone took the jar, and he reached for the next jar, pulling it forward. When he'd gotten the last one, he took the two and backed out of the cabinet, sitting down on the ground with a jar in each hand. A dark-skinned girl in servant livery held her hands out.

"I can take those," she said.

Aven handed her the jars, then slowly got to his feet. "Are you Gathi?"

She turned pink. "Yes, Healer. Housekeeper says I'm to attend you. That it's my punishment for almost—" She bit her lip, then blurted, "I'm sorry!"

Aven nodded. "I know. It was an accident. And this isn't a punishment. It's a lesson. When I'm done with you, you'll never make that sort of mistake again." He grinned. "You might make new and better ones, but you'll never make *that* one again."

As he hoped, she giggled and relaxed. "I'm not in trouble?"

"You weren't trying to hurt me," Aven answered. "You knew I needed salt in my tea. You just picked the wrong salt. Do you know why it's the wrong one?"

She shook her head. "I didn't even know there was more than one kind of salt!"

"There are, and that particular salt is only poison when mixed with tannin, and things that contain tannin. Like tea," Aven answered. "So you, Gathi, are going to learn the basics of healing, starting with possets and potions, and you're going to learn which are safe all the time, which are safe only in small doses, and which should never be mixed. Can you read?"

She nodded. "Housekeeper is strict. I had to start learning when I came here. But I don't read well yet."

"You'll get better. There's a lot of reading when you're a healer. And if you apply yourself, then perhaps you can become a healing assistant. If you have the gift, maybe you can even become a Healer." He gestured to the jars on the table. "We'll start here. These have been stored for a long time. The herbs in these jars will make a lotion against joint pain, but only if the oil is still good. We are going to open each jar and smell them." He picked up the closest jar and pulled the cork, sniffing the contents. Then he held the jar out. "What do you smell?"

Gathi sniffed, then took a deeper breath. "Nothing," she answered. She looked up. "That means it's dead, doesn't it? There's no more oil to make a smell?"

Aven smiled. "Exactly." He picked up another jar and uncorked that one. "This one was closer to the front," he said as he held it out to Gathi. She sniffed, then coughed.

"There's oil in that!"

"It's pretty strong, too," Aven said as he replaced the cork. "I'll admit, I checked the first few. I think that whoever was working here put the fresher herbs in the front and pushed the older ones to the back, instead of rotating the jars, or putting them into the still room where they should have been stored. The fresh jars are at that end of the table, and the older jars are closer to us. Now, let's see if any of the older jars were well-sealed enough to keep."

They worked their way through the jars, setting the old herbs aside to be disposed of, and carrying all but two of the other jars into the still room. When they went back for the last two jars, Gathi picked one up.

"What are we going to do with these?" Gathi asked. "I mean, we could have carried them in. We didn't. So I imagine that's my next lesson?"

Aven grinned. "You're quick. This will be fun. Yes. You're going to learn to make joint lotion. It's a process that takes several days, so we'll start it now. This is one where if you don't follow the directions exactly, you won't end up with anything worth using."

Gathi nodded. "So I have to be slow and careful," she said.

"And read your labels," Aven added. "Everything in the still room is labeled. And there are cards with the recipes for each ointment and lotion. So I'll be assigning you some reading to practice." He led Gathi back into the cool, dimly-lit still room. "Why do we use a still room?" he asked.

"Because some of the herbs will go off in bright light," Gathi answered. "My gran knew a little about healing, and she had a bit of the healing touch, like you do. She had herbs hanging in a dark corner of her house. Told me they liked the dark."

Aven nodded. "Very good. Yes. Now, we start this lotion by soaking the herbs in alcohol. First, we have to crumble the leaves. There's a large bowl on the shelf there. We'll use that."

"Do we have to dry the leaves?" Gathi asked as she took down the large pottery bowl. "Can we take them right from the garden?"

"We can," Aven answered. "I first learned using dried, because that's what we could get trading on the deep. And we didn't have a proper still room, living on a canoe. Or alcohol. So I learned to make it very differently. But when I was learning in Terraces, Treesi taught me to do it this way, and how to use fresh leaves. It makes a better lotion than the way I originally learned. But since we have so much of the dried, we'll use the dried." He tipped one of the jars into the bowl, and nodded when Gathi lifted the other. Once she'd emptied that jar into the bowl, Aven reached in and started crumbling the herbs with one hand.

"That's it?" Gathi asked. She reached her hand into the bowl and laughed. "This isn't hard!"

"Tinctures are easy," Aven said. "And your hands will smell good when we're done."

Once the herbs were crumbled, Aven picked up the jars and filled them most of the way with the contents of the bowl. He tapped the jars on the table, then nodded.

"We need the alcohol now," he said. Then he waited. Gathi frowned at him for a moment. Then she gaped at him.

"I...you want me to find it?" She turned around. "I..." All at once she stopped. "This is like the larders," she said softly. "Everything is stored just so. So...where would they keep the alcohol?" She moved down the table, stopping to look at large jars and casks. Aven could see her lips moving as she read the labels. Then she stopped and pointed at a large cask with a spigot.

"I think it's this one," she said. "Did I read it right?"

"You did," Aven said. "Well done." He handed her a jar. "Fill it to the top, but leave room for the cork."

They left the filled jars in the still room, and Gathi was smiling from ear to ear as they walked back out into the brightly-lit healing center.

"I can be a healer!" she said with a laugh.

"You can," Aven agreed. "And if you show a real talent for it, I can arrange for you to take more training in Terraces, at the main healing complex." He leaned against the table. "It's a lot of work—"

"So is being mother to three little ones when you're still a little yourself," Gathi grumbled. "I've never not worked hard."

Aven smiled and nodded. "I think I'd have said the same thing. But healer training is entirely different." He looked up as Treesi came into the room. "Trees? Am I right?"

"Usually, but about what this time?" she asked, and Gathi giggled.

"About healer training being different from other kinds of hard work."

Treesi laughed. "Oh, yes. Healer training runs you until you drop and there's always more to do than you have time to do it, because when you're fully trained, you have to be able to do six things at once."

Gathi stared at her, then looked at Aven. "You're not teasing me? I don't like to be teased."

"No one is teasing you, little sister," Aven said. "Being a healer is hard work. Being a healing assistant is hard work, and without the benefit of a healing gift." He paused. "Trees, we should have her tested. Gathi says her grandmother was a healer."

"Oh? Well, we can have Jehan do it. Or Allie can."

Aven nodded. "I need to learn how. I think we skipped it."

"We didn't have time," Treesi said. "And it wasn't important at that point. When you came back, I think we all had forgotten." She turned and called. "Allie? Are you busy?"

"No," Alanar answered, coming out of an examination room. "I think these rooms are set up properly. I'll be able to find what I need. What is it?"

"Healer Alanar, I want you to meet my new assistant, Gathi. And I'd like it if you'd test her, please," Aven said. "Her grandmother was a healer. I'm wondering if she might not have the gift, too."

Alanar nodded. "Oh, of course." He turned toward Gathi and bowed slightly. "It's nice to meet you, Gathi."

Gathi hesitated, then bowed in return. She looked at Aven and whispered, "He can't see me?"

Alanar chuckled. "No, but my ears are just fine," he said. He closed his eyes for a moment. "Chairs by the window, yes? I'm still getting used to this new space."

"Yes, there are chairs by the window," Treesi said. "We'll get out of your way."

"May I stay?" Aven asked. "I haven't seen this done yet."

"Of course you can stay," Alanar said. He turned toward the window and headed for the chairs. Gathi darted forward and caught his arm; Alanar jerked in surprise and stumbled away from her.

"Lesson one," he said with a weak laugh as he recovered. "Don't grab a blind man's arm. Wait to be asked for help. I'm Air, Gathi. I always know where I am." He offered her his hand. "And, if you don't surprise me, I usually know where you are, too."

"Oh," Gathi whispered as she took his hand. "I'm sorry. I—"

"Never met a blind man before?" Alanar offered.

"No, my grandfa was blind. So I went to do for you what I used to have to do for him." She paused. "Except he wasn't Air. And he wasn't right in the head, either. He was very old, and his mind wandered off into memories and never came back."

Alanar stopped and smiled. "That's an enchanting way of describing what happens to some elders. I imagine he'd go off searching for things that hadn't been there for years?"

"He would," Gathi agreed. She let go of Alanar's hand as he sat down, and took a seat facing him. "What do you need me to do?"

Alanar smiled. "You already did it. You took my hand." He turned. "She's definitely going to need training, Aven. She's a healer. I can't tell how strong yet, but she has the gift."

"I am?" Gathi squeaked. "I do?"

"You do," Alanar said. "Welcome, Healer-in-training Gathi."

CHAPTER THIRTY-ONE

A ria's office was indeed very pleasant. There was a large desk with a comfortable chair, a long table with more chairs, and wide windows that looked out over the sea, with a long, low couch below them. Sitting on the couch, Aria could easily imagine being there during winter, curled in a blanket and with a mug of tea watching the snow fall. It was something that she'd started doing in Terraces when the weather had been so foul that there had been days when they couldn't leave the house. At first, she'd fretted at being confined. Then Owyn had tucked her in near the window, given her a mug of her favorite tea, and told her to count snowflakes. She hadn't realized then what Owyn was doing, how he was trying to care for her. Trying to reach her through the walls she'd built between them.

Hopefully, she'd finally mend the rift between them before the first snows fell on the Palace.

She looked out at the water, at the white-capped waves. There was something peaceful in watching them, too. It was almost the same as watching the swirling snow fall, almost the same as flying. She took a deep breath and turned away from the window as the office door opened. Steward came in with a set of rolled papers under his arm. He smiled when he saw where she was sitting.

"I've arranged for a second party of scouts to head north to start searching. Trey and his squad will ride out with them when he takes his command to the meeting site. They may have just left, as a matter of fact, so we'll see what happens. And if the view is going to be a distraction, we can put up curtains," he said.

She laughed. "I'll behave," she said. "Now, you brought the maps?" She joined him at the table where he'd already unfurled a large map, and she studied it for a moment. "The traditional route is to go out to the Water tribe first, then go south, Aleia said. Since the Water tribe is already here, we'll just go south?"

Steward nodded. "I'm surprised she knew that, since that's not how Milon's progress went. Yes, we'll go south to Terraces. Then past Terraces and east, starting about here." He tapped the map. "Normally, it would be south to Forge, and then east, following the Quench—"

"The what?" Aria asked

"The river here," Steward pointed and traced a line toward the mountains.

Aria nodded and leaned closer to the map. There were several towns marked along the river. Were they still there? "The map we had when we left Forge showed towns that were no longer there," she said. "Is this map accurate?"

Steward hummed softly, then shook his head. "Probably not. Not anymore, anyway. We'll update the maps as we go."

"Let Owyn do that," she said. "He'll enjoy it." She looked closer at the map. "What is south of Forge?" she asked. "We go south to Forge, then east. Is there nothing south of Forge?"

"Not much. The arable land was all north and east," Steward answered. "Going south, there are steam vents, then scrubland. Goats. Rather a lot of goats, from what I remember. I believe there were some nomadic goat-herders that way. And the sea, about a day's ride past the Smoking Mountain.." He reached over and tapped the mountains that ran along the eastern border of the map. "I've always been curious about what's past these, myself. But as far as I know, there are no navigable passes through. The only way is over."

Aria nodded. "My grandfather told me once that when he was young, he went past the Mother's Womb, and kept flying, up to where there is very little air, and it's so cold that your breath freezes in your chest. He said looking east from the highest peak, all he could see was water." She looked at Steward and smiled at the stunned look on his face. "Steward, is Adavar an island?"

"I...I've never given it any thought," Steward stammered. "I knew what was south, but I've never known anyone who looked over the mountains at the top of the world before. And...well, we don't know what's north, past the snowfields. But maybe." He looked thoughtful. "Which leads to the question of are there other islands? Other places like Adavar?"

"Other people?" Aria looked at the map. "Other children of the Mother?"

"Or another Mother's children," Steward suggested. "It would be interesting to learn someday. We'll have to ask Aleia what the Water tribe knows. They sail away from the shores. They might have seen something no one else has seen."

"I've been on another island," Aria said. "It was where I found my Aven. A tiny island in the middle of the sea."

Steward smiled. "Someday, we'll know. For now...let's learn what we can of our own little island in the middle of the sea." He tapped the map. "We'll update the maps as we go. And we'll take the census that Owyn suggested. We'll need an accurate count of who lives where. We'll need to get an idea of who needs what, of what repairs need to be done. We'll need to recruit people to do that work." He rubbed his forehead. "It's a massive undertaking."

"Why has none of it been done before?" Aria asked.

"Because the people sent before couldn't get honest answers to questions when the questions were asked," Steward answered.

"And because they couldn't maintain the repairs to the roads, or provide for the people to do the repairs without proper supplies." He frowned. "How are we going to supply this progress? It's spring. It's not exactly the best time to be living off the land."

"But if we put this off any longer, I'll either give birth halfway through the Progress, or I will be making the trip with a new baby," Aria pointed out. "And we cannot wait. We have to let the people see me. And we have to see what the people know. What they wouldn't say before, they will say now."

Steward nodded. "I'm counting on that," he said. "Now, I do know the road between here and Terraces. There are towns here, and here, and we'll need to stop at each of them."

"Shadow Cove and Serenity Bay," Aria said. "I know of both of them. I've only been to Serenity, though. And that only once."

"That's Jehan's sister's town, isn't it?" Steward said with a nod. "We'll spend at least a day at each—"

"They're not big towns!" Aria protested.

"But there are people who don't live in those towns, and who will want to see the Heir with their own eyes," Steward replied. "Think of your presentation — we had people come from miles around the Palace to see you. We'll time it to arrive early, so that runners can bring the news to outliers. We'll camp outside the town, so as not to put a strain on their resources. We'll bring our own supplies—"

"You've given this a great deal of thought," Aria said.

"I started thinking on it after Owyn and Alanar were here the first time." He smiled. "I kept thinking of how things might work while we were still in Terraces. It gave me something to do that wasn't fussing over Memfis."

Aria smiled and studied the map. "We'll resupply in Terraces?" she asked. "And then what? The town south of Terraces where we bought supplies is no longer there."

"Trust me, I remember that town far too well," Steward murmured. "Once we leave Terraces is where things get complicated. I—" He stopped and turned as someone knocked on the door. It opened, and Lexi peered in.

"My Heir?" she said. "I've brought Marik and Esai." She opened the door and stepped out of the way as Marik came in, followed by Esai. Marik grinned when he saw Aria.

"Look at you!" he laughed. "You're getting prettier by the day, and I did not think that was possible!"

"Flatterer," Aria said with a giggle. "You'll make Esai jealous."

"He will not," Esai said. "He's right. You are." She crossed to take Aria's hands. "You're glowing."

"Am I?" Aria asked. "I...glowing?"

"She means you look very happy, Aria," Steward said. "Pregnant women glow."

"Oh. Does it mean that?" Aria turned back to Esai. "I am happy. Even though things have been very interesting. But I will tell you all of it later. How was your trip?" She gestured to the couch, and she and Esai sat down. Marik came to stand by Esai.

"Well, we would have been here yesterday if someone hadn't surprised me." Esai looked up at Marik, and her smile softened. "He asked me if we could stop in Serenity Bay."

Aria caught her breath. "Oh, Marik! You did it?"

"You knew?" Marik asked. "How did you know? Oh...Aven told you?"

"He asked me not to tell anyone," Aria admitted. "I'm so happy for you!"

Marik smiled. "I need to talk to Aunt Aleia, and find out what's proper. Mama says that my Fa didn't ask her to build a canoe, but Esai and I... we're going to do both."

"That makes sense," Steward said. "Water goes by their women."

"They were married using Earth rites," Marik said with a nod. "So she wasn't really sure of what was the right way for all that she's been living as Water for years now."

Aria nodded. "Aleia has taken a good number of the warriors out on a mission. You may want to speak to your uncle."

Marik nodded. "I'll do that. I really don't want to wait." He smiled at Esai, then glanced around the room. "Sorry. I'm going to need to go out really soon." He blushed slightly, then looked at the desk. "Is...is that a map? A map of everything?" He stepped closer and cocked his head so that he could better see the map. "Who drew this? I think it's the nicest map I've seen."

"Do you know maps?" Steward asked.

"Owyn sort of got me interested," Marik answered as he leaned over the desk. "When I was helping him take stock in Terraces after the storms last winter. Mannon, may I copy this?"

Steward paled. "Aria?"

"Oh...oh, we have a great deal to tell you, Marik," Aria said. "Come and sit."

Marik straightened. "What? What did I miss?"

"I'll go and fetch some tea," Steward said. "This isn't going to be a short telling." He bowed slightly and left.

"He's right. It isn't going to be a short telling," Aria said as she turned back to Marik. "Can you stay inside that long, Marik?"

"I'll try," Marik answered. "Ah...Aria, I don't mean to be ungrateful, but where are we sleeping tonight? Because if we're inside this pile of rock? I'm not sleeping."

"There are arrangements being made," Aria answered. "We'll go and see once we're done here. While we wait for the tea, tell me about Terraces. How is Rhexa?"

Esai laughed. "You do remember that we left the morning after you did? There really wasn't a lot of time for anything to happen."

"Rhexa is fine," Marik added. "We had another group of refugees a few hours after you left. Other than that, there isn't much to tell. Except that she insisted on sending presents." He came over to sit next to Esai, taking her hand, and they talked about Terraces and where Rhexa was going to put everyone until Steward came back in, carrying a tray. He served them, which made Esai stare.

"I...what's happened here?" she asked.

Aria took a sip of her tea. "Well, to start, I should introduce you both to my Steward, who honestly does need to tell me his name at some point."

Steward chuckled. "What's wrong with just calling me Steward? I rather like it."

"I happen to agree with my Water," Aria said. "Steward isn't a name. It is a job."

"I answer to it," Steward said. "That makes it a name." He smiled and bowed slightly, making Aria roll her eyes.

"All right," Marik said slowly. "If you're Steward, then what happened to Mannon?"

"The Usurper was condemned for his crimes against the Mother, and his name was decreed forgotten. It has been stricken from the records and our histories. He will be known only as the Usurper." Aria looked up at Steward. "We will have to announce that first wherever we stop on the progress."

Steward nodded. "I was just thinking that. I'll draft something."

"Thank you." Aria took another sip of her tea. "We found when we got here that Risha had attacked the Palace. She was the one in control here. The Usurper was not. And when she attacked, she murdered everyone who knew the secrets that she had hidden somewhere in these walls." Aria looked up, wishing she could see through walls. "Marik, my father is alive."

Marik sputtered on his tea. "What?"

"We will be searching the hidden passages and the servant quarters. From what Owyn has seen, we think that there were servants here who tried to save Milon by hiding him, but it became something more, and he ended up a prisoner. Risha took him from the Palace when she attacked." She swallowed. "He is alive. That's where Aleia has gone — some of the Water tribe is out searching for Risha's ship. And there are guards going north to search overland."

Marik nodded, then looked at Esai. She immediately nodded. He turned back to Aria. "How can we help?"

"Personal bodyguards for the short term, I think," Steward murmured. "Aria, we can't take the chance that Alanar missed someone."

Marik turned to look at Aria. "What is that supposed to mean?"

"That there were spies left behind, and they tried to take Aven and Aria from the Palace yesterday," Steward answered.

"Definitely personal bodyguards," Esai agreed. "And...Marik, you've had enough of being inside. I can tell. Your hands are shaking. Aria, if you'll excuse us?"

"I'll walk down with you," Aria said. She set down her teacup, and went to rise, only to find Steward offering his hand.

"I'll take the map to my office and start drafting the progress plans," he said. "Esai, remember the falconer's quarters?"

Esai frowned slightly. Then her eyes widened. "Oh, in the outer wall?" She looked thoughtful. "I think those would work."

"That's what I was hoping," Steward said. "So we're preparing those for you and Marik. And we're reopening the mews. Is Wraith with you?"

Marik nodded toward the window. "He's off hunting. What are you talking about?"

"I'll show you, love," Esai said.

———— ⟨∾⟩ ————

ARIA WATCHED AS MARIK'S shoulders lowered as they passed out into the courtyard. He took a deep breath and shook his head.

"You didn't have to come inside," Aria said softly. "I would have come to you."

"I...that's not right," he said, turning so that he could see her. "I'm not asking the Heir to wait on me. I can do it, in small doses. I— Aven!"

Aria turned and smiled to see Aven leading the other healers toward them. Aven was smiling broadly. "I thought I heard your voice," he called as he approached. He hugged Marik tightly, glanced at Esai, and arched a brow. Marik laughed.

"Yes, I asked her."

"And yes, I said yes," Esai added. "We need to know what the proper rites are. Danzi didn't know."

"She and Fa did Earth rites," Marik said.

"We'll talk to my father. He's in the healing center inside," Aven said. "Or Neera. You could ask Neera. She's down at the harbor with the rest of the canoes."

"She stayed behind?" Marik asked. "Esai, where are we going?"

Esai pointed. "See where the servants are working? There. We should stay out of the way."

Aven looked, then faced his cousin. "What do you know?"

"That your mother is off hunting, and that Risha's days are numbered," Marik answered. "Treesi, Alanar, it's good to see you both. We brought your things. The housekeeper said she'd have them brought to your rooms."

"Thank you," Treesi said. "Aven, I want to go and check on Owyn. Are you going to the practice field?"

"I'm supposed to go back to the healing center," Aven answered.

"I'll take your duty," Alanar said. "I'm free otherwise, but if I go back to the suite and pretend I'm not hovering over Owyn, he'll grumble at me for hovering. Aven, you stay with your cousin. Show him the grounds." He smiled and went back into the Palace.

"He already knows his way around? That's good." Esai paused and frowned. "What's wrong with Owyn?"

"There's a lot we need to tell you," Aven said. "Aria, what are you doing now?"

"Well, Steward is starting to plan the progress, and there are some orders to draft. I may go back to my office and start going over those. Or perhaps I could go and help Grandmother and Afansa and Memfis. They are in the library looking for information on heart visions." She thought about it. "No, I will go back to my office and start doing what I'm supposed to be doing."

Aven leaned down and kissed her. "I'll come join you there once I'm done. Then we'll go see what Owyn and Del have for us." He turned back to Marik. "We're searching for hidden passages later. Do you think that you might be able to help us?"

"Hidden passages?" Marik looked up at the Palace. "I...inside there? I'm not sure. Depends on how much like cave tunnels they are." He jerked, then looked around. "Wraith says there are small humans throwing rocks!"

"Where?" Aven demanded.

Marik shook his head. "I don't know. Wraith is coming to me." He looked up, and Aria did the same, seeing Wraith appear around the side of the Palace. The large bird circled over them, then flew down to land on Marik's outstretched arm. A moment later, a group of shouting children appeared.

"It came this way!" one of them shouted. He turned, and nearly ran into Aven. The entire pack of children fell silent, huddling together and staring.

"It is named Wraith," Aven said. "And Wraith is my cousin's friend. Were you throwing rocks at him?"

The boy who had shouted turned pale. He shook his head violently. "No, sir!"

"Wraith says otherwise," Marik said, bringing his arm in and cradling the bird against his chest. He ran his hand down Wraith's wing, and showed bloody fingers.

Aria turned to the children. "You hurt him! Why?"

"He talks to you?" the boy gasped. "I—"

"Didn't expect to be caught in the lie?" Marik finished. "He was sitting on the wall, and not bothering anyone. Why would you want to hurt him?"

The children shifted, looking uncomfortable. One of the smaller ones sniffled.

"My Heir? May I?" Esai said. "I saw Lexi over at the mews. I think we now have..." she paused, pointing at each child as she counted. "Eight volunteers to help clean, and to learn why we do not throw rocks at any strange animal."

Aven nodded. "That's a very good idea. Esai, would you take them, while I see to Wraith?"

Esai kissed Marik on the cheek, gently ruffled Wraith's feathers with one finger, then turned back to the children. "All right, you lot. Move!" she snapped as she marched the children off toward Lexi, who was now watching them. Aven walked over to Marik.

"Tell him I'm not going to hurt him, will you?"

"He knows, and he says thank you," Marik said. He lowered his head and gently blew on Wraith's neck. "He'll be quiet."

Aria stepped closer, watching as Aven gently ran his hand over Wraith's injured wing. "Just a cut," Aven said softly. "Nothing broken. He'll be fine."

"Good," Aria murmured. "I'll be back." She followed Esai, who was now giving orders to the children as they helped the servants.

Lexi watched her coming closer, and bowed as Aria came up next to her. "My Heir. Was the bird hurt?"

"Nothing broken," Aria answered. "Just a cut. Aven is putting him to rights. The children. Who are their parents?"

"Those are some of the Palace fosterlings, and they should be in lessons. But the older boy, there?" She pointed at the one who'd lied about throwing stones. "That's Copper. He's their leader. Anything he proposes, they all do. Which today appears to be skipping their lessons and being cruel to animals."

"And does that mean that Palace fosterlings have no parents?" Aria asked.

Lexi sighed. "Some of them have parents who work in the Palace. Some of them are orphans, like Gathi's younger brothers and sister. Copper, though..." She paused. Then she sighed. "He was abandoned at the Palace gates. He was...four or five, we think. We've never been able to find who his people were or why they left him, or even what tribe he is. Ambaryl made something of a pet of him, but she left him behind when she went to Terraces. He's been a terror ever since, the poor thing."

Aria looked over at the mews, at the children who were helping carry things. She could see Copper among them, his small face sullen. "Poor thing?"

"Aria, he was abandoned here," Lexi said softly. "He was old enough to remember his family, but all he could tell us was that he traveled for a long time before they left him here. Then he was abandoned again by the one person he thought cared about him. He's hurting."

"He doesn't want anyone to get close, so he doesn't get hurt again." Aria turned to see that Marik had come up behind her. He shrugged one shoulder, keeping Wraith steady against his chest with his other arm.. "I kind of know how that feels. Took Esai a bit to get me to trust her, after what Teva did. Excuse me?" He walked over to the children and went down on one knee. The children clustered around them, Copper included.

"What's he doing?" Lexi asked.

Aria smiled. "He's introducing them to Wraith."

CHAPTER THIRTY-TWO

"He's feral," Marik said as they walked around the Palace. "That child is completely feral."

"What does that mean?" Aven asked. Treesi had gone to look in on Owyn, and Aria had taken Esai off into the Palace to do something, so Aven volunteered to show Marik the Palace grounds on their way to the practice field. He took the long way around, passing through the healer's garden.

"Feral? It means half-wild." Marik looked up. "Wraith says thank you, by the way. His wing is fine."

"Tell him that he's welcome," Aven answered. He opened the gate to the healer's garden, wincing at the shrill squeak. "Half-wild. Does that mean Owyn was all wild?"

"Owyn says that himself," Marik answered. "At least, he's said it to me. He said he learned to be people after Memfis bought him."

"He's said that to me, too." Aven pointed between the raised beds. "The other gate is over there." They started walking, neither saying anything. Then the gate squeaked again. Aven turned, and saw Copper behind them.

"Copper?" Marik said. "Shouldn't you be at your lessons now?"

"It's reading, and our teacher let me go early. I already know how, well enough to help the littlest ones when they need it," Copper answered. He closed the gate and tucked his hands behind him. "I asked if I could go. I wanted to say sorry." He looked up. "Where is he?"

"Wraith?" Marik tipped his head back. "Out...out over the water. He's fishing. He says he'll come back once he's eaten."

"You really can talk to him?" Copper asked. "Really?"

Marik smiled. "Really. I've more than a touch of the Earth sense with animals."

Copper blinked. He looked down, frowning. Then he looked back up. "Can you talk to other animals? And...can I show you something? And you won't get mad?"

Marik looked at Aven, then nodded. "Show me."

Copper opened the gate and led them toward the back of the courtyard. The stables were back here — Aven could smell them. Copper ducked behind a scaffold, then peered out. "Can you get back here?"

Marik looked at the space, then at Aven. "You wait here," he said, and slipped into the space behind Copper. Aven came to look, and heard Copper's voice.

"We're not supposed to keep them, but they were little, and I didn't want them to die all alone. So I hid them, and I thought your...I thought Wraith might find them and think they were dinner—"

"Oh, Copper," Marik murmured. "Aven, I'm going to hand you some babies. There are five of them."

"Baby what?" Aven asked.

"Kittens."

A few minutes later, Aven was holding two furry, mewling babies. Marik had two more, and Copper had the last one.

"Where are we taking them?" Aven asked. He looked down at the balls of fur in his hands, remembering Patience. What had happened to Lady Meris' cat? He hadn't even thought about it. "Maybe Lady Meris would want them? She had a cat in Forge."

"What do we have here?" Aven looked up as Lexi came toward them from an open door. "Copper, Master Novis said you asked to be excused. Where— kittens?" She smiled. "Oh, they're precious. Where did you find kittens?" She took one from Aven and started cooing at it.

"You like kittens?" Copper blurted out. He held his burden close to his chest. "I—"

Lexi didn't look up from her tiny bundle of fur. "I adore cats. My mother always said you can't have a proper kitchen with a cat. I never agreed...oh." She looked up. "Ambaryl. She didn't care for cats."

Copper shook his head. "She said we weren't allowed to have them, and she'd drown any she saw." He looked down at his kitten. "I been keeping these hid since right before she left. I think she killed their mother."

"Oh, Copper," Lexi breathed. She looked up. "Is that why you were throwing rocks at Marik's friend?"

Copper didn't look up, but he nodded. "There were six. One of them got out and a hawk got it. I—" He hiccupped. "I'm sorry!"

Marik knelt down in front of him. "You were trying to protect the babies?" he asked. "Copper, why didn't you just say that?"

"Cause I wasn't supposed to even have them," Copper answered. "And when Ambaryl comes back, she'll be mad at me. If she gets mad enough, she'll put me out."

Aven fought to keep his face neutral as Marik looked up at him, clearly alarmed. He shook his head quickly and Marik grimaced. Lexi arched a brow at them, then turned to Copper.

"Copper, I told you. She married in Terraces, and she's not coming back," Lexi said gently. "It's my kitchen now, and I think we could do with a kitten or two. Or five. Now, why don't we take the babies into the kitchen and get them settled? I'm sure we can find a nice basket for them and see what we can find for them to eat."

She gathered her apron up, and took the kittens from Marik and Aven. Before she turned to leave, she whispered to Aven, "Do not go anywhere. I'll be right back." She led Copper toward the open door.

"What was that about?" Marik asked as he stood up.

"Not sure, but I think we'll find out when she gets back." Aven frowned. "I...don't know if anyone told them that Ambaryl is dead, Marik."

"Oh, fuck," Marik murmured. "We'll find out in a minute."

A few minutes later, Lexi came back outside. She looked over her shoulder as she passed through the door, then closed it behind her. She crossed to Aven and Marik. "Your healer face is very good," she said to Aven. Then she turned to Marik. "You should never play cards. With anyone. It's a good thing Copper wasn't looking at you. What happened to Ambaryl?"

Aven looked at Marik, then glanced at the door. He took Lexi's arm and guided her further away. "If Copper is like Owyn, he's on the other side of that door, listening," he said softly. "Lexi, Ambaryl is dead. She was working with Risha, and when we discovered it, she killed herself." He shook his head. "We tried to save her. I tried."

"Aven," Lexi murmured. "It's not your fault."

Aven snorted. "Maybe I'll believe that someday. But for now...she's interred in the caverns at Terraces. And...I don't know. Do we tell Copper?"

Lexi pursed her lips, then sighed. "I'll do it. I'll have to think on how and when. I'm not sure how he'll take it. Why did you say that Copper is like the Fireborn?"

Aven looked up at the building. The windows of his room looked out this way. Owyn's room was across the suite. His windows must look out over the healer's garden. "Owyn was orphaned, and grew up on the streets of Forge. He says he wasn't really a person until he was adopted by Memfis, and that was only a few years ago."

Lexi nodded. "I see. Perhaps I should introduce Copper to him? Because I rather like Owyn, and having Copper looking up to him might be very good for them both."

Aven looked at Marik, who nodded slowly. "Might not be the worst idea."

OWYN LOOKED ACROSS the table at Del, and grinned. "You're all over chalk."

Del brushed his hair back, leaving a blue smear of chalk on his cheek. *"So are you."*

"Maybe, but I can't see me." Owyn straightened and winced as his back protested. He wiped his hands off on a towel and went to the sideboard, picking up a few tear nuts and popping them into his mouth. He looked back at the paper-strewn table. "Are we done?"

"I think we are." Del nodded and smiled, looking very satisfied. *"All of the passages are marked out now. And the maps are ready."* He turned to Owyn and frowned. *"Are you going to be able to do this? I don't want you hurting yourself."*

Owyn came back to the table, looking down at the maps. "I don't know," he admitted. "Maybe. Short trips, maybe. I can take the shorter passages." He reached out and tapped one of the maps. "Like this one." He looked up. "Which ones are supposed to be dangerous?"

"The ones marked in red." Del answered. *"I'm leaving those until last."*

The door opened, and Treesi came into the suite. Owyn looked past her, but she was alone.

"Alanar is taking Aven's duty shift in the healing center," she answered before he asked the question. "Aven is showing Marik the grounds. Aria and Esai are around here somewhere. And I found my way back here without help, and without getting lost!"

Owyn laughed and walked over to kiss her. "Well done."

She slid her arm around him, resting her head on his shoulder. "How do you feel?"

"I'm fine. My back is sore because I was leaning over the table, but I'm fine." He hugged her to his side. "There's nibble food. And...you're awfully tense. Worried about Othi?"

She nodded. "A little. I thought being a warrior meant that he knew what he was doing. But Aven said he's never really been in a fight before. So I'm worried."

"He'll be fine," Owyn said. "He'll be back. Hopefully, with news."

"*And hopefully before we start the progress,*" Del signed.

"Before the progress?" Treesi repeated. "Do we know when that will be?"

Owyn shook his head. "No. And I haven't seen Steward since he took Aria off to show her where her office is. Del? Do we have offices?"

Del nodded. "*Each Companion does. So we can keep our tribal business separate from the others. They're all right by Aria's, and down from Fa's. I can show you.*"

Owyn whistled. "Tribal business. I keep forgetting that we're supposed to speak for our tribes. Who's gonna listen to me?"

"The entire Fire tribe?" Treesi said, leaning into his side. "Owyn, the Mother picked you. They'll talk to you. And listen to you."

Del snorted. "*The Air tribes don't even know me,*" he signed. "*I don't know what's going to happen when we get to the Solstice village.*"

Owyn frowned slightly. Then he shook his head. "Let's worry about one thing at the time. The first thing we need to do is search the passages. We need people. It can't be just the four and a half of us."

Treesi laughed. "Four and a half? There are six of us!"

"Allie can't help search," Owyn said. "And I know I'm not going to be good for much." He brought Treesi over to the table. "Mem and Jehan will want to help. Steward, too. But really, this is a lot of searching, and not that many of us. And we all have other work to do, don't we? You have to stand your watches in the healing center, and we have to do.... I don't know...ruling stuff? Whatever we need to do with Aria?"

"We need training," Del signed. *"And fast. People are going to start coming to us soon, now that we're here and Aria holds the Palace."*

"Well, then I think we all need to start school," Owyn said. "Let's go find Steward."

Del nodded. *"I'll bring the maps. I'm not leaving them here. They'll disappear."*

Treesi looked startled as Owyn translated for her. "You think they will? I thought we found everyone loyal to Risha?"

"I'm not any taking chances. Oh, and I know how to arrange the searching. I'll tell you as we go."

"COME IN!"

Owyn opened the door, and saw Steward sitting at his desk. The older man glanced up from his work, then straightened. "Owyn? Del? And Treesi? Is something wrong?" He pushed his chair back and started to stand up.

"No, no," Owyn blurted. "It's fine. Nothing is wrong. That I know of, anyway." He looked back at Treesi. "We just...we have questions."

Steward nodded, and gestured to the pair of chairs facing his desk. "I don't have enough chairs," he said as Owyn led Treesi to one of the chairs. "And...Del, are those your maps?"

Del nodded. He put the rolls of paper on top of the low bookcases and signed, "*I didn't want to leave them behind, in case we missed any of Risha's people.*"

Steward frowned, then nodded. He stood up and walked around the desk, going to the chalkboard. He stretched up, then shook his head. "I'll need that chair."

Owyn dragged the chair over and held it while Steward climbed up onto the seat and reached over the top of the chalkboard; he heard something click, and the board swung away from the wall.

"Is that where the box was? And the books?" Owyn asked. "Who knows about this?"

"Us," Steward answered. "And Lexi. Othi and three Water warriors who aren't in the Palace at the moment. Jehan, I think." He frowned, resting his hand against the wall. "Yes, Jehan. And Memfis."

"That's quite a lot of people for a secret hiding place," Owyn said. "I wouldn't use this more than you have to."

"Honestly, I wasn't going to use it at all," Steward said. "Mostly because I can't reach it. But that will work in our favor, don't you think?"

"Why? Because no one else knows how to stand on a chair?" Owyn asked.

Steward snorted. "Fine. We'll use it now, and I'll have it sealed later. Del, put your maps inside."

Once the maps were hidden and the chalkboard closed, Steward climbed down from the chair and dusted the seat. "Now that those are hidden, what can I help you with?" He dragged his chair out from behind the desk. "Owyn, Del, sit down," he added. He leaned against his desk. "Questions, you said. About what?"

Owyn looked at Treesi and Del. The both of them looked back at him, and Treesi smiled.

"Oh, I'm speaker for Companions now?" Owyn asked. He turned back to Steward. "Now what?" he asked. "That's the question. Now what do we do?" He waved one arm. "We're here. We're supposed to speak for our tribes, and to our tribes. But...yeah, we don't know what we need to know, and people are going to start showing up and asking questions soon, now that Aria holds the Palace. So how do we get what we need to know so we can do what we're supposed to do?"

Steward smiled. "Well, if things were the way they were supposed to be, you'd have lessons to bring you all up to the same level, and then there would be lessons in law, in statesmanship, in history, and you'd learn from your counterparts from the Firstborn's Companions." He looked thoughtful. "We can still do all of that, to a point. Treesi, you can work with Jehan, and Owyn with your father and with Lady Meris. Aven can work with his mother when she returns. But we don't have a proper Air Companion for Del to learn from — I never had the training Liara did, and there was no one to teach me. But there are texts for all of you—"

"More reading?" Treesi groaned.

"I'll read to you, Trees," Owyn said, taking her hand. "You know I will."

"You're going to have to," she said. "They won't be in the right typeface."

"I know which type you mean, and if we don't have copies yet, then we'll see about having a set printed," Steward said. He took a piece of paper and scrawled a note. "I won't lie. It's going to be hard work. You're not supposed to have to rule and learn to rule at the same time."

Owyn snorted, rubbing his thumb over Treesi's fingers, feeling the callouses. "I don't think there's any of us scared of hard work, Steward. Where do we start?"

Steward straightened. "We'll start with finding Memfis. And finding the Air journals for Del. They'll both be in the library. Then we'll find Jehan. I assume he's in the healing center?"

"He was when I left," Treesi said. She tugged her hand free of Owyn's and stood up. "Let's go."

OWYN SMILED AS THEY walked into the library. "I need to spend more time here."

"There are so many books!" Treesi gasped. "I've never seen so many books!"

Del took her hand, leading her over to one set of shelves. He took a book down and handed it to her. She frowned as she took it.

"Del, you know I have trouble with reading—" she started to say. Then she opened the book. "This...this is in the right type!" She looked up. "Are there others?"

Steward came up behind her. "That entire section is printed for the word-blind," he said. He turned to the trio sitting at one of the tables. "Lady Meris, which Firstborn was word-blind? I forget. It wasn't my...it wasn't Riga."

Meris looked up from her book and smiled. "No, it was Firstborn Kalanthe."

"Oh, yes," Steward said. "She was the Firstborn before Riga."

"His mother?" Treesi asked.

Owyn frowned, thinking back to his reading and Antiri's *History of the Tribes*. "His...aunt? Yeah, I think Riga was Kalanthe's brother's son. Steward, we need to update the *History of the Tribes*."

Steward nodded. "We'll do that after the progress. It's needed updating for quite a while. Fath...Elcam was never really interested in anything intellectual."

Meris laughed. "He wasn't. Getting him to sit for his lessons as a boy was a chore."

"He always kept putting it off. Even when Ankem offered to do it for him. It was tradition that the Firstborn update the history, though. So he'd never allow someone else to do it. But he also never did it." He sighed and shook his head, looking distant.

"He's still your father, Steward," Meris said.

"No, Elcam only had two sons," Steward said. "One was Jehan, and the other was...the other one. The Usurper. I don't have a past. I don't have a bloodline to put into the *Book of Silver*. What I have is the family that's claimed me." He looked at Owyn, then over at Treesi and Del. "It's enough."

CHAPTER THIRTY-
THREE

"Granna, do we have a copy, by the way?" Owyn asked. "Of the *Book of Silver*?"

"I have the actual book," Meris said. "It was in the bags that Karse and Trey brought from Forge, bless them both."

"We can put it here, if you want," Steward said. "Until Forge rises again."

Meris nodded. "A good idea. Yes. And we can update the copy that's kept here. I can't even remember when that was last done." She rubbed her eyes. "We haven't found anything on heart visions. At least, not yet. The Smoke Dancer lore apparently wasn't copied to the Palace libraries."

"That means it's gone?" Owyn gasped. "All of it?"

Meris sighed. "It may very well have been lost. Perhaps we'll be able to send someone into the ashes and find out. The archives were built to withstand fire and flood. Perhaps they were able to withstand a flood of fire." She shook her head. "We're going through the Fire tribe histories, but haven't found anything. Perhaps the information may be in the healer archives, which means we may not find those records until we return to Terraces. But we can send a message to Rhexa and have her start looking."

"And we can look at them when we go there on Progress," Owyn said. He sat down next to Memfis, smiling across at Afansa. "How are you liking the Palace, Afansa?"

"It's more than a little daunting," she answered. "I'm not sure where to find anything! And I'm not used to having servants do things for me." She glanced at Meris, who smiled. "Lady Meris says I'm her assistant? But I'm not sure what that means."

"For now, it means you're going to learn to read and write, and you'll help me with Fire tribe business." Meris answered. "And help Memfis as he learns what he needs to do to follow me."

"I really don't think I'm—" Memfis protested, then sighed as Meris waved her hand at him. "Yes, Mother."

"Better. Now, Steward, are you just showing off the library?"

"No," Steward said. "We need to start arranging intensive lessons for Aria's Companions. None of them have the training they need. Memfis, you and Lady Meris can teach Owyn. I'll talk to Jehan about teaching Treesi, and Aleia will have Aven. But we need Forsiri's journals. And Arkady's."

"Because we don't have someone who has had the Air training for Del to learn from." Memfis nodded. "Meris, is Forsiri still alive?"

"Mother bless, I have no idea. He went back to his mountains when Riga died and Elcam took the Crown." She looked thoughtful. "Our Earth, Destri, he passed...two years after Riga. Hara died the year after. Forsiri was the oldest of us. I was the youngest." She shook her head. "I may be the last of Riga's Companions. Mother knows I'm feeling every one of my years these days."

Del looked at Meris, then at Owyn, and Owyn heard his mental voice, "*Riga was my great-grandfather. By adoption, anyway. He was born over a hundred years ago. Owyn, how* old *is she?*" Owyn smiled and shook his head. Del nodded. "*Later. You tell me later.*"

Owyn turned back to Memfis. "So that's what we came to ask. We need to learn what to do when people come looking for answers. Because they're going to start coming. And we're going to be going to them."

"On the Progress," Meris said. "A proper Progress. When?"

Steward hummed softly. "I've been laying plans. I haven't shown them to Aria yet, nor have I finalized anything, but I'm thinking we'll leave in a few weeks. Possibly a month. South to the edge of the destruction, east to the foothills, north through the Earth lands until we reach the Solstice village, then make the journey to the Temple."

"We need to order that rebuilt, don't we?" Treesi asked. "Is that something we do?"

Steward nodded. "When we get there, we'll make the plans." He looked over at the bookshelves. "Lyan kept journals, too. We'll need to have those printed in the right type for Treesi to read. And the codices on tribal law."

Treesi sighed. "Well, it will give me something to do when we're traveling, I suppose."

Meris chuckled. "At least you'll experience the entire progress. I missed the first half." She smiled. "The trip north through the foothills was exceptionally boring."

"I like boring," Owyn said. "Boring is good. We've had far too much interesting this past year." He looked around again. "Really nothing about heart visions? In any of these?"

"Mouse, we haven't had time to look at all of them," Memfis grumbled. "We went looking for the Smoke Dancer lore first, and there's nothing here. The healing texts aren't in here. I'm not sure what else to look for here."

"*What about mythology?*" Del signed. "*Did you read any stories?*"

"Mythology?" Steward repeated. "Why mythology?"

"Oh," Meris breathed. "Oh, of course. I said it myself, didn't I? It's all stories now, because they're so rare, and it's been so long. We know more than most because of being Smoke Dancers. The rest of the tribes...it may very well be part of their mythology by now."

"What good will that do, though?" Memfis asked as Meris got up and walked over to the bookcases on the far side of the room. "Owyn needs more than 'and they lived in peace for the rest of their days.'"

"Of course he does," Meris said without turning. "If we find a reference in a story from any of the tribes, we can see when it was recorded, which would lead us to the histories of that time and prior to it."

"Because if it was something people could do, it would wind up in their bedtime stories?" Owyn asked. "I don't know, Granna."

"We don't have much else to go on," Afansa said. "We should also listen to the stories that aren't in books." She blushed when everyone looked at her. "Are all the stories written down here?" she asked, waving one arm. "They can't all be. Some of us who tell stories can't write them down."

Memfis nodded slowly. "There's something to that," he said. "Oral traditions. Telling about events that happened, and telling them so often that they became stories. We'll have to listen as we go."

"*Can I do that?*" Del signed. "*That sounds interesting! Maybe we can find more versions of the moon story!*"

Steward laughed. "You have seven!"

"*Eight now. Aven's canoe had a version that wasn't like the one Skela told me, and it wasn't like the Water version written down here. Othi told me, and I need to get him to tell me again so I can write it down. And if there are eight, there might be nine!*"

"The moon story?" Owyn asked. "What's the moon story?"

Del looked at him, smiling. "*How the Mother Hung the Moon,*" he answered. "*There are four different versions of the story in books here, one from each tribe. But when Skela told it to me, it was different from what's in the books. So I started looking. Teva told me the one that they tell in Terraces, and one of Fandor's servants told a different one from Forge. I want to see if there's a different Air version. I should ask Aria.*" He shook his hands out. "*Later. I can ask her when we're traveling.*"

"And then you can tell me all of them," Owyn said. "Because I don't know that story."

Del stared at him. "*You don't?*"

"I didn't get bedtime stories growing up," Owyn said with a shrug. "I only knew *The Stars Dance*. And not even all of it."

Del's eyes widened. "*I don't know that one.*"

"Later, Del," Steward said gently. "You can collect more stories later. For now, we're arranging lessons." He walked over to the shelves near the window, ran his finger over book spines for a moment, then pulled two large books down. "These are the first two of Forsiri's journals. There are two more when you're done with these. There are two volumes of Arkady's writings, too." He took down two more books. "And these are Tirine's. I'll give them to Aria."

"Will we be expected to keep journals?" Treesi asked.

"It probably would be a good idea," Owyn answered. "You can dictate to me, and I'll write it for you."

She smiled at him. "Have I told you today how much I love you?" she asked. "Thank you."

Owyn got up and walked around the table to Treesi so that he could kiss her cheek. "Love you, too." He turned to look at the others. "So, when do we start lessons? We wanted to start searching the passages today."

"Then we can start lessons tomorrow," Meris said. "It will give me a chance to look through the storybooks."

–––––––– ⟡ ––––––––

WHEN THE GUARDS WERE done with their morning practice, Aven left Marik with Karse, then walked through the healer's garden and into the healing center. To his surprise, there was a small crowd — Owyn, Treesi, Del and Steward were there, talking with Jehan and Alanar.

"Is everything all right?" he asked. "Owyn?"

"I'm fine," Owyn answered. "No, we're arranging lessons. On account of none of us knowing what we're doing now that we're here."

Aven blinked. "I..." he started. Then he laughed. "You're right. I hadn't thought about that at all. We've been so busy staying alive that we sort of forgot about what happened next."

"True," Jehan said. "And we can't really do what's been done in the past, because you can't learn from the Firstborn and their Companions. You have to rule, and learn while you're doing it." He nodded. "Treesi, we'll start tomorrow."

"Am I learning from Ama?" Aven asked. "When she gets back?"

"And until she does, you'll learn from Persin's journals, and from your great-grandmother's journals." Steward smiled at Aven. "You look confused. Persin was Tirine's Water. And Hara was Riga's Water, and Elcam's mother."

Aven nodded. "There's one missing, though. Isn't there? What about Elcam's Water?"

"That was Betha, and he didn't keep one," Steward answered. "Elcam didn't like anything to do with books. He preferred being active. His Companions took their temper from him, and the only one who kept a journal was Toman, his Fire. I'll find those for you, Owyn."

Owyn nodded. "So, we start tomorrow?"

"Why not today?" Aven asked.

"We're starting to search today," Owyn answered. "Del and I finished the maps. They're locked up."

Aven nodded. "Have you eaten?"

Owyn grinned. "I ate something before we left the suite. And I should go back and eat something again. And we need to get everyone together. Where?"

"In the suite?" Treesi asked.

"No, in the Little Council room," Owyn said.

Del nodded his agreement. "*There are passages that start near there. It's a good place to start from.*"

"In an hour?" Steward asked. "I'll bring the maps there, and we'll collect everyone who intends to search."

AN HOUR LATER, THERE were so many people ready to search the hidden passages that they moved from the Little Council room to the Hall. Steward had a table brought in, and the maps were laid out there. Aria took her seat on the dais, and nodded to Owyn and Del.

"Whenever you're ready," she said.

He nodded and turned, raising his voice. "All right! Can everyone hear me? We're going to be sending people out in pairs, so everyone pair up." He looked around as people started shuffling into pairs. Jehan and Memfis. Lexi and Steward. Karse and Esai. Danir and a boy that Owyn didn't know. Neera, who joined Aven near the dais. Guards pairing with Water warriors, and Owyn wondered why the guards weren't pairing with guards. Then he saw Karse watching them, and realized what it meant — Karse wasn't sure who was true to Aria, and who might still be a traitor. But he did trust the Water warriors. So every guard had a Water warrior to watch them. It made sense.

"Right," Owyn said, giving voice to Del's plan. "Every pair will get a map. And on every map is a different symbol. You get a piece of chalk, and when you go through your map, mark the beginning of your route with the symbol, and mark the end. If everything is the way it should be on the map, that's all you'll do. If you find something that's not on the map, mark it on the map. Just mark it. Don't search it. That's not this round. Right now, this pass is to rule out what we think is there already." He picked up the stacks of maps. "There are two of each map," he added. "So if anybody is thinking of keeping things hid...well, I don't think that there's anyone here wanting to keep things hid."

A ripple of nervous laughter through the guard, and some of them looked at each other. Owyn glanced at Karse. Interesting. They weren't sure of each other anymore either. He cleared his throat.

"There are a lot of passages. So we're doing this in sections. When you're done, come back here, turn in your map and get a new one." He gestured to the table. "Come up and get your maps."

People lined up, and Del wrote down who got each map, pointing out the symbol on each map and handing out pieces of colored chalk and lanterns. Finally, the only people left in the Hall were Aria, Alanar, Del and Owyn.

"Who did Aven go with?" Owyn asked.

"Neera," Aria answered. "And Treesi is with Gathi. How long do you think this will take them?"

Owyn looked at Del, who closed his eyes and tapped his fingers on the table.

"*An hour?*" he suggested. "*Under an hour, some of them.*"

Owyn nodded. "Right. Oh, who was that other boy? The one with Danir?"

Del nodded. "*His name is Copper. He's a foundling. I don't know him well. Ambaryl raised him, and he parroted her.*"

"If I heard Lexi right, he brought her a litter of kittens today," Alanar said. "She's very excited over that. Apparently, Ambaryl didn't like cats, and wouldn't have them in the kitchens?"

"She didn't like cats?" Aria repeated. "I didn't think I needed another reason to dislike her." She took a deep breath and closed her eyes. "What do we do while we wait?"

The Hall door opened, and Marik peered inside. "I...is Esai in here? They said she was in the Hall." He stepped inside. "This..." He looked up. "This is enormous! How can you have a room this big?"

"Marik, you didn't need to come inside!" Aria said. She got up and came down from the dais. "You're not to hurt yourself!"

Marik shook his head. "I'm fine. Well, for now I'm fine. Esai?"

"Is searching the tunnels with Karse," Aria answered.

"Oh, yes. She told me that," Marik looked up again. Then he shook his head. "I'd try, but I don't think I'd get far. It's a roof, not a cave. My brain knows the difference." He looked around. "Oh, Owyn, did Aven introduce you to Copper yet?"

"We were just talking about him," Owyn said. "And no. But he's helping to search. Why?"

"Can we step out?" Marik asked. He blushed slightly. "It's a big room, but it's still too much."

Owyn nodded and followed Marik out of the Hall and through the large entryway into the courtyard. Once outside, Marik visibly relaxed. Then he looked up and laughed.

"Wraith wants to know why I keep doing this to myself," he said. "Why I keep going inside when he knows I don't like it."

"It's a fair question," Owyn said. "Now, why am I being introduced to Copper?"

"Because he needs someone other than Ambaryl to look to," Marik answered. "Lexi said he was abandoned here when he was small. He's a Palace fosterling, but it looks to me like he bonded to Ambaryl, and she treated him..." he paused. "I doubt she hit him.

Someone would have stopped her if she'd been hitting him. But he said that if she got mad enough at him, she'd put him out."

"Oh, fuck," Owyn breathed. "No, that's not right."

"He was throwing rocks at Wraith earlier," Marik continued. "He didn't tell us why at first. But he decided to trust me. Trust us, since he came to me and to Aven. He was doing it to protect a litter of kittens that he was keeping hidden from Ambaryl. Because he was afraid she was going to come back and find them." He looked at Owyn. "No one told them that she's dead, Owyn. Lexi knows now, and she'll tell him. But he's going to need someone to help him."

"And you all think it's me," Owyn said. "Because...what, because I can understand him?" He considered it. "I don't know a lot about children, Marik."

"You need the practice," Marik answered. "There's going to be one this time next year."

"Yeah, but I'll have time to get used to the idea before it can argue with me," Owyn said. Marik laughed. "Look, introduce me and we'll see what happens. He might want you more than me, if he's coming to you."

Marik nodded. "He might. And if he does, then we'll see what happens." He smiled. "Didn't think I'd be a father this soon after getting married. Especially since we're not technically married yet." He looked around. "I'm...well, I suppose I can go work on moving us into the falconer's quarters. Want to see?"

"They have a place for you out here?" Owyn asked. "And you're good with it?"

"It's built into the walls. It's sort of a cave. I think I'll be all right. And since it's not really a cave, it makes Esai happy." He gestured. "It's over here."

The falconer's quarters were very cave-like, but not enough to bother Owyn — there were two wide windows built into the outward-facing wall. There was a large front room, and a pair of smaller, inner rooms that Owyn assumed were bedrooms.

"This is the best part," Marik said, and opened a door in the left hand wall of the outer room. The room on the other side was large and open, with a floor that was part dirt, part gravel. There were two perches, and the windows here were open, but covered with wooden slats. Between the windows was a long drape, which Owyn assumed covered the door. "I'll need to open up one of the windows, or prop the door open," Marik added. "Wraith wants to be able to come and go as he pleases."

"What does he think of it?" Owyn asked.

"He likes it," Marik answered. "It's comfortable and quiet."

"Good," Owyn said. "That's good." He looked around again and nodded. "I should be going back in."

"Go ahead. I'll get us unpacked here." Marik walked him back to the other room, and Owyn trotted back across the courtyard to the Palace. The first groups should be coming back soon to exchange their maps.

He was right. The first group — Neera and Aven — reached the Hall just as he did.

"Nothing untoward," Aven announced. "Everything was exactly the way it was on the map."

Everything exactly as it was on the map was what each group said as they came back. They all took their new maps and went back out, repeating until there was only one map left in the pile, and Del was frowning at his list. Owyn knew why. He'd noticed who hadn't come back.

"Where did Danir and Copper go?"

CHAPTER THIRTY-FOUR

O wyn looked at the larger map. "Which section did you assign them?"

Del came over to point. "*This one. Aven and Neera were there earlier and said they found nothing unusual. That's why I gave it to the boys.*"

Owyn studied the map, then traced the outline of the section where the boys had last been seen. It was marked in green.

"Lexi?" Owyn called. "What can you tell me about this section?"

Lexi joined him at the table. "That section is off the primary servant passages. The kitchens are here." She pointed. "It's not a passage that was in use, really. It was a renovated section, and there really isn't anything we use off that passage. There's nothing unusual about this section at all."

Owyn nodded. Something that should have been completely harmless, completely known to Danir. They weren't anywhere near any of the red passages that had been saved and assigned to guards and warriors. But there was something nagging at him. Knowing where the kitchens were gave him a sense of location for the building that he still wasn't sure of. He reached over and touched an empty place on the page. "What's here?"

Lexi sniffed. "There's nothing there."

Owyn shook his head. "That's...that's an awful lot of nothing," He reached over and picked up a piece of chalk. "The kitchens are here," he said, and started drawing. "The wall is...here, right? And the door to the courtyard?" He sketched a line, making a right angle. "The healer gardens are here, and the practice yards...about here, yeah?" He looked up, seeing the puzzled look on Lexi's face. "Do I have this right?"

"Yes," she said softly. "And...you're right. That is an awful lot of nothing. That space can't be solid wall. It just can't. Especially since there are rooms over that—"

"I know. My room is over that." He stepped back from the map and looked across at Steward, who was staring with wide-eyed fascination. "I think we found it. And I think the boys found it first."

"And now we need to find them," Aven said. "Right. I'm going back in. Del, I'll need you to update the small map with the area where they might be. Steward? Lexi? You both know those tunnels better than I do." Del nodded and grabbed the small map, started sketching. Aven turned. "Aria, my father went off with Mem. You and Treesi, see if you can find them? I think we'll want him ready, just in case. Owyn, would you tell Alanar to be ready in the healing center?"

"Aven, what other help can we be?" Aria asked. "What else can we do?"

Aven frowned slightly and tucked his chin. Then he nodded. "Find Karse. Tell him we're going to need guards he can trust to properly map this area when we're done, and to seal it if necessary."

Aria and Treesi left as Del stood up, a new map in his hand. He came over to join Aven, Lexi and Steward, showing them the sketch. Steward took it, and they headed toward the door.

Owyn watched them go, then closed his eyes, swallowed hard, and said, "I'm coming with you."

Aven turned. "No, you're not. I'm not letting you hurt yourself—"

"I'm going with you. If it gets to be too much, I'll come back." Owyn ran his fingers through his hair. "I can do it."

Aven came to stand in front of Owyn, studying his face, close enough that Owyn could see the hints of green and gold in his hazel eyes.

"Are you sure?" Aven asked, his voice just as quiet. "Mouse, I love you, but this is not the time to test your limits."

"I need to do this, Fishie," he said softly. He looked at Del. "When did they go out?"

Del frowned, then signed, "*Third or fourth round. I'd have to look.*"

"That's a couple of hours they've been back there, then," Owyn said. "And the lanterns...they're going to be in the dark really soon. We can't waste time arguing. I'm going."

Aven nodded. "Then let's go."

Lexi led them first to the kitchens, where she gave them all fresh lanterns. Owyn watched as she filled one with oil — her hands were shaking.

"We're going to find them," he said softly. She looked up at him.

"Of course we're going to find them," she snapped back at him. Steward put his hand on her shoulder, and she shuddered. "I'm sorry. I...I shouldn't bite at you."

"If it helps, feel free to bite all you want," Owyn said. "Just don't break the skin, or Allie will get angry."

She smiled slightly. "This way," she said, and led them out of the kitchen.

Owyn was second to last into the passage, and immediately felt the walls starting to close in. It got worse as the door swung closed behind him.

"Owyn?" Steward said. "You've gone white as a sheet."

"I'm..." Owyn stopped and swallowed. "Well, not fine. But I'm doing this. Just...just give me a minute." He closed his eyes, took a deep breath. Tried to force his heart to slow and all his migratory body parts to go back where they were supposed to be. When he opened his eyes, everyone was looking at him. "I'm fine."

"You're not," Aven said. "Come walk with me." He held his hand out.

"Aven, I don't need to hold your hand," Owyn grumbled. But he took Aven's hand, and let him lead them down the corridor. In the lantern light, he saw two chalk marks on the wall — a star, and a crescent. "Which one is yours, Fishie?"

"The star," Aven answered. "Del, where are we going?"

Del gestured, moving to lead the way. His voice was soft in Owyn's mind. "*It's not a long corridor,*" he said. "*I don't know where they could have gotten to.*"

"If they found something, it would be on the right-hand wall," Steward said, holding the map to the light.

Owyn started to study the wall. It didn't seem all that remarkable — the walls here looked very much like the walls outside the Heir's suite, except that the plaster was flaking off to reveal the dark stone beneath.

"You said this was closed off in renovations?" he asked. "When?"

"I'm not even sure, to be honest," Lexi said. "And I never asked. These passages don't go anywhere useful, and they dead-end...there."

Aven stopped, letting Owyn's hand fall. "There's nowhere for them to go," he said. "They knew they had to come back and turn in the map. They wouldn't have run off."

"Especially since Copper was supposed to come back to the kitchens and help me with the kittens," Lexi said.

"All right. Spread out and search the wall," Aven said. "Owyn, if you start feeling off—"

"Start?" Owyn managed not to squeak when he said it, but just barely. Aven smiled.

"If you start feeling more off than you already are, tell me and I'll take you out."

Owyn nodded and moved off, frowning at the wall. There had to be something. Another door, maybe? Something that the boys might have opened by accident? Which would mean that the mechanisms would be lower. He looked down slightly, studying the plaster. Then he coughed.

"Check the floor," he said. "The plaster is falling off. Look for piles. If something moved, the plaster probably fell off a lot." He stepped back, saw a scattering of plaster, then saw something he had missed. Half a crescent, scrawled in chalk on the wall. He crouched, and found a bit of plaster in the litter on the floor with the rest of the crescent. "Here," he called. "It's here." He pointed as the others joined him. "They marked the wall. It's...it's something here."

Steward came closer, and ran his hand over the wall. "There's a catch. There has to be a catch—"

"And it has to be low," Owyn said. "Low enough for someone Danir's size, or Copper's size." He stepped back. "If it was me, I'd be running my hand on the wall. And Danir... wait." There was decorative scrollwork that ran the length of the wall, just like in the corridor that led to the suite. He walked back a short distance, then came back toward the mark, doing something he'd seen Danir doing in the hall outside the suite — he ran his fingers along the top of the scrollwork. As he reached the place where the symbol had been scrawled, his fingers touched something that sank under pressure. He heard a click, and a section of the wall shifted. There was a deafening screech of tortured gears, and plaster rained down onto the floor. Behind the door was another corridor, and no signs of Danir or Copper.

"That's a servant corridor," Lexi said. "Probably like the ones that run behind the rooms on the upper levels of this wing. I had no idea this was here. I didn't even know there were suites here. There will be doors that open into them—"

"And I'll bet one of those suites was where they were hiding Milon," Aven said. "Right. Someone needs to stay and make sure this door doesn't close on us."

"I'll stay," Steward said. "Unless Owyn wants to."

Owyn looked over at him. "Why didn't you volunteer me to stay? Not that I'm complaining."

"Because you got yourself this far," Steward answered. "I'm not stopping you from going further."

Owyn blinked, then looked down the dark corridor. "All right. You saw where the catch was?"

"I saw. Go on." Steward handed Del the map, and they started walking. The light from the lanterns illuminated doors on one side.

"Open the doors," Lexi said. "That way, we know there's nothing in them."

"Are we sure there's nothing in them?" Aven asked. "I didn't bring a weapon. Not that there's enough room to swing a sword in here."

"Open them carefully, then?" Lexi said. Owyn moved to the closest one and stood with his back against the wall next to the door. He reached out and touched the knob, then looked at Aven. Aven took a position on the other side of the door, the lantern hanging from his hand.

All at once, Owyn heard Aven's voice in his mind, *"When you open the door, move. If there's someone in there, they're going to get hit with burning oil. I don't want to get you."*

Owyn nodded. Then he turned the knob and pushed the door open. It swung wide and banged into the wall, bouncing almost closed again. The sound echoed, and almost immediately they heard more banging from down the hall, and faint voices.

"Danir?" Lexi gasped. "Danir!"

"Go," Aven said. "We'll open the rest of the rooms. Del, go with her."

Lexi and Del ran down the corridor. Aven and Owyn followed, moving slowly down the hall, opening doors into empty rooms. After the third one, Aven relaxed.

"There's no one here," he said. "Look at the dust inside. There hasn't been anyone in here for years."

Owyn nodded. "We'll want to search them all anyway. See if anything was stored in them. Or hidden."

"Aven?" Lexi called. "Owyn? You want to see this."

"How are you feeling?" Aven asked. Owyn blinked, then looked around.

"I...fine until you asked me?" Owyn said with a weak laugh. "I was distracted enough that I wasn't thinking about it. Now...yeah, can we finish?"

Aven smiled. "Let's go see what the boys found."

At the end of the corridor, Lexi was standing outside a doorway that had a chair propped in it to keep it from closing. She was holding two boys to her sides, murmuring soft words of comfort. Danir straightened when he saw Owyn and Aven.

"I..." He looked at Copper, then clasped his hands behind his back. "We weren't supposed to search. But we found the door, and it wasn't on the map, and it didn't look like it was that long, and we thought maybe we'd just see a little. And the door at the end was open but it closed on us and locked, and..." He stopped. "There's stuff in there. A lot of stuff."

"You may have found exactly what we were looking for," Aven said. "But you went against instructions to do it. You're lucky we found you."

Danir shook his head. "I knew you were going to find us. You all promised to look after us. I knew you'd come find us." He grinned. "Copper was scared—"

"So were you!" Copper retorted.

"We were all scared," Owyn said. "Where's Del?"

"He went in to take a look," Lexi said. "And we made sure the door wasn't going to close on him."

Owyn nodded and went to the door, peering into the room. It wasn't dark, but it wasn't as brightly lit as Owyn would have expected for the time of day. Unless they'd been searching long enough for the sun to go down? He didn't think so.

"Found anything?" he called.

"*The windows are boarded up on the bottom halves. All of them. It must have been horribly hot in here in high summer,*" Del answered. "*This was definitely a prison. A comfortable prison, but a prison.*"

Owyn looked up at Aven. "This is it," he said. "Do we want Aria to see this?"

Aven bit his lip, then shook his head. "I don't want to upset her. Lexi, take the boys out. We'll need better light, and a way to disable the locks on these doors. I'll want my father and Mem—"

"No. Not Mem," Owyn said. "Same reason we don't want Aria in here. Not yet. Your fa, yes. Not mine."

Aven nodded. "Lexi, my father, please. And Karse. And...don't tell Aria or Mem what you want them for. If you can help it."

Lexi nodded. "I'll try. Come on, the both of you. You've had a grand adventure, and now there's some warm milk and honeycakes for you both."

"Honeycakes?" Copper gasped. "Really?"

"Really," Lexi answered. "You've both done men's work today. It's time to go back to being boys." She led them down the corridor.

Owyn turned to face Aven. "You first?" he asked. Aven smiled and headed into the room. Owyn followed him.

The short hall opened up into the back of what looked like a large sitting room. There was hardly any furniture in the room. Two tables. Several bookcases. A desk. The windows were boarded over, but the boards stopped just over the level of Aven's head, allowing light in through the tops of the glass. There was a boarded-up double door on the right hand wall, and another door on the left. Del appeared through the left hand doors, and put his lantern down on the table to free his hands.

"*This is a bedroom,*" he signed. "*And there's a bathing room. There are clothes in the bedroom, and books.*"

Owyn nodded and walked over to the desk. There was a pen laying on the desk, and an uncapped inkwell. An open book, the page half-filled with small, neat handwriting. He leaned close and realized what he was looking at.

"A journal," he said. "He kept journals, just like we thought. And we were right. They didn't have time to take them with them."

"*There's something else.*"

Owyn turned to see Del, still standing at the double door. Aven was with him, and he waved Owyn closer. "You were right," he said, and pointed. Owyn looked through the doors, into the bedroom.

Resting on its side in the middle of the floor was a wheeled chair.

CHAPTER THIRTY-FIVE

Jehan arrived with Karse as Aven and Owyn tugged the last board down from over the sitting room windows, filling the room with light. Jehan stopped just inside the room and closed his eyes.

"He was here," he murmured. "The entire time. He was here." He looked around. "You were right to keep Mem out. Although I'm not sure how long you can keep Mem out."

Aven nodded, dropping the board he was holding on the floor. "Del's collected all the journals. There are dozens of them. Given how many, I'm not surprised that Risha left them. There were too many to carry quickly."

Karse walked around the room, stopping at the pile of boards under one window. "The windows were boarded up?"

"Only halfway," Owyn said. "The bedroom is still boarded, if you want to see."

Karse headed to the double doors and went into the bedroom. Jehan went to the table, looking at the piles of books.

"*They're numbered,*" Del signed. "*So they're in order. We can take them back to the suite and read them there.*"

Jehan nodded. He picked up one of the books and flipped it open, tipping it slightly toward the light. He smiled slightly. "His handwriting. He wrote so small. He could get more words on the page than anyone I'd ever seen." His brow furrowed, and the smile faded. "Oh, Mother. Listen to this. *I am alive. I don't know why. Agisti tells me that my Companions sacrificed themselves to save my life. She tells me that I will survive, that I will stand again, but that for now, I must hide, and heal. And then? I don't know what I will do then. How can I go forward, without them? Without my Mem, without Jehan or Aleia. At least Liara is safe, and will stay safe. Agisti has promised to see that word is sent to her, that she must stay safe in the mountains, for the sake of our child.*"

Owyn cleared his throat. "He told me that they told him you all were dead."

Jehan nodded. "I wonder. Did Agisti ever send the message? Is that why Liara never came down from the mountain? There's no way she could have known it wasn't safe."

"I don't know if it matters," Aven answered. "Agisti is the one who started all this. She might have meant well, but..." He waved one arm, trying to encompass the entire Palace, the entirety of Adavar, and every moment of the past twenty-five years in one gesture. He must have succeeded, because his father sighed and nodded.

"Truth." He looked around. "When did it change, I wonder? From meaning well to...this? All right. I'll take over here. You three go and rest. You have other work to do. Send Steward in, and if you see Neera inside, tell her I want as many cousins as she can muster to carry things."

Aven nodded. "All right." He studied his father for a moment, then added, "Fa, it's not your fault."

Jehan didn't look up. "We should have stayed with him."

"If you'd stayed with him, then they'd might have been telling him the truth when they told him you died," Owyn said. "They'd either have handed you over to the Usurper, or you and Aleia and Mem would all be in rooms down the hall." He paused. "Fuck, if you hadn't done what you did, we wouldn't have Aven. Or me!"

Aven turned to look at Owyn. "What?"

"Fishie," Owyn said. "Think about it. If your parents and Mem were taken prisoner when they took Milon, they'd each have been in one of the other rooms...fuck. There were three other rooms." He looked toward the door. "Were...were they *planning* this? How could they plan for this?"

"Doesn't matter, Mouse. Go on," Aven said. His throat felt dry.

Owyn nodded. "If they'd locked up Jehan and Aleia and Mem, they wouldn't have put them together. They wouldn't have put them so they could plan anything. Which means no you—"

"Aleia was already pregnant," Jehan said. "She told me the morning of the attacks."

Aven looked at his father. "If they'd taken you both, locked each of you up in those rooms in the name of hiding you—"

"They probably would have taken you from your mother the minute you were born. Assuming you both even survived," Jehan finished.

Aven blinked. "I...what?"

"There's a reason you never had any brothers or sisters, for all that we wanted them. Your mother didn't have the easiest time birthing you, Ven," Jehan said. "It's a good thing we were at the main healing complex when you were born, and that Mother is as good a healer as she is." He looked around. "So...yes, I agree with Owyn. If we'd been kept here, the way they kept Milon, then you wouldn't be here now. And if Mem didn't go back to Forge, Owyn wouldn't be here either."

"Oh, I'd have been dead years ago," Owyn said, sounding oddly cheerful. "But I'm not. And Aven's here. So...yeah, things happened the way they needed to happen. No more should haves. You did what you did, and now...well, now we're here."

"Fixing what happened because we did what we did?" Jehan asked. He grinned.

"Nope," Owyn answered. "Fixing what happened because the Usurper did what he did." He looked up. "This isn't too bad, now that the windows are open. But I want to go out. I think I need to eat."

Aven nodded, coming around the table and held his hand out to Owyn. "Del, are you coming?" he asked, turning. Del was standing near the fireplace, biting his thumbnail. He shook his head.

"*No,*" he signed. "*I'll stay and help. Go feed Owyn, and tell Aria we found it, and we found her father's journals. She'll want them.*"

Aven glanced at his father, who nodded and walked over to rest his hand on Del's shoulder. Aven turned back toward the door and led Owyn out.

"Any idea what's bothering Del?" Owyn asked as they walked down the dark corridor. They could see Steward at the end.

Aven shook his head. "I don't know. Let me get a chair, so we can prop the door open and Steward doesn't have to hold it." He let go of Owyn's hand and went into one of the other rooms. The curtains were closed, and he went to one and tugged them open, filling the room with light.

Would this have been his mother's room? Or his father's? He shook his head and picked up a chair, walking back out into the corridor. Owyn had kept walking, and was at the head of the corridor, talking to Steward.

"This was definitely it?" Steward said as Aven came within earshot. "This was where they hid him?"

Aven put the chair down and shoved it against the door. "Yes," he said. "And you can go see if you want."

Steward looked down the corridor. "The other one, he thought he was ruling. He honestly did think that. He thought he'd been raised to rule, and he thought he was a good ruler. For years, he thought he was the one in control of everything." He sighed and shook his head. "He's better off forgotten, the Usurper. No matter what he thought, he wasn't very good at being a ruler. Not if his own servants could keep something like this hidden from him for twenty-five years."

Owyn snorted. "One of the last times I talked to him when we were in the Palace, I asked him if he was a clerk at heart. He told me he was a librarian. So maybe he wasn't good at ruling, but he was good at organizing. Good at taking care of things and people. Everyone who came to the Palace to see him judged said he was good at taking care of them. That's not the same as ruling."

Steward nodded. Then he smiled. "I'm very glad, then, that I'm not a ruler, and I just have to take care of the Palace and the people."

Aven laughed. "And we're glad to have you caring for us. Fa says you should go in. I think cataloging exactly what's in there would be a good thing. And I'll send some of my cousins in to help carry the journals out."

Steward nodded and headed down the corridor. Aven took Owyn's hand again as they started walking.

"Are you all right?" he asked. He didn't try to examine Owyn — he wasn't worried about physical ills this time.

"You're the healer," Owyn answered. "Am I?"

"Mouse..."

"I'm fine," Owyn said with a laugh. He looked back over his shoulder. "I...that wasn't as hard as the caves in Terraces were. Maybe because I was doing something. I was distracted."

"Probably," Aven agreed. "Let's go get you something to eat. Then we'll find Aria."

Owyn nodded. He leaned into Aven's arm, and Aven let go of his hand and put his arm around Owyn's shoulders.

"I'm tired, Ven," Owyn murmured.

"We'll get some food for you, and you'll feel better."

"No, it's not that," Owyn said. He stopped and turned to face Aven. "I...the people who did this. To Milon. They meant well, when it started. Right? I mean, they were trying to protect him." He paused, looked down the hall. Then he looked back up at Aven. "I don't understand why they lied to him. About Mem and your parents. And I don't understand how it changed from protecting him to keeping him prisoner. And...they meant well." He paused. "We mean well. How do we not make that mistake? I mean, we don't know what we're doing. How do we not do...that?"

Aven shook his head. "I don't know the answer to that," he said. "Maybe it's something we'll learn from Fa and Mem and Ama. Or maybe it's something we'll find in the journals. The ones from the other Companions Steward says we have to read, and the ones Milon left us."

"Aria gets to see those first." Owyn said. "Then Granna and Mem. I have to tell Granna and Mem what we found. I don't know how Mem is going to take it. I mean...he smashed his gem because he thought Milon was dead. I don't understand why he didn't see the truth in the smoke. Why the Mother kept that from him." He reached up and touched the Fire gem at his throat, then closed his eyes and took a deep breath. "I need to eat. I'm getting really fucking maudlin."

"Let's go."

THERE WAS NO ONE IN the suite when Aven and Owyn got there.

"Aria might be in her office," Owyn said. "We have offices, too. Did Del tell you that?"

"No," Aven said. "Sit down. I'll make a plate for you." He hugged Owyn to his side, then let him go and went to the sideboard. He filled a plate up — ignoring the platter of various cheeses in favor of nuts and cured meats. And somehow, it didn't surprise him at all that Owyn was asleep by the time he got back to the chair. He put the plate down on the table next to Owyn's chair, then sat down on the couch across from him to think.

How would they know how to not make the same kinds of mistakes that had left them with these problems? He knew he didn't know nearly enough. None of them did. If things had been the way they were supposed to have been, they'd have been trained to this since childhood. He'd have grown up here, with Aria...

Which would have made being her Companion very strange. Would they be lovers...or siblings? He shuddered at the idea, and shook his head. No, being in the Palace, being trained to this, that wouldn't have made a difference. According to Owyn, the Usurper had been trained to this, but he'd gone horribly wrong.

They had no training. How could they keep from doing the same? Or doing worse?

He looked up as the door opened, and smiled as Aria came in. She looked surprised to see him.

"You're done?" she asked. "What did you find?"

"Yes, we're done," Aven answered. "And I was going to come find you once I'd made sure that Owyn ate something. But he fell asleep before he could eat." He nodded toward the chair. Aria sighed.

"Oh, my Owyn," she murmured. "The Mother is using him so much harder than the rest of us."

"Don't let him hear you say that," Aven warned. He reached out and took her hand, tugging her into his lap. She chuckled and cuddled close.

"I know him well enough to know that," she said. "I'm going to be too heavy to do this soon."

"And I'll still hold you anyway," Aven said. He slid his arm around her lower back, smiling as her feathers brushed his skin.

"So...do we talk about what we found first, or do I tell you what I was thinking first?"

"What you found," Aria said. "Tell me."

Aven nodded. "The boys found it. There was a servant corridor that wasn't on the maps, hidden off a corridor that we searched. Neera and I missed it, but the boys found it. There were four suites there...oh. I don't know where the other doors to those suites are. There have to be more passages not on the maps. We'll have to ask Steward."

"Aven..."

"Sorry," Aven said, giving a soft laugh. "Just thought of that. There were four rooms. Owyn thinks the other three were for my parents and Mem. I don't know. But the last one...that was your father's room. His prison. Aria, he left journals. Too many for Risha to take with her. Fa will bring them here."

He felt her shiver. "Journals. What else? What else did you find?"

"Proof that Owyn was right," Aven said. "Remember he said that when he was in Milon's head, he couldn't feel anything below the waist? And we thought it might be because he was stabbed in the back? There was a wheeled chair in the room." He left out that it had been tipped over. He didn't like the implications of that, and upsetting Aria was the last thing he wanted to do.

"When can I see this room?" Aria asked.

"Fa and Karse are searching it now, seeing what's been left behind, and they'll be bringing the journals here," Aven answered. "We need to give them time to search properly. So...you'll see it tomorrow? You and Memfis and Lady Meris?"

Aria nodded. "Have you told Memfis yet?"

Aven shook his head. "No. We were going to tell them after we told you. Now, I think we'll tell them after Owyn wakes up and eats." He tightened his arm around Aria. "It means I get to have you to myself for a little while longer."

She smiled and rested her head on his shoulder. "It was so simple, when it was just the three of us. It's never going to be that simple again."

Aven sighed. "That leads into what I was thinking. Aria, how do we keep from making the same mistakes?"

She raised her head and looked at him. "I don't understand."

Aven took a deep breath. "We don't have any of the training we need. We were supposed to be raised to this, you and I. We were supposed to have been trained by the Companions before us. I don't know what your mother taught you, but Ama never said a single word about any of this to me. Now...we're here, and we're supposed to rule. And we don't know what we're doing. How do we keep from making the mistakes the Usurper did?"

"Well, if you even think of trying to kill the rest of us, I'll break both your legs," Owyn muttered from the other chair. "So there's that. And we'll get training so it doesn't come to that."

Aria giggled. "How long have you been awake?"

"Long enough to hear you being nostalgic for the days when it was just the three of us trying to get killed." Owyn sat up and stretched, and Aven heard his back crackle and pop from where he was sitting. "This is for me?" he asked, pointing to the plate.

"Yes," Aven said. "Eat, and we'll go find Memfis and Meris."

Owyn nodded. He picked his plate up, then got up and crossed to sit on the couch next to Aven. "That's better," he said, pulling Aria's legs over his own so that he could move in closer to Aven. Aven put his free arm around Owyn's shoulders, and Owyn sighed. "Sometimes, I miss it, too," he said. "Those early days, before we all changed. It was simpler then. More simple? Which is right?"

"It doesn't matter," Aria said. "I'm not criticizing your grammar. So, if one of us decides to murder the others and take over—"

"The others will stop them," Owyn answered. He picked up a piece of meat and popped it into his mouth. "Because we're all of us in this together. The Mother picked us, and put us here. Right? So we're the right people. We might make mistakes, but they're not going to be huge, destroy-the-world mistakes. Because we're balanced. And we'll learn. No cheese, Fishie?"

"I wasn't sure which you'd want, and I don't want to taste them," Aven answered. "I'm not sure which color you like better."

"I'll get up and get some," Owyn said. Then he set his plate down next to him and cuddled closer, resting his hand on Aria's thigh. "Later. This is nice. Sitting like this with Allie is nice, but it's nice with you, too. We need to make sure we have time for this. Just being together. We're too busy."

"We are going to be busy quite a lot, and for quite a while," Aria said. "The progress...as much as I am looking forward to going, to seeing if we can find answers, and finding my father, I'm not looking forward to leaving. This...I like this. I like the Palace. I like having everyone I care for under one roof."

"One extremely massive roof," Owyn muttered under his breath.

"Yes, one extremely massive roof," Aria agreed. "You are all here. Everyone I love is here. And now we have to go." She paused. "And possibly find him."

"We'll find him, Aria," Owyn said. "He wants to know you."

"And when we find him, what then?" Aria asked. "Will he take the crown and the throne?"

"I suppose the question is will he want it?" Aven asked. "After all this time, and losing everything? Will he want to take the throne, or will he want to live the rest of his life in peace? We won't know that until we find him."

Owyn shifted in his seat. "Well, I could—"

"No!" Aria and Aven answered in one voice. They looked at each other, then at Owyn, and they all started laughing.

"Very well," Aria said. "We will find out what his answer will be when we find him. And we will learn then what we need to do. But first, we need to find him. And to do that, we need to leave." She took a deep breath. "Let's go find Memfis and Grandmother."

CHAPTER THIRTY-SIX

Aven, Aria and Owyn went down to the practice yards, hoping to find Neera. It would, Aven hoped, save them from having to go down to the dock, and would let them move on to searching for Meris and Memfis.

"Aven, there she is," Owyn said, pointing at the mossy dancing floor. She was standing at the railing, watching an older man on the dancing floor. "And...who's that with her? And what's he doing?"

As the old man turned, Aven recognized him. "That's Skela," he said.

"Skela," Owyn repeated. "Del's Skela? His tutor?" Owyn looked at the dancing man, then back at Aven. "I thought he was dead. Did you know he was alive? You had to. You know who he is."

Aven nodded. "Del knows, too. Skela spent some time with us after we went to the family. His family canoes range further..." he stopped, his breath catching as he realized something. "Further north."

Aria's brows rose. "Is that so?" she murmured. "Then perhaps I should speak with him."

They walked toward the dancing floor. Neera turned and smiled at them.

"You wanted to know if we could find anyone who used falling stars," she said as they joined her. "I found someone."

"Skela uses falling stars?" Aven repeated. "That's a stroke of luck."

"He says he may very well be the last person you'll find who uses them. He hasn't heard of anyone or seen anyone who uses them at all at the big gatherings, and he wants to know where Othi heard of them," Neera said. "He hasn't touched them since before he was Del's tutor. He said he would be happy to teach Del, once he's back in practice. Where is Del?" She looked around, then up at Aven. "Did you find what we were looking for?"

Aven nodded. "We found it. And he's still in there, helping them clear the room out. We'll need a couple of volunteers to help carry books to the Heir's suite."

Neera nodded. "I'll send a few of the cousins up. Four?"

"Six," Owyn said. "There were quite a few books." Neera arched a brow at him, and he grinned. "I stopped counting when I hit twenty."

Neera snorted. "I know you can count higher than that, Owyn," she teased. She turned to the dance floor. "Skela!"

The old man stopped moving slowly, letting the two long pendulums he was holding settle so that they dangled from his hands. He turned, and smiled. "Well, I have an audience. Waterborn, and...oh." He took both pendulums in one hand and saluted, thumping his chest with his fist. "My Heir. I didn't realize you were watching."

"It was interesting to watch," Aria answered. "They remind me a little of Owyn's whip chain."

Skela nodded. "I have seen the whip chain. They are similar. I'm not sure which inspired the other." He smiled impishly. "I'm not that old."

"So, instead of one long chain, you have two short ones?" Owyn asked. He stepped closer. "What's on the end?"

"It depends," Skela answered. He picked up one of the pendulums. "These are training stars. They're filled with sand. They'll bruise, if you hit someone hard enough. Or hit yourself hard enough. But they won't break bones."

Owyn nodded. "My whip chain has a ball and a blade. I can change them out. What do you use when you fight with these?"

Skela studied Owyn for a moment. "You're the Fireborn, then? The Twiceborn?"

Owyn smiled. "You can just call me Owyn," he said.

"Well, Owyn. Do you know what a wolf-singer is?"

Owyn nodded. "Marik told me about them. I wasn't sure I believed him. Are they real?"

Skela nodded. "They are real. When we hunt them, we take the teeth, and we embed them into koa gourds—"

"Those are about the size of a large apple," Aven interjected.

"They're soft when you pick them, so you can hollow them out and push the teeth through the rind," Skela continued. "Then you put the cord through the rind, fill them with sand, seal them, and hang them to dry. They get hard as stone as they dry."

Owyn coughed. "So you get a hard ball with razor spikes?"

Skela grinned. "They're a fearsome weapon, but hard to master. Not many want to take the time anymore. But if my Del wants to learn, I'll be happy to teach him." He nodded. "I have to say, when Neera told me that you all were looking for someone to teach Del to fight, I thought she was talking about someone else named Del. Because I didn't think that boy would ever be able to pick up a weapon to defend himself. Not after what that monster did to him."

"He killed a man to save our lives yesterday," Aven said. "He's a fine shot with a crossbow."

Skela paused in turning away, then turned back. "My Del killed a man? He raised a weapon to defend someone?"

"Why do you keep calling him your Del?" Owyn asked. "And...yeah. He freezes up solid if you attack him, but don't let him get you in his sights if you're trying to hurt someone else."

Skela chuckled. "That sounds like him. Yes. And yes, I do call him my Del. He reminds me of my grandson. When I first came here, Del was about the same age my Adar was when he disappeared and went back to the deep."

"Oh," Aria murmured. "He must have been very young. The Usurper told us that Del didn't have enough of the signs to tell him what really happened in the tower until he was sixteen."

"And the weapons master had him from the age of twelve," Owyn added. "When did you come to the Palace?"

"Del was nine," Skela said. "And as wild and frightened as a young water-cat. It took time to gentle him and to help him to learn." He shrugged. "Antavi came three years later. And Del...well, I thought it was because he was growing, becoming a man. He wanted his privacy. I had no idea what was happening until he was late to his lesson that day."

Owyn nodded. "He told me." He looked around, then lowered his voice, "And he told me that he helped you. Thank you."

Skela smiled slightly. "I wasn't going to lose my grandson again. My Del...I've missed him. It was good to see him out on the deep. Good to have time with him again. So when Neera said that he needed me to teach him again? I came to teach. Where is he?"

Aven nodded toward the Palace. "He's helping with clearing up some secrets we just found." He paused, glanced at Aria, then looked back at Skela. "Your canoes ranged further north than my grandmother's did."

Skela nodded. "That's right."

Aven hesitated and looked down at his hands. "Did many people in the northern canoes just disappear? Like your grandson?"

He heard Aria's breath catch, and looked up to see Skela's surprised look.

"Why do you ask?" Skela asked slowly. "Because...yes. Women, children. My Adar was not the only one who went to the deep without us ever knowing the reason why."

"Risha has been preying on our tribe, and on the children of Air. She thinks we're animals to be experimented on. To try to make us human, like Fire and Earth," Aven answered. "Del isn't the only Air that has lost their wings to her."

Skela went pale. "And what does she do to us?" he asked, his voice harsh.

"She kills us," Aven answered. "The man Del killed yesterday was trying to bring Aria and me back to her, so she could finish what she started. She's trying to break the cycle of change—"

"She what?" Skela gasped. "She...how? How could she do that? How is that possible?"

"Do you mind if I don't say it?" Aven asked. "Just...somehow, I am the only one to survive her torture since she started. She wants to know why."

Skela's eyes narrowed. "You limp," he said, pointing at Aven. "And I have seen you change. Forgive me, but how you change is not...not normal for someone so young. It is slower than it should be, and you are in pain when you do, and when you swim."

"To be honest, I'm in pain most of the time, on land or in the deep," Aven said. "What she did to me destroyed my hip. My change may never be without pain again."

Skela swallowed and closed his eyes. "I...I see. I think I understand. I will not ask you more. And I will speak to the others of my canoe, and find out what they might know."

Aria reached out and touched his arm. "Skela, anything they might know will be valuable to us," she said. "We are very certain that Risha has my father."

"Milon the Heir? But he died here, did he not?" Skela asked, gesturing to the Palace.

"He didn't," Aria answered. "He was hidden, kept away from the Usurper. But somehow...his protectors became his keepers, and he became a prisoner. Risha knew he was here, and now she has him. We have to find him—"

"And if she has a place to hide near my canoe's water, we may be the ones to find her, or her ship," Skela nodded. "I will go down to the water now, and speak to the others." He bowed slightly and walked away, heading toward the courtyard.

"I'll go with him," Neera said. "And I'll send the cousins up to help. Is there anything else we can do?"

Aven looked at Aria, who shook her head.

"There's nothing we can think of, Neera. Thank you."

DEL STACKED THE LAST of Milon's journals in a box and stepped back, letting the tall Water warrior take it. He knew Fara from his time on the canoes. She was one of Aven's side-cousins, and she'd been very interested in Del, and very clear in making her interest known. He hadn't seen her since he'd refused her advances.

"Where am I taking this?" she asked.

Del nodded and signed, "*The Heir's suite. Do you know where that is?*"

She chuckled. "I don't know where anything is in here. How can you find anything when you can't see the sky?"

Jehan laughed as he came out of the bedroom. "I heard that," he said. "And Del, I think we're done here. At least, we're done with the books. If you want to show Fara where to go, we'll be fine."

Del turned to him. "*You haven't packed anything else.*"

"Karse and I were talking, and we're not going to," Jehan replied. "We're leaving everything else where it is until Memfis has a chance to see the room." He looked around. "Mem knew Milon better than any of us. If there's anything important here, he'll see it. Karse and I might not. So we'll wait for him. Go on. You're done."

Dell nodded and gestured to Fara, leading her back down the now well-lit passage to the main corridor. As they passed through the propped-open door, Fara nudged him.

"Del, you're feeling...not right," she said. "What is it?"

Del forced a smile. "*Swimming in murky waters,*" he signed. "*I'm not sure. I'm trying to get my thoughts in order. There was something about that room and what they did that's bothering me.*"

She nodded. "There was something that bothered me, too. Being locked away like that, without being able to see the sky?" She shook her head. "It's really obvious that it's bothering you. Your stone face is slipping." She stopped walking. "Is it anything I can help with?"

Del stopped and turned to face her. "*No, but thank you. I need to puzzle it out.*"

Fara shifted her burden and started walking again, and Del caught up with her. "You'll do it. You're good at puzzling things out," she said. "I just...I don't like seeing you upset." She looked at him. "I know you told me no, but...we're friends, aren't we?"

"*Of course we are,*" Del signed. "*I just don't know what help you'll be when I'm not entirely certain what's bothering me.*"

"Fair enough," she said with a nod. "Come swimming with us tonight. Maybe that will help."

Del smiled. "*Maybe I will. I'll see.*"

"You don't play anymore," Fara said, nudging his shoulder with her own. "You're too serious now."

Del laughed and nudged her back. "*I'm busy!*"

"See? You're too serious!" She laughed. "You need to play, Del."

Del gestured as they reached the turn, and led her to the door to the Heir's suite. He opened the door and looked inside, smiling when he saw Alanar sitting in one of the armchairs. The tall healer had his head tipped back, and his eyes closed.

"Who's there?" Alanar asked, raising his head and opening his eyes. Del sighed and rolled his eyes, looking at Fara.

"Del," Fara answered. "And me. I'm Fara."

Alanar smiled. "Nice to meet you, Fara. I'm Alanar." He cocked his head to the side. "Water? Which canoe?"

"Varsi's canoe," Fara answered. "Aven is a side-cousin." She shifted her box. "Where should I put this, Del?"

"Oh, is there another box?" Alanar asked. "We've been putting them in Aria's room. She gets them first."

Fara nodded. "Del, which door?"

Del showed her, pointing out the row of identical boxes. Fara put the box down, then followed him back out into the main room.

"Sunset?" she asked. Del nodded, and she grinned, looking at Alanar. "Good. Bring your tall friend here."

"*He's married, Fara,*" Del signed. "*To the Twiceborn.*"

She laughed. "Bring them both," she said, and left. Del wondered if she'd be able to find her way out.

As the door clicked, Alanar sighed. "There's no one else here at the moment. I'm not sure where anyone is." He grimaced. "That's not exactly true. I know Treesi is with Lady Meris and Memfis, in the library. They're collecting the journals that she'll need to read, so that they can be printed in the right type." He took a deep breath. "So, you're stuck with me."

Del smiled and went over to Alanar's chair. He leaned down and kissed Alanar's cheek. Alanar smiled and reached up to catch Del by the wrist.

"Sit with me," Alanar said. "Things have been so crazed, and it's unsettling."

Del nodded and let Alanar pull him down into his lap, settling against the healer. He rested his head on Alanar's shoulder and closed his eyes.

"Your heart is quick," Alanar said. "And your blood is high. Are you all right?" He snorted. "You can't answer me. Why did I even ask?"

Del laughed and shook his head.

"You're not all right?" Alanar asked.

Del shrugged the shoulder against Alanar's chest, making Alanar laugh.

"You're not sure if you're all right or not?" Alanar guessed. "Something is bothering you?"

Del tapped Alanar on the nose, then clung to him as Alanar howled with laughter, shaking hard enough to rock the chair, laughing loud enough that Del missed the sound of the door opening.

"Look, they're having fun without us."

Del turned, seeing Owyn, Aria and Aven in the doorway. He shifted to get off Alanar's lap, only to have Alanar's arm around him tighten.

"Nope," Alanar said. "Pay a forfeit."

Del blinked. "*Forfeit?*"

"He wants a kiss, Del," Owyn answered.

"*What if I don't want to?*" he asked, feeling the first flutter of panic.

Immediately, Alanar's arm fell away, and Del scrambled off his lap. "Fuck. I didn't mean to frighten you, Del," Alanar said. "I just...I was teasing." He let his hands fall into his lap, a stricken look on his face. "I'm sorry!"

Del bit his lip, looked at Owyn, then turned back to Alanar and leaned down to kiss him on the cheek. Alanar smiled slightly.

"Thank you," he murmured. "You know, there aren't many times I wish I wasn't blind, but this is one." He leaned his head on his hand. "I've never seen the face of the man I love. I've never seen any of the people I love. And...because I can't see to even learn basic Water signs, I just scared someone I care a lot about. That..." He let out a short, sharp breath. "You know, I don't often feel crippled. But this is one of those times when I just feel broken." He sighed, then grimaced. "Aria, all the boxes with the journals are in your room."

"We need to find Mem and Granna, so that they can see the rooms," Owyn said.

"In the library with Treesi," Alanar answered. "Tell me about this room? Since, you know, I can't see it." He grimaced. "I haven't felt this frustrated in a long time."

Owyn moved over to sit with his husband, and Del went to sit by himself in a corner. He could hear Owyn describing the suite, but tried to ignore them. There was something about what Alanar said...

"Del?" Aven came to stand by his chair. "What is it?"

"I'm not sure," Del signed. *"There was something about that room."* He frowned. *"No, not the room. The room was...it was part of it. Just..."* He paused. Looked at Alanar.

Broken.

Del's breath caught, and he got up. *"Owyn? Ask Aria if I can look at the books?"*

Owyn turned. "What? Aria, Del wants to look at the books. Del, why?"

Del bit his lip, trying to get his racing thoughts in order. Then he started signing, *"Jehan asked when it went from meaning well to keeping Milon prisoner. Milon wrote that Agisti told him that he'd stand again. I want to see when they stopped trying to heal him, when they told him that he wouldn't stand again. And who told him."*

Owyn sat up. "What are you thinking?" He frowned. "Wait...Del, where are you going with this? Because if you're going where I think you're going...oh, fuck." He rubbed his hand over his face. "We need to look at the books. And we need to talk to Jehan."

"Will you two please finish a thought?" Aria demanded. "This is exhausting."

Owyn looked at Del. "It's your idea. I'll translate."

Del nodded and raised his hands. "*Ambaryl thought I was broken, that I was an idiot. What would she have thought of Milon? He couldn't walk.*"

Aria sat down on the couch. "She'd have called him broken, too. Wouldn't she?"

"She called Allie broken because he was blind, so yeah," Owyn said.

"She did what?" Alanar asked. "When was this?"

"You were at the healing center. And I didn't tell you because I didn't want you to break her arms. It was before we knew she'd been betraying us."

"If I'd know, I wouldn't have fought so hard to try and save her," Alanar grumbled. "All right. So, I'm broken, Del is broken, Milon...she probably thought he was broken, too. So?"

"*So I think that's when Milon went from being protected to being a prisoner.*" He shook his hands out. "*Remember the books from the hiding place in my father's office? They started out saying that the healers needed to keep working. That was Ankem. Nestor only said they needed a healer because of the ague. Because Milon must have gotten sick.*"

Aven scowled. "I think I want my father to hear this. Because Ambaryl had healer training. Risha was a healer. Was this something they learned? And from who?"

Aria nodded slowly. "Del, come with me. We will look through the books together. Aven, go and get Jehan and Steward."

Del nodded and followed Aria into her bedroom. He sat down on the floor and took a book from one of the boxes, handing it to Aria.

"We're looking for what they told him originally, and how it changed when Waran died," he signed. *"He died about sixteen years ago. That's when they brought Ambary! into the secret."*

Aria nodded. She sat down on the bed and started turning pages. Del picked up another book and started searching.

CHAPTER THIRTY-SEVEN

Aven turned down the corridor that would take him to the passage, and stopped. Meris, Memfis, Afansa and Treesi were coming out of the library. Treesi saw him first.

"Aven! We were going to come find you. Lexi said you found the boys, but wouldn't tell us what else. What did the boys find?"

Aven looked at Memfis and didn't turn away. "We found where they were keeping him. And he found his journals. Aria has them. Fa wants you and Lady Meris to see the rooms. But I need him first. Del...he may have an idea why they kept Milon locked away."

It took a moment before Memfis reacted, until slow horror crept over his face. "Where is it?"

"I'll show you," Aven said. "This way." He offered his arm to Meris, and led them through the halls to the propped-open door to the hidden passage. He stopped there and turned to face Memfis again.

"There are four rooms on this hall," he said. "Owyn thinks that if you had still been in the Palace when they found Milon, that you and Ama and Fa would have been in here along with Milon."

Memfis closed his eyes and swore softly. "I...how? How could they do this to him?"

"Del might be able to answer that," Aven answered. "Fa wants you to see the rooms. See if you see anything before they pack everything and take it out." He led them down the hall and stopped at the door to the suite. "Fa? I've brought Memfis and Lady Meris."

Jehan came and met them at the door. "Mem," he said. "I...this isn't going to be easy—"

"Just show me," Memfis growled. "Get out of my way."

Jehan nodded and stepped back, but not fast enough; Memfis shoved past him on his way into the room. Jehan fell backward into the wall. Aven stepped forward, but Jehan shook his head and signed, "*I'm fine. He's not.*"

"*Go be with him,*" Aven signed back. "*Send Steward out. We need him. And you, when you can come to the Heir's suite. Del may have an answer.*"

Jehan nodded and turned to Meris. "Lady Meris?" He escorted her and Afansa into the room. A moment later, Steward came out.

"Jehan said you needed me," he said. "What is it?"

"Remember how Del was off when Owyn and I left?" Aven said. "He might have figured something out. He said the room bothered him, and he thinks he knows why. He and Aria are going through the journals."

Steward nodded. "Right. And you need me for...what?"

Aven grinned. "Because Aria said she wanted you. Other than that? I don't know."

They started walking, and were about halfway down the corridor when an unearthly howl echoed from behind them. Aven whipped around, nearly throwing himself off-balance, stumbling until Steward caught him by one arm, and Treesi caught the other. The howl went on for several minutes, and Aven realized it was Memfis' voice.

"Mother of us all," Treesi breathed. "Do...should we go back?"

Aven looked at her, but before he could answer, Steward did, "No," he said softly. "Let him be. Jehan has him. And Meris and Karse. They'll be better able to help him."

A moment later, Afansa appeared in the door. She saw them, and came toward them. "Waterborn, your father says that you're to keep doing whatever you were doing," she said, her voice shaking. "And I'm to go with you. Or go do something else." She looked over her shoulder. "They want privacy."

"Then come with us," Aven said.

OWYN LOOKED UP FROM the plate he was filling as the door opened. "You're back," he said as Aven came in, then smiled when he saw Treesi, Steward and Afansa. "Wait...where's Jehan?"

Aven licked his lips. "I...I ran into Memfis and Lady Meris," he said. "And I took them to see. Fa is with Memfis. He...he was needed there."

"Needed?" Owyn repeated. "Needed how?"

"Mem is hurting," Treesi said. "A lot. Jehan and Meris and Karse, they're with him."

"Should I go?" Owyn asked. He put his plate down on the table hard enough that it rattled. "Does he need me?"

"I think you should let Jehan do his work," Steward said. "They'll be along later. Do you want to wait on what you've learned until they're here, or tell me now?"

Owyn looked at the closed door to Aria's room. "They haven't come out yet. I don't really know anything. I think I have an idea where Del's going with this, but I'm not sure." He sniffed. "Until he tells me what he's thinking, I'm in murky waters." He sighed. "I've got about half, I think. Afansa, come in and sit. Make yourself comfortable. And eat something. There's nibble food over there."

"I'm fine, thank you. But something to drink would be nice." She went to the sideboard, poured a glass of water. "Where should I sit?" she asked.

"You're welcome at the table," Owyn answered. He pulled a chair out for her, then took his own seat, pulling his plate toward him. Aven sat down facing him, and Treesi filled her own plate and came to sit next to him.

Aven looked around. "Where's Alanar?" he asked.

Owyn gestured behind himself. "Our room. He's still upset because he scared Del."

Steward sat down next to Aven. "Alanar frightened Del?"

Owyn sighed, rubbing his face. "When Allie likes someone, he teases them. Plays. It's all in play. If you're sitting with him, and you go to get up, he'll hold on, and won't let you up unless you pay a forfeit. It means he wants a kiss. He does it to me all the time. Aven, he do it to you yet?"

"No, but I'm too tall to sit in his lap the way you and Treesi do, and the way Del was sitting." Aven answered. "But I've seen him do it."

Owyn nodded. "He did it to Del," he said. "And Del got scared." He sighed and picked up a piece of hard cheese, taking a bite. He chewed and swallowed, then shook his head. "He apologized. Del forgave him. But he's still feeling about an inch tall."

Steward nodded. "I see," he said slowly. "We'll see how he is feeling when he comes out. What are you thinking?"

Owyn looked down at his plate. "What we read in Ankem's journal, and the little bit that Jehan read in Milon's first journal, they both seemed to say that the healers were working on Milon. That they were trying to heal whatever happened to him that killed his legs. But that changed somewhere. They stopped trying to help him." He frowned. "When I talked to him, he said that he didn't have a name anymore. That everyone had forgotten him. We need to know why." He looked up at Steward. "Del thinks it has something to do with how Ambaryl thought he was broken.

Because if she thought that about him, and about Allie, then what did she think of Milon?"

"And was it just Ambaryl?" Aven added. "Was Risha in on this, too? I mean...she doesn't think Air or Water are human, what does she think about someone like Del, or Alanar?" He laced his fingers and rested his chin on his interlaced thumbs. "Is that why she held Treesi and Alanar back? Not because they were going to be stronger than her, but because she didn't think they could, because of Alanar's eyes and the way Treesi sees?" He shook his head. "We don't know. And we don't know where they learned it. Ambaryl grew up in Terraces, didn't she?"

"No. She and Auntie Rhexa are from a smaller village. Not sure where. But near Terraces," Owyn answered.

"And Risha's from someplace near the border of Earth and Fire lands, near the mountains." Aven's brow furrowed. "The only thing they have in common is healing training. And I really, really am worried about that."

"Why?" Treesi asked. "I mean, it's not anything I remember hearing, ever. I know what they tried to make us think about the Waterborn and the Airborn, that they weren't human, but I don't think they ever said anything about someone not being human if they were disabled. And I don't know if she'd even have said something like that to me." She frowned. "No, I don't think she would have. I mean, she worked with me, to teach me how to work with what I can do, instead of letting it work against me. I don't know."

Owyn snorted. "Not sub-human. Just broken. That's what Ambaryl said."

"Regardless, we won't know until we know what's in those books." Aven let his hands fall and leaned back in his chair. "She might not have said anything, Trees. She never said anything to me about not being human. Not until she was trying to kill me."

"She was very good at keeping her thoughts to herself," Steward murmured. "I never suspected anything like this about her."

Owyn closed his eyes and rubbed one hand over his face. They needed better answers...real answers. The journals would help, but...

"I need to try and reach Milon again," he said.

"No," Aven answered immediately. "You'll kill yourself. We'll see what's in the books first."

Owyn nodded. "I wasn't saying I'm going to run off and do it right now. But we're going to need answers that I think we can only get from the man himself." He looked down at his plate. It was empty again. "You know, this whole not remembering that I've eaten is getting really old."

"Do you want more?" Afansa asked. "I can make another plate for you."

"Afansa, you don't need to—"

"Let me do something," she protested. "Meris told me to go out so she could take care of her son. I can't help any other way." She rose from her chair and rested her hand on his shoulder, reaching over for his plate. "A little of everything?"

"Yes," Owyn answered. "And thank you. For taking care of Granna, and for helping out where you can."

She took the plate and walked away, coming back with it heavily laden. "There. That should keep you for a few minutes."

Aven chuckled. "Maybe you should be taking care of Owyn and not his grandmother."

She laughed as she sat back down. "He does seem to need more taking care of than any other man I've ever met, but I'm not sure what his husband would say if I volunteered."

Owyn snorted. "Fuck the both of you."

"Didn't anyone ever tell you that you shouldn't make promises you don't intend to keep?" Afansa asked. Owyn turned to stare at her, and she blushed. "I was married, Fireborn," she murmured. "Up until last winter. I've been alone ever since. So don't tease me. I might bite."

Owyn chuckled. "Right. No teasing." He looked at Aven. "Maybe introduce her to one of your cousins?"

Aven grinned. "Maybe. Afansa, do you know how to swim?"

The door to Aria's room opened, cutting off Afansa's answer. Del came out, stopping when he saw them all at the table.

"What have you found?" Aven asked.

"*No answers. Not yet,*" Del answered. "*We started at the beginning, and we're still in parts where he says they tell him he'll walk again, and that once he does, they'll help him overthrow the Usurper. We've gone through five of the books, and we're tired, the both of us.*" He looked at Afansa. "*Where's Lady Meris?*"

"Aven took her and Mem to see the room," Owyn answered.

"And Memfis...he's upset. So she's with him, and she asked me to leave them in private," Afansa added. "I need to learn the hand-talking."

Del smiled. Then he looked around. "*Owyn, where's Alanar?*"

Owyn sighed and nodded toward his door. "He's in our room. He's still upset that he scared you."

Del looked at the door. "*Will you come with me to talk to him?*" he signed. Then he turned slightly. "*Fara invited us to come swim tonight. Is it sunset yet?*"

Aven shook his head. "Not yet. Are you going?"

"*I was thinking about it. But I want to talk to Alanar first.*" He walked over to Owyn, who stood up.

"Come on," Owyn said. "Let's go talk to him."

OWYN LED DEL TO THE bedroom door, knocked, then opened it. "Allie?" he called as they entered the room. "It's me and

Del." He closed the door, and the room disappeared into shadow. Owyn snorted. "Love, I know you don't need the curtain opened, but I do."

A moment later, the curtains were pulled back, letting the room fill with late afternoon sunlight. Alanar tied the curtain back, then went and slumped into a chair. Del looked at Owyn, who shrugged.

"*Tell him I'm not angry,*" Del signed.

"Allie, Del said he's not angry at you," Owyn repeated.

Alanar nodded. "I know he's not. Del is too sweet to stay angry." He smiled slightly, then shook his head. "I'm angry. At myself. Wyn, don't leave me alone with Del again? I can't be trusted with him. Not when I can't see to know what he's saying. Or if I'm doing something wrong." He growled. "Fucking useless broken thing—"

"*He is not!*" Del signed.

"Del says you are not," Owyn translated. "And I agree. You're not useless. You're not broken."

"*And he isn't a thing,*" Del added.

"I'm still not to be trusted around you," Alanar said once Owyn translated. "I can't tell if I've gone too far until I'm past it. I care about you too much to hurt you again, just because I can't understand your language."

Del swallowed. He went over to Alanar's chair, kneeling on the floor between Alanar's knees. He rested his hands on Alanar's legs, then closed his eyes.

How long had it been since he'd last tried this?

He opened his mouth.

"Ahhh...." He swallowed again. "Ahh...k...k...ssspek..."

Alanar sat bolt upright. "Del?"

"Fuck me," Owyn breathed. "Sideways." He came over and dropped to his knees next to Del. "You have a voice?"

Del nodded. He took another breath, then jerked when Alanar touched him, his fingertips pressed to Del's lips. The look on the healer's face was almost like pain.

"No. You're not doing this. You are not going to hurt yourself to try and make me feel better," he whispered. "You're not." He reached down and pulled Del up, embracing him tightly. Del clung to him, his cheek pressed to Alanar's broad shoulder.

"You said you couldn't speak," Owyn said softly. "You hid this?"

"*From everyone,*" Del said into Owyn's mind. "*My father doesn't even know.*" He pulled free of Alanar's arms and sat back on his heels, raising his hands. "*There's something wrong between my head and my mouth,*" he signed. "*I can think the words, but I can't say the words. When I used to try, it came out as noise. Grunting, mostly. No one understood me.*"

"Skela said you were wild when he got here," Owyn said. "We saw him, by the by. He's going to teach you falling stars."

Del smiled. "*I was wild. I was angry, and frustrated. I had so much to say, and no way to do it. Then Skela came, and taught me to speak with my hands. And taught my father to understand me. So I could tell him everything.*" He sighed as Owyn repeated his words to Alanar. "*It changed my world.*"

"I think I understood you, though," Alanar said. "You said you can speak, didn't you?"

"*I practiced in front of my mirror for years, where no one could see me or hear me. I practiced moving my mouth and making the sounds until they almost sounded like words. But they never really sounded close enough, and Ambaryl already thought I was an idiot. I wasn't going to feed that flame. So everyone thinks I can't. And I don't even try anymore. I don't have a voice. I have noises.*"

Alanar nodded slowly as Owyn translated. "You came close. You almost taught yourself again. Maybe, with more work, we could get further. If you wanted. There are exercises—"

Del shook his head. "*I don't need it. Unless it's with you. I want you to understand me.*"

Alanar's brows rose as Owyn translated. Then he reached his hands out. Del blinked, then put his hands into Alanar's; the healer drew Del's hands to his mouth and kissed them. "Del, I don't know what to say. That's the sweetest thing I think anyone has ever said to me. Owyn, he's got you beat."

"I think you're right," Owyn said. "Del, that's a lovely gesture."

"It is, and I want you to understand that I appreciate you offering this more than I can say," Alanar continued. "And I absolutely refuse."

Del blinked. "*What? Why?*"

Owyn translated, and Alanar nodded. "Because you are not going to torture yourself for me." He smiled and squeezed Del's fingers. "We'll make things work, Del. We'll find a way that doesn't make you miserable."

Owyn shifted to kneel behind Del, pressing against his back. "Stay with us tonight," he said, putting his arms around Del. "Just...sleeping."

Alanar still had Del's hands, so he turned his head and told Owyn, "*We're invited to go swim with the cousins. Fara wants you and Alanar to come down.*"

"Does she?" Owyn said with a laugh. "Allie, Fara wants to see you with your trousers off."

Alanar looked puzzled. He started rubbing his thumbs over the backs of Del's fingers. "Fara was here earlier. Have I met her before? Which one is Fara?"

"Aven's side-cousin—"

"Which helps me not at all," Alanar said with a laugh. "Aven has a ridiculous number of cousins." He raised Del's hands and kissed them again. "All right. Let's go swim. And let Fara look."

Del tugged on Alanar's hands, pulling him forward. Alanar frowned, then slid out of the chair to kneel on the floor in front of Del. Del tugged his hands free and wrapped them around Alanar, who laughed low.

"Owyn, come here," he said, his voice rumbling in Del's ear.

Owyn moved, pressing against Del's back, pressing him against Alanar's chest. Arms tightened around him, steadying him. Grounding him. Del took a deep breath and sighed happily.

"*I love you both*," he thought.

"We love you, too, Del," Owyn answered, his breath ruffling Del's hair.

CHAPTER THIRTY-EIGHT

A few minutes after Del and Owyn disappeared into Owyn's room, Aria came out of her bedroom. She looked around, clearly looking for someone.

"Del is with Owyn and Alanar," Aven said. "Alanar is still upset about scaring Del."

Aria nodded and walked around the table, stopping to kiss Treesi in passing. She smiled at Steward, then turned further. "And where is Jehan?" She noticed Afansa, and blinked. "And my grandmother?"

Aven grimaced. "With Memfis. I ran into Memfis and Lady Meris in the hall, and I took them to see the rooms. And...Memfis needed them more than we needed my Fa."

"Lady Meris sent me out," Afansa added.

Aria turned to look at Aven, then realization dawned on her face. "Oh. Oh, dear. Then it may be some time before we see Jehan."

"I'm not sure we'll be waiting quite that long," Steward said. "I mean, if they were alone, possibly. But in front of Lady Meris? And Karse?"

Aria moved to sit next to Aven. "We've found nothing yet. My father wrote quite a bit. He wrote about Agisti, how she promised him that he would walk again. That the damage in his back was severe, and that he needed to remain immobile to keep from permanently damaging himself until the injuries healed naturally.

415

It...it made sense to him. And to me. I wanted to show that to Jehan." She laced her fingers together. "He wrote every day, I think. Sometimes multiple times. Notes to my mother. Questions that he thought he'd be able to answer eventually. Plans for how he was going to retake the Palace, and for what would happen after. He asked himself many times how he was going to continue without Memfis, without Jehan and Aleia. He wondered if he'd ever dance again." She paused. "There are letters to Grandmother in those books. Drafts, I think. He made reference to letters that he gave to Agisti, that she promised to deliver."

"I wonder what happened to those," Treesi asked. She got up from her chair and went to the sideboard. "You know, nibble food is all well and good, but when did any of you have a proper meal last?"

Aria frowned. "Breakfast? Did we have something at midday?"

"Not really," Aven said.

Treesi nodded. "I thought not." She went to the bell pulls and tugged on the one that would bring someone from the kitchens. "Once we eat something, then what?"

"Fara invited Del down to swim. We can all go," Aven suggested.

Aria looked thoughtful, then glanced at her door. "I should—"

"Go swimming," Steward interrupted. "Aria, you're not to work yourself to ash. There's so much for all of us to do, so many things for you to learn. Take time for yourself. The books will still be there in the morning." He smiled. "But before anyone gets here, you wanted me for something?"

"I wanted you and Jehan to hear what Del had to say. But Jehan is busy, and so is Del," Aria answered. "So it will wait." She rested one hand on her stomach. "We need to plan this progress. Steward, I don't want us to leave until after Aleia returns."

Steward nodded. "I was thinking along those lines as well. But I'm just not sure when she will be back, and we do have to keep a schedule." He pointed toward her. "Are you going to travel with a baby in your belly, or in your arms?"

Aria nodded. "I have given that thought. And I would rather do the former than the latter."

"Then we'll need to leave sooner rather than later," Steward said. He frowned and counted on his fingers. "The storm, you said?"

Aven realized what he was counting. "The baby will come in mid to late summer," he said.

Steward nodded. Then he grinned. "I know how long it takes, Aven," he said. "And...I know roughly how long the progress will take. I remember Tirine's. We'll be cutting it very fine."

"Even with not having to go out to the Water tribe?" Treesi asked.

"Even leaving the sea journey out. Not going to the deep will save us two or three weeks, but that's not much." Steward looked up. "With your permission, Aria, I think I'll be asking Zarai to travel with us. Sometimes babies don't adhere to schedules."

"I'll have four healers traveling with me," Aria protested. Aven reached out and covered her hand with his.

"Three of whom haven't delivered a baby," he said softly. "Ask Zarai."

She met his eyes. "Will it make you feel better?"

"It will make me feel safer," Aven corrected.

"Then ask Zarai," Aria said. Steward nodded.

"I'll send a messenger down to her tomorrow." Steward stood up and bowed. "Now, after you eat, you should go swim. Relax, just for tonight. Tomorrow is soon enough to—"

The suite door opened with a bang, and Aven was out of his chair and on his feet before he had a chance to register that it was

Danir. The boy was panting and pale. Behind him, also breathing hard, was Copper.

"Healer Aven," Danir wheezed. "They need you now. All the healers. Now."

Aven raised his voice. "Alanar!"

The door to Owyn and Alanar's room opened, and Alanar hurried out. "What is it?"

"Emergency. And my father is busy. Let's go." Aven turned, saw Treesi standing behind him. "Where are we going, Danir? The healing center?"

Danir shook his head. "The entryway. Mama says he won't make it to the healing center if you don't hurry."

"Fuck," Alanar breathed. "Who can grab my hand?"

"I can," Copper said. He ran over to Alanar and took his hand. "Come on."

"Go ahead," Aven called as Treesi and Alanar headed toward the door. "I'll catch up!" He followed, and Danir fell in next to him.

"What's happening, Danir?" he asked as they hurried through the halls.

"One of the guards who went north came back," Danir answered. "Just one."

Aven turned his head to look at the boy. "Trey?"

"Not Trey," Danir said. "I don't know his name. But he came with Trey and Karse."

Aven swallowed and silently cursed his hip. He needed to run. "Go get Steward," he said. Then he started running.

By the time he reached the entryway, Alanar and Treesi were both on their knees, flanking a body on the ground. Treesi looked up as he reached them.

"Good, you're here," she said. "We need to merge."

Aven dropped to his knees, realizing that he knew the guard. Garrity, from Terraces. Had he known that Garrity had come north with them? "Who's leading?"

"Alanar," Treesi said. "He's already holding Garrity stable."

"But I won't be able to keep him that way if we don't hurry," Alanar growled. "I don't know how he got here like this." He held out one bloody hand. "Now."

Aven rested his hand on top of Alanar's, closing his eyes and feeling Treesi's hand covering his. He took a deep breath and opened his power to Alanar, watching as Alanar worked.

No, there was no way that Garrity got to the Palace in this condition. He was barely alive. Between internal damage and blood loss...he would barely have been able to stay on a horse, let alone walk.

"Focus, Aven," Alanar chided. Aven forced his thoughts to silence, focused himself on healing, letting Alanar direct their combined power.

Letting him save a friend's life.

OWYN FOLLOWED ALANAR out of their room, staying back as the healers ran out of the suite. Danir returned a moment later. "Steward! Aven says you should come, too!"

Steward turned. "They need me?"

Danir nodded. "Aven says you should come. He asked me what happened, and I told him that it was one of the guards who went north—"

"Trey?" Owyn blurted, his heart suddenly in his throat.

Danir shook his head. "It wasn't Trey. But Aven said Steward needed to come down."

"I'm coming," Steward said. He didn't stop to bow, hurrying out after Danir.

"There were two parties that went north," Aria said softly. "There was Trey's group, and there was another. A scouting party." She wrapped her arms around herself. "Where is Karse?"

"*With Memfis,*" Del signed. "*Should I get him?*"

Aria closed her eyes, then nodded. "Yes. Owyn, will you go with me?"

"To the entryway?" Owyn asked.

"Yes. We should be there."

"My Heir? Is there anything I should be doing?" Afansa asked. "Is there any help I can be?"

Owyn looked up at Aria. "I...maybe?" he stammered. Then he cleared his throat and nodded. "Yes. Go with Del. You can help Granna and Jehan with Mem. Or just help Granna, since I'm pretty sure that Jehan is going to head for the entryway once Del tells him what's happening."

Afansa nodded, and followed Del out of the room. Aria stood up and took the arm that Owyn offered her, and they left the suite.

The entryway was crowded, but only around the perimeter. The area around the healers was completely clear. Owyn saw Lexi standing with Steward, and led Aria toward her.

"My Heir," Lexi said in a quiet voice. "I'm not sure if he'll live yet."

"There are three healers working, and Jehan will be coming," Aria said. "Don't give up on him yet. Who is it?"

"A Terraces guard," Lexi said. "A young man named Garrity—"

"What?" Owyn gasped. "No!"

Steward looked shocked. "Garrity. That's one of the guards who rode with you when we first met."

"Yeah, yeah, he is," Owyn agreed. "Oh, fuck. Where's Evarra? Did she go out with him?"

The bleak look on Steward's face answered him, and Owyn had to force himself to ask the next question.

"Did they go with the scouting group, or with Trey?"

Steward closed his eyes. "They were with Trey."

Owyn bit his lip. He could hear a commotion, raised voices coming down one of the corridors. He saw Jehan first — the healer came into the entryway at a run, and dropped to his knees next to Alanar with a thump that made Owyn wince. He placed his hand on top of the other three healers' stacked hands, and closed his eyes.

"What happened?"

Owyn turned to see that Karse had come up behind him.

"Where is Del?" Aria asked.

"Coming with Meris and Afansa," Karse answered. "Memfis is asleep. What happened? Del said it wasn't Trey."

"It's Garrity," Owyn answered. He looked back at the healers.

"And what happened?"

Lexi didn't turn. "The gate guards said there was a rider. He came in fast, and threw the body...threw Garrity down. He was bundled up in a cloak, and the rider was gone before anyone realized what was happening."

"Did anyone follow?"

Lexi nodded. "We sent out a pair. They're not back yet." She finally turned to face them. "I wish I could tell you more."

"A pair?" Karse repeated. "As in...two?" When Lexi nodded, Karse swore. "Why didn't anyone come and get me?" he demanded. "And you only sent two? Something may have wiped out an entire squad, and you only sent two?" He turned to look over his shoulder, and for a moment, he froze. He looked confused. Then he shook his head. "Right. I'm going."

Steward stepped closer. "Captain—"

"I'm going," Karse repeated. "That's my man out there. And my men."

"I'm going with you." The words were out of Owyn's mouth before the thought had even finished forming.

Aria stared at him in horror. "No!"

"Aria, I have to," Owyn said. He lowered his voice. "Aria, I can hear him. You know what that means."

She closed her eyes, and Owyn remembered too late that he couldn't hear her...and she knew what that meant. Then she opened her eyes and nodded. "Go armed. And be careful."

"No shit," Owyn muttered, and saw the flash of her smile. "Aria, when I get back...we'll...we'll see about that...that other thing?"

More than a flash of a smile. "That means you have to come back."

He stepped closer and kissed her. "I'll be back. Karse, I'll meet you in the stables." He turned and took off running. He heard someone behind him, but didn't see who it was until he reached the suite.

"Del, you are not coming with me!"

"*No, I'm not,*" Del agreed, not even bothering to sign. "*I heard, and I'm helping you get ready. Go get your weapons, and I'll put together some food that you can travel with. You can't fall over. Not now.*"

Owyn nodded and headed into his room. He stripped, pulling on clothes that were better suited to riding. To fighting. He stamped into his boots, and pulled on a tight-laced vest that might serve as armor, if he was very lucky. He swallowed hard as he fumbled with the lacings. Trey had been the one who insisted that he have something like this. He grabbed the pouch that held his whip-chain and hung it from his belt, then went out into the main room. Del handed him a rucksack.

"*One bundle has nuts. The other has that hard cheese you like. There's a bottle of the tea you like, too.*"

"Thank you." Owyn slung the bag across his body. He kissed Del quickly, then licked his lips. "Stay with Allie tonight. I'm not going to be able to wait to say goodbye to him. Just...be with him?"

"Even if you hadn't asked. Go."

Owyn went, running out of the suite and down the corridors, heading for the doors that would take him to the stables.

KARSE WAS WAITING IN the courtyard with a groom and two horses, and at the sight, Owyn couldn't help but laugh.

"Freckles!" he called. He went to the horse and held his palm out, letting the spotted gelding sniff his palm. "I wondered what happened to you."

"He came back to the stable here," the groom said. "We've been taking care of him. He's a good boy."

"He is," Owyn agreed, stroking Freckles' neck. "Right. Karse, where are we going?"

"I have a copy of the map," Karse said, and swung up onto his horse. "Let's go."

Owyn nodded and mounted, turning Freckles to follow Karse out of the courtyard and out onto the road. The road branched, and they took the north fork, following it around the Palace and along the coast.

"How far?" Owyn shouted as Karse urged his horse into a trot.

"About ten miles," Karse called back. "It'll be dark by the time we get there."

"Oh, fuck," Owyn grumbled. "Do we have torches?"

"In the packs!"

They fell silent and rode, alternating between trotting, galloping and walking, and it seemed like forever before Karse called for a stop.

"We need to rest," he said. "Let them breathe."

Owyn dismounted and slowly started walking Freckles, then let the gelding graze. "Is there water?"

Karse pulled the map out and looked at it. Then he nodded. "A stream. It's not far from here, and it crosses the road." He took his reins and started leading his horse further down the road. Owyn caught Freckles' reins and followed, stretching his legs to catch up with Karse.

"Glad it's coming on to summer," Karse said. "A month ago it would be dark already."

"It's still going to be dark long before we get there," Owyn said. "How are we going to do this?"

Karse scowled. Then he shook his head. "Don't know. But we're not going back. Not until we know something."

"I wasn't saying go back," Owyn protested. "I was asking how we were going to do this. If we go on in the dark, we risk breaking a leg or a neck. These roads are horrible. We can't walk the horses the rest of the way — it'll take all night. So how do we do this?"

Karse stopped and looked at Owyn. Then he started to look over his shoulder again. This time, Owyn realized why.

He was looking for Trey.

"We'll find him, Karse," he said.

Karse nodded. "Yeah, we will. Let's let them drink, then we'll get moving again. See how much ground we can cover before it gets too dark."

They let the horses drink from the stream, then mounted up and moved on, starting at a slow walk to let the horses get warm again. A walk became a trot. Then a gallop, and the ground flew by. Owyn leaned over Freckles' neck, feeling the wind and the sting as Freckles' mane whipped at his cheeks. They'd find Trey. They had to.

The shadows were long and dark when Karse slowed his horse to a walk. "We need to stop again. It's getting too dark."

"What now?" Owyn asked. He guided Freckles off the road and slid from the saddle, letting the tired horse start to graze. He reached into the rucksack and took out one of the bundles Del had packed for him, pouring a handful of nuts into his palm and starting to eat. Karse came over and rubbed his hand over his face.

"I didn't plan this," he admitted. "I reacted. I didn't think. We shouldn't be out here alone. Not in the dark, not when we know there's something hunting out here."

"We couldn't not come," Owyn said. "We couldn't wait until morning. Not when there's a chance he's still out here."

"By the time we get there, it'll be black as the bottom of a tar barrel," Karse said. "Moonrise isn't for hours yet."

"Yeah, but we won't get there for hours yet," Owyn pointed out. Karse scowled at him. Owyn looked north along the dark road and frowned. "Karse, the place we're going. That's where they were going to take Aria and Aven, right?"

"Yeah. So?"

"So how were they going to get them this far?" Owyn asked. "This...ten miles? With two unwilling prisoners, one of whom is a Water warrior and a healer, and can make you hurt in ways you never thought possible?" He shook his head. "Something isn't right."

"Alanar said he was telling us the truth," Karse said.

"Alanar also told me that if someone is delusional, they believe their madness. To them, that is the truth." He looked around again. "Just because he thought it was true doesn't mean it actually was. Maybe they didn't tell him the truth." He groaned. "Risha knows about truth-telling. She can't do it, but she has to know. And she knows Allie is a level five healer."

"Oh, fuck," Karse breathed. "They told him the wrong thing, in case we found out. That means..." He stopped. "Owyn, I have to find him."

Owyn looked around. "Ground is pretty flat here."

Karse frowned. "Yeah? And?" He coughed as he realized what Owyn was saying. "No! No, you're not going to dance. Not here. I don't have anything you'd need if you go into shock again."

"We don't have a choice, do we?" Owyn asked. He handed the rucksack to Karse, then walked out to the middle of the road and took his whip-chain out of its pouch. "It might not work. This isn't how I usually do it." He looked down at the road, then over at Karse. "Stay over there until I stop. Don't come close until you can see the chain. And I'll need that bag when I'm done. I'll need to eat."

Karse nodded, and Owyn closed his eyes. One breath. Two breaths. Three breaths, and he snapped the whip-chain out and started to dance.

And the vision rose to meet him.

CHAPTER THIRTY-NINE

He was standing on the road. There was a field, marked by two standing stones that stood like doorposts off to Owyn's left. Looking through the stones, he could see that the field was littered with bodies — Water warriors, men in guard uniforms. Owyn moved through the field and counted them. Then he counted again.

Eleven.

A squadron was fourteen. Garrity would be twelve. That meant there were two people missing. Owyn went back through the carnage, looking at the bodies, and identifying the ones he knew. He felt sick.

Trey wasn't there.

Where was he?

The world blurred, and Owyn was looking at the field from a different angle. He could still see the stones, but now they were further away, and off to his right. He heard a distant moan. It could have been the wind.

He didn't think it was the wind.

The world blurred again, and he saw another rock, a large one shaped roughly like a turtle shell. He looked around, saw the standing stones, still off to his right but much farther away. He heard the moaning again. It was louder. Closer. And it seemed to be coming from the rock.

He moved closer, and heard movement. There was a hollow, under the rock. And he could see something moving inside. It was too dark to see who, or how many. Was it both missing guards, or only Trey?

And, more importantly, where was this place?

He stopped, dropping to one knee and hearing his whip-chain clattering around him. Karse rushed over, dropping to his knees next to Owyn. He shoved Owyn's rucksack into his hand.

"Eat something," he said. Owyn nodded and sat down, crossing his legs and opening the rucksack. The bundle he pulled out was the one of nuts, and he nearly choked on them, trying to eat them too fast. He pulled out the bottle and took a drink, then ate some more.

"See if you can see any standing stones around here," he said. "While we still have light. I saw something. Might be him."

"Might be?" Karse repeated, standing up. He squinted. "Can't see shit."

"I couldn't tell if it was him," Owyn said. He ate another handful of nuts, then drank more of the tea. "I saw the battlefield, but I only counted eleven bodies, and Trey wasn't one of them. Garrity makes twelve..."

"So two are missing," Karse finished.

"And there was something moving underneath a rock that looked like a turtle shell," Owyn finished. He took out the other packet and ate a piece of cheese, then closed the rucksack. "All right. I think I can ride," he said as he stood up. He picked up his whip-chain and coiled it up, putting it back into its pouch. "Do you think we can find it?"

"Standing stones?" Karse asked.

"Yeah. Just off the road. On the left." Owyn went over to Freckles, slowly got up into the saddle. "They looked like doorposts."

"Well, we didn't pass anything like that," Karse said. He mounted his own horse. "Let's keep on. Was it close, do you think? Any idea?"

Owyn clicked to Freckles, guiding him back onto the road. "I...I don't think it was far. But we can't waste time. What did you say about tar barrels?"

They rode on, going slower than they had been. It was too dark for the breakneck pace they'd kept before they stopped, and Owyn remembered his talk with the Usurper, about how the roads hadn't been maintained, and was surprised that the section where he'd danced was as smooth as it had been. He blinked. Blinked again.

"Karse," he called. "Are you seeing what I'm seeing? Something dark?"

"I see it," Karse called back. They rode up to the standing stones and stopped.

"The battle was here," Owyn said. "In the vision, I could see them through the stones, like I was looking into a room."

"And where was the turtle stone?" Karse asked.

Owyn closed his eyes, remembering. "The stones were on my right, and...maybe a half mile away?" He looked around and pointed. "That way."

"Lead the way," Karse said.

Owyn turned Freckles, and they started across the field. He shuddered, wondering if the horse could see well enough not to walk on any of the bodies by accident. "We'll have to send people with carts," he said over his shoulder. "We have to do right by them. We can't leave them here. Not the Water warriors. They have to go back to the deep."

"When we get back," Karse said. "I'll bring men back with carts and torches. We'll bring them home."

They rode on in silence, until Owyn was sure they were getting close. "You said that we had torches? We'll need them."

He dismounted, and heard Karse do the same. He heard Karse moving around and saw the spark from a flint and steel. A torch started burning, and Karse used it to light a second one that he passed to Owyn.

"I'll stay with the horses," Karse said.

Owyn nodded and started walking. The circle of light cast by the torch was oddly comforting, as was the fact that there didn't seem to be any bodies this far out. Where was the rock?

Then he heard the moan. He turned, closing his eyes to try and pinpoint the sound...there!

"Trey!" he called as he started walking. "Trey, can you hear me? It's Owyn!"

He heard the moan again, and started running. A dark shape loomed in front of him, and he slowed before he ran into the rock. He walked around it, searching for the hollow. "Trey?"

"Owyn?"

A barest whisper of his name.

A *woman's* voice.

Owyn found the hollow and dropped to his knees, holding the torch so he could see into the hollow. "I found you," he said. "It'll be all right." He raised his head. "Karse! This way!"

"Did you find him?" Karse called, and Owyn watched as the light of his torch grew closer. "Please tell me you found him."

"No," he answered as Karse reached him. "It's Evarra down here. Trey isn't here."

Getting Evarra out from under the rock was something that Owyn never wanted to do again. He never wanted to hear her scream again, or beg for him to stop hurting her. By the time she passed out from the pain, by the time they got her out from under the rock, he was in tears.

"How are we going to get her back to the Palace?" he asked. "We can barely touch her!"

"You're going back," Karse answered. "You're going back and getting a rescue party. I'll stay with her. I'll build a fire. Keep her warm and stable until you get back." He looked around. "And see if I can find anything else."

"And make yourself a huge fucking target for any of Risha's men that might still be out here," Owyn pointed out. "A fire is going to draw them in."

Karse nodded. "I know. But not much choice, is there?"

Owyn scowled at him, knowing the look was lost in the darkness and not caring. Karse needed to be scowled at. He was right, but it still needed doing. He scrubbed his hand over his face and got up. "Right. It'll take me a while to get back."

"I know. At least the moon will be up by the time you get there. And back." Karse came over and clapped his hand on Owyn's shoulder. "Be careful."

"You, too," Owyn said. He bit his lip, then gave in to impulse and hugged Karse, drawing a startled laugh from the man.

"Go on," Karse said, ruffling Owyn's hair. "Off with you."

AVEN LEANED AGAINST the wall and closed his eyes. Garrity would live, but it had taken all four of them to heal him, and they'd had to pull him back from the edge twice, once while they were still trying to stabilize him to bring him to the healing center, and once after they'd gotten him there. Now he was resting in a healing trance, and Jehan was with him. Aven, Alanar and Treesi were all supposed to go to bed...but Aven was pretty sure that Treesi had fallen asleep in her chair, and Alanar was stretched out on the bed in another examination room.

"Healer Aven?"

Aven opened his eyes. "Gathi. What are you doing awake?"

"I'm supposed to be helping you," she said. She handed him a mug. "Drink this. It's fish broth."

Aven took it and sipped the hot, salty broth. "Oh, that's good," he murmured, and noticed the tray with three more mugs. "Fish broth for everyone?"

"No, the others have chicken," Gathi answered. "It's very late. Are you going to sleep here tonight, or will you go back to the suite?"

"I'm not sure," Aven answered. "I'm tired enough that I might get lost between here and there."

Gathi nodded. "I understand. The Heir asked me to tell you that if you decided to sleep here, she understands."

Aven nodded again, sipping more of the broth. "Why don't you go see if anyone else is awake? I think my father—" He stopped, straightening and turning toward the door, hearing someone shouting in the distance. Someone familiar... "Is that Owyn?"

A moment later, the door flew open. Owyn grabbed onto the doorframe, panting. His clothes were streaked with dirt and what looked like blood.

"Need...fuck...we need carts. For...for recovery. For bringing the bodies back. But we need a healer. We need a bunch of healers, or Evarra won't make it," he gasped. "The squad...the whole fucking squad is gone."

Aven stared for a moment, then raised his voice, "Fa!" He turned to Gathi. "Go find Steward. Tell him we need carts and horses and armed men, as soon as he can have them ready."

Gathi nodded and bolted from the healing center. Owyn stumbled the rest of the way into the room and sank into a chair. Aven grabbed one of the mugs of broth and handed it to him.

"Drink this," he said.

Owyn stared at it for a moment, then took a sip. Then a gulp. "Oh. Oh, that's good," he breathed. He closed his eyes and kept on drinking, and Aven rested his hand on Owyn's shoulder.

"I feel that. You don't have to. I'm fine, Fishie," Owyn said. "Tired. I need to eat. But I'm not hurt."

"What's going on out here?" Jehan said as he came out of Garrity's room. "What's all the...Owyn?" He looked around. "Where's Karse?"

"Still out there," Owyn answered. "We found the place. Most of the squadron is dead. But Evarra...she's hurt bad. We need a healer out there, Or six. Six would be excellent, if we had them. But we need one out there two hours ago." He frowned. "Or six. Healers. Not hours."

"Mother of us all," Jehan breathed. "Aven, stay with Garrity. I'll go."

"You should both go," Owyn said. "She's bad. As bad as he was."

"Oh, fuck," Aven murmured. "Fa?"

"I'll wake Treesi and Alanar up. We'll have to see who stays behind to monitor Garrity." He closed his eyes, then swore. "It took all four of us. And we're all of us exhausted. I don't know—"

"We can't not try," Aven said.

"I know. You, me and Alanar. We're the strongest—"

"But you're all exhausted," Treesi repeated Jehan's words back to him as she came to join them. "I heard the shouting. Alanar is the worst of the three of you, because he led the merge. He needs to stay, and Gathi can help him, and watch Garrity. That way, Allie can sleep, and she'll get him if he's needed." Treesi folded her arms. "Tell me I'm wrong. I dare you."

Jehan chuckled. "You're not wrong. Get a kit together, Mistress Smart Healer."

Treesi dimpled and ran into the examination room, brushing past Alanar where he stood in the doorway. Alanar frowned and leaned against the wall.

"I heard Owyn's voice," he said. "And...what's going on? I'm staying behind? What happened?"

"Trey's squad," Owyn answered. "They were wiped out. We found Evarra, and she was alive when I left. Karse is still out there, with her."

"And Trey?" Alanar asked.

"We didn't find him," Owyn answered softly. "He wasn't...he's not there. Not that we could find. Karse was going to build a fire, try to keep Evarra stable, and he was going to keep looking. But she's bad, and we need as many healers as we can get out there."

Alanar nodded. "And I heard the last of that. Treesi's right. I couldn't heal a paper cut at the moment. I can't focus." He scowled. "I don't like that he's still out there. And with a fire? Might as well put up a flag saying 'Here I am, attack me.'"

Owyn nodded, putting his empty mug down. "I know. And he knows. But there wasn't much of a choice." He got up, swaying a little.

Aven steadied him, glancing at his father. Jehan shook his head slightly, confirming Aven's opinion. "Wyn, stay here. Rest. You've done enough."

"You don't know where to go," Owyn protested.

"North. How far?" Jehan asked.

"Couple of hours. There are standing stones that look like doorposts—"

"Those are still there?" Jehan interrupted. "I know exactly where they are. That used to be an open market for an artisan village out there. Leather-workers, mostly. The place was called Turtle Rock."

"That's where we found Evarra," Owyn said. "Under the turtle-shaped rock." He paused, then looked up at Aven. "She crawled underneath it, like a dying animal. Getting her out— she's never going to forgive me for hurting her like that."

"She'll understand," Aven said. "Owyn, go lay down with Alanar. You..." Aven frowned as he finally made sense of what he was feeling from Owyn. "You're off balance. Owyn, did you dance?"

Owyn nodded. "I had to find them. And I didn't find Trey." He sagged slightly. "I couldn't find him." His voice cracked on the last word, and he started crying. Aven pulled him close, letting him cry into his chest until Alanar reached them. Then he surrendered Owyn to his husband, who took him off to the examination room and closed the door behind him. Treesi came out a moment later, slinging the strap of a carry-bag over her shoulder.

"You'll tell me what happened on the way," she said. "Let's go."

They stopped only long enough to give a returning Gathi her instructions about monitoring Garrity and to wake Alanar if anything happened. Then they headed for the entryway. Steward met them there.

"There are carts being readied. Do you want to wait for them, or do you want to ride ahead?" he asked. "The moon is rising. You should be able to see well enough. Do you know where you're going?"

"Turtle Rock," Jehan answered. "Owyn described the standing stones. And we need to go now." He looked back at Aven and Treesi. "Are you both up for hard riding? I'll warn you right now, Ven—"

"I know I won't be able to walk a straight line when we get there," Aven interrupted. "But it can't be helped."

"And I'll keep up," Treesi said. "I'm a better rider than I was. I'll be all right."

Steward nodded. He turned and gestured, and a servant appeared from the shadows. "Go to the stables and tell them to have the three fastest horses saddled for the healers. Run now." The girl ran off, and Steward turned back to Jehan. "I'll tell Aria where you've gone. What's happening with the patient?"

"Gathi is monitoring, and Alanar is resting in the healing center. She'll wake him if anything." Jehan answered. "Steward, Owyn is in with him. Send some food down there, as soon as you can."

Steward nodded. "I'll wake the cook," he said. "And Lexi. I'll never hear the end of it if I let her sleep through this." He looked over his shoulder. "You should go. Hurry."

Jehan nodded. He looked at Aven and Treesi, and the three of them hurried down the corridor that led out to the stables.

TREESI GRITTED HER teeth and leaned over her horse's neck. She'd been regretting saying that she'd be able to keep up since Jehan had set the pace — a ground-eating something that she wasn't even sure had a name, but that threatened to rattle the teeth out of her head. But she could see the standing stones, and off to her left...

"Can you see the fire?" she called.

"I see it," Jehan called back, and slowed his horse to a walk. Treesi straightened in her saddle and let her horse follow, drawing up next to Aven. She looked at him, and saw the pinched look on his face. She could feel the pain radiating from him.

"How bad?" she whispered.

"I don't think I'm going to be able to walk," he whispered back. "I don't have my walking stick."

"I'll be your walking stick," Treesi said. "You can lean on me. And I'll take care of you on the way back. In the cart. Neither of us is riding."

The look that he gave her was one of pure gratitude. Then he snorted. "How are we going to go on progress? Neither of us can ride."

"There are these things called coaches," Treesi told him in a conspiratorial whisper. He barked with laughter.

"Fancy box on wheels," he said. "I remember. Meris had one."

"I think she still does," Treesi said. "It's in Terraces."

Aven nodded. He drew his horse to a stop; Treesi looked forward and saw that Jehan had already dismounted. She slid to the ground and walked around to take Aven's horse by the bridle.

"Can you get down?" she asked. "I don't think I can catch you."

"I'll make it to the ground," Aven said. "Back into the saddle? That's not happening tonight." He grimaced as he leaned back, swinging his right leg over the pommel so that he was sitting sideways in the saddle. He didn't so much dismount as he slid down to the ground, falling forward and gasping as he stretched his length out on the ground.

"Ven?" Jehan called.

"I've got him," Treesi called back. "Go see about Evarra. We'll be there in a minute." She let go of the horses and went to help Aven get back to his feet. He tried to walk, and would have fallen again if Treesi hadn't caught him.

"No more riding for you," she said as she slung his arm over her shoulders. "Lean on me. You undid a lot of our work."

"Couldn't be helped," Aven growled. "Let's go."

They started walking, with Aven leaning heavily on Treesi and hobbling alongside her. Jehan and Karse met them halfway to the fire. Karse looked at Aven, then looked away, and Treesi knew.

"When?" she asked.

"A little before moonrise," Karse answered. "She never woke back up. Just...between one breath and another, she was gone."

"And...Trey?" Aven asked.

Karse shook his head. "He's not here. I went out with a torch. I found every body in this field, and I brought them all to the rock. Trey isn't out there. Not anywhere." He looked around. "Either he crawled off and hid like Evarra did, or...they took him."

CHAPTER FORTY

O wyn paced the width of the courtyard, back and forth, watching his footprints in the dust as they slowly formed a distinct groove.

"*You're going to make yourself sick.*"

"I am not," he answered, and turned to walk back toward Del, Aria and Alanar. "I'm fine. I'm just—"

"Worried," Aria finished. "We all are." She looked up. "Good morning."

Owyn looked back toward the Palace and saw Memfis and Lady Meris coming toward them.

"Nothing?"

Owyn shook his head. "Nothing yet. Want to take a ride?" He looked up at his father. "If we head out on the north road, we'll meet them coming back."

"Wyn, I'm not sure that's a good idea," Alanar said. "You're still off-balance."

"Fuck that," Owyn snapped. "I'm never going to be *on* balance. I'm always going to be just this side of sick, and I can't let it stop me. There's too much that needs doing." He turned back to Memfis. "Ride?"

"No," Memfis answered. "And apologize to your husband. Owyn, I taught you to behave better than that."

Owyn stared at him for a moment. Then he sighed and turned back to Alanar. "Allie, I shouldn't have snapped at you," he said. "I'm sorry. I'm just—"

"Worried?" Alanar finished, and smiled. "I know, Wyn. I'm worried, too. To quote someone, we all are." He grinned as Aria smacked his arm. Then he turned his head. "Horses. I hear horses. Wyn, stay here so you don't get run down." He put his arm around Owyn, as if he was afraid Owyn wouldn't listen. Maybe he was right — Owyn had a strong urge to run out the gates and out to the road to try and see them coming. Then Del took his hand, and Aria rested her hand on his shoulder.

"Am I really that obvious?" he muttered.

"*Yes, you really are,*" Del answered in his head.

A moment later, the first wagons rolled through the gates. Owyn saw Jehan, Aven and Treesi sitting in the first one. He didn't see Karse, but he didn't look. The healers were all in the first cart. That meant...

"Evarra must be in that first one," he whispered. "Allie, they're going to need you."

Alanar nodded. "Take me to them?"

The other hands fell away, and Owyn took Alanar's arm and led him to the wagon that had rolled to a stop, and where Treesi was helping Aven to the ground. Aria went to Aven's side, helping steady him.

"I can feel that hip from here," Alanar called. "Aven, what did you do?"

"I learned that all that time I spent learning to ride was a complete waste," Aven answered. He leaned against the wagon, keeping his left foot off the ground. "Owyn—"

"How's Evarra?" Owyn blurted. "And...did you find him? Did you find Trey?"

Aven took a deep breath. "There's no sign of Trey. They searched once the sun came up. That's why it took us so long. And...Owyn, Evarra died before we reached her. Karse said she was gone not long before the moon rose. I'm sorry."

"Evarra died?" Owyn repeated. "But...no. She was alive when I left. I needed to apologize. I hurt her, getting her out. I made her cry." He looked up at Alanar. "She died before the moon rose. That was before I even got back here. Allie...I...I moved her. I hurt her, when I moved her. I...I killed her, didn't I?"

"No."

The answer came from four different directions — Alanar, Aven, Treesi and Jehan all said it at the same time. Owyn shook his head.

"I pulled her out from under the rock," he protested. "I moved her wrong...or made things worse...or..." He slumped against Alanar as his husband put his arms around him. "I killed her," he moaned.

"Owyn, trust me," Aven said, his voice gentle. "You didn't kill her. She was too badly hurt, and too far from help." He took a deep breath and rubbed his hand over his face, holding tightly to the wagon with the other.

"Owyn, how did you move her? Tell me what you did," Jehan said.

Owyn frowned, closing his eyes and thinking back. "I...She wedged herself in the hollow under the rock. I had to grab her under the arms, and Karse pulled me out by the ankles."

Jehan took a deep breath, then shook his head. "You didn't do anything we wouldn't have done," he said. "Under those circumstances? You did the best thing you could have."

"And she still died!" Owyn said. "If I'd left her where she was—"

"She still would have died," Jehan interrupted. "Owyn, she was too badly hurt. There wasn't anything that could have been done without at least three healers you didn't have." He shook his head again. "I am sorry," he added. "Alanar, how is Garrity?"

"He was still asleep when we came down," Alanar answered. "Gathi is with him, with Copper to come for us if he wakes." He tightened his arms around Owyn. "Help me, Wyn? Aven hurts enough that it's making my hips hurt in sympathy. We need to get him to the healing center and lying down."

"And we need to get word down to Neera," Aven said. "There are seven who need to go back to the deep tonight."

"Oh, Aven," Aria breathed. "Can you lean on me?"

"Not without knocking you down," Aven answered. "I can't put weight on the left at all."

"I've got you, Ven," Jehan said. "Alanar, Treesi, I'll need you. Aria, will you send someone to the canoes?"

"Of course," Aria said. She stepped away. Jehan slung Aven's left arm over his shoulders, and the two started moving slowly toward the Palace. They passed Steward, who turned and stared, then came to join them at the wagons.

"My Heir," he said. He looked at the wagons and closed his eyes. "Mother hold them all."

Aria nodded. "Steward, send a runner down to the canoes. Tell Neera that seven of her warriors fell in our service," she said. "And arrange for the appropriate rites for the others. I want them all to be laid to rest with honors."

Steward nodded. "And...Trey?"

"She took him," Karse growled. Owyn turned, saw Karse standing with Memfis and Meris. "That bitch butchered my men and she took my man."

"We'll find him," Memfis said. "We'll find him, and we'll find Milon."

"It don't make any sense," Karse said. "Why? Why take him? I mean, she don't even know him!"

"You're sure that she took him?" Alanar asked. Owyn winced, and Alanar sighed. "I'm sorry. It's just...you're right. It doesn't make any sense."

"We searched that entire area. We went back under the rocks, and we went a full mile in every direction. He wasn't out there. There weren't any other bodies." Karse closed his eyes and shook his head.

"It doesn't make sense," Owyn murmured. "When I went looking, I went looking for him. Not Evarra. I should have found him. Shouldn't I?" He looked at Memfis and Meris. "Shouldn't I have seen him?"

"Sometimes you see what you need to see," Meris said. "Not what you want to see." She put her hand on Karse's arm. "Owyn, you shouldn't be dancing at all. Not until we have these new talents of yours under better control. I still haven't had the chance to test you."

"I needed to do it, Granna," Owyn said. He frowned, closing his eyes as he pictured the field. The stones. The rock. Hearing the moaning.

Hearing moaning from halfway between the standing stones and the turtle rock.

"Wait," he murmured. "Wait...I...I think I missed something." He looked up. "First part of the vision. I was at the standing stones, looking at the bodies. Second part, I was in the field, and I heard moaning. Then I moved, and I was at the turtle rock, and I heard Evarra." He went cold. "Maybe...maybe I missed him. Maybe we all missed him. Maybe he's still out there, and we missed him! Jehan said there used to be a village there. A village means houses—"

"Houses? In Turtle Rock?"

Owyn turned to see that Steward had come up behind him. "Yeah, that's what Jehan called it. Said it was an artisan village."

ELIZABETH SCHECHTER

Steward nodded. "It was. But there weren't houses there. The Turtle Rock community were itinerant herders and leather-workers. They had their regular markets at Turtle Rock in the spring, but there's no good source of water there, and the land is too rocky to dig a well. When the water dried up in the summer, they moved on."

"No houses?" Owyn said.

Steward shook his head. "Tents. Some temporary booths. No houses. You were thinking cellars, weren't you?"

Owyn nodded. "Yeah. But... yeah, that was stupid. There's no ruins there. If there'd been houses, there would be ruins, yeah?" He frowned. "So...where is he?"

Steward frowned slightly, then looked at Karse. "Send another squad out?" he asked. "Better armed, better prepared? Turn over every rock in that field?"

"Turn them back, you mean," Karse said. "I already turned them all over myself." He closed his eyes, tucking his chin down his chest. After a moment, he nodded. "Yeah. Yeah, we'll go back out. Couldn't hurt."

"Come inside," Memfis said. "You're worn out. You need to eat something." He slung his arm around Karse's shoulders, and Meris took Karse's other hand. Karse didn't move.

"Captain, go and eat something," Steward said. "I'll arrange things. But if you don't go take care of yourself, then you're not going."

"You can't—"

"I can," Aria interrupted. "Captain, go take care of yourself. Things will be ready for you when you get back."

Owyn hung back and watched as Karse seemed to sink into himself. As he let himself be led into the Palace.

"He's hurting," Treesi murmured. "He's hurting so much."

Owyn nodded. "You don't hear him talk like the streets unless he's really tired, or really upset. Or both," he said. "He might have been born here, but he came up in the streets of Forge. He sounds it, when he forgets."

"It's understandable," Alanar said. "Owyn, Treesi and I are needed in the healing center. Are you going to be all right?"

"Yeah," Owyn said. "Yeah, I'll be fine. Go on and help Aven." He smiled slightly when Alanar and Treesi both kissed him, but let it fade as they hurried away.

"You should rest," Aria said. "You've had a long night. Del, take him back to the suite?" She turned to Steward. "What can I do to help?"

As they walked away, Del took Owyn's hand. When Owyn looked at him, he smiled.

"*You're not going to rest, are you?*" Del whispered in his mind. "*What are you planning, and how can I help?*"

Owyn blinked. Then he grinned. "I wasn't planning until you said something," he whispered. "You sure?"

"*He's my brother,*" Del answered. "*Whatever trouble you want to cause, I'm going to help.*"

Owyn nodded. The idea that had sparked with Del's offer to help now seemed like a very good idea indeed. "You get to figure out where we're not going to be disturbed for however long it takes me to find answers. I can't use the dance floor. We'll be seen."

Del frowned. "*Your grandmother told you not to dance.*"

"I thought we were getting into trouble," Owyn countered. "Del—"

"*I know where we can go,*" Del interrupted. "*But we'll need food.*"

OWYN LOOKED AROUND. "Tell me how we're not going to be caught?" he asked. "I mean...the Hall?"

"*Which no one uses when there's nothing happening,*" Del answered. "*Servants will come in and clean every morning, but that's it. They don't even use the Hall as a shortcut. They don't need to. There are passages that are shorter. It's big, it's open, and no one will come in here now that they've cleaned.*" He set his bundle on the dais step, then came to join Owyn. "*Are you feeling well enough to do this?*"

Owyn looked down at the smoke blades in his hands. He nodded. "I'll be fine." He looked up and leaned over to kiss Del. "Go sit. I might be a while."

Del nodded and went back to the dais, and Owyn took the first of his three breaths.

The vision enveloped him in darkness. He could feel rocking and bumping. It didn't feel like a ship, though. And he could hear something.

A man's warm laughter.

"*I feel you. I was starting to think I'd gone insane, you know.*"

Owyn smiled. "*Hello, Milon. Should...should I be calling you Firstborn? I mean, you are.*"

"*In my own head, we won't stand on ceremony. Thank you, for giving me my name back. For telling me about my daughter. For giving me hope.*" He laughed again. "*Even though I did think I'd lost what was left of my mind.*"

"*I'm not sure why I'm hearing you,*" Owyn admitted. "*I wasn't looking for you.*"

"*Were you looking for someone else? A young man, perhaps?*"

"*Trey?*" Owyn nearly fell out of the vision. "*He's with you? Tell me he's with you!*"

"*Is that his name? He wouldn't tell me.*"

Owyn laughed. "*Yes, that's his name! Tell him you're talking to me. Tell him...tell him we're coming for him. Tell him we turned every fucking stone in Turtle Rock over looking for him.*"

Silence, then more laughter. "*He says I'm insane.*"

"*He said you're* fucking *insane, didn't he?*" Owyn asked, and felt Milon's mirth. "*Now tell him that Karse would slap him silly for swearing at the Firstborn.*"

"*And now he's just sputtering. Who is Karse?*"

"*His husband. And you wouldn't have known that. I know that. So now he knows you're talking to me.*" Owyn took a deep breath. His head was starting to spin. "*Tell him we're coming. We'll find you both. But I'm going to need help. Where are you?*"

More silence, then Milon said, "*We're not at sea anymore. There was a battle, and the ship just barely made land. That's really all I know. I think that's why Risha brought Trey to me. She needed someone who would be able to help me. I can't walk, you see.*"

"*I figured that part out,*" Owyn said. "*When I'm in your head, I can't feel anything below the waist.*"

"*You're very good. You're very strong. I don't know that I've ever heard of a Dancer being able to do this.*" Milon went silent again. "*Trey says that he thinks they brought him north from where his squadron was attacked. He doesn't know how far. We're locked in a cart, and we can't see out. So that's all I can tell you.*" He paused. "*You're fading. I can feel it. Go back.*" Silence. "*Trey asks that you tell his husband he loves him. And tells you not to worry. He'll look after me.*" Another pause. "*And I'll look after him.*" Another pause. "*We're stopping. Tell Memfis I love him. Tell them all I love them. And tell my daughter I can't wait to meet her. Now go!*"

Owyn opened his eyes. He blinked, then looked around. He wasn't in the Hall. He was in a bed in the healing center, and Alanar was sitting in a chair next to the bed.

"Allie? How did I get here?" he asked.

Alanar just growled at him. "Six. Fucking. Hours. Owyn."

"What?" Owyn gasped. "No. No, that...and you moved me? How did you move me without pulling me out?" He sat up and winced. "My head is pounding."

Alanar stood up and walked over to the door. He opened it and called, "He's awake."

The first person through the door was Meris, and she was as angry as Owyn had ever seen her.

"I told you that you weren't supposed to be dancing!" she snapped. "You could have killed yourself!"

"I found him," Owyn answered. "I found Trey. And I talked to Milon again. He says there was a fight, and the ship barely made land. So the Water tribe, they'll be back soon, I think. And they're on land. Risha is, I mean. They're on the move. And Trey thinks they're in the north."

"You..." Meris stopped. She came into the room and took Alanar's abandoned chair. As she sat down, Aria entered the room, followed by Treesi, Del, and Aven. Aven was leaning heavily on his walking stick, and he was frowning. Memfis, Jehan and Steward stayed in the doorway. Meris looked around, then turned back to Owyn.

"Tell us."

"Where's Karse?" Owyn asked. "He needs to hear this."

"I sent Copper for him," Jehan said. He walked over to the table and poured a mug full of something, and handed it to Owyn. "Drink that. Slowly. If you keep it down, you can eat."

Owyn took a sip of what proved to be barely warm broth, and nodded. "Right. I went looking for Trey, and I hit Milon." He told them about his conversation with Milon, repeating himself when he saw Karse come to stand next to Steward.

"So...that's what I know," he said, and finished his second mug of broth. "Trey's alive. Milon's alive. They're moving, and they're north. At least, Trey thinks that they were north." He frowned. "Carts can't really go off road, can they? So they're somewhere you can get to by road. And it wasn't a bad road, either. No big bumps." He looked around. "So, you tell me. Was it worth it?"

Silence. Until Aria took a deep breath.

"Steward," she said slowly. "How soon can the progress be on the road?"

Also by Elizabeth Schechter

Heir to the Firstborn
Worlds Begin
Written in Water
Forged in Fire
Bones of Earth
Wings of Air

Rebel Mage
Counsel of the Wicked
Haven's Fall
Where Home Lies

Swords of Charlemagne
Hidden Things
The Lady and the Sword
Ashes and Light
Table of Stone
Swords of Charlemagne: The Complete Series

Don't miss out!

Visit the website below and you can sign up to receive emails whenever Elizabeth Schechter publishes a new book. There's no charge and no obligation.

https://books2read.com/r/B-A-KGBH-JQJLB

BOOKS 2 READ

Connecting independent readers to independent writers.

Standalone
The Rape of Persephone
Fools Rush In
Her Captive
To Market
Infernal Machine
Chains of Light

Watch for more at elizabethschechterwrites.com.

About the Author

Elizabeth Schechter has been called one of the top erotica and alternative sexuality writers in the world. Her writing credits include the award-winning steampunk erotic romance *House of Sable Locks*, the Celtic fantasy *Princes of Air,* and the dystopian fantasy *Rebel Mage* trilogy. Her shorter work has appeared in anthologies edited by D.L King (*Carnal Machines*), Laura Antoniou (*No Safewords*), and Cecilia Tan (*Jingle Balls*; *Like a Prince*).

With *Written in Water*, the first in the *Heir to the Firstborn* series, Elizabeth is exploring new ground, with her first new adult romance that was written entirely in real time on Patreon.

She was born in New York at some point in the past. She is officially old enough to know better, but refuses to grow up. She lives in Central Florida with her husband and son.

Elizabeth can be found online at http://elizabethschechterwrites.com, or on Facebook at https://www.facebook.com/Elizabeth.A.Schechter. You can also find her on Patreon, at https://www.patreon.com/EASchechter.

Subscribe to Elizabeth's newsletter at https://www.subscribepage.com/k4u7k2

Read more at elizabethschechterwrites.com.

www.ingramcontent.com/pod-product-compliance
Lightning Source LLC
Chambersburg PA
CBHW020248030726
47499CB00001B/109

* 9 7 8 1 9 5 2 5 9 8 1 5 9 *